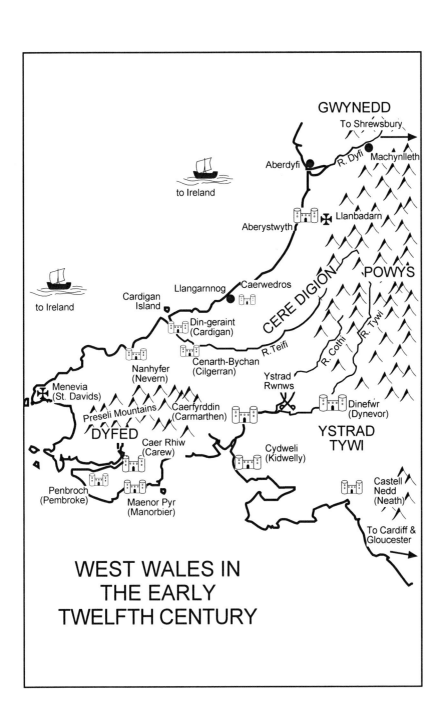

WEST WALES IN
THE EARLY
TWELFTH CENTURY

Lion Rampant

The Story of Owain and Nest

Bernard Knight

Back-In-Print Books Ltd

Published by Back-In-Print Books Ltd 2004
ISBN 1 903552 47 8
Previously published in Great Britain by
Robert Hale under ISBN 0 7091 3082 1

Printed and bound on demand in Great Britain by
Lightningsource.

Back-In-Print Books Ltd
PO Box 47057
London SW18 1YW
020 8637 0975
info@backinprint.co.uk
www.backinprint.co.uk

BERNARD KNIGHT

Bernard Knight CBE is a retired Home Office pathologist and Professor of Forensic Pathology in the University of Wales. He has been writing for over forty years and has had some thirty books published, as well as radio and television dramas and documentaries. He reviews crime books for the *Tangled Web* site on the Internet and is one of the judges for the *Silver Dagger Award* of the Crime Writers Association.

He continues to write the successful *Crowner John* series of historical mysteries, based on the first coroner for Devon the 12th century. He previously published two novels about that century, *Lion Rampant* being one, the other *Madoc, Prince of America*.

Bernard Knight was born and lives in Cardiff.

Other novels include:

The Sanctuary Seeker
The Poisoned Chalice
Crowner's Quest
The Awful Secret
The Grim Reaper
The Tinnerís Corpse
Fear in the Forest
The Witch Hunter
Brennan
Madoc, Prince of America

CONTENTS

AUTHOR'S NOTE

Most of the events described in this book actually happened and to the best of the author's knowledge, none of them could not have happened. All the characters, apart from the most minor ones, have a solid existence in the pages of history. Even after eight hundred and sixty years, some of the dialogue – especially that of Henry I – is given verbatim, as recorded by chroniclers later in the same century.

The author gratefully acknowledges the help given by so many people, especially Miss Eleanor Fairburn (author of *The Golden Hive*, another novel about Nest), Mr. Tom Hopkins, Archivist of Cardiff Public Library, Dr. Geraint Dyfnallt Owen of the Royal Commission on Historical Manuscripts (and author of two novels in Welsh on Nest and Owain), Mrs. Nesta Trollope-Bellew of Carew Castle (a descendant of the original Nest), Dr. Ffransis Payne of the St. Fagans Welsh Folk Museum, Mr. A.D. Carr of the University College of North Wales, Mr. Dafydd Morris Jones, Secretary of the Cardiganshire Antiquarian Society, Major Francis Jones, Herald of Wales Extraordinary, and Mr. Alun Edwards, Cardiganshire County Librarian.

B.K.

(from original edition, dated 1972)

PROLOGUE

WITHIN a few years of 1066, all England had been conquered by the Norman invaders. However, the Celtic princedoms of Scotland, Ireland and Wales retained their independence in varying degree for centuries longer. The Princes of Wales, in spite of constant in-fighting amongst themselves, owed their freedom to the mountains which had also protected them from the Romans and Saxons. These same mountains posed too difficult a problem for William the Conqueror to deal with himself – he and his successors were too interested in England and Normandy. He delegated the problem to a few of his favourite henchmen, who became Lords of the Marches along the Welsh border. In effect, these became subsidiary kingdoms under the overall sovereignty of the Monarch. The Marcher Lords had absolute power in their realms and were free to enlarge their territory westwards at the expense of the Welsh princes.

The Marcher Barons themselves delegated a lesser power to their own knights, adventurers who were willing to cut out estates for themselves by force of arms. Both they and the Lords themselves drove into Wales, their success varying greatly at different periods and in different areas.

From the first, the coastal plains at the extreme north and south fell easy prey, but the central mountain mass continued to give it age-old protection, both to the peaks of Gwynedd and part of Powys in the north and to the remote coastal area in the west, especially Ceredigion (the modern Cardiganshire).

Dyfed (the modern Pembrokeshire), being continuous with the South Wales coastal strip, was more vulnerable. William the Conqueror made a sabre-rattling procession there in 1081, under the pretext of a pilgrimage to the shrine of St. David. Whilst there, he came to an arrangement with Rhys ap Tewdwr*, supreme Prince of South Wales, by which, on payment of tribute to the Conqueror, Rhys' lands would be safe from invasion by the hovering Marcher Barons. Though William was able to control these rapacious Lords during his lifetime, their ambition tore loose on several occasions during the reigns of his sons, William Rufus and Henry I, leading to the open revolt of the great Montgomery family against the Crown at the turn of the century.

William's pact with Rhys was honoured for his lifetime, but within weeks of Rhys' assassination in 1093 – by an over-ambitious Norman occupier of

* *Rees ap Tudor*

Brecon – both Normans and opportunist Welsh princes tore into Dyfed and Ceredigion to begin a wrestling match for territory that was to last for another two hundred years.

Prince Rhys had a daughter, Nest, whose reputed beauty has caused her to be called 'Helen of Wales'. Her name is woven into Welsh history – and into that of Ireland and England – more deeply than any other Welsh woman before or since.

Her beauty plunged West Wales into battle, fire and vendetta that was to flare up again and again for years to come.

This is the story of the seven most eventful of those years.

PART ONE

CHAPTER ONE
CHRISTMAS DAY, 1109

THE frosty moonlight gave the scene an ethereal brilliance. To the Porter at the outer gate, the royal compound seemed carved from silver, suspended against the blackness of the woods across the river.

There was not a breath of wind to disturb the hazy smoke which filtered through the wattled eaves of the great hall. It climbed slowly into the diamond-studded sky, as if undecided whether to drift over the sea to Ireland, or back up the Teifi valley to lose itself in the hills of West Wales.

The Porter had eaten his Christmas meal some hours before, snug in his own hut with a buxom wife and three children. Now he was resigned to spending the rest of the night at the opening in the stockade, unlikely to be disturbed by anyone save late-comers to the Prince's feast. His spear could lie idle and his dagger could rust in its scabbard: although there were Normans across the river in Dyfed, the gate would not need defending against them this night. Prince Cadwgan* ruled all Ceredigion and most of Powys. There had been peace these last few years – albeit an uneasy one.

The Porter scratched himself and pulled his sheep's fleece closer against the frost. His woman would bring him a bowl of soup at midnight, but until then all he had to do was imagine the rich food and drink that was being poured down the throats of the revellers inside the hall. This was the first Christmas for the new building and Cadwgan was celebrating with an extravagant feast. The old hall had burned down last spring and the Prince had had it re-built in the fancy new style, with dry stone walls up to a man's height, pierced with openings to let in the light. Many thought it mere aping of the new fortresses of the French and suspected that Cadwgan's Norman wife had nagged him into it. The Porter scowled at the thought. She would be in there now, glutting her fat body on good food, the old cow! He hoped that she choked on it.

Looking up at the full moon, he calculated that there was little more than three hours before midnight and his dish of *cawl*. Getting late, he mused. Owain and his hot-heads had better be quick or they'll miss the best of the food. Everyone else that Prince Cadwgan had invited had arrived long ago, so where was his eldest son and heir? There had been a lot of speculation in the

* *Cadogan.*

armoury that morning as to whether Owain would get an invitation at all, after that business in Powys last week. Cadwgan had just about despaired of his eldest son, they said – and that old French bitch did all she could to twist the knife in the wound.

The Porter looked around again at the wooden palisade of the Welsh castle, enclosing its two acres of ground. The other guard should be patrolling there somewhere, unless he'd slipped back into his dwelling for a quick fumble with his new wife! His eye fell on the Hall again, with its steeply-pitched roof of rush-thatch and turf. A faint buzz of voices and the clatter of dishes came tantalizingly across the compound, but a moment later his keen ears picked up another sound.

From the north, where the coast track ran down the length of Ceredigion to this fortress of Din-geraint*, the rumble of hooves came faintly through the night air, as they hammered across the open moorland beyond the woods.

The Porter smiled to himself in the brittle cold. Owain ap Cadwgan was coming! Owain, favourite of the men, idol of the little boys – and devastator of the maidens!

Owain was coming – now the Christmas feast should really come to life!

Inside the hall of Din-geraint, enough drink had flowed to get the party well under way. This was one of the three feasts of the year when the womenfolk were allowed to share the Hall with the men and their presence added spice to the revels. Both young men and old fools showed off before them, their eager tongues wagging from too much mead, bragget and new beer. In the centre of the earthen floor, between the middle pair of the six huge tree trunks that supported the roof, was a great fire, piled with peat and topped with a massive yule log.

Through the blue haze of smoke which hung amongst the rough rafters, a hubbub of gossip, laughter and the clatter of wooden dishes confirmed the good spirits of the hundred or so people in the Hall. Cadwgan himself was already half drunk and full of the expansive good nature that a dozen horns of spiced mead had induced. Even his snobbish, patronizing wife, her fat buttocks drooped over the chair next to him, permitted herself a few strained smiles from time to time.

'Well, lady, what do you think of our new hall?'

The Prince waved an unsteady hand at the low stone walls, hung with Christmas garlands of laurel and holly.

Her once handsome face, thickened by two dropsical pregnancies, cracked into a supercilious sneer.

'It would make a good cottage for a serf in England,' she rasped, 'or a fair pig-sty in Normandy…why can't you build all in stone, like civilized people?'

Cadwgan scowled and turned his head away. His good humour drained away as if the woman had pulled a plug from the bottom of his soul. Pig-sty, be damned! Old pig herself! He had had six sons by different women and

* *Later called 'Cardigan' by the Normans and 'Aberteifi' by the Welsh.*

daughters by too many others to remember, but had managed to avoid marrying any of them, until he got saddled with a wife like this – and a Norman into the bargain. No wonder a man took to drink! The thought brought him back to the present and he banged furiously on the table with his gold-banded drinking horn. His cup-bearer, hovering nervously nearby, leapt to re-fill the vessel and spilt some mead on the scrubbed table alongside the Prince's silver plate.

'You clumsy fool!' snarled Cadwgan, giving the man a vicious backward blow in the stomach with his elbow.

As the man slunk away, Cadwgan felt instant remorse. He knew that he was getting old and losing his grip. Ten years ago, a clumsy servant would have a cheerful clout on the ear, followed by a hearty slap on the back – and gone away grinning with pride. Now his serfs hated him, his free-men pitied him and his gentlemen despised him. When they went to battle – which thank God was now rarely enough – instead of clamouring to die for him, they found every excuse to slink away and only recovered their old vigour when Owain appeared on the scene.

Tears of drunken self-pity began to well up in Cadwgan's red-rimmed eyes as he gulped the strong mead. He stared mistily out across the raised upper hall at his guests and his officers, then sniffed noisily, rubbing at his eyes with the linen sleeve of his tunic. No one took much notice of him – he was respected there not for himself, but for his princely rank in the strict hierarchy of Welsh royal protocol. He was the son of Bleddyn – and Bleddyn was long dead. By this token, Cadwgan was Prince of Powys and Ceredigion – at least, for so long as the French condescended to respect their pact leaving him in authority there.

But there was little love for Cadwgan himself. He knew that when his sons looked at him, they were mentally calculating how long he might live, so that their chance would come. And the way he felt some days, with these attacks of the yellow skin and vomiting of blood, they would not have very long to wait.

His eyes pricked again, but with a sudden flare of his old spirit he jumped to his feet and slammed a horny hand on to the table. Immediately, the Silentiary – one of the ten officers of the Court entitled to a chair in the privileged upper hall – sprang to his feet, struck the nearest roof-pillar with his staff and bellowed in a resounding voice:

'Silence! *Yr Argwlydd** speaks!'

The tumult melted away like snow in a flame and one young woman in the lower hall who giggled in the silence got an ear-warming buffet from the matron next to her.

Prince Cadwgan ap Bleddyn ap Cynfyn leaned heavily with his fists on the table, to steady himself. He raised one arm in the tired gesture of an old man, though he was hardly turned fifty.

* *The Lord.*

'My guests…my kindred…my people! I give you welcome on this day of Jesus Christ.'

The arm drooped and Cadwgan swayed slightly and fell silent. The Chief Guest, sitting two chairs away on the Prince's right hand, looked decidedly embarrassed.

Rhydderch ap Tewdwr had married Cadwgan's sister Hunydd, but had no particular wish to be present when the Prince of Powys fell flat on his face in the dishes at his own Christmas feast.

But his brother-in-law pulled himself together and gazed blearily down into the main hall, where crowded tables lined the walls.

'Seven years of peace have I given you…seven years since we last fought for our land against King Henry!'

His voice was strong again, but his tongue sounded too big for his mouth.

You bloody old liar, thought Rhydderch cynically. You joined your brothers in helping Norman against Norman – and when you found that you had backed the loser, you changed sides within the hour.

Even Cadwgan seemed to realize in his fuddled mind that he was on the wrong tack. He switched his platitudes to less delicate matters.

'Tonight we sit in the greatest hall in Ceredigion.' He swept his hand uncertainly up to the dark recesses of the roof. 'Eat your fill and drink well! When the tables are cleared, we will have a night of entertainment before us. I have called bards from the ten commotes and beyond, to compete before us.'

He swayed slightly again and his Chancellor half rose to grab him. But the Prince gripped the table edge with one hand and threw up his drinking-horn with the other.

'The day of Jesus Christ!' he yelled hoarsely.

'The day of Jesus Christ!' echoed another roar from the Chief of the Household of Din-geraint, jumping from his chair at the far end of the lower hall. Reluctantly, the whole assembly lumbered to its feet and raggedly repeated the Holy toast.

Then, as their voices died and the gulping of mead and beer subsided, there was the sudden sound of hooves rattling on the frozen ground outside. The tinkle of harness and the sound of voices came through the woollen drapes that hung over the entrance.

The Doorward rushed forward, but he was too late. Though a big man himself, he was brushed aside by the solid mass of youthful humanity that erupted through the curtains.

All eyes were on the doorway as the leader, a red-head with shoulders like an ox, stopped on the threshold and stood grinning at the standing crowd.

'God be with you all!' he cried. 'But there's no need for you to rise to your feet for me…I'm not Prince yet!'

It was a perfect entrance and, with the typical Welsh sense of drama, the assembly took full advantage. The drinking cups went up again, with about twenty times as much enthusiasm as for Cadwgan's toast.

'Owain…Owain.…Owain!' they chanted exuberantly, 'Owain the Valiant,

Lion of Powys!'

Smiling hugely, the auburn-haired princeling strode forward, closely followed by eight other young men. The Penteulu – the Chief of the Household – came forward to clasp Owain's arm in an affectionate greeting. The young man threw back his great riding cloak of green wool and unbuckled his sword-belt.

'Take this, friend...there are no French to do battle with in here tonight...at least, no French*men*,' he added wickedly, with a pointed glance up the Hall towards Marie de Sai, his stepmother.

As surreptitious giggles and guffaws rippled round the Hall, the other men were throwing off their cloaks and removing their arms, as courtesy demanded.

Immediately behind Owain was his closest brother, Morgan. They began striding up towards the fire to greet their father.

Cadwgan ap Bleddyn watched them approach with mixed feelings. Pride at fathering such men battled with anxiety and not a little jealousy. The eternal strife between the generations was far stronger here than usual and most of it was directed at his eldest boy.

Owain Morgan, son of a different mother – as all his sons were, except the two recent brats of the Frenchwoman – was Owain's satellite. Though strong, brave and clever in his own right, Morgan stood in the shadow of his elder brother's vibrant personality. The heir was self-assured to the point of arrogance – Morgan watched his flank and his rear and made up in calculating coolness for what he lacked in his brother's fire and impulsiveness.

The two young men stepped up between the low screen that separated the lower from the upper Hall and stopped before the Prince.

They bent their heads dutifully to him.

'*Arglwydd*, we wish you well,' said Owain simply.

'Greetings, our father, on this day of Christ,' added Morgan.

Cadwgan looked suspiciously at Owain, who was smiling innocently. He saw that his son was strikingly dressed in a mottled wolf-skin hung over a fine green tunic. Around his neck was a slim torc of twisted gold.

The father glared from Owain across to the dark face of the swarthy Morgan, then back to his eldest son.

'I greet both my sons and welcome them to this house, which is as much theirs as mine,' he muttered formally. His watery gaze remained fixed on Owain. 'I trust that you have been acting with some restraint since we last met?' he growled thickly, thinking of the journey he must make the very next day, to smooth over some feathers that Owain had recently ruffled in Powys.

The auburn-haired young man gave a little bow. 'I only try to keep your Lord's domain free from traitors and to slit a few filthy French throats.'

As he said the last words, he looked pointedly at where the obese Marie de Sai sat champing a boiled fowl. She reddened and only a mouthful of meat gave Morgan time to grab Owain's tunic and pull him across to a vacant space at a table against the opposite wall. While the woman spat insults into

Cadwgan's ear, Owain and his brother squeezed themselves behind the tables and slid their legs over a long bench. Though the heir was entitled to one of the coveted chairs allotted to persons of distinction, he had long ago refused to take one while his other brothers had to do without. The battle with his father over this breach of tradition had long ago been fought and no one raised their eyebrows when the Edling* slid on to a common bench.

He now found himself next to the pretty young daughter of the Chief Judge, who sat on his privileged chair on the other side of the girl.

As he sat down, two beaming servants hurried up with wooden bowls of steaming broth. There were hunks of *bara canryg* to steep in it – bread made from wheat and rye, as well as plain wheaten loaves and rye cakes. The table groaned with food, though it was restricted in variety at this time of year. Almost all the cattle were slaughtered in November, as only breeding animals could be fed through the winter, but there was plenty of salted beef, and pork and poultry in plenty. Fish, eggs, apples, honey, curds and hot oat-cakes lay on wooden platters, the rare metal dishes being reserved for the highest folk and their chief guests.

A servant jogged up with a great joint of boar's flesh sizzling on a skewer, the fat still burning at one end. Owain courteously sliced off a few pieces for the girl and laid them on the scrubbed boards before her, where she expertly barricaded them with bread crusts to keep the gravy and molten fat from running on to the white linen of her best robe.

After hacking off some great chunks for himself with his dagger, Owain settled down to eat with one hand and drink with the other. When his first thirst had been quenched, he used the free arm to better purpose by slipping it around the slim waist of the giggling girl next to him, her mantle shielding it from the judicial stare of her stately father.

Gwenllian was sixteen, a mature age for a spinster in days when girls became marriageable at twelve. She was spoken for by the son of the Penteulu in Gwynionydd, another commote** of Ceredigion, but he was miles away tonight and a last chance flirt with Owain the Valiant was one to be grasped eagerly. She slid closer along the bench and gently used her elbow to coax his hand nearer her breast.

Though he responded readily, she noticed petulantly that there was not a second's hesitation in the rhythm of his jaws. The young bloods had arrived late from Powys and had to catch up on the food before the tables were taken away for the entertainments. Gwenllian had already eaten her fill and was merely playing with the food that Owain had cut for her. She slipped pieces down to the sleek hunting dogs and corgis that crouched wide-eyed beneath the tables.

As Owain crunched his way through pig, game and beef, he watched his profile against the glow of the fire and the flicker of the rush lights. There

---

* *Welsh equivalent of Saxon 'aethling' or heir.*
** *An administrative area, several of which comprised a 'Cantref' ('hundred').*

was strength in every line of his face, from the rather heavy brows to the clean-shaven chin, aggressive and pugnacious. Though most Welshmen shaved their heads up to a circular rim, Owain kept his hair longer and an unruly russet lock bobbed over his forehead. As he tore pieces from the boar's shin-bone, Gwenllian noticed his gleaming teeth. Even in a land where cleaning them with hazel twig was a ritual, his were unusually white and strong – most other men of twenty-five had lost a few from either fighting or disease.

She wriggled contentedly and felt his hand slide up her cloak to cup her breast. 'And how is my Gwenllian these days?' Owain swallowed his meat and bent his face to her ear. He had known her about the court since she was a baby, but that did not prevent him from fully appreciating her lately developed attractions.

'All the better for seeing you, my Owain – it's half a year now, I feared to hear of you being married!'

He laughed and squeezed her playfully. 'Married! Why should I ever marry when there are lively girls like you about? Or do you want me to end up like my father, driven to the mead horn by that haughty French cow!'

He picked up a pheasant drum-stick and pointed it across at Cadwgan's Norman wife, spitting out the words with a virulence that surprised even the resilient Gwenllian. She decided to change the subject in case Owain's volatile moods swung again and made him stop massaging her under the mantle.

'What do you think of our Prince's choice of Chief Guest tonight, Owain? He never had much love of Rhydderch before, even if he was wed to his sister.'

Owain shrugged, not taking his eyes off Marie de Sai nor his lips from the food.

The girl spoke again, with the worrying persistence of her sex. 'Do you think your father has designs on Cantref Mawr*, that he's playing up so to his brother-in-law?'

The eldest son switched his gaze to the Chief Guest, who sat immediately opposite, a few seats from the Prince. In the courts of Welsh princes, the Lord sat on the right hand, not at the top of the hall as with the Saxons and Normans.

Owain saw a handsome man, with a black beard and moustache. Rhydderch wore unusually fine garments and had a magnificent golden torc around his neck.

'Rhydderch ap Tewdwr, brother of the great Rhys,' he mused aloud. 'My dear uncle-in-law, who I wouldn't trust with half a groat when my back was turned.'

Gwenllian giggled again. 'He doesn't look short of half a groat, nor even a hundred pounds. Look at that satin robe on his wife – and his own neck-plate!'

Owain stopped eating and glared across the upper hall with a fixety that made his uncle stare back in annoyance.

'That torc belonged to his brother, Rhys ap Tewdwr, the last true Prince of Deheubarth,' declared Owain in a loud, carrying voice. 'And he wore it by strength of arms, not as a lick-spittle of the damned French!'

* Part of Ystrad Tywi, the modern Carmarthenshire.

The powerful voice happened to hit a lull in the babble of voices and Gwenllian suddenly felt like sinking under the table with the dogs.

Alongside Owain, Morgan sighed and automatically felt for the absent hilt of his sword.

The Judge turned to glare at the heir, who blithely ignored him, but on the opposite table Rhydderch turned red above his beard, twisting to see if Cadwgan was taking any notice.

The Prince, however, had chosen not to hear, though Marie de Sai began hissing a commentary into his unwelcome ear.

Owain calmly tore a wheaten loaf in half and began to pour honey along its length. Though Gwenllian's ear was no more than a foot away, he carried on in a conversational tone that could be heard half-way down the Hall.

'Rhys ap Tewdwr was a great man – he gave his life at Brecon Gaer in trying to keep de Neufmarche's vultures out of these lands. He would turn in his grave to see a Welsh vassal of the French playing at being Prince in his old palace of Dinefwr!'*

He intended his words to be insulting and he succeeded. Rhydderch sprang to his feet, his heavy chair going over backwards with a crash. The black brows hung like thunderclouds over his furious face. He turned and shouted, not at Owain, but at Cadwgan the host.

'Prince and brother – I have watched this son of yours grow bigger and more insolent as the years went by. But did you invite me to your feast only to be a sport for your unruly offspring?'

His neck veins stood out like purple worms as he pointed a quivering finger in Owain's direction. He was no coward and the heir's brash insults were unfair, even if it was true that he held his lands in Cantref Mawr by condescension of the Normans. When his brother Rhys had been killed sixteen years earlier, the Kingdom of Deheubarth had been fragmented by Welsh and Norman alike. Rhydderch, like Cadwgan, was at least managing to keep a Welsh hold on some of the land, not like the utter subjection of Penbroch and Morgannwg** by the Normans and their Flemish underlings.

Owain ate on with insolent unconcern, but this time Cadwgan could not continue his pretence of sudden deafness. He lumbered to his feet, groaning inwardly at his fate in having such a wayward son. Morgan watched anxiously, his deeper sensitivity feeling a great foreboding for his brother.

'Owain, come here!' The Prince's voice grated through the ominous quiet in the hall.

Though dissipated and tired, the enormity of having his Chief Guest so grossly insulted by his own son, brought an edge to his voice that rang subconscious echoes of childhood chastisements to Owain.

---

* *Now called Dynevor Castle, the ancient capital of Deheubarth, the Kingdom of South Wales.*
** *Pembroke and Glamorgan.*

His grin vanished and he climbed sullenly off his bench to walk across to face his father once more.

The whole hall fell deadly quiet. Family quarrels, even those of the Chief of the Kindred, were not things to be hidden beneath a polite veneer of manners. A squabble was public property, something to be talked over across the hut fires in the long winter evenings. Everyone watched, their eyes flicking from father to son, as Owain stood with hands on hips, defiant yet wary, for Lord Cadwgan was not yet written off as a power in his lands.

They faced each other across the table, the Prince's Foot-holder doubled up on his stool to miss any buffets that may be let fly. A full quarter of a minute passed in utter silence as they eyed each other. Morgan waited anxiously as the figure of his brother stood erect, the flames flickering on his wolf-skin and his slim-legged buff trousers.

Then Owain's head bowed slightly and Morgan – and the whole court – knew that he had submitted, without a word being spoken.

'Owain, you are a trial to my soul!' Cadwgan's voice held a trace of a whine, rather than of towering rage. 'As a child you were quarrelsome and as a youth you caused me ceaseless anxiety. Three years ago you murdered Meurig and Griffi, your own cousins – and evil seems to have followed you ever since.'

His son's head jerked up, his green eyes blazing in the torch light.

'Murdered? You call that murder! Is every man killed in a fight to be accounted a murder at the gates of heaven?'

His flaring temper had exploded again and Morgan's fingers dug deep into the crust he was holding as a spasm of anxiety gripped him again. Owain flung up an arm dramatically. 'If ridding Powys of the sons of Trahearne was murder, then how many score of murders can be laid at your feet, my father! How many men did you *murder* that day at Coed Yspwys?'

The mention of Cadwgan's greatest battle against the Normans, many years ago, made his old head jerk up. Owain, who could sometimes be as wily as he was rash, had spiked his father's anger with a single sentence. Cadwgan, who had been going to dismiss his son ignominiously from the Hall, softened his voice.

'You have offended against the rules of hospitality, my son. You have insulted not only my guest, but a kinsman beneath our own roof. I can only think it was your youth, your thoughtlessness and the new mead. You will ask Rhydderch's pardon – or leave this Hall.' He ended bluntly and sat down with a thud of finality.

The Hall waited with bated breath.

Would their Owain yield or not? Much as they hated the thought of him submitting to the unpopular Rhydderch, the rest of the evening would be sterile without his presence.

Owain hesitated before his father, as if calculating how much he could get away with. Behind him, Morgan willed him desperately not to get deeper into trouble and to take the face-saver that his father was offering.

'Apologize!' rasped Cadwgan, uncompromisingly. He pointed down the table with a finger that was an ultimatum.

Owain scowled. 'I had better leave, *Arglwydd*,' he muttered.

There was a clatter behind him, as Morgan rose quickly to his feet. 'Then I go too,' said the brother.

Even Gwenllian started to get up, but her father pulled her down with a bump that made her teeth rattle.

Owain looked over his shoulder at Morgan standing ready to share his disgrace. A split-second went by in weighing up the situation, then he shrugged philosophically, his temper having fallen as quickly as it had risen.

'Sit, my brother!' He walked the few steps to stand before Rhydderch and smiled down as charmingly as if he was wishing him the best of a fine spring morning.

'Lord, my kinsman – I fear the cold air of our ride from Llanbadarn and the over-strong drink of my father's knavish brewer combined to make my tongue wag foolishly. To be beneath the roof of my own kindred makes my sin the greater. I pray that the goodwill of this day of Jesus Christ will allow you to pardon me.'

Rhydderch looked up from beneath his black brows. The insolence of this young man was notorious and it was time he was taught a lesson. Yet it was a difficult time and place for such teaching. Rhydderch turned his head to look down the table at his brother-in-law, but his eyes fell first on his own wife.

Hunydd was staring up at the handsome Owain in moist-lipped admiration. Though he was her nephew, he was only eight years younger and Rhydderch well knew that she shared all the other women's adoration of Cadwgan's heir.

She had even insisted on calling their second-born son after him and Rhydderch knew that if he rejected Owain's sweet apology, Hunydd would punish him with a month's frigidity, as well as endless wagging of her tongue.

The Lord of Cantref Mawr sighed and turned his eyes back to Owain, who stood there as innocent as any choirboy.

'Your tongue would charm bees from a hive,' he said harshly, 'but inside that manly body you still have the mind and manners of a brash child. Go back now to your place and employ your hasty tongue on meat and wenches – not in idle insults about which you know little truth.'

Owain's face hardened, but he kept his temper in check for once in his life. He had expected counter-insults in return and was prepared to swallow them while under his father's roof. He nodded curtly to Rhydderch, gave his aunt a flashing smile which made her toes curl, then swung away and returned to his place at the table.

Morgan gave his arm a comradely squeeze as he sat down, but Owain's mercurial moods had swung to the depths for the moment. He ignored Gwenllian and fell to eating and drinking as if he were crunching Rhydderch's bones and drinking his blood.

The hall returned to normal, partly relieved at Owain's apology and partly disappointed at the mildness of the royal squabble. Cadwgan, sweating with relief, felt suddenly sober and called for more liquor, under the disapproving eye of his wife, who was about the only woman not susceptible to Owain's charms.

'You'll go down in history as a drunkard, not a Prince,' she grated in his ear. 'Am I to tell my fine sons that their father died of drink?'

Cadwgan turned his big, heavily-lined face to hers, emboldened by a new horn-full of mead. 'Tell them what you like – even the truth!' he muttered.

'What do you mean?' she snapped.

'Tell them that they exist on this earth only because their father needed to protect his lands by scraping favour with the invaders from the Marches. You don't think I would have married you otherwise, do you – you fat daughter of a petty French adventurer!'

Marie's face purpled with rage. 'Don't you talk of my father like that, you Welsh savage! Sir Picot de Sai was a gentleman, not aborigine scum like your kind, living in huts in a rain-drenched forest!'

Cadwgan pushed his yellowed cheeks nearer to hers, reckless of her powerful personality. 'Yes, a real gentleman, your Lord of Clun! Slaughtered bare-foot peasants, castrated the men, hunted the women and children for sport – that's your Norman chivalry!'

This furious sotto-voce battle was brought to an abrupt end by the appearance before the table of the Chief of the Household, the permanent custodian of Din-geraint.

'*Arglwydd*, it only wants two hours to midnight – will you give the order for the feasting to end, so that we may begin the entertainment?'

Cadgwan tore his furious gaze from the spiteful face of Marie de Sai and brought his wits to bear on matters of the moment.

'Eh?…entertainments? Yes, get on with it then.'

'You must give the command, Lord,' the Penteulu reminded him gently. He signalled across to the Silentiary, who jumped to his feet and struck three resounding blows with his staff on the rough-hewn roof pillar.

'Silence, *Yr Arglwydd* speaks!' he yelled.

Cadwgan ap Bleddyn hauled himself to his feet once more. 'Eat what you have before you, but keep your cups and horns. Bards, see to your strings and voices – we begin the night's revel!'

Almost before he had finished speaking, the Penteulu waved at the serfs hovering in the shadows. They dashed in to start clearing the debris on the tables – the choice remnants were stuffed into the servants' tunics as Christmas treats for their families, while the scraps were thrown on to the rushes for the dogs to snarl over. The tables were taken off their trestles and stacked against the wall, while the revellers arranged their benches in ranks facing the great fire.

In the upper hall Owain crammed down the last mouthful of meat and cleaned his fingers on a piece of bread. His volatile spirits began to lift again and he slid a hand under the table to squeeze Gwenllian's thigh.

'Oh, so you're speaking to me again?' she said petulantly.

'I'll do more than just speak to you this night,' he promised in a whisper, 'if we can tie an oat-sack over your father's head first – he seems to disapprove of me.'

The bright-eyed girl giggled as the table was suddenly whipped away and Owain had to remove his hand hastily.

The hall was now in noisy confusion as a jostling throng pushed for the best places. The Doorward stalked around, ejecting those lowly ones with no right to remain. The only serfs left were those waiting with pitchers of mead and beer, ready to quench the thirst of the assembly through the night.

When the hubbub had settled, the Silentiary again struck the centre pillar and called for the Pencerdd, the Prince's Chief of Song. He was a venerable old man, dressed in flowing robes of red, green, black and blue stripes. On his head was a kind of skull-cap with an upturned brim and his long, white hair was plaited into a coil on the back of his neck. Standing on the step above the fire, he bowed to Cadwgan and raised the small harp given to him long ago by Bleddyn, the father of the present Prince of Powys.

Instantly, the last whispers died in the great hall and a religious hush fell on the assembly. Expectancy and suspense stiffened the smoky air. The fingers moved and a liquid ripple of sweet music flowed over the Kindred, bringing wonderment and ecstasy to the hearts of rough men who might be killing and plundering the next day.

As the plaintive chords wafted through the night air, the soul-strings of his audience began to vibrate in sympathy. Then the Chief of Song began to sing and all thoughts of family feuds, princely politics and even the ever-present Norman thundercloud began to evaporate under the magic of the *hengerdd*, the ancient verse handed down with jealous care from generation to generation of bards.

Owain was affected as much as anyone. Brought up in the mystique of the old songs, this was as much magic for him as the next man. Of all the men in the royal court, he respected the Pencerdd most. He had been his teacher, his friend and as much a father-figure as Cadwgan himself. As Owain sat in that enchanted place, the thought of now making a disturbance as he had earlier, would have been akin to high treason.

The old man, head thrown back and eyes closed, was singing in a high, clear voice to the roof-trees. The first song, as tradition demanded, was a hymn of glory to God. Then he changed to the equally traditional eulogy of praise to his Prince. The bravery, resourcefulness, mercy and godliness of Cadwgan were extolled at great length. The Pencerdd had obviously been working on the song for this special feast, as he had added some new verses, in which Cadwgan's great battle of Coed Yspwys in 1094 largely figured.

He came to the end of his songs and received a gold ring from the Prince for his services. It was now the turn of the lower hall to provide the singer and the Bard of the Household of Din-geraint – a protégé of the Penteulu – got to his feet.

Slowly circling the rush-strewn floor, he drew his own brand of evocative music from his harp and then launched into song. He was a much younger man and his melodious throat rendered the well-loved tales of old – Taliesin and Aneurin and all the verbal half-history, half-legend of the dark but glorious years since the Roman legions had left Britain.

Though every man in the hall knew the verses word-perfect for himself, the whole audience listened enthralled, as with searing passion one moment and velvety caress the next, the Bard Teulu acted out the six-hundred years' history of their land.

When he finished, there was no crude clapping or shouting in the Norman or Saxon fashion. The best compliment he could have was dead silence and some long sighs as his audience slowly came down to earth from the temporary emotional paradise that he had created for them.

Then the mood changed, as there were to be jesters, storytellers and minstrels, who were to inject a light-hearted interlude before the contest of the rival bards. This was a far less serious part of the evening's entertainment and many of the audience took the opportunity to shift their seats, refill their cups or go outside to relieve themselves. Gwenllian slipped away for some feminine purpose and Owain prodded Morgan's shoulder. He jerked his head and they slipped away through a small door in the upper hall, which led to the royal – and only – chamber, a smaller wattle building adjacent to the hall itself.

The brothers stepped out on to the hard turf of the compound and walked slowly towards the stockade. Owain shivered in the chill air and pulled his wolf-skin more closely around him.

'This sea-bound Ceredigion can get as cold as our own mountain land in Powys,' he muttered.

Morgan, the thoughtful one, was silent for a few more frost-crunching paces.

'Owain, why in God's name do you provoke your own kinsfolk? You came near to permanent exile and disinheritance tonight.'

'Ah, a pox on them, the grovelling herd!' snapped his brother impatiently. 'My fellow-Welshmen sicken me. They boast of their ancient battles and in the same breath talk of their latest bargain with the French. I tell you, Morgan, I hope I never live long enough to grow so feeble that I have to kiss dirty Norman feet.'

Morgan gripped his brother's elbow. 'It's the only way sometimes, Owain. When we are so outnumbered and disunited, what else can we do? Every time we fight, you know the result – the slaughter of our people, blinding, maiming, burning! Better to live and fight another day.'

Owain shrugged impatiently. 'Sometimes, Morgan – but it gets a habit with these smug Princes. Rhydderch, what has *he* ever done to keep the French out? When his brother Rhys was killed, he was one of the first to grab a piece of Ystrad Tywi for himself and make a treaty with the French for them to let him keep it.'

They walked on in silence past the huts and out-buildings of the main fortress of Ceredigion, a pitifully weak structure by Norman military standards. Here and there, the brittle silence was broken by a child's cry, and from one wattle shack came the moans of a woman in labour, giving birth to a Christmas babe.

Faint sounds of laughter drifted to them from the storyteller's jokes, but when they reached the further end of the camp, there was only the lapping of the river as the flowing tide came up the estuary and washed the southern face of the castle rock. Climbing an empty guard platform, the brothers leaned on the top of the palisade and looked down at the river's edge at the foot of the low cliff. A couple of flimsy coracles and a long Irish sea curragh lay on the narrow bank but beyond them the moonlight shimmered on the waters of the Teifi.

For a few moments neither man spoke, glad to fill their lungs with clear night air after the effects of peat smoke and strong drink. Morgan broke the silence first, banging a hand on the rough wood of the stockade.

'Strange that this wall should have been built by the damned French – about the only good thing they ever did for us.'

The fortress had been erected on an old Welsh site by the Normans who invaded immediately after Rhys's death back in '93, but Earl Roger Montgomery soon found himself overstretched and abandoned the new stockade within a year.

Owain was unimpressed by their unwitting generosity. 'I wonder what those pigs will do next,' he snorted. 'The swine have been too quiet for my liking these past few years.'

The brothers looked out in the moonlight to the opposite bank of the river, which divided Ceredigion from Dyfed. A few miles of no-man's land separated them from the Norman Lordship of Cemais along the coast. Inland, the castle of Cenarth Bychan was even nearer, there being only three miles of wooded valley between them. Neither place was much of a threat to the Welsh across the river – the real strength in Dyfed was King Henry's great castle at Penbroch*, thirty miles to the south.

'One day, they'll walk straight into Ceredigion and slaughter the lot of us,' muttered Morgan pessimistically.

His elder brother made a derisive noise in the direction of Dyfed, as if challenging the whole land that lay frozen under the moon.

'If we all got together, we could fling every Frenchman and Fleming back over Offa's Dyke. It's these weak fools like Rhydderch and our own father who play into their hands. United, we could free Wales again...but we spend our time squabbling amongst ourselves and bleeding each other in petty family feuds.' He slammed a fist into his palm in excited irritation. 'That's why I'm so impatient to rule this land, Morgan. One strong man could repair all the harm that's been done since Rhys died at Brecon.'

Morgan spat pensively over the stockade. 'Then Rhys's son, Gruffydd, should come back from Ireland to do it.'

* *The modern Pembroke.*

Owain snorted, 'To hell with Deheubarth now…let our land of Powys gain strength by their default.'

'And what do you think the Normans are going to do while you go about this master plan? I can't see why they are content to sit on their bottoms at Penbroch and Shrewsbury at present, let alone if you started a revolt against their precious truce.'

Owain shrugged. 'They've got their hands full in Normandy. And Rufus burnt his fingers so badly in his Welsh campaigns, that his wiser brother Henry has taken the hint and leaves us alone.'

The night air began to bite too sharply and the brothers cut short their political meditations to start walking back to the hall.

'Rhydderch is a fine looking man, for all your dislike of him,' observed Morgan.

Owain grunted. 'His brother Rhys was a fine figure of a man. His children used to visit us at Mathrafal. I just remember them, you were a little too young.'

'That was the Gruffydd we spoke of just now?…the one that vanished as a boy to Ireland?'

Owain nodded. 'There was also a younger brother and an elder sister, Nest. She is the one they say is the fairest woman in Wales – she was certainly a pretty child as I remember her.'

Morgan grinned in the moonlight. 'We must get our own good looks from that branch of the family, brother! We have the same grandfather as they, so must be second-cousins.'

Back in the hall, the contest between the rival bards had just begun. One from each commote of Ceredigion and several from Powys and Ystrad Tywi were competing for an oaken chair donated by Cadwgan. The songs varied from the traditional sagas to impromptu ballads, the judges being the Pencerdd, the Bard Teulu and the Prince himself.

Owain and Morgan went down to the lower hall to join their travelling companions from Powys, and sat to listen with new horns of bragget in their hands.

The rivalry between the bards grew stronger as the contest progressed; the excitement in the hall became more and more evident as the contestants became fewer in this 'knock-out' competition. Between each song there were heated arguments amongst the audience as to the relative merits of the singers and when the opinion of the judges was given by the Silentiary, the partisan groups became more and more vociferous. On the next bench to Owain and Morgan were two more of their half-brothers, Maredudd,* son of Euron and Einion, son of Sannan.

There was not the same relationship between the two pairs as between the elder brothers. Owain and Morgan had stayed at their father's court all through boyhood, but Einion and Maredudd, with another one Madoc, had been fostered out, as was the common practice. Although blood bound them

* *Meredith.*

together against any outsider, within the family it was usually Owain and Morgan versus the rest – and as the elder pair were always dominant, further jealousies were aroused.

Between the rendering of the songs, there was increasingly active banter between the two groups, aided by the crowd of younger men who were the satellites of the various brothers. Though it began light-heartedly, it developed into an acidulous combat of tongues centred around their opinions of the contestants. Only the actual start of the singing silenced their comments.

Of the last two competitors left in the contest, the first to sing in the final round was the Bard Teulu of Caer-wedros, a commote on the coast of Ceredigion. After his magnificent delivery of a lover's plaintive lament, most of the audience felt that nothing could possibly surpass it, but as Owain was of this opinion, Einion felt bound to differ.

'You say that only because the last man is the household bard of Rhydderch ap Tewdwr,' he sneered at Owain. 'You cannot have your hated uncle the winner beneath our own roof.'

His brother's retort was cut short by the announcement of Rhydderch's Bard Teulu, who stepped forward into the centre of the Hall once again. The dark-browed Lord of Cantref Mawr rubbed his hands expectantly and nudged his wife, Hunydd, in premature triumph as the singer raised his small harp.

After the first few words, all the young men in the Hall listened enthralled, for the song was an impassioned and highly coloured account of a woman's charms. And it was no vague generalization of a woman, but one particular lady, known to some in the hall and actually related to not a few.

This eulogy was of the Princess Nest, daughter of the great Rhys ap Tewdwr and hence a niece of Rhydderch himself. He had obviously commissioned his bard to extol her virtues, to emphasize his own close ties with the last ruler of Deheubarth and to gain some reflected glory.

And his singer had done him full justice. He sang with a fervent first-hand knowledge of the glorious woman, whom he compared with the legendary Helen. Her raven-black hair, skin like cream velvet and a supple body like that of a young doe – the bard, sweating himself into a lather with the effort of extemporization, sang of Nest's great eyes, the glistening lamps of her soul that could reduce any man's will to water at a single glance...He seemed to have an endless fund of metaphors to illustrate the matchless allurements of this wondrous daughter of Wales, as well as a bottomless pool of simile to describe her gentleness, compassion, meekness, nobility and charity!

When he at last ran dry on these scores, the bard from Ystrad Tywi turned to the history of this fabulous woman. Owain's ears, already straining to catch every syllable of praise for his apparently angelic second cousin, almost flapped when the sad story of her life rolled off the golden lips of the singer.

He sat forward on his bench, hands clenched in front of him, as the bard began to portray Princess Nest as the beautiful martyr of Welsh nobility, caught in the toils of the dastardly Normans! Singing of the destruction of

Rhys's family immediately after his death, the bard lamented the capture of Nest when she was but eleven years old and her exile in Shrewsbury and Gloucester castle as a hostage and ward of King William Rufus. He went on to bemoan her bestowal in marriage on the hated castellan of Pembroke, Gerald de Windsore, and her permanent separation from her infant brothers, one of whom had been a prisoner of the French since he was two years old.

It all made a heart-rending story which added greatly to the appeal of the ballad. No one was surprised when Rhydderch's man won the coveted chair and the Lord of Cantref Mawr was fully restored to good humour, after the episode of Owain's insults earlier in the evening.

The contest over, the folk in the hall broke up into noisy groups. The evening was far from finished though it was well past midnight – the women retired to their beds, but the men seemed fit for drinking, gossiping and arguing until the dawn

Gwenllian went off in a pout, as Owain failed to carry out his promise to seduce her – she could see him buried in the biggest throng of young men in the lower hall, gesticulating and throwing his russet hair about with angry tosses of his fine head.

'If that's what happens to the daughter of the great Rhys, we Welsh should be ashamed to rest in our beds until we have avenged her!' he was declaiming, pounding his knee with a massive fist. 'Are we mice or men, that we let Frenchmen take our royal women and give them like prizes to castle caretakers?'

Einion sneered back at him. 'Mention a fair woman and brother Owain is pawing the ground like a stallion...you can't bear the thought of a kinswoman sharing the bed of a Norman, is that it?'

Owain, inflamed by drink and his habitual temper, grabbed his half-brother by the slack of his tunic and shook him angrily.

'You've just got yourself a wife, Einion – would you like to have her captured and thrust into the lecherous arms of the likes of this Gerald of Windsore?'

Einion pulled himself free and brushed down the creases in his tunic. 'Forced into marrying she may have been...but not by the King of England. She was given to de Windsore by Arnulf de Montgomery and her own brother, with Rhydderch's connivance, for she lived with her uncle after she was leased from her stay in the Border castles.'

Owain scoffed at him. 'Since when are you a scholar of story? How could she be given in marriage by her brother, who was both in Ireland and but ten years old when she was wedded in eleven-hundred? And whatever you say with your clever tongue, Einion, it's still a disgrace before God for the best royal lady in Wales to be handed out like a handful of silver for some slimy trick of Rhydderch's, to ingratiate himself with the French!'

Maredudd, a skinny youth with a bad squint, came to his brother's support. He was to Einion as Morgan was to Owain.

'Spoken like a hero, Owain,' he sneered. 'Go and rescue the damsel from the clutches of her oppressor, then – the bards can sing *englyns* about you for the next thousand years!'

Guffaws from Einion's men made Maredudd even bolder. 'They can also sing of how Gerald de Windsore stuck your severed head over his gate at Penbroch, with your entrails rapped round it like a necklace!'

Morgan, his own blood aroused, suddenly gave the youngest brother a push in the chest that sent him sprawling on the floor.

'Keep your impudence for old men and the womenfolk,' he growled, afraid that Owain's unpredictable temper might be fanned into some new folly.

A new, deeper voice cut into the developing brawl.

'I thought as much – whenever the name of my niece is mentioned, young men begin to get red in the face and push each other around!'

All the young bloods turned and saw Rhydderch ap Tewdwr standing behind them. The mead and the success of his bard had mellowed him and he stood smiling benignly at them all. Though he was rocking slightly on his heels, he was still a handsome, commanding figure and the younger men waited on his words.

Einion stood up from his bench and motioned to a hovering serf to fill up the elder man's mead horn. 'Lord Rhydderch,' he said, 'can you settle this argument, if you will. This lady of whom your Bard Teulu sang, our kinswoman Nest – she was nearer to you than any of us in Powys?'

It was a statement of fact more than a question, but Rhydderch nodded gravely, only the drooping of his eyelids giving away his mild intoxication. 'Nest – my beautiful Nest!…I can tell you most things about her. What was it that led to your argument?'

Owain cut in sharply, his previous joust with Rhydderch forgotten in the more interesting matter of a woman. 'Was she as beautiful when grown to womanhood as she promised to be as a child?'

Rhydderch nodded slowly. 'I have never seen fairer. I tell you, I often wish that I was both younger and not her near kinsman. Nest has a beauty that has never been seen before in this land. My bard tonight sang with eloquence, but not exaggeration.'

Maredudd, keeping out of range of Morgan's fist, turned his horrible eye on his uncle-in-law. 'Sir, we have argued here about her wardship with the King of Normandy. Was she, fact, his ward? Some say that she was even his mistress. And how came she to be tied to that miserable castle keeper at Penbroch?'

Rhydderch slung a leg over the nearest bench and sat down heavily.

'No one knows the answers better than I. When my brother Rhys fell in Easter Week of 1093 at the hands of Bernard de Neufmarche, his eldest child Nest was in the palace of Dinefwr, his main court in Ystrad Tywi. Both her younger brothers, Gruffydd and Hywel, were at the lesser court of Caer Rhiw,* near Penbroch, in the care of kinsfolk, their mother Gwladys having died the previous year giving birth to Hywel.' He paused for a long swig from

* *The modern Carew.*

his mead horn. 'Your father, Cadwgan, invaded Dyfed within the week, but was himself overwhelmed two months later by a massive invasion of the French, sweeping down from Shrewsbury and Brecon under Roger Montgomery and his son Robert de Belesme. His other son Arnulf already had a foothold by sea at Penbroch.'

Rhydderch swept his arm unsteadily around the smoke-filled hall. 'It was then that this old fortress of Din-geraint was rebuilt by Earl Roger...'

Owain cut in with an impatient gesture. 'All this is common knowledge, but what of Nest?'

Rhydderch, now too drunk to take offence at the young man's tone, waved a finger at him. 'Ah, Nest...my lovely Nest. She was taken at Dinefwr with all the palace household when Neufmarche over-ran it. There was slaughter amongst the men, of course, but the daughter was taken as hostage. Old King William the Bastard had had a pact with her father, so Neufmarche hesitated to do anything rash without consulting Rufus, the new King.' Rhydderch sniggered. 'But William the Red wasn't interested in girls, no matter how beautiful – boys were more in his line.'

This raised a lewd laugh from some of the youths, but Owain continued to scowl. 'Then what?' he grunted impatiently.

Rhydderch bobbed his head knowingly. 'Wait...Wait! Rufus made her his ward, though he took no interest in the matter and never set eyes on her, to my knowledge. When his brother Henry took the throne after that unfortunate arrow shot in the great forest' – this drew more sniggers from the boys – 'the wardship was automatically transferred to him, along with a few score other diplomatic hostages up and down the country.'

The Lord of Cantref Mawr tapped the side of his nose. 'Nest was lodged in Shrewsbury Castle for some years before Henry came to be King and I know he met her more than once there, when he was but Prince Henry...If anything happened between them, I know nothing of it, but she would be about sixteen then, being eleven when captured...and eighteen when married.'

Owain banged an angry fist into his palm. 'Now we come to the meat of the matter – how came she to be wed to that damned castle-keeper at Penbroch?'

But he was to be further frustrated for an answer. Just then, the Penteulu hurried up and tapped Rhydderch respectfully on the shoulder. 'My Lord, Prince Cadwgan is retiring and bids me invite you to his chamber for a last horn of mead.'

Rhydderch was a stickler for etiquette and immediately swayed to his feet to obey the royal request. After straightening his tunic and settling his yellow mantle over his shoulder, he waved his hand in flamboyant farewell to the young men.

'I bid you good night! This talk of Nest ferch Rhys wastes your time, as she is guarded like the Holy Grail itself by her jealous husband. Only her close family have seen her to speak to, these eight years. So if your hot blood needs a sight of her beauty, you'll have to storm the walls of Cenarth Bychan for it!'

As he began to walk away behind the Penteulu, Owain called out to him. 'Cenarth Bychan?...why so?'

Rhydderch twisted his saturnine head for a last call over his shoulder. 'Because Gerald de Windsore and his wife travel there tomorrow from Penbroch!'

Without further explanation, the Lord from Ystrad Tywi strode off with the exaggerated care of the slightly inebriated.

Einion rounded on his elder brother. 'There's your chance, great hero! The lady is but a few miles away tomorrow,' he mocked, his sneering face stuck out towards Owain.

'He'd never get within arrow shot of the lady,' gibed Maredudd. 'Her husband is well known to hate Welshmen even more than Saxons, though his own mother was from Gwynedd.'

Einion nodded with calculated contempt. 'True...he'd throw you in the Teifi...and it's a long drop off the rock of Cilgerran.'

Morgan jabbed a hard finger into Einion's shoulder. 'Don't tempt him, brother,' he snapped. 'You know his pride. And this cousin of ours is a mature woman with a brood of children, not some young virgin to be carried off for fun.'

Maredudd's swivel eye rolled with delight. 'Yes, she's probably as happy with her French husband as Saint Caranog with his pigeon – she'd not want some hairy-chested kinsman breaking in on her elegant Norman ways.'

Owain jumped up, his bench crashing backwards. 'How do you know, you flat-faced fool,' he snarled, gripping Maredudd by the slack of his tunic and shaking him. 'What has age and children to do with it. She was a hostage, given in marriage to a Norman – of course she would want to be free!'

Einion spat on the floor. 'They say she was King Henry's mistress – before and after she was wed...There are even rumours that the King's eldest bastard, Robert, is a whelp of hers. She seems well content to sleep with Frenchmen!'

Owain released Maredudd to thrust his reddened face close to Einion's. 'You know nothing of it – none of you,' he shouted furiously, his temper beyond control. 'The only way to discover it is to ask her.'

Morgan laid a calming hand on his brother's shoulder. 'You heard what Rhydderch said, Owain...none but her close family come near her these days. This Gerald keeps her locked up like a chest of treasure.'

'And what a treasure, if all they say is right,' sniggered the trouble-making Maredudd. 'A pity to keep such a sight for French eyes alone.'

Owain kicked over another bench in pure rage. 'By Christ Jesus, I'd go to Cenarth Bychan myself for a half a groat and discover how she fares!'

Einion clapped his hands together in delight. 'Half a groat be damned! I'll wager you my best horse that you could never get into de Windsore's castle, let alone have speech with the lady.'

Owain glowered at him. 'I could do that blindfold, brother – if I chose to.'

'Ha...if you chose to! But I'll bet you don't choose to...unless you want to end up floating face down in the Teifi with your throat cut and your members missing!' This came from Maredudd, sheltering behind his larger brother, out of range of Owain's vicious fist.

'Right...right then!' Owain was wagging his hand at them in suppressed fury. 'I'll not only get audience with her, but I'll be invited to sup there. A good horse and pair of gold cloak buckles to each of you if I don't.'

Einion sneered. 'Talk is cheap...our father's mead must have been witched by Merlin this Christmas.'

Owain grabbed him by the shoulder and poked a furious finger almost up his nostrils. 'Listen, brother – have you ever known me go back on my word? When I say I will do it, I will do it – and only God can stop me!'

His vehemence silenced even Maredudd and Einion, but as usual the diplomatic Morgan stepped into the breach. 'Ay, brother, we well know that you would try it – no one doubts your courage. But come, the drink has flown too freely, let's not be all at each other's throat like dogs. We are brothers, after all is said – hands on it now, and forget these squabbles.'

Owain stepped back a pace and ignored Morgan's outstretched arm. 'No, by God, I'll not forget it! I care nothing for all your sneers, Einion, but the lady is our kinswoman and I must see her to satisfy myself, if nothing else.'

Morgan sighed and gave up his attempts at peace-making. When Owain had that hard look on his face, his jaw clamped like a blacksmith's vice, it was waste of time to argue.

'You'll go, then?' said Einion, suddenly uneasy. He, too, knew his elder brother's stubborn ways and was uncomfortable at what his own roguish tongue had done. 'There's no need,' he muttered harshly, 'I'll absolve you from the wager. It was but a stupid jest.'

Owain looked at him bleakly. 'Are you now so mean or so poor that you fear the price of a horse, Einion? I said I'll go to Cenarth Bychan and go I will...at tomorrow's sunset to claim a free meal from that Frenchman.'

Sobered by the foolhardy risk that Owain was intent on running, Einion and Maredudd tried to shake his resolve, but as Morgan had feared, they only strengthened it.

Eventually Einion became nasty. 'Go then, and be damned to you, brother. De Windsore will cut your guts out!'

'How do we know you will succeed?' cut in the evil-minded Maredudd. 'What's to stop you resting up in the woods for a few hours and then coming back with some trumped-up tale of dining with your cousin and her charming husband?'

Livid in an instant, Owain grabbed Maredudd by the hair and forced him to his knees. 'Brother, some day I'll kill you...My word is my bond and you question it at your peril!' He hissed the last words into the squinting eyes, then flung Maredudd to the rushes with a contemptuous flick of his brawny arm.

His blazing eyes came up to meet Einion's. 'But if you want proof, I'll take one of your men with me – and one of yours, Morgan, so that there'll be no scurvy lies told.'

'I'll come myself, brother,' said Morgan simply.

Owain shook his head. 'No, if anything goes wrong, the Frenchman's treachery will need avenging by the strongest arms. I suppose I can at least count on you for that, Einion,' he added sarcastically.

The other man scowled. 'Rhys Ddu will go with you.' He beckoned to a sullen-looking young man, with such a black head of hair and devil's eyebrows that Rhys the Black was the only possible name for him.

'And I'll send my Iolo,' added Morgan, pulling the arm of a powerfully-built blond youth, of obvious Norse ancestry.

Owain looked at them both, the one dark, the other fair.

'Will you come? I'll not lead anyone into hazard against their wish.'

Iolo grinned. 'Try and stop me, Lord...I've heard of the Lady Nest from my mother. I'll take the risk to see her beauty.'

Owain looked at the dark man. 'And you, Rhys Ddu...will you come to be a true witness?'

Rhys nodded abruptly, his deep-set eyes fixed unwinkingly on the elder brother's face.

Morgan made one last attempt. 'Look, we all know that you can do it, Owain, so for the Virgin's sake, why go to all this trouble to prove it?'

Owain stared into the depths of his drinking horn for a second, then tossed down the contents with an air of absolute finality.

'We ride at sunset,' he said, and stalked off to find his bed.

CHAPTER TWO

THE SECOND DAY OF CHRISTMAS, 1109

A SMALL, heavily armed cavalcade wound its way slowly down the heavily wooded valley which led the Plysgog stream to its meeting with the Teifi. Almost a quarter of a mile ahead, an advance party had already come within sight of the castle of Cenarth Bychan perched on its rock of Cilgerran, high above the river.

The leader of the main party, a burly man-at-arms with a huge ginger moustache, glowered suspiciously from side to side.

'I hate these bloody Welsh valleys,' he rumbled in his throaty Norman-French. 'You can't see more than twenty paces, even now when there's no leaves on the damn trees.'

Behind him rode six more warriors, nothing of them visible except a pair of eyes and a mouth. Conical steel helmets with a guard covering their noses, chain-mail hauberks down to their knees and long, pear-shaped shields gave them a menacing look that had struck fear – with ample reason – into most of the population of Britain during the past forty years.

They plodded on uneasily through the fading light of late afternoon. This was the very edge of the Norman territory of Dyfed. Across the Teifi were the lands of Cadwgan ap Bleddyn. Although, in theory, he held these lands by the grace of the Norman King, a theory would not save their throats in a country where armed bands of Welshmen roamed like pirates and politics changed locally like the phases of the moon. Most of the time, the sergeant thought thankfully, the Welsh were squabbling amongst themselves, but every now and then, they would combine to wipe out some travelling Norman party, then vanish into the wilderness of forest, moor and mountain.

He shivered in the dank air and strained his eyes ahead for a glimpse of the vanguard. 'The sight of Sir Gerald's castle will be more than welcome,' he growled over his shoulder to the next man, 'even though it be only half built.' He turned further in his saddle to look back along the cavalcade of twenty riders to see that all was well – these Welsh had a nasty trick of putting their superb bow-men to pick off stragglers at the rear.

Immediately behind the first group of soldiers, he saw the erect figure of Sir Gerald de Windsore, sitting solidly on his big, grey horse. His armour was identical, but he wore a scarlet surcoat over his hauberk in the new fashion brought back from the Holy Land, though he had never himself gone a-crusading.

Following him was a litter slung between a pair of horses, then the Lady rode her white pony side-saddle, with two of her children jogging close by.

Another dozen soldiers were strung out behind and a separate rearguard was still out of sight, the whole party being about thirty souls, including a few scouts and outriders. Sir Gerald was not one to take chances where his family was concerned.

Satisfied, the sergeant-at-arms turned his thoughts to the castle kitchen and the soup that would be heating up there for them.

Behind him, Lady Nest was also thinking of Cenarth Bychan – yearning for the journey to be over, not for her own sake but for the children.

Her eldest, William, was almost nine years old and scorned the 'babies' carriage', as he called the litter. He rode nearby on his own pony, alongside Gerald's twelve-year-old bastard, whose name was also William, though they called him Hubert to avoid confusion.

Though the discomfort of the thirty-mile journey from Caer Rhiw to Cenarth Bychan was bad enough on the back of a horse, Lady Nest preferred it to the litter, which swayed and bumped like a ship in a storm. Her over-active maternal feelings constantly ached for poor little Maurice and baby Angharad, as well as for her faithful maid, Rhiannon. Once more she felt exasperation at Gerald for insisting on this midwinter journey right across Dyfed, merely to gloat over the building of his new fortress. He could have gone alone – or even been content with her coming alone to bolster his pride – but to drag along the little ones was ridiculous. She had refused to bring Gwladys, only six months old – not that Gerald was much interested in his girl children, and David, their four-year-old son, had stayed home with a mild fever.

Her children were her life, she thought, with a sudden flash of inward-looking pensiveness – she had little else to console her. Feeling the all too familiar depression creeping over her, she mentally shook herself and concentrated on the castle to divert her.

Cenarth Bychan – an ancient Welsh stronghold once belonging to her father – had been rebuilt in wood in the French fashion by Arnulf de Montgomery back in '93. It became his brother's property, the black Robert de Bellesme, then fell derelict after their disgrace eight years ago. Several years later, when Henry the King had given it to Gerald, he had received it with the delight of a child with a new toy. Nest understood why this was – it was the first land he had ever owned in his own right. Pembroke was the King's, Gerald being but the castellan. Even Caer Rhiw itself, though Gerald's by right of marriage, had come as Nest's dowry, given by her brother Gruffydd from what was left of the vast possessions of their royal father.

Though Gerald must have guessed whose influence had persuaded the King to hand over Cenarth, he preferred not to acknowledge the fact and threw himself into its rebuilding with the zeal of a missionary.

For two years he had been planning the reconstruction in stone, which had been started six months earlier. Now he was anxious to look at the progress of the work and to show it proudly to his sons, who would one day inherit Cenarth Bychan.

Suddenly her thoughts were disturbed by a shout from the man at the head of the column. The sergeant-at-arms threw up his gloved hand to point ahead. The track had begun to climb and the saplings seemed thinner. Nest presumed that they were within sight of their destination and she was soon proved right. The soldiers stopped and her husband wheeled his stallion about to trot back down the line.

Reining in her own pony, she pulled her fur-lined cloak closer about her and waited for Gerald to come near.

'Are we there, sire?' asked William excitedly. He looked half-frozen, but his young face was alight with anticipation.

'Aye, boy, up there beyond the trees. You'll see it in a moment.' De Windsore was a big man, but his voice was too high-pitched to suit his frame. It always held a querulous note. He was forty years old last spring and Nest often felt that far more than thirteen years separated them.

He moved past the boys and stopped alongside her. She looked again at his face, wondering as she often did whether she was tied to this stranger for life. For stranger he would always be, a Norman with a trace of Florentine – as unlike a Welshman as she could imagine, for all his mother's Celtic blood.

His face was square and had high cheekbones and small eyes. It gave him a slightly Oriental look, an impression that was heightened by the habitual impassiveness of his expression.

Gerald sported no beard or moustache. His straight narrow-lipped mouth was in full view, the mouth of a man who loved order and discipline, of a man who knew what he wanted and spared no one, especially himself, to get it.

He sat on the great horse and looked down at his beautiful wife, his mood concealed by the mask of his face.

'We shall be at my castle in a few minutes, Lady.'

There was no enquiry about her fatigue or the comfort of the infants.

'You may settle the children in the gallery of the old hall, we shall sleep in the lower chamber. There is no other accommodation, as all except the keep and gatehouse have been demolished to make way for the rebuilding.'

She noticed that he said 'my' castle, another sign of his intense possessiveness for the place.

'Where will the men-at-arms bed down, sir?' she murmured, trying to show some interest.

'They can sleep in the hall tonight – on the floor. Most are returning to Pembroke tomorrow. There's no need for such a heavy guard as this except when travelling. These local Welsh savages like sneaking shots from behind a tree, they've no stomach for storming a palisade.'

Her husband seemed quite insensitive to the fact that he was talking to a princess of the royal Welsh line, one who could trace her ancestry back to Cunedda.

She made no answer, and the knight wheeled his horse around and rode past the column to its head.

They moved off again and soon broke through the trees to find that the rock of Cilgerran was in sight.

The light had almost gone when Nest first laid eyes on the castle perched on its summit. Its black shape was outlined ominously against the pinkish-grey clouds which reflected the last rays of the western sun. Something about that gaunt, jagged silhouette sent a shiver through Nest, a shiver that was not born of the biting cold.

As her steed stumbled up the steep path beyond the trees, she looked up again and saw the grim outline of a wooden palisade, with the tip of the central keep just visible. There was no typical Norman mound, partly because this had been a Welsh fortress and anyway, there was little earth on that rocky spur.

The castle sat on a great rounded promontory that looked as if it should have been jutting out into the sea, not the Teifi. The path from the valley terraced up and after a few more laborious moments, they were at the top.

Nest saw that there was no moat on that stony outcrop, but a deep, dry ditch had been hacked on the landward side and a drawbridge led across it to a massive gate set in the old wooden walls.

It rumbled down as they approached and the gate swung open.

Sir Gerald pulled his stallion aside and waited until the procession passed him. As his wife drew level he gave a rare, bleak smile.

'Welcome to this place, Lady Nesta. We'll have to find a good Norman name for it in place of that outlandish native one it bears at present, eh?'

With a vague foreboding, she heard her pony's hooves echo hollowly on the drawbridge as she entered Cenarth Bychan for the first time.

Their evening meal was a far more sombre affair than the one held the previous night at Din-geraint. There were no guests and the Lady Nest and Sir Gerald sat alone in the hall, apart from two hovering servants.

William had eaten with them, along with Hubert, but they had been packed off to bed after eating their fill. The hall was small, by Pembroke standards, but it seemed vast and gloomy to the two silent diners.

The long table across the head of the hall was lit by some guttering torches stuck into rings on the wall, and a few tallow candles stood by their plates. A stone hearth was built into the wooden wall behind them and a crackling fire added some flickering light, but even this was not sufficient to dispel the darkness in the empty corners and up amongst the rough timbers of the high roof.

Gerald had eaten a great deal, but in almost complete silence. Nest had long ago given up trying to make conversation at meals with her aloof husband and merely answered politely when he deigned to address her. She was not actively unhappy with her lot, but merely resigned to it. There had never been any pretence at love on either side. It had been a business transaction on his part and she had had no choice on hers. At least, she thought wryly, he was always civil and grudgingly polite. Gerald's attractions were all negative – he never abused her, never struck her and never criticized her before others. So far, he had never displayed any positive attractions for her, though she never doubted that he was a clever soldier, an able administrator and a brave man.

As far as their marriage was concerned, he 'possessed her' in the true sense – she was his wife, a valuable piece of property, capable of producing strong children at almost yearly intervals.

His sexual drive was spasmodic – switched on and off under complete control. Between times, there was no word of affection, as there was neither word of reproof. She often wondered why he bothered with the occasional mistress – without conceit, she recognized that not one was one-tenth as attractive as herself. His love-making was typical of the rest of his personality – rapid, silent and efficient.

'Is the meat to your liking, Lady?' he asked suddenly.

The silence had been so long that it took her a second to shake off her reverie. 'Very good, Gerald – your cook here is an acquisition.' She always called him by his first name in private, but was never anything but 'my lady' or 'Lady Nest' in return, even in the rare moments of his passion.

'The cook is a Fleming. They are good at everything,' he said flatly. Nest knew his admiration for this big-boned, impassive people who had been imported in great numbers from Brabant and other parts of Flanders the previous year, mainly at the instigation of King Henry, who wanted the Welsh driven from their lands in southern Dyfed.

The thought of Henry Beauclerk conjured up disturbing old images, which she hastily put aside in her husband's company, almost as if she was afraid that he might penetrate her very thoughts.

'How long will we stay, Gerald?' she asked, mainly to exorcise her wayward memories.

He reached for more venison, killed in preparation for their visit.

'About three days – I wish to call at our lordships in Cemais, then Nevern and perhaps Fishguard before returning to Pembroke.' He offered her more meat, but she held up a hand. 'Three days should be enough for me to see every stone here and talk with the masons about the direction the work must take.'

He was a great builder, this Gerald, she thought. It must be hereditary, as his father had built Windsor soon after the Bastard's conquest. The old man, William fitz Otho, sometimes called Walter, had been obsessively devoted to King William and his Norman ways, even though his own father, Dominus Otho, had been one of the Italian Gherardini living at the court of the Confessor even before the conquest. Nest pondered on the same trait in the father as in her husband...with Florentine and even a trace of Turkish blood and a wife who was a daughter of the Prince of North Wales, old fitz Otho had been aggressively French and had cast his third son, Gerald, in the same mould. It looked as if Gerald was going to repeat the process with his own sons – a continuing example of how those who adopt a culture become more ferocious champions than those naturally born to it.

Castle building seemed to be in their blood – Gerald had taken his name from the huge pile built by his father, then himself had supervised the building of the first fortress at Pembroke for his Lord Arnulf. Later he had rebuilt it in stone and now was in the process of doing the same with Cenarth Bychan.

Nest wondered again how much he guessed about the reason for Henry granting him the gift of Bellesme's forfeited land. Gerald had so studiously avoided the matter that he must well know that it was her intercession with the King that had won it, just as her whispers on the pillow had brought Gerald back from imprisonment after the rebellion, to be restored once more to the wardship of Pembroke. He preferred not to remember these things – she had the feeling that his cold politeness to her was in great part due to these submerged feelings of indebtedness to her.

They ate on in silence.

The hall was icy in spite of the fire. Draughts whistled from every corner and came in through the roughly panelled boards that lined the hewn logs of the square building.

Nest wore a plum-coloured velvet cloak that covered her from throat to ankle, but still she shivered when a serving man opened the side door to bring dishes from the kitchen building on the other side of the courtyard.

She looked up into the shadows to seek the primitive minstrel gallery that had been built opposite the high table. It was being used tonight as a bedroom for the children. The elder boys were rolled up in blankets at one side and the cot for little Angharad was alongside a mattress for Rhiannon, who slept cuddling young Maurice to her.

Nest and her husband had a small chamber on the ground floor, which opened off the main hall opposite the door to the kitchen. A bed had been built against the wall and long, woollen drapes hung around it in an attempt to stave off the worst of the draughts.

'In a year's time, I'll have quarters fit for royal guests,' Gerald had said smugly, when he had taken her to the primitive accommodation on their arrival. He even showed her the new privies, built in stone. They formed part of the new masonry now going up around the old keep. The latrine opened from the bedroom by a short passage and boasted a modern 'garde-robe' shaft excavated in the solid rock.

She still had enough royal blood in her to be little interested in the mechanics of sewage disposal, but Gerald insisted on conducting her on a tour of the rebuilding, preceded by a soldier bearing a blazing flambeau. The frosty sky was quite black when they came back indoors and now, two hours later, his sporadic talk was only concerned with building operations in his beloved fortress.

She pushed her plate away and motioned to a lurking servant to pull back her chair. Gerald rose, as he always did, a frown disturbing his meditations of building methods.

'You retire early, my lady?' he suggested in a tone of rebuke.

'Only to see that the children are well settled – I shall be down again in a moment.'

She walked towards the rough staircase in the corner, the servant following her with a torch. Gerald watched the slim, straight shape of his wife gliding away, the dark velvet of her mantle rippling and the sheen of her black hair glistening in the torchlight. He felt a sudden itch of desire. The well recognized feeling stole through him like a creeping fire as he sat staring at his empty plate. He had the most beautiful wife in Wales, yet there could never be anything but this barrier between them. He felt more at ease with a Saxon or Flemish concubine than with his Lady Nesta. Staring unseeingly at the greasy silver, he hated the Welsh all over again. He hated the half of him that was of their blood, hated the twist of fate that made him despise the race yet made his loins ache for one of their princesses.

He looked up to glimpse the torch flickering along the gallery high up in front of him, then his gaze was distracted by some movement at the great oaken door below. It had opened a fraction and a draught of icy air streamed in, as a head poked through to speak to the mailed guard standing woodenly inside.

'Shut that damned door!'

De Windsore's voice cut across the hall in a penetrating hiss. The children were right above and he had no wish to waken them – the boys were dearer to him than his castles and far more so than a dozen royal wives.

The head vanished rapidly from the doorway and the heavy oak door closed with a dull thud. The guard strode stiffly across the flagged hall, his armoured hauberk clinking as approached. He stopped before the glowering Gerald and crossed his mailed fist across his breast in salute.

'Sire, there are three Welshmen beyond the outer ditch asking to be admitted.'

De Windsore's scowl changed to an expression of disbelief. Though technically the land was at peace, Welshmen and Norman were in a perpetual state of war.

For three Welshmen to come knocking on the gate of Norman outpost at night was more than unusual – it was incredible! They risked a shower of arrows first and question afterwards.

'Welsh! nonsense!' he grated. 'Whoever they are, do they say what they want?'

'The leader seems to be a minstrel, sire. He held up a small harp. Then he called out in good French that he wished to give my Lady Nesta greetings on this feast of Christ.'

'Was he a vagabond – or a fighting man?' demanded de Windsore.

'I know not, sire…the gate guard said he could see shields lying on the ground, but nought else.'

Gerald reached for his goblet. 'Send word for them to be given a quiver-full of arrows – in the chest if possible!'

The guard hesitated for a fraction of a second, then saluted and strode back to the door. No one argued with Sir Gerald – he had a reputation for ruthless dealing with the slightest wavering of discipline.

Nest was still upstairs with the children when the man-at-arms came back five minutes later. Uneasily, he clanked up to the high table once more.

'What now?' snapped de Windsore. 'Couldn't they hit the fellow in full moonlight?'

'Sire, the man dodged behind some building stones on the edge of the ditch. The only arrow to get near him was turned on his shield. Then he cried out again that he came in peace to see his kinswoman, the Lady Nesta. He claims entry on the grounds that he is her cousin, sire.'

Gerald was annoyed more than intrigued. Half the native population was related to each other in this damned country, he reflected impatiently. Inbreeding and incest was as common as in ancient Egypt.

He looked up to the gallery to see if his wife was coming down and saw her peering over the balustrade.

'Is there anything wrong?' came her low, musical voice.

'Three Welshmen are outside.' He refused to say 'three of your country-men' – for the sake of his sons, she must be stripped of native connections. 'One claims kinship with you and asks to be admitted.'

Nest was silent for a moment. For years she had not seen anyone of her *teulu*,* apart from infrequent visits from her uncle Rhydderch. Then Gerald saw her head vanish from the gallery and a rapid bobbing of the flame along the narrow side-walk showed that she was hurrying down. A moment later, she was at the table, her face looking flushed in the firelight and her dark eyes sparkling with almost fearful anticipation.

'Who is it?' In spite of herself, she felt a sudden quickening of her heart fluttering inside her chest.

'I know not – neither do I care overmuch,' growled Gerald. He looked across at the waiting soldier. 'What device was on the shield?' Like his own red surcoat, the returning crusaders had brought home this new habit of emblazoning their shields as recognition signs.

'A golden lion rampant on a field of scarlet, sire.'

De Windsore had no need to consult his wife on this military matter. 'The royal arms of the House of Powys,' he muttered. He looked up at his wife standing by his side. 'What kinsman have you there, lady?' Nest was of the rival kingdom of Deheubarth.

The white brow above the perfect oval of her face wrinkled slightly. 'Very many, sir. Through Rhydderch ap Tewdwr's wife, the whole family of Cadwgan ap Bleddyn. But also through my mother, who was Cadwgan's cousin.'

Gerald snorted derisively. Interlaced like rabbits kept in a box, he thought. Aloud, he said, 'Well, lady, one is outside – and a flight of arrows has not chased him off.'

* *Family or clan.*

He felt the sudden descent of her hand on to his shoulder – a rare thing, as they never touched except when his desire became intolerable.

'Gerald, let him in…please! It is Christmas and I have a great longing for news of my people.' Her voice was still low, but it was vibrant with yearning emotion.

'But this is a man of Powys, not your old family.' It was an effort for him to talk about them at all.

She looked down at him with a trace of her old regal spirit. 'My own kindred are scattered abroad, sire, but Powys remains. I have many kinsfolk there and spent happy days in childhood at their court.'

Gerald sighed and motioned her to sit down. He turned back to the motionless guard. 'Enquire this man's name. Make sure he is unarmed. Let his companions be seized and held as surety for his good behaviour.'

He signalled the soldier away with a flick of his finger, but called to him as he was half-way to the door. The guard snapped around and stood at attention.

'Be sure this is no treacherous plan to storm the gate. Have all the guard train their bows on the nearest trees and let the drawbridge down only enough to let them climb in.'

When the man had gone, Gerald held his goblet to his servant for re-filling. Nest refused more wine.

'I trust these Welsh brigands no further than the tip of my sword,' he said flatly. 'I do this for you, lady, as it is Christmas.'

Nest normally bottled up her pride, not because she was in the slightest way cowed, but for a smoother passage through the life that seemed inevitably carved out for her. But now the cork was pulled slightly, with a man of Powys at their gate.

'Sire, they are no brigands. They fight as best they can to defend their land. It is leather against chain mail and bare feet against a long hauberk.' Her voice softened. 'And they are – my people, sire.'

It was a long time since she had reminded him of that – in nine years of marriage, they had tacitly avoided giving voice to the root cause of their polite estrangement.

He looked at her and saw the spots of colour on her ivory cheeks. The full, open lips seemed ready to go into battle against him on behalf of her countrymen; he felt the spur of his desire quicken again and, afraid that an open breach might quench it by the time they got to bed, he smothered his sneering reply.

Then there were faint shouts from the castle bailey and the rumble of the drawbridge windlass came clearly through the frosty air.

'Go to the bed chamber for a moment, lady,' ordered Gerald, 'I still fear some treachery in this.'

Again he rubbed in the untrustworthiness of her compatriots, but this was a direct order and Nest obeyed, walking silently into the shadow of the further corner, where she stood concealed behind the heavy curtain that concealed their sleeping-quarters.

Gerald de Windsore was sitting alone at the centre of the high table when the main door opened wide. The scene was like some tableau from a dream. The light from a pair of branched candlesticks fell on his impassive face, throwing the high cheek-bones into strong relief.

Darkness lay all around him and when Owain entered, the young prince wondered for a moment whether he had walked into a place of summary execution, so dramatic was the gloom and so striking the pale blur of the castellan's face.

He started across the bare floor of the hall, but the two men-at-arms who had closely followed him from the gate, grabbed his arms as they waited for a word from their lord.

Angrily, the Prince of Powys shook off the common fingers of French soldiers and advanced to the centre of the hall.

He stopped, his eyes leaving Gerald to search for his kinswoman and to take in some details of the place where he had perhaps ventured too rashly.

He dimly saw the canopy hanging over the high table and the helmets and shields emblazoned with the diagonal red cross on silver that was Gerald's device*. Two servants slunk in the shadows, but of Nest there was no sign.

He moved nearer, followed by the uneasy guards, and stopped just outside the circle of candlelight to address the castellan.

'Greeting be unto thee, Sir Knight, and be this greeting no less unto the lowest than unto the highest and be it equally unto thy guests and thy warriors. Let all partake of it as completely as thyself.'

This traditional Welsh greeting was glaringly inappropriate, as Gerald sat alone, with not a single guest or lieutenant to grace his table. It was a subtle insult and was not lost on Gerald.

He said nothing, but sat looking down at the young man who had so audaciously thrust himself into his presence. He saw a broad-shouldered figure who, though of little above average height, had the easy bearing of a royal heir. He had a self-assured erectness, the stance of a man born to rule, an almost arrogant self-confidence that gave him stature beyond his inches. Dark russet hair glinted in the torchlight as the visitor nonchalantly flung back his heavy woollen riding cloak, to reveal his toga-like garment of spotted animal-skin over a slim, green tunic. His belt sported a glistening gold buckle, but his scabbard was empty, the dagger having been snatched from him by the gate-guard.

Gerald sat immobile, one hand on the base of his half-full goblet and the other on the hilt of his own dagger below the level of the table. He needed no knowledge of the lion rampant device to sense that here was a man of royal blood; his Norman disdain was tempered by his own inverted snobbery that so envied kingship, even in so primitive a race as the Welsh.

'Who are you, boy?' Gerald tried to inject as much offensiveness into the words as possible.

* *Now embodied in the 'Union Jack'.*

Owain ap Cadwgan moved a few more paces until he was at the foot of the few steps that led up to the dais of the high table.

'I am Owain, Prince of Powys, Sir Knight – and, as for being a boy, alas, eleven years have passed since that happy time.'

This was pert reply to Gerald's sarcasm. Welsh lads come of age at fourteen, two years later than their girls.

De Windsore remained impassive, his Oriental features hiding his thoughts as well as the other's displayed his every mood.

'And what want you here, Owain ap Cadwgan?'

Gerald knew this one by repute – the eldest and most troublesome by far of Cadwgan's many sons.

Owain's eyes roved the back of the hall before he answered.

'I was in the neighbourhood and thought it well to call upon my dear cousin, *yr Arglwyddes* Nest ferch Rhys ap Tewdwr.' He deliberately used her full Welsh title, sensing that it would annoy this stony-faced Frenchman who looked as if his ancestors had come from Tartary.

Owain stepped abruptly up on to the dais, the two men-at-arms hesitatingly closing up behind him at the lower level. He came well into the ring of light thrown by the candles and Nest, watching through the draperies, saw his face clearly for the first time since he had entered the hall.

She recognized him immediately from the painful depths of her childhood memories, but recognition was shockingly swamped by sheer animal desire. Though he was indeed handsome, this shattering sensual thunderstorm was really born of years of emotional starvation. Here was not only a young and comely man, but the incarnation of everything that she had lost – a royal heir, a man of her own race and her own kin, the epitome of resistance to the subjection brought by Normandy. A man who radiated everything her husband lacked, as far as she was concerned. She gazed at the two men now, her heart hammering as if it was trying to escape her body. The candlelight fell on the two faces and though no words were spoken, she recognized the battle of wills that was being waged.

Owain, for the first time since entering, had the advantage of height over the seated Gerald, who refused to rise to greet even the heir to lands a hundred times the size of his own paltry possessions in Dyfed. The Welshman was fifteen years his junior and even de Windsore's obsession with royalty did not allow him to stand before a stripling from this subject race.

Owain suddenly moved his hands in a smooth movement to rest them on the edge of the table. Though Gerald did not move his body, from her position at the door Nest saw his hand pull his dagger half from its sheath, then slowly slide it back as he realized that Owain was not about to leap across the table at him.

'I dearly wish to offer the Lady Nest the greetings of her royal kinsmen at the court of Powys, Sir Knight,' said the young Prince. It was the first time he had spoken in Nest's hearing and the words were clear and slow as if he were delivering an ultimatum. The sound struck her ears like the tolling of a silver bell. Owain's voice was just as she would wish it – he spoke in Welsh and the musical accents sent a shiver of delight down her spine.

Nest saw her husband hesitate and she knew the reason. Even though he affected not to understand the native tongue, this time he made no disclaimer. His built-in awe of royalty was preventing him from having this insolent young man ejected, mutilated or killed.

Partly from fear for Owain's safety, but mainly from her strong desire to be nearer him, Nest stepped quickly through the curtain and stood directly beneath the torch that flickered on the wall above her head.

The sudden movement caught Owain's eye and, like Gerald, a fighting man's reflex sent his hand shooting towards his empty scabbard. As his head turned to the source of the distraction, he forgot dagger, Gerald, hall and everything else.

Nest had experienced sudden desire from years of deprivation, but the young man's passion exploded from nothing but uncomplicated admiration and lust.

Like Nest, he recognized her straight away from childhood memories at the court at Mathrafal, but the recognition was swamped by a tumultuous awareness that this was the most beautiful woman in the world and that, *ergo*, she must become his.

Oblivious of her husband, Owain's eyes devoured her. Her velvet mantle had fallen aside as her hands held the curtains and a white silk gown glistened beneath it. A girdle of gold thread encircled her waist three times, the ends falling almost to her ankles. The same gold shone on her bodice, but it was not the apparel that absorbed his eyes, even though the gown accentuated the sinuous grace of her slim waist and the exciting swell of her breasts. It was that face, a face framed between the long, raven hair that fell down to her shoulders, that diverted his attention. The face was perfection, an oval of sublime virginal calm, yet the dark eyes and full lips gave a clear promise of unbridled passion. It was a face devoid of Nordic coolness or even his own brand of auburn Celtic rashness. The features were those of the ancient Iberian people of Wales, like his brother Morgan or Rhys Ddu, who was still shivering outside in the castle yard.

They stood for a long moment looking at each other, those second cousins, these great-grandchildren of King Cynfyn.

They looked into each other's eyes across the dimness of the upper hall and knew that for both of them, life would never again be the same.

Nest's appearance had been utterly silent, but Owain's movement and the long pregnant stare made Gerald slowly turn his head.

He opened his mouth to speak, but Owain's deep voice cut him short.

'Nest ferch Rhys ap Tewdwr, I bring you the greetings of my kinsmen and the felicitations of one who has long listened with impatience to the inadequate praises of our bards and minstrels.'

Nest glided forward to stand opposite Owain, only the table now separating them. She seemed oblivious of Gerald's presence, her eyes clinging to Owain's. The Constable of Pembroke rose to his feet for the first time. He was slightly taller than Owain, but narrower in the shoulders and had a slight crouch which detracted from his height. His dark hair had gone from his temples and a sharp 'widow's peak' slashed his forehead in two. His lips narrowed as he looked from one to the other.

'You seem to know each other,' he said harshly in French, the voice sounding shrill after the deep tone of the Welshman.

The scrape of his chair on the stone flags and the sound of his voice jerked Nest back to reality.

Her eyes dropped from Owain's and she looked across at her husband, not at his face, but at his hands, now hooked pugnaciously into his heavily embossed belt.

'It is many years since we met, Gerald...yet the memories of childhood are the ones we carry to our graves.'

Her husband stored away these ambiguous words for later digestion.

'You wish him to remain?' he said shortly.

Nest's head snapped up this time, her eyes glinting with anger and not a little shame.

'Remain! My husband, in all these years, I still fail to understand your French ways. In my royal house, as in all Wales, hospitality is the yardstick of honour, not prowess with the lance.'

Gerald's sallow skin was incapable of flushing, but it came near to it at that moment. Honour, the force that drove a Norman above everything except perhaps territorial ambition, was not something to be thrown in his face before some native intruder. Yet...the man was the next king of Powys, if his father's claims survived King Henry's wishes.

Gerald's eyes pierced Nest's face, not with hate – for no man born could hate her – but with complete incomprehension. If they had been born on different planets, they could not have been less in sympathy.

He saw nothing in her eyes but the shutters which kept him from her soul. Turning back to Owain, he waved a hand awards the table.

'Join us, son of Cadwgan,' he said heavily and sat down. As the young man came around the end of the table, Gerald motioned impatiently to a servant hovering in the dark corner and ordered the man to bring more utensils and meat.

Owain came to the opposite side of Nest from her husband and again their eyes locked as he held the back of her chair for her to be seated. His gaze followed her down and he gave quick bow of his head before taking his own seat.

Gerald watched with a trace of a sardonic smile on his lips. He was not jealous – yet, but was allowing his slow anger to kindle at the ease with which a Welsh stranger could achieve better relationship with his wife in two minutes than he himself had managed in nine years.

A servant hurried up with plate and goblet, whilst another brought wine. A moment later, another joint and a roast fowl appeared before Owain.

'We had almost finished eating, Owain,' said Nest softly, the more mellow Welsh of Deheubarth than her kinsman's northern accents. 'So you set to with a will.'

They began conversing in Welsh in low tones, which Gerald could not catch, but he broke in on them abruptly.

'You just happened to be "passing by" tonight…an odd time to be riding on this side of the river, on a frosty night?'

Owain looked at him coldly. 'I like to ride the boundaries of my father's kingdom, to see that no liberties are taken by our neighbours,' he said with calculated insolence. 'And the few miles from Din-geraint is nothing compared with the prospect of seeing the princess of whom I have heard nothing but flowery praises.'

Nest flashed him a look of warning, but he ignored it.

'Our bards are almost at each other's throats, vying for the honour of singing your praises, Nest ferch Rhys. Yet not until now have I realized how feable were their efforts to do justice to your beauty.'

Nest's feelings of exultation began to be mingled with fear. She looked quickly from Owain to her husband and in case her kinsman's rashness might be due to the fact that he had not realized that Gerald spoke Welsh, she raised her own voice in that tongue.

'Gerald, please ask that serving man to bring more wine.'

Her husband looked at her and understood exactly what was worrying her – she could have easily called the servant herself.

In spite of his slowly rising anger, Gerald was amused. His dear wife was fearful for the safety of this impudent dandy. Owain had thrown his cloak off, carelessly draping it over the next chair. His showy wolf-pelt, bright tunic and white linen trousers were in almost gaudy contrast to the long, dark robe that Gerald wore.

The castellan leant forward on his table to look past the slightly troubled features of his wife to where his unwelcome guest sat.

'Owain ap Cadwgan, what was your real reason for coming here tonight?' he asked harshly.

The young prince lifted his head reluctantly from his intense study of Nest's face. 'My real reason, Sir Knight? Since you have been enjoying the real reason for so many years, need you ask?' He inclined his hand graciously towards the lady.

Gerald took a deep breath. This farce was going on too long.

'I feel it strange that on the very first night that my family has ever spent in this castle, you should fortuitously appear. Have you your usual damned spies in the woods, watching every move with the intent of some barbarous raid on my property?'

Nest paled, sensing the inevitable conflict that was to come. She had heard tales of the temper of this cousin of hers – of his violent execution of the sons of Llywarch some years before. That she should be the cause of a further feud was awful to contemplate, yet with Owain there, part of her felt too exhilarated to care. But the breach was not yet upon them. Owain grinned suddenly, his face lighting up with the almost impish delight of a child.

'No chance of that, Sir Knight...no spies in the woods, only the wagging tongue of a close kinsman of this most fair lady. Her uncle, Rhydderch ap Tewdwr, spoke of your coming from Caer Rhiw to Cenarth Bychan today.'

Gerald scowled, allowing his normally blank features the luxury of some expression. 'That be damned for a tale,' he snorted rudely, 'how would that paltry tenant know my movements?'

Owain looked the picture of sincere innocence when he replied, 'I think he is at this moment attacking the castle of Penbroch in your absence, sir – a place I think of which you are also the paltry tenant.'

Two red spots glowed in de Windsore's sallow cheeks. His mere caretaker capacity in Pembroke was a very sore point, as Owain well knew.

'Watch your tongue, Welshman!' snapped the castellan.

Owain shrugged. 'Let us not bicker at Christmastide. There are far more pleasant things to contemplate.'

He swung his head around to stare at Nest and laid a hand on her arm in an unmistakable gesture of affection, rapidly asking some pleasantry about her family.

Gerald's fingers began to tap on the linen cloth of the table, a sure sign of the mounting pressures within him. He had no quick temper like Owain, one that could explode into red rage at a second's notice, but his was a more dangerous sort. It rose more slowly, but fell with equal reluctance. De Windsore was a good soldier because he never allowed his rage to rule his reason, even in the blood-mist of battle.

But now the actions of this arrogant native were raising his temper up to a pitch where action was called for. Many a man had made a fool of himself over the lovely Nest, but never with such open contempt for her husband as this. Her lack of encouragement or response to those others was less of a compliment to himself than a dislike of everything Norman, but now that a dashing young Welsh prince had arrived on the scene, a blind man could tell the difference in her attitude.

He was not jealous in the normal sense – he had never possessed anything of her but her body and her loyalty as a mother to his children. But his present jealousy was one of a threat to a prized chattel. Nest was his property and his resentment of Owain's open flirtation was more akin to finding him with his arm in the treasure chest than as a potential cuckold.

The tension at the table in that silent, gloomy hall could be sensed by the granite-faced soldiers and uneasy servants in the background. De Windsore's little black eyes blazed at the visitor. Nest sat immobile, as if by freezing she could neutralize the enmity between the two men.

Of them all, Owain seemed the least concerned. He tucked into the meats and stuffed down bread and wine quite cheerfully, apparently oblivious of the glowering host on his right.

Nest began to move, trying to break the oppressive silence of her husband. Fiddling with the golden cord of her gown, she spoke in a low voice, using French for Gerald's benefit.

'Owain, do you ride further tonight?'

He ran a hand carelessly through the red plume of hair that swung over his forehead. 'Ride further? I arrived but ten minutes past, *arglwyddes*! I have come only to feast my eyes on your loveliness – and on your excellent meats, Sir Knight!' he added in an afterthought that could be nothing but scathing, as the fare at the table was far from lavish, compared with the previous night's feast at his father's court.

'We are not settled yet, Owain – the castle is being rebuilt and our kitchens are half-dismantled,' Nest cut in hurriedly, and Owain could not decide whether she was defending Gerald's hospitality or trying to smooth over the implied insult in her cousin's comments.

Gerald broke his sullen silence at this. 'In six months, this will be a fortress of stone – impregnable!' In spite of his anger, he could not resist flaunting his favourite topic before his Welshman. 'Soon there will be a town and burgesses clustered round this rock – the start of real civilization in this wilderness.'

Owain grunted, no smile on his face now. 'Flemish burgesses, no doubt. And more Welsh lands taken from their rightful owners on pain of blinding, castration or death!'

'God helps those who help themselves,' sneered Gerald. 'If King Henry could only tear himself away from his disputes in Normandy to attend to his English possessions, he would take all Wales from Pembroke to Anglesey.'

This was a fuse that was guaranteed to ignite Owain ap Cadwgan. His eyes blazed and even Nest was forgotten for brief moment.

'You bloody thieves and murderers! What is it that drives you Frenchmen to covet land as if it were the only thing in life?'

Gerald thumped the table with his fist, delighted that he had roused his antagonist. 'The only thing!' he retorted. 'We Normans are the most devout race in Christendom, so what talk is this of obsession with earthly property? Our brand of churchmen have done more for Christ in this land in forty years than your watery blooded Saxon priests have done in four hundred.'

Owain was red in the face now and almost incoherent with anger.

'Saxon priests!' he snarled. 'What have Saxon priests to do with us? We had saints in Wales before Saxons stepped from their pagan boats on to dirty English soil. And speaking of pagans, you Northmen worshipped the underworld gods no more than a century or two past, before you robbed the French of their religion as well as their language and their lands.'

Nest looked from one to the other, bewildered at the sudden twist of events. She had been quaking for fear of a fight over her own charms, then within half a minute the two men were at each other's throats over politics and religion.

Perhaps it was safer that way, she thought hopefully, but her optimism was short-lived.

'Savages...that's all you Welsh are,' snapped Gerald in retaliation, riding his high horse of Norman arrogance 'Even the Saxons, poor lot though they are, look down on you. You've not a single town in your rain-sodden country, not even a village worthy of the name. You all live in mud-plastered wooden shacks, you shift around the countryside like a pack of the mangy sheep you herd.'

Owain slammed down his goblet and jumped to his feet, his russet lock swinging wildly across his temple.

'Then tell me, Norman, how far back can you trace you music, your poetry, your laws? You have nothing except facility for shedding blood and building ugly fortresses. You steal everything from the lands you conquer, even their tongue and their laws. Normandy, Sicilia, then England, now poor Wales. Your religion is the sword – do you think that this blessed lady would be your wife by choice if it were not for the blood of her royal father and his kindred that you and your kind spilt on our own soil?'

This time it was Gerald's turn to leap to his feet. 'Talk of battles and lands and stratagems, if you wish, Welshman – but not of my wife, do you hear!'

The two men were shouting at each other over the head of the seated woman. Owain impulsively laid a hand on her shoulder as he bellowed at her husband.

'You pillaged her and ravished her just as your kind pillaged and ravished our land,' he raved. 'She was bought for you by your master, Arnulph – he tried to make you a gentleman with some dower lands and a royal wife, instead of a scurvy half-breed Florentine, a castle caretaker, a mere servant!'

If he had rehearsed it for a week, Owain could not have struck de Windsore on a more sensitive spot. The castellan whipped out his dagger and yelled for his guard.

Nest screamed and flung herself at Gerald, taking his knife arm in a grip that was about as effective as a sparrow against his muscles.

Owain, teeth bared in a grimace of desperate frustration at having no weapon, seized his chair by the back and retreated towards the small door leading to the kitchens. He was almost there when one of the mailed guards from the main door careered across the floor and lunged at him with his spear.

Owain dodged and the man skidded into the wall, but the other guard hacked at him with his heavy sword and only the tough wood of the chair saved his right arm from being lopped off at the shoulder. Nest screamed again. 'Stop him, Gerald...man, get away!'

Gerald had so far done nothing but stand in a watchful crouch with his dagger at the ready. The second guard, his sword irretrievably skewered into the chair, hesitated. The lady had told him to stop and his master had said nothing at all. His momentary indecision was his undoing, as Owain swung the chair and hit him a terrible blow across the head, which even his helmet could not withstand. As he fell, Owain leapt up on to the table, dishes and candles scattering in all directions. In a single, smooth movement, he vaulted cleanly down on the other side and sped across to the now unguarded main door.

Gerald, his face impassive, still stood at his place, with Nest clinging uselessly to his arm.

'Guard!' he yelled again, but it was unnecessary. As Owain raced to the door, it flew open and a flood of armed men burst in from the bailey outside.

Owain had no chance – he ran straight into their midst and within seconds his arms were pinioned by the soldiers, who dragged him back to the foot of the high table.

He was still in a flaming temper, with no trace of fear or even apprehension. 'Is this how you treat a guest at your table, Norman!' he snarled. 'Tell your Flemings to take their earthy hands from a Prince of Powys.'

He tried to shake them off, but as Gerald still gave no sign, the stolid-faced guards continued to hold him in a grip of iron.

Nest released Gerald's arm and stood white-faced and trembling. 'The children...the noise will awaken them,' she whispered, as if this was more important than the prospect of her cousin having his throat cut.

The impassive castellan raised his eyes to the balcony, then lowered them to Owain.

'Take him outside,' he said woodenly.

'Gerald! What are you going to do?' cried Nest, now heedless of any more noise.

Her husband ignored her and followed the half-dozen men across the cold flagstones and out into the even colder moon light of the castle courtyard.

Nest, her cloak pulled tightly around her, stood shivering in the doorway as Gerald walked up to Owain, now wriggling impotently in the grasp of his captors.

De Windsore looked at him silently for a few seconds. 'Well, Welshman, why should I not kill you now and save either myself or one of my men the trouble in months to come?' The voice was flat and controlled. In the pale light from the sky, the cheekbones of the castellan's face seemed almost like those of a skull.

Owain was still almost incoherent with rage. 'I came in peace – you took my arms from me at the gate. You admit me to your hall. You invite me to break bread with you...then you attack me with a dagger and set your poxy men upon me. Now you offer to murder me! Frenchmen, you have much to learn about chivalry, I think, for all your aping of nobility.'

Nest groaned softly. Of all the things he could have said, must Owain repeat the jibes about Gerald's common station in life. He was as good as dead now, she thought.

Though a woman not given to tears, she wept silently. It was too much to bear – half an hour ago, she was in raptures at having found a handsome kinsman, a man who had set her soul singing as it had never sung in a lifetime. Now she was about to see him slain at the casual behest of her husband.

The cold tears that coursed quietly down her cheeks suddenly stopped. This awful thing could not be allowed to happen. Her years of quiet acceptance of Norman overlordship fell from her in an instant. In the blinking of a wet eyelid, she became, not my Lady Nesta of Pembroke, but Nest ferch Rhys ap Tewdwr, eldest child of the King of South Wales. She ran out into the chill moonlight, her hair and cloak streaming behind her.

'Gerald – let him be, for my sake.' Though pleading, her voice had suddenly become commanding. She grasped his arm again. 'He is my kinsman – he was here at my request, I asked you to admit him. My cousin is unarmed, it is the feast of Christ.'

Gerald looked at his wife, the expressionless face giving no clue as to his thoughts.

Nest threw back her hair and ran a quick hand under her eyes to remove her tears. Her voice was still strong and almost imperious as she spoke again. 'Will it do you any good to have the blood of a Prince of Powys and Ceredigion on your hands, especially when it becomes known that he was defenceless. The King, too – Cadwgan holds his lands at the behest of Henry. The death of the heir will bring no pleasure to Woodstock or Westminster, Gerald.' She dropped her voice. 'Especially when the King realizes that he is my kinsman.'

Gerald's bead-like eyes gazed steadily at her. She must be in an extremity of fear for the Welshman's life for her even to hint at the forbidden subject of her relationship with Henry Beauclerk. Yet, as usual, her words were full of sense. If he slit the gizzard of this insolent youth, he would have the full fury of half Wales about his ears. Even those vassal chieftains like Rhydderch might be moved to join with Cadwgan and the more militant men of the north in uniting to overthrow the Normans. In combination, they were quite capable of doing so – it was only the fragmentation of the Welsh that had allowed the invaders to keep their present precarious foothold.

Nest was right – the King would be far from pleased if his minor servant, Gerald de Windsore, was the instrument that shattered the present balance of power in Wales. He had been in enough misadventure already with the Montgomery débâcle to risk another breach with the King.

He turned back to Owain and deliberately hit him twice in the face with his open hand. The blows were hard and vicious, causing blood to appear at Owain's lips and nose.

'Go then, Welshman...the next time I meet you, I shall kill you. Do you understand?'

Owain was speechless with rage. He hardly noticed the blows, so full was he with passion and incredulity that a mere French castle-keeper could slap the face of a Welsh prince and not suffer instant death from heaven as retribution.

Before he could find his tongue, there was a bellow from the shadow of the gatehouse and a slim figure came streaking across the frozen grass, pursued by two mailed guards.

'Lord Owain,' screamed Iolo, the youth of Morgan's band who had come with Rhys Ddu. He had been held with Rhys by the gate guards as soon as the disturbance broke out in the great hall, but had torn himself away at the sight of his prince's face being slapped by a Norman.

Dodging under the arm of the first soldier who tried to catch him, the boy rushed towards Gerald, his arms flailing in blind fury. The next pair of mailed men grabbed his wrists and hauled him clear of the crowd, his legs still kicking in a futile effort to avenge his lord.

The captain of the guard, a young squire with a thin, cruel face, looked enquiringly at Gerald.

'Dispatch him!' snapped Gerald, calmly and callously.

De Turberville, the captain, drew his dagger and drove it with an upward lunge into Iolo's belly as he was held by his captors.

A look of utter disbelief crossed the boy's face as the long blade tore up through his organs into his chest. Every face watched in the moonlight as his eyes rolled up and a volcano of blood erupted from his mouth, some of it spattering the hauberk of his killer.

The guards released him and he fell full length on to the frozen ground, twitching for a moment in his own blood before he became still for eternity.

To the men, a death like this was commonplace – the soldiers looked at his passing with professional interest in its efficiency. Neither was Owain shocked by the manner of his death – only by the utter needlessness of the act and the audacity of these low-class foreigners in killing the servant of a prince before his very eyes.

Shaking with rage, he strained his chest toward Gerald.

'Now, Sir Knight – do you the same to me! Come, God blast your black soul, slay me too and see what a hornet's nest it brings down on you and your kind in Dyfed! Go on, Frenchman, strike me as you struck that faithful lad!'

He really meant it – Nest, witness of more than one such violent death as this, was not too shaken to see that he would willingly have died to encompass de Windsore's destruction in a Welsh revolt.

But Gerald's calculating mind was now well under control.

'I'll make no martyr out of you, for your tribe of savages to avenge. We will pick our own time for disposing of your ragged army of bandits. Guards, throw him out!'

Contemptuously, he turned on his heel and walked back to the door of the hall. As he reached it, he turned and shouted a last insult, before striding inside. 'Welshman, the next time we meet, I shall kill you!'

Nest was standing alone in the icy air, watching her kinsman being dragged towards the gate, kicking as he went.

He yelled furiously at the door which Gerald had slammed contemptuously behind him. 'We shall meet again, Norman...but if I do not kill you then, I will cut my own throat in penance!' he raged in French.

Suddenly, he dug his heels in and twisted around to face the still figure of his cousin standing alone in the light of the moon. 'Nest ferch Rhys, most lovely of women,' he called in a softer tone, using their native language, 'we also shall meet again – much sooner than you think.'

The soldiers threw him forward by brute force and abruptly Nest turned around and ran to the dark doorway in the wooden keep. The drawbridge windlass clanked and Owain was hustled to its end. It was still at a steep angle when de Turberville, the guard captain, motioned to his men to thrust the captive off. Owain fell a painful ten or twelve feet into the frosted soil of the ditch, with Rhys Ddu suffering the same indignity close after him. Before they could stumble to their feet, a volley of small stones was hurled at them from the parapet of the gate-house. A rock the size of an egg struck Owain on the head as he staggered out of range, a volley of jeering abuse following them in the clear night air.

Grinding his teeth, he stumbled behind some masonry blocks intended for the new castle and waited for the dark Rhys to crawl up to him. Though he had little in common with this acolyte of Einion, this adventure had joined them with bonds of steel.

They crouched side by side, their hearts too full to reply to the raucous shouts in bad Welsh that echoed from the gate-house roof.

'Iolo – the boy died needlessly,' grated Rhys Ddu. 'He must be revenged in double measure.'

Owain, quivering with emotion and exertion, wiped the blood from his head with the back of his hand. 'By Saint David's bones, Rhys, I swear that I'll not rest until this night is paid for in more than double measure.'

Before he could say more, there was a muffled 'thunk' and an arrow ricocheted off the flinty ground nearby, narrowly missing his leg. More followed, and though they were deliberately mis-aimed, the message was clear.

Owain pulled at Rhys's arm and they made for the dark line of the woods where they had tethered their horses.

The two men swung themselves into their saddles and sat under the leafless trees looking back at Cenarth Bychan, its grim outline black against the hoar frost on the ground.

'Look well on it, Rhys. It will be but a memory in the minds of men before that moon stands as high in the sky tomorrow night.'

Pulling his horse around fiercely, Owain ap Cadwgan led the way into the dark cavern of the forest.

CHAPTER THREE

THE THIRD DAY OF CHRISTMAS, 1109
NEST thought that they were all asleep, but as she bent to pull the blanket over Maurice's shoulder, he raised his head from the pillow.

'Madame, what really did happen last night, when there was all that shouting?'

She wished that he would call her 'mother', as did little Angharad. The boys, Normans to their fingertips, persisted in this formality.

'Hush, Maurice. I've told you, it was only an unruly wassailer who had to be put out when he became a nuisance.'

'There was blood on the grass – I saw it this morning.'

Nest hesitated. 'An accident, child – there was an accident. Now go to sleep like William and Hubert and your sister.'

She gently pushed his head down and moved along the gallery to where a more bulky shape lay next to the little girl's cradle.

'All well, Rhiannon?' It was a sudden relief to stop speaking French.

'Yes, *arglwyddes*...the babe has been fast asleep this past hour.'

Nest looked down at her maid-servant, then spoke softly again. 'Rhiannon, did you hear anything of what passed last evening?'

The maid's plump face took on a wary expression and her eyes moved involuntarily to the gallery entrance. 'A little, only a little. It was Owain, the Lion of Powys.'

Her mistress looked at her with the calm trust of a life-time's companionship. Nest could not remember a time when Rhiannon was not there, even though the other was only thirty-five, a bare seven years older than herself..

'Did you hear all that happened, Rhiannon?'

The maid's mouth tightened. 'There was trouble, I know. That man Turberville...I feel more trouble to come, lady. I saw three magpies in one tree today – not that I need omens to forecast trouble when Lord Owain is in the neighbourhood!'

Nest was unsure whether Rhiannon meant this in disapproval or pride, but she was reluctant to launch her on her favourite topic of sooth-saying. Leaving her, Nest made her way along the narrow catwalk down to the main hall.

The meal had finished some time before. It was only two hours to midnight, but Gerald, not content with a whole day of parading the new building works, had gone out with a horn lantern to haunt the bailey and walk the parapet, dreaming of the day when all would be replaced with great, grey stones, instead of the present warped and splintered timbers.

As Nest sat alone in the hall, he was on the roof of the gate-house with the sardonic young squire who had slain Iolo the previous night. Gerald gazed around his possessions in the moonlight. The outer palisade was roughly circular, with no towers or bastions except at the gate where it was ten feet higher. Here there was this two-storeyed gatehouse to accommodate the drawbridge windlass and to provide shelter for the guards. There was no portcullis, only great oaken half-doors secured by massive bars on the inside. The rest of the palisade had crude castellations made by varying the height of the timbers every few feet. There was a narrow parapet on the inner side, reached by openings in the gatehouse and by rough ladders here and there.

Much of the outer wall was built right on the brink of the precipice that dropped steeply into the Teifi river below. The keep occupied the centre of the enclosure, being a squat tower a few feet higher than the palisade.

'I have been worried in your absence about the weakness of the gate foundations, sire,' said de Turberville. 'The masons have mined under this floor to make a foundation for the new entry passage. They have taken away the timbers that lie beneath the pivots of the drawbridge.'

Gerald shrugged under his heavy cloak. 'Removed timbers, maybe – but they have replaced them in stone, man. The only danger will be in a month or two when they have to remove the gates to build up the gateposts. But then I will send up a troop of men from Pembroke to stand extra guard for that period.'

Turberville grunted. 'I hope so, sire. Since you sent your travelling escort off to Fishguard today, I have but twenty men here.'

De Windsore banged his gloved hands together in the icy air. 'All you need is two men to raise the drawbridge, lad. The river border here has been quiet these past five years. Cadwgan knows when he is well off. Any trouble from him and Bishop Richard would be on him like a fiery angel...our Lord Bishop of London sits in Shrewsbury since the King made him Warden of the Marches and watches Henry's interest like the old hawk he is. We need have no fear of the Welsh, de Turberville.'

The squire did not share his senior's disdain of the people across the Teifi. 'What of that hot-head last night? Could he not stir his father into action?'

Gerald laughed, a harsh, humourless sound. 'The very opposite! The old prince spends half his time trying to repair the mischief done by his wayward sons, of whom that insolent braggart Owain is by far the worst.' He slapped de Turberville on the shoulder. 'Watch easy, boy, keep those beasts out, that's all I ask this night!'

He pointed over the timbers to the black line of the woods, from which came the distant howling of wolves.

A quarter of a mile away, Owain ap Cadwgan looked up at the moon and cursed it under his breath.

'Not a cloud to be seen,' he fretted to Morgan. 'That bank on the horizon has hardly moved this half hour.'

His brother moved silently out from the cover of the high bushes on the river's edge and looked up at the sky. The moon had a great halo around it and a few woollen wisps of vapour hurried past its disc.

'There's a good breeze coming up and it's not so cold,' he said optimistically. Shifting his gaze to the west, he saw the crag of Cenarth Bychan rising above them, the castle crouched on the summit like a black eagle.

The two brothers and fourteen men had left their horses well back in the trees and were waiting impatiently for complete darkness before making the difficult climb up the rock-strewn cliff to the fortress. They were all as heavily armed as Welsh fighters could be – they lacked the long chain-mail of the French and indeed, only Owain and Morgan wore any sort of armour.

Around the chests of these two were light cuirasses of overlapping iron plates. Their upper arms were covered with chainmail sleevelets but the rest of their protection was only leather. Leather helmets strengthened by metal plates and a leather tunic reaching to the knees were their only protection against the heavy swords, maces, spears and arrows of the Normans.

Their men fared even worse, having nothing but a leather helmet and a leather tunic each. Most were barelegged and barefooted, though three who carried spears wore a single shoe on their left foot to support the end of their shaft. Another two men carried bows, but the rest had short swords. All had wicked-looking daggers on their hips and a round wooden shield with a spiked boss in the centre.

They were all followers of either Morgan or Owain, except Rhys Ddu who had insisted on returning with them. He gave no reason but Owain knew that Iolo's cruel death was a matter of personal vengeance for the dark, sullen youth. For youth he was, as were all the warriors on that river bank. Owain, at twenty-five, was easily the eldest, most of the others being well under twenty, except Morgan.

After their ignominious departure from Cenarth Bychan the night before, the two survivors had ridden grimly to Castell Caerwedros, the court of the commote some ten miles north. There they had stayed the rest of the night with the Penteulu, but had sent a rider straight away back to Din-geraint, to call out Morgan and anyone else willing to avenge the insult.

Morgan came immediately with all his own and Owain's friends, but their father and other brothers had left the previous day to ride to Powys.

Both Morgan and Owain were thankful that their father was absent. Though all his sons flouted his wishes daily, he was still the Prince. The revenge that Owain had in mind was almost sure to blow apart the precarious truce that had existed in this part of Wales for almost a decade.

Morgan had spent half the day trying to talk Owain out of the adventure, without the slightest success. Now his conscience spurred him to make one last attempt, knowing that he was wasting the breath that drifted away in the cold night air.

'Brother, are you still determined to go on with this? Our father will surely disinherit us and we will be banished – and the French will hunt us to the end of our days.'

Owain gripped his favourite brother's arm, the mail jingling as he shook it. 'Morgan, can men such as we look the other way when a French castle-keeper assaults a prince of the royal blood, murders his unarmed squire and then throws him like a dog into the castle ditch? Can we ignore this and turn the other cheek just for the sake of some truce made at the Frenchmen's convenience – a truce that will be ignored by them as soon as they think fit?'

His argument was unanswerable. Morgan took a deep breath. 'Let's get it done, then – though God knows what the consequences will be, Owain. I fear that tonight we will set a torch to a fire that will consume us all!'

The first stray fingers of black cloud crept across the cold face of the moon, thickened, then blotted it out. For a few minutes, the bright orb flashed intermittently through gaps, but soon a solid mass rolled in from the west and the distant crag of Cilgerran vanished in the midnight gloom.

'Come…this is our hour!' hissed Owain, and led the way silently out from under the trees.

This was the kind of warfare at which the Welsh excelled. They usually had little choice, as conflict on an open field of battle was merely a bloody form of suicide against the heavily armed and armoured Normans. Ambush, harrying the flanks of marching columns and nocturnal raids such as this were the only means by which they could partly restore the imbalance of strength.

The sixteen shadowy figures padded in single file along the narrow path that followed the edge of the river. The Teifi here was deep and sluggish, utterly different from the roaring cataracts at Cenarth Mawr, a few miles upstream. Normally the river was active with leaping salmon and busy beavers, but tonight all was silent apart from the soughing of the wind.

Owain wished that the waters would make some sound to cover their approach, as once beneath the loom of the castle rock, they had to leave the path and scramble up the rugged slope, with the inevitable noise of scuffling feet and dislodged stones.

As arranged, once the raiders started the climb, they fanned out, each climbed the steep scarp individually, forming an irregular line across the high bluff. Owain was in the centre, with Morgan and Rhys Ddu on either hand.

They picked their way carefully, as every stone that rolled down was a threat to the lives of them all, if it attracted attention from the ramparts above. In daylight – or if the moon broke through too soon – a pair of archers on the palisade could slaughter the whole band within minutes.

But the cloud looked set for the night as Morgan looked up. He could see Owain dimly on his right, with one hand on the ground and the other clutching his scabbard to prevent the sword from rattling. Beyond him, the saturnine Rhys walked upright, his nimble feet finding the best footholds as naturally as a goat.

Halfway up, Owain raised his hand to the pair on each side and the same sign was passed along silently to the end of the line. All stopped and carefully slid to the ground for a rest, as had been arranged in the battle council held in the woods on the way from Caerwedros.

As they all hugged the ground, Owain slid across to Morgan and put his mouth close to his ear. 'Have you seen any movement on the parapet?'

Morgan shook his head. They both looked up at the outline of the wooden battlements directly above them. They watched for some minutes, but no pacing figure broke the faint squares of grey sky between the projecting timbers.

Owain was just about to give the signal to press on when, far to the west, beyond Din-geraint and over the sea, a low rumble of thunder rolled upon their ears.

'An omen, Morgan...the Gods are with us in our anger!' whispered Owain exultantly. He was keyed up to fever pitch and his brother knew that he valued this chance to break the deadlock with the Normans, as well as to wreak his personal vengeance.

There was a distant flicker of lightning on the horizon – not enough to light up the hill-side, but enough to worry Morgan.

'Lightning, Owain...thunder would be welcome to cover our sounds, but I have no fancy to be caught in front of the gate in the glare of heaven's lights!'

'It will be a long time before it reaches us – that is sea lightning,' murmured Owain. 'But come, give the signal – and you, Rhys.'

They rose to their feet and immediately one of the men further down the line dislodged a stone. It tumbled down the cliff, cannoning against others and starting a minor avalanche in the still night.

'Down!' hissed Owain and Morgan together, and immediately the whole party froze to the ground.

This time there was a movement overhead. A helmeted figure slowly leaned over the battlements and stared for what seemed an eternity before pulling back and vanishing. A loud peal of thunder marked his going but this time there was no flash.

Owain waited a moment longer, then signalled a move. More rapidly this time, they scaled the hill to reach the shelter of the fortress wall, paradoxically being safer crouched against the bosom of the castle than they had been some distance away. The last few yards were solid rock instead of loose shale and were much steeper. The band of 'hot-heads', as the elders would call them, were breathless and sweating as they nestled against the rough timbers. Unless a guard hung out and looked directly down, they were safe for the time being.

After a brief respite, the two leaders and six others began to crawl softly around the base of the wall towards the gate, leaving the other eight crouched at the top of the cliff. Two of the waiting party had ropes coiled over their shoulders with three-pronged grapnels on the ends. Their part in the escapade waited on the success of the other group, who had now slunk into the dry ditch that encircled the landward half of Cenarth Bychan. Away from the cliff, the land was flat and here a deep trench had been cut, a pale imitation of the usual Norman moat.

Owain led his party along this in a hurried half-crouch, until they reached the side of the gateway.

The thunder had increased and in spite of his forecast, the lightning came every few moments, though still not bright enough to illuminate the walls or the nearby woods.

Some whispers of wind had sprung up with the arrival of the clouds and a loose shutter high up on the gatehouse creaked and banged, forming a useful cover for their low voices.

'There, look!' whispered Owain, 'Rhys and I noticed this last night while we waited admission to this accursed place.' He pointed to the wall beneath the drawbridge hinges, where splintered timber and debris marked a recent transition from the old wood to new masonry. The eight-foot high gap from the bottom of the ditch to the underside of the drawbridge had just been replaced by freshly-hewn stone.

'They have no mortar between the outer joints yet – and that in the deep cracks is still soft.' As he murmured this, Owain pushed his fingers between two blocks and scraped out a handful of limey paste. 'We can pull out half a dozen stones at the top, enough to squeeze ourselves through into the space beneath the doors.'

Last night, Owain's keen eyes, always on the lookout for faults such as this, had seen that there was enough room at the edges of the slatted floor of the entrance passage to allow a man to climb up from the space beneath.

He tapped one of the youngest lads on the shoulder, one of those carrying a bow. 'Ifor, you're the smallest, so climb up on Rhys's back and start scraping...we'll give these arrogant murderers a night to remember!'

Nest lay uneasily on the strange bed, unable to sleep. Thunder had always frightened her, the learned explanations of her priestly tutors never having dispelled her childhood fears of angry gods shouting across the sky.

She lay on the feather-filled palette, covered by a heavy beaver-skin coverlet and watched the narrow window slit flickering with distant lightning. All the old Celtic superstitions came flooding back in the lonely night. She wondered what the materialistic, unimaginative Normans thought of thunder – it was not the sort of thing that Gerald would think worthy of his attention.

He slept soundly alongside her, on a separate mattress as always, but close enough for her to hear the heavy whistle of his breathing and the occasional snorting grunt that sometimes almost woke him. After a lifetime as a soldier, he never removed his clothes to sleep, only discarding his over-tunic and accoutrements like belt, shoes and gartering.

For her part, she always felt the need to be unfettered in bed. Unlike most of her female acquaintances, there was some animal spirit in her that made her seek freedom from constraint even in the depths of winter. She wore nothing but a linen shift now, and in summer she shed even that beneath the covers.

The thunder grumbled away and between peals she heard the irregular banging of some distant shutter. The cold wind puffed mournfully through the window slit, came under the curtain that hung in the doorway from the hall and also whispered down the narrow passage that led from beyond Gerald's bed into the new privy.

Even the walls themselves leaked air between the timbers – the fur on her bed-cover bent this way and that as draughts hit it from every direction. Though her face was cold, she kept her head high on the silk pillow. Her eyes roved alertly around the dark room, now watching the red flickering under the curtain, where the hall fire still blazed, then switching back to the window to wait for the mysterious flashes from heaven. She was usually a good sleeper, but something about this night made her uneasy.

The senseless death of the young Welsh boy had saddened her, but in an age where most deaths were violent, this in itself was no cause for prolonged horror or even loss of sleep.

It was Owain himself – his very existence and personality – that had ruined the previous night's slumber. Naturally, she had known much about him before – as eldest son of the Prince of Powys, Owain was known to everyone throughout the country. Known for his wild nature, his almost foolhardy courage and his habit of ruining the most carefully contrived diplomatic moves.

Even in her Norman isolation in Caer Rhiw and Penbroch, all the news of Wales filtered through to Nest sooner or later. Rhiannon was the best source, passing on the gossip gleaned from her numerous relatives in Caerfyrddin.* In the sixth year of Nest's marriage, the local grapevine – and even the Normans – had been discussing the assassination by Owain of the two sons of Trahearne, a usurping petty prince of North Wales. Though this episode had caused poor Cadwgan endless trouble, the general consensus of opinion was that Owain had performed a public service by ridding Powys of two treacherous troublemakers. Richard, Lord Bishop of London, was delighted, as two Welshmen fewer was itself cause for rejoicing, as well as anything that added fuel to the eternal fire of internal strife among the Welsh factions.

Nest ferch Rhys lay and thought about these things while the cold breeze played about her and the pale flashes trembled at the window. Nest ferch Rhys... she had almost stopped thinking about herself as that. Month in, month out, she was 'Lady Nesta, wife of the Constable of Pembroke'. Her life was almost purely French. Her two eldest sons were Normans from head to heels and David, the younger, would go the same way in time. Only little Angharad and Gwladys had any hopes of retaining some Welshness about them, as their

* *Carmarthen*

father paid scant attention to daughters. Though Gerald had said nothing openly, Nest knew that he was displeased at having two girl children in succession. Ever since the birth of Gwladys, six months before, she felt that every occasion when he came silently into her bed, it was a conscious act to beget another son. Their irregular mating – one could not call it 'lovemaking' by any stretch of imagination – seemed to be solely to provide more male fitzGeralds to inherit the estates that their father was cutting out with such unswerving determination.

There were long hours and days in which she was alone, idling away time with unnecessary needlework and waiting for Angharad to grow older so that she could hold a proper conversation with her. In these long hours, Nest had ample opportunity to re-live the days of her youth. So much had happened in her twenty-seven years that she felt already that she was at the door of old age...until she looked in the mirror and saw with shy pleasure that she had never looked lovelier.

But she had plenty to look back on. The glorious days of her childhood as eldest daughter in the household of her father, the King. The terrible days after the news of his death had arrived...the frantic flight of her little brother Gruffydd. He was the male heir, taken by night to Ireland, where he still dragged out his endless exile. Her younger sister was away in the north and had escaped capture to be later married to a nobleman of Gwynedd, but Nest and her baby brother Hywel had been seized by the mailed demons of Bernard de Neufmarche. The memory of the armoured Normans tramping through the royal court still coloured her nightmares. Though many of the household had been butchered, the two royal children had been taken to Pembroke to be delivered into the hands of Arnulf de Montgomery. As offspring of royalty – even Welsh royalty – they were useful bargaining counters in the complicated chess-game of politics and treaties. But Arnulf lost one of his pieces in the game to the King, William Rufus, who demanded the elder captive, Nest, to be delivered to him, as his ward. He had never laid eyes on her during the seven remaining years of his kingship, before Walter Tyrel's arrow laid him low in the New Forest, but his omission was repaired by Prince Henry, both before and after his accession to the throne in the first year of the century. Whilst Nest was an open captive at Shrewsbury, the scheming Prince added her to his long list of conquests until, during a false alarm of pregnancy, she had been hurriedly returned to Arnulf at Pembroke for him to find a suitable husband to provide a home for yet another royal bastard.

It soon became obvious that Nest was not with child, but by then the Montgomery plot was thickening against the King and she became caught up in its toils. Gerald de Windsore had just been sent to Dublin to bring back an Irish bride for Arnulf, together with the promise of Irish troops to assist them in their revolt against Henry. Meeting the young Gruffydd ap Rhys and his guardians there, the wily castellan arranged his own marriage with the deposed princess, swallowing his pride at taking a cast-off royal mistress for the dowry lands of Caer Rhiw and Maenor Pyr* and the reflected status of entering a royal family. When the revolt crashed, Gerald fell with it and owed his very survival to his wife's return to King Henry's bedchamber, this time at Gloucester Castle.

Nest's mind was wandering through these arcades of memory, when her attention was suddenly focused on a sound that emerged from the tail end of a rolling peal of thunder.

Instantly alert, she felt her scalp tighten as some vestiges of primaeval muscle tried to direct her ears towards the half-heard sound. It came again, seconds later, the faint cry of a man in terror. She sat bolt upright, heedless of the icy cold, her mother's senses flying at once to her children up in the gallery of the hall. Undecided for a second, she looked across at Gerald, still humped under his blankets, breathing heavily.

If she had been sleeping, she would have thought the faint noise the product of some dream. Hesitating to wake him for nothing – he was never sweet-tempered after sleep – she slid from the mattress and groped for her heavy mantle that was spread over the foot of her bed. Her feet slithered around the rushes on the floor to find her soft doeskin slippers, but just as she was tying a knot in the silken rope of her girdle, her doubts about waking her husband were rudely decided.

A series of blood-curdling yells from the courtyard were followed by the unmistakable 'thwack' of an arrow into the wooden wall alongside the window slit.

Years of campaigning sent the meaning of that sound straight from de Windsore's ears to his limbs, without reference to his brain. In a spasmodic lurch, he threw back the clothes and jumped out of bed, yelling some incomprehensible words from his vanishing sleep.

The window now showed flickers of light that were too ruddy to be lightning. Pounding feet came across the hall and as Nest stood paralysed by indecision, the curtain was torn aside and one of the door guards charged in without ceremony.

'Sire, we are attacked…there are Welsh in the courtyard!' He gabbled this, then turned tail and rushed off to bar the small door that led to the kitchen in the bailey.

Though only seconds had passed, Gerald was already buckling on the sword that always stood at the head of his bed. Feeling for his foot-gear, he rapidly tied the cross gartering, looking up at Nest in the dim light from the window and door.

'Go to the children, lady, while I see what is amiss. Hurry!' he snapped.

Nest found her feet moving toward the hall before she realized it. 'Gerald, what's happening?'

He charged across the room, pushing her aside.

* *The modern Carew and Manorbier.*

'How in God's name do I know?' he snarled. 'Get upstairs whilst I find out.'

Without mail or helmet, he rushed into the great hall and she followed him, turning at the end of the dais to run up the narrow stairs to the minstrel gallery. The rush lights had long gone out and the fire had dulled, but she could see well enough by the frequent flashes of lightning and the ominous red glow that came in through the high window slits just below the roof beams.

Gerald clattered across the stone floor to the guards at the main door. Only two men slept in the keep, the rest of the garrison being billeted in the gatehouse.

'What goes…are we attacked?' he shouted to the men at the door. One had opened it cautiously and was peering out. Almost immediately, the flying figure of a Norman flung itself upon them.

'Open for me…it is Turberville!' shrieked the man. Nest clearly heard the terror in his voice as she peered over the balcony. As Turberville squeezed through the partly opened door, an angry yell from strange voices went up from outside and a rapid succession of arrow blows rained on the oaken door. Turberville's cry of terror instantly changed to a scream of mortal agony as a shaft entered between his shoulder-blades.

'In with him…bar the door!' howled Gerald, and three bodies threw themselves at the inside of the panels. The great bar was dropped into its sockets an instant before there was a frustrated battering on the outside.

'What about the rest of the men?' snapped Gerald to the man on the floor. 'And what about the door to the kitchen?' he rasped to the guards before waiting for an answer from the dying squire. In spite of her lack of love for him, a part of Nest that was not preoccupied with the safety of her children found time to admire Gerald's iron self-control and his undoubted bravery.

As he ran to the small door to check it, she knew that he was at that moment giving short odds on his own life. He was trapped with three men, one mortally wounded, in a ramshackle wooden hall, with two women and four children as an added burden.

In the gallery, confusion was being born as the noise wakened the young ones. Rhiannon, heavy with sleep, was terrified and seemed to think that some supernatural event was taking place. Nest slapped her face vigorously to bring her to her senses and picked up Angharad, who was the only one still slumbering.

Maurice and Hubert were sitting up on their palettes, white-faced and apprehensive at the sudden clamour. William was struggling out of his coverlet, trying to stand up. 'What's happening, my lady?' he asked almost tearfully. 'Are we attacked by the Welsh?'

Nest cradled Angharad in one arm and put the other around her eldest son. 'Some disturbance is going on, William, but your father will deal with it, never fear,' she said firmly, with a conviction that she did not feel.

So far, she had had little time to wonder herself what was really going on. Kicking Rhiannon with her toes, to hurry her to her feet, Nest peered down over the balustrade of the gallery.

Turberville was dragging himself painfully across the floor, blood streaming from his back where a broken arrow-shaft still protruded. Nest realized with a shock that she could now see quite clearly – a bright pulsating light was coming through the high windows. She could now hear the crackling of burning timbers and the smell of burning wood. Along with strident shouts from outside, the first wreaths of smoke came into the hall.

'Is the building on fire, Gerald?' she screamed across the hall, to where de Windsore was helping one of the guards to drag the great dining table across the small corner door.

He raised his head briefly. 'Not yet – that must be the guardhouse. This is what comes of admitting your maniac relatives to our presence. We will pay for it with our lives, it seems.'

The bitterness and accusation in his voice came clearly through the confusion. For the first time, Nest realized that what he said must be true...This must be the work of Owain, come to avenge the insult and the murder of his companion on the previous night.

'Owain ap Cadwgan...it is he, then?' she found herself calling over the balcony to her husband.

'Of course it is he!' snarled Gerald. 'Turberville fought him face to face just now, until he broke off to come to warn us – and got an arrow in his spine for his trouble.'

De Windsore stood frustrated in the centre of the hall, his sword out, but hanging low in useless impotency. Turberville lay moaning at his feet and one guard was against each door with a mace and drawn sword.

Apart from the crackling of flames, occasional shouts and a desultory banging on the main door, the tableau was quite still as Nest looked down from above, her agile mind already seeing a glimmer of hope where no hope should survive.

In the bailey of the castle the initial confusion was dying down, though yellow flames were rising higher and higher and falling beams sent cascades of sparks up into the windy sky. The whole gatehouse was burning furiously, thanks to a barrel of oil that Morgan had found in the guard-room. Sprinkled over the old weathered timbers, this had caused such a rapid conflagration that one side of the gatehouse and a large section of palisade had already collapsed outwards into the ditch beyond.

Owain stood facing the hall, concealed behind a pile of newly dressed stones, in case any archer in the hall found him silhouetted against the flames. Morgan ran up from the gatehouse and shared his shelter.

'No one left, Owain,' he reported. 'We chased the two serving men and an old woman out through the gate before we fired it. Everyone else is dead.'

'And our men...what of them?' demanded Owain. His face was covered in smuts and he had a long scratch down one cheek which, though trivial, had bled all down his face and neck.

'Two dead, that's all. And Ifor has a wound of the head which will certainly kill him before morning. But apart from cuts and burns, the rest are unharmed.'

Owain took a quiet look around the courtyard. 'We did well...those loose stones under the gate cost these Frenchmen their lives.'

Morgan waved his sword towards the still intact palisade next to the cliff edge, from which Rhys Ddu was removing their ropes and grapnels before firing it. 'Having his men attack from the rear, while we assaulted the gatehouse was a good stroke, too. But what now? I have put men all about the hall.'

Owain stuck his head around the new blocks of masonry to study the scene. Though new flames were leaping up all around the palisade and outbuildings, the men had kept strictly to his orders in leaving the central keep well alone.

He saw one man outside the main door, striking at it futilely with a war axe, but the old oak was too stout to give in to such an attack.

Owain rubbed impatiently at the trickling blood on his chin.

'Right, brother...let's get to the real business of the night. De Windsore is in there somewhere.' He gave a piercing whistle that carried above the roar and crackle of the inferno. The dozen or so men scattered about the bailey looked towards him and waved their weapons in reply as he motioned with his sword towards the keep.

Morgan walked beside him as they all advanced cautiously on the tall wooden building. The ring of unarmoured men were sitting targets for any bowmen, but Owain was correctly gambling that there would be few Normans within and probably no archers.

The more prudent Morgan kept a sharp eye on the parapet for any movement, but no feathered death came whistling down. In a moment, they were at the foot of the tower, safe at least from arrows. Owain had no true idea of how many men had been in the garrison, but expected no more than half a dozen to be with the castellan.

Silently, the warriors waited for Owain's next move, standing expectantly against the rough timbers, the fire glinting on the metal of their weapons or the iron plates that reinforced the leather helmets of the more fortunate ones.

'Take three men and start breaking in the kitchen entrance,' snapped Owain to Rhys. 'We'll try the main door, Morgan...Dafydd, Hywel, Geraint...bring one of those stones, we'll use part of de Windsore's precious new castle to smash down his old one.'

Three of the younger men grinned back at him, their teeth flashing like Nubians in their grimed faces. They grunted as they lifted an oblong slab of newly quarried masonry between them, at least two hundred pounds in weight. Moving to the door of the keep, they began swinging it like a pendulum, between the full reach of their arms. When it was moving fast, a yell from Morgan spurred them to a combined lunge at the door. With a terrific crash, the oaken planks shivered, but held firm. The stone fell to the ground, leaving the boys ruefully rubbing their tingling arms, but another trio took their place and repeated the operation.

'This will take time, Owain,' muttered Morgan. 'We have nothing to use as a ram, unless we take a stake from the palisade.'

Owain stamped about impatiently, whistling his naked sword blade through the cold night air.

Then he ran impetuously to the small door at the side, where Rhys Ddu was battering it with a post torn from the cook-house.

'They have some great weight jammed behind it, Lord Owain,' grunted the dark one. 'I doubt we'll shift it with this bit of twig.'

Another man shouted over the noise of the fire and the rhythmic crash of the ram, 'There's a new stone building on the other side – a privy by the look of it. It's joined to the keep by a wooden passage. If we fired it with more oil, we could break in that way.'

Owain slashed his blade down on to the post, missing the man's finger by a bare inch. 'I'll skewer any man who puts a light to this before I say so,' he yelled. '*Yr Arglwyddes* Nest is in there and I mean to get her out...after that you can cremate de Windsore with my blessing – but not until I say so.'

Going back to Morgan, he looked with frustration on the stubborn resistance of the six-inch thick door to the ministrations of the men with the stone block. Holding up his sword to stop them for the moment, he stepped forward and put his mouth to the ill-fitting joint between the tortured door and its splintered frame.

'De Windsore!' he yelled in Norman French at the top of his voice, 'De Windsore, send out your lady and your children, I'll not harm them. My business is with you alone!'

For an answer, there was a tremendous buffet against the inside of the door, as if it had been struck with a mace. Owain's face was against it and he jumped back, rubbing his stinging cheek.

'Right, you murdering knave,' he roared, 'I'm coming in for you.' Pushing Hywel aside, he furiously motioned to the others to help him lift the stone. Like a man possessed, he began hurling the great boulder at the groaning door which kept him from his mortal enemy.

The inside of the keep felt like a great bell, with two great clappers rhythmically smashing against the walls. The children were crying with fright, in spite of Nest's and Rhiannon's efforts to calm them, as their eardrums reverberated with each blow on the doors.

Then the booming of the clappers stopped for a moment as Owain yelled his ultimatum through the door. The words came clearly, but Gerald, now wearing his hauberk and helmet, replied with a ferocious jab at the door with the butt of a great war axe taken from the wall, where it had hung as an ornament for many years.

The battering began again, faster and more urgent, but Owain's challenge had spurred Nest into action. She pushed the boys across to Rhiannon and ran down the stairs to her husband.

'Gerald... listen to me.' She grabbed his arm and shook him, as he seemed oblivious of her presence and stared only at the door, through which certain death for him must enter within the next few minutes.

'Gerald…listen, will you!' she hissed at him, dragging his arm, trying to pull him away from the door and the white-faced men-at-arms who stood in futile readiness behind it.

'What is it, woman…go to the children, will you!' he snapped, when she had made him aware of her.

She ignored him and beat her fist against his mailed shoulder.

'Gerald, you can save yourself and go for aid…I'll not be harmed, nor the children. It's you that Owain wants, in revenge for last night.'

The hard face looked down at her in a half sneer. 'And he'll get me, by the looks of it, blast him!' snarled de Windsore. 'But I'll take him with me, unless he skulks behind and gets his knavish brigands do the killing.'

'There is no need,' she wailed in desperate urgency. 'You can go out through the new privy shaft and ride to Cemais for help. If you stay here, you'll certainly die and I and the children will be taken, so what use is that?'

Some devil was giving insistence to her tongue and Gerald at last listened to her.

'What nonsense is this, woman? Since when does a Norman knight leave his wife and children to fight his battles?'

'This is no battle,' she retorted. 'You are but three against God knows how many outside. You will surely be dead inside the next five minutes, Gerald – and what chance then will your sons have of being recaptured or even ransomed?' Though she was hardly aware of it herself, some inspiration was lending wings to her tongue, giving her arguments every ounce of influence. The mention of his sons, those extensions his body who would inherit his hard-won lands and make the Geraldine line a perpetuation of his memory, was the most subtle and forcible argument she could have uttered, even if she had spent a century considering what to say to him. Gerald tried to push her words aside, but she could tell that the battle was being won. 'It's impossible…I must stay,' muttered unconvincingly.

Nest clung to his arm and tried to shake the solid steel and muscle into doing her will.

'Your defence will last but a few seconds, Gerald…and what good will that be then to William and Maurice and David? Go, go, I pray you…take these two men-at-arms or they will only be slain for nothing. The three of you can find horses…steal those of the attackers, they must be nearby. Then ride to Nevern, it's but seven miles away…or you could find one of the nearer forts with Norman troops…Eglwyswrw or somewhere.. . anywhere!'

'It would be morning before we could return, lady,' he grated, uncertainly. His thoughts were on his sons, she knew. He looked away from the door to her earnest face, pleading with him in the red flickering light. 'It would be morning and too late,' he repeated.

'It will be eternity if you do not, Gerald,' she burst out impassionedly. 'Owain will not harm a hair of my head. He is my kinsman, we played together as children. He is a royal man, a prince, with a prince's honour. I will see to it that the children are safely returned to you, Gerald, I swear it!'

The impassioned sincerity in her voice cut through all his confusion and indecision in this, his greatest moment of peril. As she saw him waver, she pulled again at his arm and he stumbled a step, like a child being persuaded against its will.

'Quickly, you will need all the start you can get. I shall delay them but you must be well into the trees before they discover you are missing.'

He looked once more up at the balcony, where Rhiannon was peering fearfully over the rail, her arms clasped around the tousle-headed boys.

A crack suddenly appeared in the upper part of the door and the sudden urgency of the situation seemed to settle de Windsore's indecision.

'I like this less than anything else in my whole life, lady,' he snapped, with a return of the hard, efficient soldier's voice 'I shall take you all with me.'

He waved to the two soldiers to follow and beckoned to Rhiannon. 'Girl, bring down the children.'

Nest clung wildly to his arm again. 'No...no, Gerald. It would be the end of us all. Women and children cannot take that route. This is a man's escapade...go and return with a war band. The others will be here till dawn, looting and burning – their trail will still be fresh.'

Nest suddenly felt surprised at her own eloquence. She had not spoken with such animation to him for most of the years of their marriage. Did it need mortal peril to bring them together, she thought – or was it something else. She pushed the thoughts aside and dragged at his wrist. 'Quickly, to the bedchamber!'

Reluctantly, de Windsore followed her and the two mailed soldiers stumbled behind, bewildered, but disciplined to obey without question.

Still muttering protests, Gerald let himself be pulled by his slim wife down the narrow tunnel that joined the bedroom to his new latrine. For convenience in building, these new ablutions had been constructed first, before the rest of the keep was rebuilt. A deep culvert had been driven into the rock from outside the palisade which turned abruptly up into a vertical shaft that led directly into the garde-robe.

The four people crowded into the tiny stone chamber, which was almost in utter darkness.

Gerald made one last stand. 'This is madness,' he rasped. 'I'll not skulk away through some stink-hole and leave my family to the mercy of a damned Welsh bandit.'

Nest, acting as she never would have done in saner moments, pushed him unceremoniously towards the crude wooden seat.

'Fine use you'll be to your sons and heirs with your head struck from your body by Owain ap Cadwgan...think of your children, for the sake of Christ!'

Gerald capitulated and groping in the gloom, with the sound of the battering rams still loud in their ears, found the seat and ripped it from its supports. 'Soldier, you first,' he snarled.

Though this was the latest thing in sanitary engineering, the odour was far from inviting, but with a muttered oath, de Windsore thrust the reluctant man-at-arms forwards. The soldier took off his sword belt and dropped it down the shaft, where it struck with an ominous squelch a dozen feet below. Then he squeezed himself into the eighteen-inch hole and, cursing fluently, began to wriggle and squeeze himself down, his hands above his head.

As soon as he had vanished, the next man went, dropping his sword belt on to the head of the other, producing muffled curses from the depths.

Whilst they struggled to get around the sharp bend into the culvert that led to freedom, Gerald turned to his wife in the darkness.

'I charge you, Nesta, to look to my sons...I will spend the rest of my life in seeking them if they are not returned.'

She nodded in the gloom, 'By Our Lady, Gerald, I swear that I will not rest until they are returned to you. I give my word, that that is the word of a princess, daughter of my father Rhys.'

Why she said that, she could not tell. She might equally as well have sworn on her word as the wife of a Norman gallant, hidebound with traditional chivalry, but instead she chose to emphasize her royal Welshness.

Gerald made no comment. He made no move to embrace her nor even to say a word of fond farewell. All he did was to hiss a last command to guard his precious sons...he made no mention of little Angharad, nor even Hubert, a mere bastard.

Then he swung his legs into the latrine shaft and with an unseen grimace into the darkness at the stench and ominous soiling of the stonework, he slid from sight – what sight there was in that dark cubicle.

Nest waited not a moment to see how he fared, but hurried back along the passage and through the bedroom to the hall.

As she walked alone into that great, dark cavern, throbbing with the crash of the battering rams, she felt a strange thrill of exultation. For the first time in nine years, she felt free. She was away from Gerald, he could never reclimb that foetid shaft now, even if he changed his mind.

She looked up at the balcony and called out almost gaily in Welsh. 'Rhiannon, we are alone. All will be well, my kinsman will see that we come to no harm.'

She strode to the great door and with a feminine gesture out of keeping with the dangerous circumstances, she tossed back her hair and used both hands to settle the long, black tresses down the outside of her cloak.

Waiting until she saw that the massive oaken barrier was last about to give way, she filled her lungs with the smoke-tinged air. 'Owain...Owain ap

Cadwgan ap Bleddyn...my kinsman!' Her clear voice rang out and echoed around the bare hall. Immediately, the battering on the door stopped and after a few seconds of yelling outside, the assault on the smaller kitchen door was also halted.

'Who calls?...is that the *Arglwyddes* Nest ferch Rhys?' A strange thrill flitted through her body. It was so many years since a Welsh voice had called her that.

The shouts were renewed outside, then another voice, recognizably Owain's, called out, 'Nest...is that you at the door? Where is your Norman master, then, that he sends his wife to guard his gate?'

Her eyes glistened in the flame-light and her tongue flicked round her full lips.

'Yes, it is I...Nest, your kinswoman. Why do you shout in vain, Owain ap Cadwgan? He whom you were seeking has escaped.'

There was a babble of voices outside as the clear tones penetrated the door.

One thunderous crash came on the door, as if in blind rage, then Owain yelled for silence again.

'Nest, my cousin – what are you saying? You cannot save that Frenchman. He has done us much wrong and you well know it. I claim him for myself. It will be fair combat between us.'

She sighed with relief and felt shaken to the very marrow of her bones. Thank God that she had persuaded Gerald to leave. If a personal combat had been fought, would not her husband, a seasoned soldier, have been sure to win...and Owain to lose?

'He is not here, I tell you. I and my children and my maidservant are alone in this place,' she cried again.

The battering on the door began with renewed frenzy, but judging that Gerald and the two men would by now have reached the safety of the trees, she used all her lung power to reach the Welshmen outside for the last time.

'Stop...save your strength to fight we women and children. Stand back, I shall take the bar from the door.'

The Lion of Powys excitedly thrust back his angry follower and stood close to the outside of the door as the beam was rattled free from its sockets. Morgan, less trusting than his impetuous brother, snatched a spear from Dafydd and stood close by Owain, the weapon aimed directly at the door in case of treachery.

'Have a care, brother,' he muttered. 'That sly Norman pig may be using the lady as a snare. For where could he have gone?'

Owain ignored him, quivering as the heavy wooden bar was painfully lifted by Nest's slender arms.

Then it fell with a clatter on to the stone floor.

'Stand back, Nest, my princess,' yelled Owain. Lifting his foot, he kicked and kicked again as the distorted planks jammed against the frame.

Though Morgan tensed himself, no flight of arrows or vengeful sword flashed through the opening and seconds later the door creaked aside to reveal the proud figure of Nest.

She stood erect, the white of her night robe gleaming beneath the graceful fall of her dark velvet cloak as she stood calmly her hands clasped at her waist.

'Am I to be your prisoner or your guest, Owain?' she asked.

Owain stared at her for a long moment, then with a fluid movement slammed his sword back into its scabbard and fell on one knee.

He took her hand in his and bowed over it, his lips brushing her fingers. He immediately rose again.

'I wish this first time that I kissed you had been in happier circumstances, my cousin.' His eyes blazed into hers and in the space of a heart beat, she felt all the adoration, admiration and desire that had been denied her during nine long years of marriage. Lustful looks she had had in plenty from the full-blooded Normans who had been entertained at Pembroke, but they were mere carnal insults compared to this pure desire that flashed from Owain's face.

The moment passed, but would never be forgotten.

'Gerald de Windsore is not here,' she said calmly. 'But you may search for him.'

Owain's eyes still held hers in the dancing fires from the dancing castle. 'What need is there to seek, Nest?' he asked softly. 'You said he had gone – who am I to doubt your word. And suddenly I find that I care little about hunting the Constable of Penbroch.'

Morgan spoke up from behind his shoulder. 'You may not, brother, but the rest of us do. My cousin, tell us what happened. We are men in the heat of anger, we cannot match agility of Owain's moods.'

Nest smiled at Morgan and he, too, was lost to her for life.

'My husband and two men-at-arms went through the garde-robe shaft. They will be well into the woods by now, on their way to Cemais or another outpost. They will have a troop of men here by dawn, so I suggest you go about your business with some speed.' Her eyes returned to Owain and he had not moved his own from her face.

While the practical Morgan sent men running to the gate to look for the fugitives, Dafydd slipped into the hall to search every nook and cranny. The two cousins stood motionless in the doorway. Slowly, Owain reached out and took both her hands in his.

'Nest, all will be well, I swear it. I came here to kill and plunder – now I find I have no heart for slaughter and all I wish to plunder is your beauty.'

She flushed slightly and pulled her hands down, though gently. 'You speak plainly, cousin. Remember I am the wife of a Norman and have borne him five children, three of which are above us here on the gallery. Let us get on with this business. What will you do with us?'

Owain stared blindly at her. Her beauty last night had excited him as would that of any lovely woman – then the anger that followed had filled every corner of his being with a different passion. But now that he had her in front of him again – submissive, helpless, yet infinitely more desirable – he felt different from any other moment in his whole life.

He wanted her – not only because she was the most beautiful woman he had ever seen – but because some magic had just touched him. Some spell had fallen on him, compounded of animal attraction, the drama of the moment and the ecstatic fulfilment of an almost dream-like situation. He had fallen love not only with Nest, the woman, but with the awareness that he was playing a role straight out of mythology, with the handsome young prince rescuing the maiden from the clutches of an ogre…this capture of a Norman's Welsh wife crystallized into a moment of triumph that must be marked by some even greater ecstasy.

He held out his arms and pulled her to him. With his face buried in her dark hair, he groaned into her neck, 'Nest, why did you not meet me again ten years ago…though I was then but a boy. Oh, Nest, Nest.' The last words were almost as if he were in pain and she could not tell if it was anguish or sheer, unbridled desire.

A husband and a royal lover had taught her well enough to recognize uncontrolled passion, but never had she felt urgently wanted…and this time by a young man of her own kind, a prince and one who had so obviously capsized emotionally within the space of five minutes.

She shivered, partly with a sudden chill, partly from the nearness of Owain. 'My children are on the balcony…what do you do with us?'

Owain mentally shook himself and shifted one iron-bound arm so that it lay across her shoulders. 'We ride for Castell Caerwedros as soon as our business is done…come, let us gather your belongings. The children will be cared for by your woman. There are plenty of horses for all.'

She walked slowly into the hall, his arm still around her.

Dafydd ran past them to the door, but Owain grabbed his shoulder.

'Tell Morgan we leave in an hour…send for the horses. And do everything the maidservant requires for the children's comfort. Load anything else worth taking, then we fire the keep.'

In the centre of the hall, Owain paused to look round with incurious eyes. 'In here your husband insulted me. In here, I should have repaid him with the sword. Nest, from now onwards, you have no husband in my eyes, only a cowardly French knave who sired your children.'

She turned to face him. 'No, not even you must say that, cousin. He went at my instigation – I told him it would save the children. I swore that you would return them to him.'

Owain's brow furrowed. 'Save them?…do you think, then, that I would have harmed them? We will speak of children later – but why did you baulk me of my revenge, Nest? It was fair that he should pay for the murder of young Iolo – and the insult to myself.'

She shook her head. 'If you had been the instrument of Gerald's death, I could never stand with you like this, Owain. You could never touch me or even speak to me other than in enmity. It is better like this.'

He looked eagerly at her, his face alive with expectation.

'Nest, then you feel what I feel…I know it! There is something between us that needs no human lips to frame. In the minutes we have been together, some bond has been tied between us. I have never felt like this before, though God knows, I have dallied with girls in plenty.'

She gazed steadily at him, knowing exactly what he was trying to say. He had pulled off his helmet and the unruly auburn hair wreathed down on to his forehead. The strong features were flushed and the smear of dried blood and the smuts did nothing to lessen his intense attraction for her.

'You are taking us away,' she murmured, for something to say.

'Not far…some fourteen miles to Caerwedros – a commote where the Penteulu is my especial friend. We shall be there within three hours. Your children shall be sleeping safely again before dawn.'

She nodded, then shivered again within the circle of his leather-clad arm. 'I must get warm clothing – for them and myself.'

Gently, she pulled herself away and moved towards the curtained doorway where the bed-chamber lay.

Like steel following a lodestone, Owain followed her. Once through the door, he took one look around the dim chamber, then pulled the door shut and dropped the bar into its sockets.

The sound made Nest turn round quickly. They stood staring at each other in the flickering red light, almost like opponents ready for combat.

'What is this, Owain?' she asked in a low voice.

He knew that her words held no fear, only awareness. Two steps brought him to her and then his arms were around her again and his lips were on hers.

The fire within him rapidly outstripped that which was flaming outside in Castell Cenarth and within seconds its sparks had set her alight also, smouldering at first then flaring as high as his.

The abandon which any man could ignite within her was magnified to a degree she had never known before as his mouth leapt and caressed her face and neck. His arms slid beneath her cloak and around the thin linen of her night robe, crushing her lithe body against his tight sheathing of steel and leather.

For a long moment passion obliterated all other sensation but the pressure of his sword hilt and armour began dully to penetrate her consciousness and her fingers started to tear blindly at the buckles at his waist.

Still trying to keep his mouth on hers and with her arms locked around his neck, he frantically tore off his belt and dropped his scabbard to join his helmet on the floor.

He kissed her fiercely again, then stepped back and ripped feverishly at the lacing of his short tunic of mail, dragging it off, then the leather cuirass beneath.

Once free of these encumbrances, he seized Nest with renewed passion and twisted his fingers in her raven hair as their mouths met again. Not a word had been spoken since they entered, apart from her still unanswered question, but as he lifted her easily from the floor and laid her on the tumbled furs and blankets of the bed, he whispered hoarsely in her ear, 'Nest, my Nest...'

No other word was spoken until they lay spent amongst the chaos of the bedclothes.

Nest came back to earth first, from the sweetly frightening heights of ecstasy. Owain lay heavily on her, his sobbing breath hot on her bare shoulder. She stared at the window slit and found herself thinking vaguely that not half an hour before, she had been lying here alongside her sleeping husband, watching the play of lightning. Now she had had her own sweet thunderstorm and made her own orgasmal lightning.

The thoughts suddenly brought her back to reality. Her husband had fled, his castle – her home – was being reduced to ashes, she was being abducted, her children going to a fate unknown...yet lying on her body, on her own bed, was someone she had known as a man for no more than a few minutes, recovering from what would have been rape if she had not offered such avid co-operation.

'Owain...for God's sake...the children. And Gerald, he might be on his way back, if he has met some men from Cemais...are you quite mad?'

He raised his head with an effort and she saw his face in the light from the window. Something in it made her forget her words and kiss him, kiss him so hard that it hurt, her hands fondling his tumbled hair and rubbing the iron-hard muscles of his back through the thin undershirt, the only clothing that had not joined the debris of his garments on the floor beside the bed.

For answer, he rolled to one side, then cradled her in his arms. He kissed her gently, expertly, without the explosive violence of a few minutes before.

Then he stood up and held out a hand to her. 'You are right, we must go. But from this moment on, my life is yours. You shall never lose me now, Nest...nor I you.'

This was said with no melodrama, it was a plain statement of fact.

Though her mind was still numb from the avalanche of events, she knew clearly enough that this indeed was the man of her life.

Reaching up, Nest took his hand and rose gracefully to her feet. 'Give me some minutes, Owain. Send my maid to me, we must dress for a cold night's journey.'

Owain nodded gravely, then with regal assurance, began to step into his fallen clothes.

'Our love will last more than that journey, Nest...it will end only when breath leaves our bodies.' Then he snapped back into a brisk alertness. 'Take whatever you need – all your robes, you may not get a chance to replenish your wardrobe if events now go as I fear...' Then he corrected himself. 'I should say "expect"...there can be no fear for me in a life that holds you, Nest.'

She smiled and went to a curtained alcove, taking out clothes and throwing them into a leather trunk that had come with her from Caer Rhiw.

Owain had speedily dressed and was walking to the door 'I will send the girl – Rhiannon, you called her.'

Back in the hall, now arrayed again in his full battle outfit, Owain sent the maidservant and the children into the bed chamber. The two elder boys stared at him with mixed fear and awe. William knew enough of adult life to wonder what had been going on behind that barred door, but his mother's composure when they entered soon chased the thought out of his head.

'What is he to do with us, madam?' he asked solemnly. 'Where is my father?'

Nest pulled the boys close, all three of them. 'He has escaped to get help from the Lord of Cemais – though it seems he will be too late. But you will join him very soon, perhaps even in the morning.'

'And you, madam?' asked Maurice, who was much younger and seemed only half aware that anything but some elaborate game was going on.

Nest hesitated. 'I maybe going away for a time – not long, but you may have to return to Pembroke or Caer Rhiw without me.'

As Nest and Rhiannon hastily began pulling clothes from the wall niche and stuffing them into the trunk and tying some up in a blanket, the servant looked at her mistress with gossip-hungry eyes. They had been together so many years that they were more like sisters than lady and serf.

'I may have to stay with the Lord Owain for a time, Rhiannon,' said Nest as they worked. 'You will go back to Dyfed with the children.'

The girl stopped packing, her wise face stubborn in the gloom. 'Where you go, I go, lady. It has always been so.'

Nest shook her head. 'Angharad needs you, Rhiannon.'

'Not so much as you do, *arglwyddes*…let Gwenllian care for the little maid, she can do that as well as suckle Gwladys. The children will need for nothing in Caer Rhiw, there are enough servants there to trip over…I go with you.'

As the problem was still in the future, Nest refused to argue and the minutes soon passed in a bustle of packing up the children against the cold. Hubert and William, still uneasy at the absence of their father, were silent and sullen, but Maurice was sleepily delighted and the infant girl had never fully wakened.

Ten minutes later, strong hands were passing them all down into the dry moat through a large gap in the palisade, where a long section of burnt timbers had been pulled aside by the same grappling hooks that had got Rhys Ddu and his men over the wall.

The gatehouse was still impassable with fire and the drawbridge itself was flaming as it hung drunkenly on one hinge.

Owain himself took Nest's slim body as Morgan handed her down. He took her up the sloping further bank in his arms – with others about, he made no gesture of love, but as he lifted her on to his horse, he whispered in her ear.

'Nest, do not look behind, look forwards, where our life lies!'

In spite of his words, she twisted on the horse and gazed back through the gap in the castle wall. With a great gush of flame feeding on oil, the wall of the keep suddenly erupted into an inferno. Arrows with oil-soaked straw tied to them were shot up in flaming arcs to land on the thatched roof that lay behind the parapet, and within seconds, the whole of the central building became a crackling pyre to end Gerald's ambitions at Cenarth Bychan. Nest looked back at Owain with steady gaze. 'This place means nothing to me, cousin. Before yesterday, I had never seen it – and if I never see it again, little will I care.'

Owain stared at the flames and the showering sparks with some regret. 'To me, it will always be the place where my life started anew…where I first saw you as a woman, Nest. But come, you'll look even more beautiful in a Welsh court…let's be off to Caerwedros!'

He swung himself up into the saddle and Nest clung to his waist. With two of Morgan's men leading the way, they walked sedately along the edge of the trees, dipping down towards the river as they made their way upstream to a ford on the winter-swollen Teifi.

Once across the river, they were in Ceredigion. Heading north, they passed up a wooded valley, then up on to low, bare hills, alternating with lonely tree-filled vales. Years of war, both Welsh and Norman, had decimated the population and in the first five miles they came across nothing but two ruined homesteads.

The first habitation was at Tan-y-groes, seven miles from Cilgerran Rock. A few fearful faces peered from a rude shack, wondering what these armed night-raiders had to do with the ruddy glow that stained the clouds pink on the southern horizon.

As they came over a rise near the old Celtic camp, the fresh smell of the sea slightly mellowed the bite of the frost.

Owain turned his head and waved an arm ahead. 'Welcome home, lady,' he murmured. 'Here lies a Wales free of Frenchmen!'

CHAPTER FOUR

NEW YEAR'S EVE, 1109

THEY lay together on an outspread cloak, basking in the winter sun that could shine so mildly in Geredigion even on the last day of the year.

Owain propped himself up on one elbow and looked into the serene face alongside him, which stared up into the pale blue sky.

'Four days and three nights, my love,' he murmured. Nest moved her eyes and looked at him steadily. His face was as eager as a young boy in his first calf love. She loved him so much, as she smiled back. 'Such days as I've never had before, Owain...but what's to happen to us?'

He sat up with a sudden movement. 'Happen? We'll live and get happier every day!'

Nest's face clouded slightly. 'The children, Owain...the boys at least. Send them back, Owain.'

A slight breeze wafted over them, bringing a reminder that it was still a midwinter afternoon. The Lion of Powys jumped to his feet and bent to catch her hand. 'It's getting cold, my love.'

She still lay on the cloak...'Answer me, Owain ap Cadwgan...what about the children?'

His mouth tightened. 'We've talked long of this already, Nest. Until I know what de Windsore has in mind, I must keep them here.'

She turned her head away. 'Do you shelter behind little lads, Owain?'

His face darkened, but he was saved from answering by a sudden commotion from the direction of the court of Caerwedros, a hundred yards away. Several horns blew urgent blasts and the sound of horses on the stony track came simultaneously with the flying figure of the Porter, who raced down the grassy slope towards them. 'Your father, *Arglwydd*...Prince Cadwgan is coming.'

Owain groaned. It had to happen sooner or later, but the prospect of his honeymoon being shattered by a stand-up fight with his father was not to be relished. 'Come, Nest...help me wage the battle with our ancestors.'

By the time they walked back to the gate in the small stockade on the hill top, Cadwgan's party was breaking through the trees in the distance.

Owain and Nest stood hand in hand as the royal party trotted into the courtyard outside the hall.

Almost before his horse had stopped, Cadwgan had slid from his saddle and stalked into the hall, swinging a furious arm at Owain to follow him inside.

Owain, taking a deep breath, loped after his father, pulling Nest along by his side.

Cadwgan stopped near the fire and threw his great, grey cloak back over his shoulders. His watery eyes glared at the pair as they approached. Owain spoke. 'Greetings, father. This is Nest ferch Tewdwr, daughter of the Prince Rhys…you last saw her as a child.'

Cadwgan nodded perfunctorily. 'Nest ferch Tewdwr!…I think you are Lady de Windsore, madam. I wish you no ill, but I likewise wish you fifty miles from here!'

He turned his yellowed face towards his son. 'And you…no sooner do I turn my back to go and heal your last breach of the peace, when you directly get up to the greatest folly of your life. Are you crazed, Owain…was there some seed of madness in your mother that you commit these maniac deeds?'

Owain flushed. He knew that it would come to a shouting match; even when forewarned, nothing could help him control the temper begotten by his red hair.

'Wait, father! You must have heard the story…This Gerald killed my man, struck me and threw me out like a dog. Are you to see some French castellan – with no royal blood to match ours, not even the filth that Normandy calls royal blood…will you see him insult the Heir of Powys and murder a man without retribution?'

Cadwgan pointed a shaking finger at Nest. 'Retribution you call this? Abducting a ward of King Henry, of whom we hold all our lands…You madman, what have you done!'

Owain shouted back, hands on hips and head stuck forward. 'What then, send the man a posy of flowers and ask forgiveness for staining his castle bailey with Welsh blood! Come, tell me!'

Cadwgan tore off his helmet and threw it on the floor. 'You could have raided some outpost…slain a few men-at-arms…even burn his castle, slay the man, though God knows that would set the land afire again. But to abduct his wife and children…his wife of all the women in Wales...you crazy fool! We'll have an English army on our necks as soon as messengers can cross the land.'

'My father, you set too much store by kissing the buttocks of the French…you once carved out your inheritance by arms, alongside Gruffydd of Gwynedd. Now you quake in your shoes at the thought that some offence might make your Norman masters chastise you like a naughty boy. I care nothing for their charity. This Wales is ours and has been since the Romans left. If we deserve to keep it, then we should fight for it.'

'And fight you will, you rash knave…and you'll lose.' Cadwgan had flecks of froth at the corners of his lips as he screamed the words. Already he could see the Norman columns winding down from England to annihilate him.

Owain sneered at him. 'Your heart has withered since Coed Yspws…if that's how you feel, then give up Powys and Ceredigion to a man who still likes to feel a sword hilt in his hand.'

Cadwgan ignored him, his mind obsessed with finding some way of making amends.

'What is to be done? What salvage can we make out of the wreckage of your folly? The woman and children must go back at once, and any loot from Cenarth. And we must make restitution, in gold and hostages.'

Owain's face went livid. 'What! Give our people as hostage for that barbarian to wreak his revenge upon…blinding and maiming! Over my dead body, Prince…and not a groat of his treasure, either. And the sons stay, and so does Nest, who shall be my wife as soon as I can find Gerald to slit his throat!'

Cadwgan threw a shaking finger almost into Owain's eye. At the back of the hall, the Penteulu was sweating even in the cooling air, and half the kindred of Caerwedros crowded into the doorway to take in the royal quarrel.

'Owain, you will do as I say!' snarled the Prince. 'This very afternoon, all shall set out from here for Cemais. I hear you took two boxes of silver coin, the pay of the stone-masons, as well as accoutrements from the castle of de Windsore. These shall be doubled as recompense, in the hope that any revenge will be by Dyfed Normans only and not a royal army from Shrewsbury.'

'Nothing – not one thing goes back!' snapped his son. 'If de Windsore or Henry want anything, they must come and get it!'

Nest pulled at his arm. 'Owain, let the children go…the boys. Keep the pillage, fight whom you wish, but let the boys go. They are their father's sons, but you have no quarrel with them, for they are of my flesh also.'

Owain, still simmering, looked down at her and shook his head. 'They are bargaining counters, Nest. Hostages of war.'

She looked straight into his eyes and he felt uneasy. No woman had ever moved his senses like Nest and he knew no defence against her.

'Owain, I tell you for the last time. I swore to de Windsore that I would do all I could to return his sons. If I had not done that, I would be dead now, along with him and the children, for he would have fought to all our deaths. Owain, if thou will have me true, release my sons to their father.'

With one of the sudden shifts of mood that were typical of his volatile nature, he abruptly gave in. 'Very well, for you and your love, I agree. But nothing else…the booty is my men's by right, and they shall keep it.'

'And the little girl, Angharad, and Hubert?'

Owain nodded impatiently. 'What care I for a French bastard…and the girl child, she will be better with her brothers.'

Cadwgan listened to this with some satisfaction.

'Nest ferch Tewdwr, you at least have some sense…more than this lout that I mistakenly conceived. But you, too, must return and make intercession for us with your husband.'

Nest looked at Owain and he drank in her glance. They ignored Cadwgan and slowly their hands met.

'And what about you, Nest ferch Tewdwr?'

She looked at Owain, then at Cadwgan. 'I shall stay.'

'She stays – for ever,' said Owain quietly.

CHAPTER FIVE

NEW YEAR'S DAY, 1110

IN the turret chamber that he used as an audience room, Richard, Bishop of London, sat grimly behind a heavy table. Having just come from the celebration of Mass for New Year's Day, he still wore his rich vestments, though his cope and elaborate headgear had been discarded.

Behind him stood a sleek chaplain and a richly-dressed squire, contrasting strangely with the two mud-spattered Welshmen who stood solemnly on the other side of the table. There was no trace of servility in their manner, only a grudging wariness. Both were young, in their early twenties and in all their surliness, showed the traces of arrogance that went with royal blood.

Richard, a tall, gaunt man with pale hair and ruthless eyes, looked at them with distaste. One of the men, Ithel, had just had the temerity to wish him well for the New Year.

'There's little good about it,' retorted the Bishop. 'It could hardly be worse, especially for your damned countrymen!'

Ithel and his brother, Madog, sons of Rhiryd ap Bleddyn, Cadwgan's brother, had heard some rumours of a great scandal in southern Ceredigion during the past few days. The details were hazy in a country where news travelled only as fast as a horse could walk through wooded vales and rugged mountains. They guessed that their cousin Owain would be involved, as he usually was mixed up in any local disturbance. Richard soon confirmed their suspicions.

'Your kinsman Cadwgan, your father's brother, was allowed by us to rule over Ceredigion and half Powys. Weak and feeble though he is, he has caused King Henry little trouble until lately – and then not through his own default, except in the lack of constraint over those mad-men sons of his...especially the one Owen!' The Bishop almost spat out the words, epitomizing his hatred and contempt of all Celts.

Ithel shifted his leather helmet uneasily from one hand to the other. 'Owain?...the Valiant, they call him, or the Lion of Powys. He will fight anything that moves, from a stray dog to a tree swaying in the wind!'

Madog, almost two years his junior, though as alike as a twin, spoke for the first time. 'We have heard of trouble at Din-geraint this Christmas – is it because of this that you have called us here to Shrewsbury?'

Richard banged a fist on the table. 'Trouble, you call it! We have had peace on the Welsh border since the Montgomery traitors were banished. King Henry placed me here as his steward to stop other ambitious Marcher barons from stirring up revolt, but now we get the same trouble from your pestilent tribes!'

The sons of Rhiryd scowled. They might hate half their own countrymen enough to kill them, but when a Norman started to call Welshmen names, their hot blood began to simmer.

'What trouble was this?' growled Ithel.

'Owen has razed the castle at Cenarth Bychan, slain all the garrison, except Gerald de Windsore, who managed to escape. But worst of all, he has made off with his wife, Nesta, and four of de Windsore's children.'

The kernel of the rumour was a surprise even to the phlegmatic Ithel. 'Nest ferch Rhys! But she was a royal ward.'

The martial bishop slammed the table again. 'Exactly! A ward of King Henry…and formerly his mistress, though naturally de Windsore's plea failed to mention that matter. Now she is taken, ravished, seduced, abducted…anything you will! And de Windsore's heir, William, is captive, to say nothing of loot taken and complete loss of the castle. This will set your Wales on fire, Welshmen!'

Madog and Ithel exchanged glances. Enmity against Norman was forgotten – where one princedom suddenly found itself in jeopardy, its neighbours turned cannibal, cousins or not.

Richard intercepted the glance and smiled sardonically. 'Do you wish to please King Henry and to win friendship from him for ever? He will honour you and exalt you over and above any of your fellow landholders and he will make all our kinsfolk envious of you.'

Another rapid glance shot between the sons of Rhiryd. They nodded. 'What do you want done, Lord Bishop?'

Richard stood up, a tall figure resplendent in his brocade robe. His blond hair was tonsured as a gesture towards his divinity, though until a year before, he had been a warrior – and still was, under the episcopal surface.

'Go you into your own country and find Owen. Seize him if you can, but if not, expel him and his father from their lands. I declare their mandate over Ceredigion and Powys void as from this moment!'

'And the lands they leave…what of them?' snapped Ithel in avaricious haste.

'You shall be dealt with handsomely, if you do as I say. For the redress of this wrong against the King and knight de Windsore, you shall be amply rewarded.'

Madog bowed his head, showing more respect than when he had entered. 'We shall raise a war band and march within two days for Din-geraint, if that be where Owain ap Cadwgan lies.'

Richard sank back on to his chair. 'You will need all the wiles and weapons you can muster to get the better of this fox. I have already arranged some assistance for you. I will give you the truest and most faithful companions,' he sneered sarcastically. 'Namely, Llywarch ap Trahearne, whose brothers Meurig and Griffi were murdered by Owen three years ago. Llywarch will find revenge most sweet. Also Uchtryd ap Edwin and his men. All these hosts will be added to yours. With such a war-band, even you can hardly fail to smoke out this lion from

Powys and his feeble father!'

In the dying sunlight of that New Year's Day, a lone figure stood on the new stone battlements of the great castle of Pembroke, high above Milford Haven.

He looked north, his eyes staring vacantly at a horizon beyond which was Ceredigion and his wife. Two hours before a messenger had ridden in with the children. Silently, Gerald had embraced William and Maurice, patted the heads of the bastard and the girl and sent them straight off to Carew, his country home a few miles up the river. 'His home...' He reminded himself with the usual masochism that it was Nest's, not his. A part of the dowry, not land cut out by his own sword.

De Windsore stared bleakly across this alien Wales, pulling his cloak more closely around his armour – which he had not taken off, except to sleep, these past six days. As he stared north, he loathed every yard of ground over which his gaze passed – the only part he could tolerate was the low-lying land around Pembroke, filled with Flemings and vaguely resembling the country around Windsor where he had been born.

Since that night in Cenarth Bychan he had lived in a dream-like state where only one thought obsessed his mind – Owain ap Cadwgan. He carried on his constable's job with machine-like efficiency, but the real Gerald was living in a fantasy world where unimaginable tortures were inflicted in monotonous rotation on Cadwgan's wild son. Of Nest he thought little, except as part of Owain's heinous offence. He had missed his children, but now that they were back, he could devote his whole attention to hatred of Owain without distraction. He felt not the slightest trace of gratitude – or slightest lessening of loathing – for the safe return of the boys and Angharad.

Above everything else that consumed him, was the destruction of Cenarth Bychan itself. The vision of its smouldering ruins on the following dawn was branded into his memory. After reaching Nevern, where the nearest Norman neighbour lived, Gerald had raced back with a strong troop of soldiers, reaching the rock of Cilgerran just after first light. The keep was still burning and the palisade was a smoking line of charred logs. The new stone foundations of the gatehouse had collapsed into the ditch and most of the trenching for the new masonry had caved in or was filled with burnt timber. Many of the new stones had split with the heat or had cracked where they had fallen. Fifteen burnt corpses lay around the castle, and three were never found, apart from some brittle bones in the ashes.

His fellow rider, de Turribus, who held the Lordship of Nevern, seemed to think the whole affair amusing. He was a crude, unimaginative man who thought only of wine, wenching and fighting. 'Saves you taking the old place down, eh, de Windsore,' he cackled. 'Done you a good turn, this Welshman. Pity about your lady, though...still, I suppose she's used to laying with Welshmen, as well as Normans!'

At any other time, this would have merited a duel to the death, but Gerald, transfixed by the ruins of his castle, appeared not to hear – not even the innuendo about 'Normans', in the plural, which his companion sneeringly used to refer to Nest's well-known liaison with the King.

Gerald left the rock without a word and stayed silent as they rode along the left bank of the Teifi almost to its mouth. They drew rein opposite the castle of Dingeraint, known to them as Kerdigan. There was no bridge yet and they sat silently in their saddles, watching the castle at the bend of the river. The only sign of life was a watchful pair of sentries lurking behind the wooden parapet. No banner flew over the hall and no horses came or went from the gate. The fields around were deserted and the whole district seemed to be holding its breath.

Gerald gazed icily across the river, then wheeled his horse around and started for Pembroke. Now he stared just as coldly into the greying sky and wondered where Owain had gone, taking Gerald's wife with him. De Windsore had never loved his wife, though in the first months his response to her beauty had prompted a mild infatuation. Since she had returned from the King, two years after their marriage, she had ceased to mean anything to him but a status symbol and a piece of decorative property – apart from her very satisfactory function as a prolific producer of children, even though the last two had been girls.

Now she was more important than ever before, by her very loss – a sign of the enormity of Owain's crime.

Gerald had struggled to get his mind into motion for long enough to send a war-band from Pembroke to Kerdigan, but they had been repulsed by the garrison, two men being killed by stray arrows. He had too few men to mount a full-scale raid into Ceredigion and in any case, he hesitated to attempt it without the approval of the King.

There was nothing else to do – all the Welsh homesteads in the Vale of Teifi had long ago been burned, their folk killed or fled. With no great army, all he could do was to send two messengers out from Pembroke. One to Shrewsbury to alert Richard, Warden of the Marches; the other to Woodstock or on to Windsore and London to seek the King.

This second one was the hardest to send. Since that day when Henry had returned Nest and given Gerald back the wardenship of Pembroke, he had had no contact whatsoever with his royal master, except through the impersonal military orders from barons and justiciars. But now it had to be done, not for Gerald's own benefit, but as his duty to report the abduction of a King's ward – for ward she would be until the end of her days, whomever she was given to in marriage.

One messenger had returned with an answer that day. He had come from Shrewsbury, telling him that Bishop Richard had mobilized rival Welsh factions against the Princes of Powys. Some of the refugees would soon be spilling out of Ceredigion. Gerald grimly promised retribution against any straying into Dyfed.

It was too soon for word from Woodstock – if there would be any. Gerald cared little either way. With a last look northward, he swung around and, with his armour clanking, he strode grimly down into the depths of the fortress.

CHAPTER SIX

THE FIFTH OF JANUARY, 1110

THE hall of Caerwedros was already quiet by the fourth hour before midnight. The evening meal had been a sober one, with no songs or tales to brighten the cold and windy evening.

All day refugees from the north and east had been limping in on their way to Din-geraint, to seek the relative safety of Cadwgan's main fortress in the south. They told pitiful tales of homesteads seized and burnt, kindred butchered and cattle driven off by the men of Madog, Ithel and Llywarch who were striking ever nearer down the length of Ceredigion.

Only half a dozen of Owain's own henchmen were in Caerwedros. Morgan and his other brothers had gone with Cadwgan, who had travelled north two days before, to see what the true situation was in Powys. Owain, loth to leave his new 'bride', had promised that he would ride after them on the Feast of Saint Hilary, eight days ahead. Until then, he intended to stay as the guest of the Penteulu of Caerwedros, who, though far too polite to say so, would rather have seen the dust flying behind the hooves of Owain's departing horse.

The east wind whined uneasily through the old reeds on the roof of the hall and found every nook and cranny in the mud-plastered walls. Most of the men had crawled under their blankets and lay in an elongated circle on the earthen floor, with their feet towards the fire. A few insomniacs crouched over the glowing peat, playing *tawlbwrdd** in the dim light. The hall door was shut tight and outside there was a full guard on the stockade – not that Caerwedros was strong enough to resist any determined attack.

Owain and Nest were in the Penteulu's chamber – the only separate room in the court – with the crude door barred against any intruder, innocent or hostile. The usual occupant was lying with his men in the hall and his wife was bundled in with the rest of the women in a hut outside.

It was many years since Nest had slept in such a decrepit old building, but she was more happy than if it had been a marble palace. Wrapped in Owain's arms beneath woollen blankets and the heavy skin of some foreign bear, the cold was defeated. They had pulled a linen undersheet right over their heads and were laughing and joking like two children.

Their love-making was over for the moment, until the next time that sudden awareness would make them throw their bodies together in reckless

* *A kind of chess played with pieces of whalebone or ivory.*

passion. But now, though almost naked, their contact was gentle and playful. Nest settled her head on Owain's shoulder, her long hair flowing over his chest. He kissed her forehead and languidly let a hand slide across her breasts.

'Nest, tell me what this King Henry was like?' he murmured.

She opened her eyes suddenly under the bedclothes and searched her mind for the right way to answer.

'It was a long time ago, Owain...you won't add him to your list of men to be fought for my sake, will you?'

Her voice was half-serious, but he chuckled and slid his hand into her armpit to pull her around, so that he could kiss her lips.

'No, Nest ferch Rhys...I have enough at the moment with your Gerald, this Richard of London and those dogs of Rhiryd. I only wanted to know what a King of a big country was really like.' In the few days that she had known him, Nest had already found his Achilles' heel. As Gerald had been obsessed by ownership of a castle, so Owain was fascinated by kingship. Even the hatred he had of Normans failed to quench the lure of a great throne like Westminster.

'Henry...Henry Beauclerk. He was a real man,' she mused aloud. 'A man less like you could not be found.'

'Why – am I not a man, then?' Owain sounded piqued and pinched her hip fiercely.

'You act with your heart – Henry with his head. Your temper, your rashness, none of these were in him. A cold, calm man who never uttered a word or performed an act until he had worked it around his mind like a baker kneads his dough.'

Owain rested his chin on her soft hair. 'And you were the mistress of this royal man...for how long?'

She sighed and moved slightly in his arms. 'Some two years – though the times we met could be counted on my fingers. Whilst I was still at Shrewsbury, a ward of Rufus, Henry took me as a lover, but very soon I thought I was with child and was sent back to Caer Rhiw. Then came my marriage with Gerald.'

Owain lay thoughtful, turning over these ways of Norman nobles in his brain. 'You were twice his mistress, then?'

She nodded in the gloom. 'In the second year of the century, when Penbroch fell and Robert and Arnulf Montgomery were disgraced, Gerald was ejected from the castellanship. I was taken to Gloucester as a royal ward once more – this time with two babes, William and Maurice.'

'What happened to de Windsore?' Owain was intrigued with this Norman feud, a change from Welsh vendettas.

'He spent months in his own dungeons. Then King Henry came to visit Gloucester and we met again. Once more I went to his bed, and for my sake Gerald was released, but lived in disgrace at Caer Rhiw, with no position and no rank. Some foul-mouthed ruffian called de Saer was appointed as warden of Penbroch.'

Owain stirred and pulled her close, as if to forgive her for her forced infidelity with the King of England.

'And Henry…you went to him willingly?'

He felt her shrug under the blankets. 'Was I in any position to do otherwise? I was a prisoner in Gloucester, though I was treated civilly enough. There was a room, and a maid to care for the babes. When Henry came and remembered me from Shrewsbury, I was told to go to him the first night…what choice had I? Gerald was closer to me in those days – perhaps his life hung on my refusal. As it turned, his restitution came from my bed talk with Henry.'

'You loved him?' murmured Owain, his curiosity of regal things still keeping his jealousy in check.

'Love? Never – though neither did I hate him. And he loved me not, either. Nor will he love anyone, save himself. But he was kind and chivalrous – and a worthy lover. I had no cause to complain – my station in Gloucester changed overnight. I became a guest, not a prisoner, though I could still not go home to Caer Rhiw.'

'And Henry – the King – came but seldom?' persisted Owain.

'Maybe one night every few months, if he chanced to be in the Marches. He spends much time in Normandy, as you must know. And his new Queen had charged him with fidelity as a condition of marriage. Poor Matilda, how little she knew that man! Not half as well as I, for all the brevity of our meetings.'

'How did it end?'

'He came less and less often, a few clandestine visits stolen from affairs of state. I was but one mistress of many, but Matilda and the Archbishop Anselm were clamouring for his fidelity. One night, he told me it would be the last time. Seizing my chance, I prevailed on him to restore Gerald to Penbroch. It was easy, as this brute de Saer was drunk half the time and the castle was reported ill-managed to Walter, Justiciar of Gloucester. As a parting gift, he sent me back to Dyfed to carry the news to Gerald.'

Owain was silent for a long time and Nest became fearful that his errant temper was grinding away at the thought of her sharing yet another Norman's bed. But she was wide of the mark.

'I will be a king one day not far hence,' he said suddenly. 'People think me a rash and fiery fool – and so I am. But this brand of rashness which has set Wales in a turmoil is not without purpose.'

'Tell me more, my Owain,' she asked. She loved him, this new man of hers, and his voice was the sound of music to her.

'My father, and others like him, such as your uncle Rhydderch, have grown old and become used to kissing the French boot. It is time that someone shook life into them or cast them out to make way for younger men. I had not planned it through you, Nest, but it is well that it happened this way. There will be bloody times ahead – as there is blood flowing and homesteads burning this very night – but what cook can avoid breaking eggs? Only one thing can unite Welshmen and that is oppression – and Lord God, enough of that will come from this escapade of ours, Nest ferch Rhys!'

'And how will you fare in it, Owain?' she whispered.

'The strongest go to the front – and I am the strongest,' he said simply. 'I and Gruffydd ap Cynan of the North. He's old and I am young. When I have recaptured all Powys and Deheubarth, with you as my queen, I can wait for him to die in Snowdonia. Then all our land this side of the Great Dyke will be one kingdom again, as it was in Rhodri Mawr's time!'

She sighed again and snuggled up to his hard chest. 'You are a dreamer, Owain ap Cadwgan...the Lion of Powys dreams of an empire,' she teased, but only half in fun, for his words sent a strange thrill through her.

'It will come, sweet love,' he said with complacent certainty.

After a moment's silence, their now familiar hunger for each other suddenly flared up again and they clutched at each other passionately. But the pattern of ten nights was broken by a distant noise. Owain flung back the coverlets and thrust his bare shoulders into the icy draughts of the bedchamber.

'Horses and shouting,' he snapped. 'When men ride at night, evil is afoot!'

He clambered out of bed and groped for his clothes. A vision of another bedchamber, another man and another night flashed into Nest's mind, but this time no thunder, no lightning and no flickering flames lit up the window slit.

Then came voices in the outer compound and the door of the hall was unbarred. 'It's Morgan, my brother,' muttered Owain, still grappling with his clothes. 'He must bear urgent news.'

Throwing a cloak over his shoulders, he walked to the chamber door just as an urgent tapping came on the rough boards.

'Stay, Nest – I will see him in the hall.'

Outside, a half-frozen and dishevelled Morgan was drinking mead and crouching at the fire. He had ridden with three men from Llanbadarn* to warn Owain of imminent danger.

'Tomorrow they'll be on us, Owain,' he growled through chattering teeth. 'Two hosts, a great one of Madog, Ithel and Llywarch, and a smaller but still dangerous band under Uchtryd ab Edwin.'

Owain scowled into the glowing peat. 'We knew already that they were on the rampage. Richard, Warden of the Marches, has set them upon us, at de Windsore's behest. But what urgency makes you ride from the banks of the Ystwyth tonight?'

'A secret messenger from Uchtryd came to us. He is joined in this venture reluctantly and bids us fly before we are trapped. There are great hosts under the other three, eager for revenge and for the chance to ravish our lands.'

Owain pulled at the quiff over his forehead as he pondered. 'Uchtryd...I wonder he consented to join this foul enterprise. He loves Normans as little as we. But why his secret messenger to you?'

* *Near the modern Aberystwyth.*

Morgan gulped the last of his drink. 'These treacherous men from Powys are now camped on the upper reaches of the Rheidol and Ystwyth. They can reach here in an easy day's march. There are also rumours of others being allowed passage through the Norman lands near Llanmyddfai*, who could storm upon us from the east through Llanbedrpont-Steffan**. We are in urgent peril, Owain.'

The elder brother snarled in temper and slammed his hands together. 'These damned sons of Rhiryd and this Llywarch – I should have sent him to hell along with his two brothers!' Morgan rubbed his numbed fingers before taking a cup of mulled bragget from the worried-looking Penteulu.

'But what's to do, Owain?' he asked. 'They'll have direct orders from this bloody bishop to take you, living or dead. And to restore Nest to her French husband.'

Owain straightened up suddenly. 'Nest! She must be put a safe place. Is there any fear of this rabble marching after you tonight?'

Morgan shrugged. 'Who can tell? Though I doubt it. The night's as dark as the devil's boot until the moon rises later, but Ithel is a sly wolf. If you wish to set Nest in a safe place, I'd not leave it beyond the dawn.'

Owain clapped his brother on his stout shoulder and gazed into the deep, dark eyes. 'You are a man without equal, my brother. I'll arrange things this very hour and be back with you in the morning. How is our dear father taking this upset in his ordered life?'

Morgan shook his head sadly. 'Don't jest about him, Owain. He has aged ten years since Christmas. We are to join him at Llanbadarn before dusk tomorrow, if our dear cousins have cut us off by then.'

'Will Cadwgan fight?' asked Owain.

His brother shrugged again. 'He sent two emissaries to Ithel. They returned the head of one, wrapped in his own cloak. The other has not been heard of since, so diplomacy seems to be ruled out.'

'Then the old man will have to fight?'

'He talks of going to Gwynedd to ask Gruffydd ap Cynan for aid…the old eagle of Eyryi*** was always one for a fight with the French, but we have to get there first.'

Owain nodded slowly. Now that the crisis was upon them, he was thinking fast without the impetuous haste that sometimes led to mistakes. With a spear or battle-axe in his hand, then the red mist of battle made him cast prudence aside, but in these quiet hours before the conflict, his quick mind could deal with many things at the same time. He called his nearest squire, a youth with flaming ginger hair, and gave orders for horses to be made ready. To another, he gave instructions for certain men to be roused and armed. With the

* *Llandovery.*
** *Lampeter.*
*** *Snowdonia.*

Penteulu, he made arrangements for a dawn march of the whole court. The women and children, with the old men and livestock, would vanish into the woods, leaving only a small garrison who were ordered to melt away if a large force of the enemy appeared.

'I'll see you soon after dawn, Morgan. Get some sleep, your buttocks must be like raw leather after that ride.'

An hour later, a small party jogged out of Caerwedros, some on foot alongside a few horses. Nest, Rhiannon, Owain and Caradog, the red-haired youth, rode whilst a few men from the court carried light arms and some bundles of clothing for the two women.

They had not far to go. Crossing the little river that bubbled from St. David's well – the patron saint was himself a son of one of the ancient kings of Ceredigion – they climbed a few ridges and dropped into the deep valley of another stream, the Hawen. As they followed this down, the clouds cleared and a full moon hung above the horizon. It glinted on the silver sea at the end of the narrow gorge and presently the distant rush of the surf echoed between the steep walls of the Hawen valley.

They did not descend to the beach yet, but stopped where the stream made its last plunge over the edge of a platform in the valley. Here, sheltered from the sight of Norse sea raiders, was the church of Saint Carannog. It was only a tiny place of mud-daubed wattle, with an even more wretched priest's cell a stone's throw away. Nearby were a few hovels belonging to the fishermen of Llangrannog, clinging to the gorse-covered slopes. Opposite were a few tilled fields, winterbare in the cold moonlight.

'Which dwelling is it, Caradog?' asked Owain, as they drew rein outside the church.

'The last one – above the Gerwn.' The young man pointed down to a hut that was slightly larger than the rest, with nets hanging blackly about the door. It stood a few yards from the Gerwn, a twenty-foot waterfall that tumbled the stream down with a roar into a rocky bowl below.

They rode towards it and Caradog dismounted to bang on the door. But the noise of their coming, in that most remote of hamlets, had already brought the occupant to peer out fearfully into the night. No Norman had ever yet set foot in the place, so obscure was it, but there had to be a first time. But as soon as the fisherman saw the outline of Welsh nobility, he threw down his feeble spear and ran out to kneel by the horse.

'They tell me in Caerwedros that you are an accomplished sea-man and have a safe boat,' said Owain, after Caradog had introduced the man.

'I could take you to Amorica* itself, if you so desired, *arglwydd*,' replied the fisherman proudly.

'Ireland will be sufficient, my friend,' grinned Owain. 'You will have the

* *Brittany*

most precious of cargoes – the daughter of Prince Rhys himself.'

After more details had been settled, they spent the rest of the night in the hut above the waterfall. It smelt of fish and smoke, but Owain and Nest barely noticed. The fisherman and his family shifted out without being asked, going to their nearby kinsfolk.

In the odorous wattle hut Nest pillowed herself on Owain's shoulder, a cloak over them both, while Rhiannon curled up on the rushes by the dying fire and slept as soundly as if she was in her own bed.

The lovers whispered and dozed together until the first grey fingers of dawn crept into the valley. The fisherman's wife brought them oat-cakes and chopped meat and by the time it was fully light, they were all down on the pebbles above the cliff-girt strip of sand.

Three fishermen slid a frail-looking vessel down to the sullen grey water and stood waiting for their passengers.

Owain, a confirmed land-lover, looked dubiously at the boat. It was a large Irish curragh, a huge, elongated coracle made of skins stretched over a wooden frame.

'Thank Dewi Sant* that the sea is flat calm,' he muttered to Caradog. 'I'd be loth to cross the Teifi in that, let alone the western sea to Ireland.'

Owain picked up his lover and waded out into the icy shallows to place her in the waist of the boat amongst her belongings. Caradog did the same with Rhiannon as the sailors of Llangrannog hoisted a tattered sail on the spindly pole that did service as a mast.

'I'll be with you in a few days, my love,' called Owain, holding Nest's hand until the craft bobbed away, 'or else I'll send a messenger to fetch you back – in a better vessel than this, too!'

The curragh gathered speed and Owain stood thigh deep in the surf, heedless of the cold.

'Give King Murketagh O'Brien my devotion and tell him I may have need of his vessels and men before long,' he shouted.

A white scarf fluttered until the pathetically small boat became a speck on the western horizon.

Owain trampled back up the beach, where Caradog and the guard waited patiently. 'She will be safe, *arglwydd*,' consoled the squire. 'That fisher fellow is the best on this coast for all his rude looks.'

Owain scowled as he swung himself into his saddle and pulled the horse's head round. 'He had better be…if anything happens to that cockleshell, he should hope to drown rather than fall into my hands!'

He kicked his steed's flank and they set off up the valley to confront their fate.

---

* *St. David.*

CHAPTER SEVEN

THE NINTH OF JANUARY, 1110

'SO WE are cut off! This is what your infatuation for that lady has brought us to.'

Cadwgan's voice was bitter. The temporary return of vigour that the emergency had brought had suddenly fallen away, leaving a defeated, hopeless old man in its place.

Some fifty men lay wearily in the little church of Saint Padarn, not so much for the sanctuary it offered, but because was the largest covered space within the stockade of the *clas** of Llanbadarn.

Owain shrugged at this interminable repetition of his father's accusation and wandered restlessly to the open door. It was dusk and dark rain clouds were scudding across the sky. Thank God, he thought, the gales had held off for a day or so after Nest had sailed from Llangrannog. In the four days since then, both natural and human storms had hit poor Ceredigion. The forces of Madog and his allies had ravished the countryside and twice scattered Cadwgan's poorly organized band.

Twice their own party had been scattered and each time fewer men managed afterwards to rejoin the main party. Once they had sheltered in the sanctuary of the other monastery of Llandewibrefi, but Madog had even violated that in his desperate anxiety to capture Owain and curry further favours with Richard and his King.

Now Cadwgan still whined complaints at his eldest son's broad back as he stood at the door. 'If they would not respect the church of David, they will not hesitate to come flying in here tomorrow – or even tonight!'

Owain turned round. 'They can't kill us all – there must be a thousand of our men out there somewhere,' he snapped, sweeping his hand at the darkening mountains that gave birth to the Ystwyth and Rheidol rivers.

'And what good are they to us out there,' quavered Cadwgan, 'scattered like lost sheep, caring only for their own skins. Unless we can get through to Gruffydd and wait for our men to creep to us in twos and threes, we will never see Ceredigion or Powys again.'

Owain prowled back and sat down on the flagged floor. The church was a rectangle, the further end under the little peaked bell-tower containing the altar raised on one step. The rest of the building, though consecrated, was held in no particular reverence by the abbot and brothers of the clas. Fiercely

* *A part monastic, part secular settlement of the Celtic Church.*

anti-Norman themselves, these priests of the Celtic Church were not at all put out by having fully-armed men use their nave as a barracks.

Owain leant forwards and appealed to his favourite brother, who, with the others of the original raiding party on Cenarth Bychan, was acting as his personal bodyguard.

'Morgan, what do you say we do? Stay the night or try to slide through the hills to the Dyfi tonight?'

The dark-browed Morgan jerked a thumb at the teeming rain outside. 'That's our best defence. We can stay in safety this night – Madog and his rascals will not stray far in that.'

Cadwgan made a rude noise. 'We are not even sure where they are, my clever sons! If you're so set on getting to Ireland to join this woman, you'd best get down the valley and find a boat in Aberystwyth.'

Owain shook his head stubbornly. 'I said I'd help you get to Gwynedd to see Gruffydd and that's what I shall do. Come the dawn, we'll leave and strike inland over the shoulder of Plynlimon. They'll not expect us there, but on the low ground of the coast. Once across the Dyfi, then around Cadair Idris and we'll be at the Mawddach river – across that and we're safe.'

'You don't have to teach me geography,' snapped Cadwgan, his face grey with fatigue. 'But our dear kinsfolk, Madog and Ithel, know it as well as you. If I am alive this time tomorrow, I'll praise God for the surprise of it…and all for you and your lust for some Norman's wife!'

'All right, don't keep ranting about it,' shouted Owain, his temper surging. 'What's done is done and I do not regret it. This is but a bad beginning. Once these wolves have gorged themselves of plunder, they'll have had enough and will go home. We can get more than enough support from old Gruffydd to come back and rout them…then organize ourselves to keep out the damned French, which is what has been needed these past ten years.'

'And what if Gruffydd of Gwynedd will not help?' grated his father.

'Then I'll go to Murketagh O'Brien and ask for his help and that of his Norse friends. He'll receive me well enough – and he's almost a brother to Gruffydd, who was born and raised in Dublin.'

'Pah…dreams again. You've wrecked years of patient dealings between me and the Normans and you'll end up with a grip of French iron on all our land!' snarled the Prince, his bitterness silencing even Owain's ready tongue.

The darkness closed down and later a meal was prepared in the kitchens of the *clas* and brought to the fugitives. As they were finishing the rough food, a tall, tonsured monk appeared, soaked to the skin and dishevelled after riding a pony through the mountains.

He bent his knee to Cadwgan and to Owain. Wiping the rain from his bushy eyebrows, he delivered his message in a deep, firm voice.

'Princes, I am come secretly from Uchtryd ap Edwin. He camped near my cell about fifteen miles away. He bids you once again know that he is out of sympathy with the venture of this so-called bishop. Already he has received many of your men who have fled from the battlefield. He has been beseeching folk to fly to him and not to Madog or Llywarch – nor especially into Dyfed, where we have heard of awful deeds wrought by the French there.'

Owain stood over the crouching figure in his sodden habit. 'How came you to find us – and you have not ridden the hills to tell us just this, brother?'

The priest shook his head, the rain flying from his hair like a dog shaking itself. 'Though we are solitary men, news travels fast between us brothers of God, arglwydd. I heard you were in Llanbadarn and not only I know it.'

Owain grunted, 'What do you mean by that, monk?'

'Uchtryd further extends his help by sending secret news to you by my mouth. There is a great host with him, and Madog and the others are camped not far distant. These others wished to march upon Llanbadarn tonight, but Uchtryd has persuaded them to stay their hand until day-break, saying that you may have gathered a great number of your men back again and the battle would be better fought where they can see you in daylight. He prays that you will use this respite to flee, else this *clas* will be ravished and you and your men will undoubtedly be taken.'

Cadwgan, huddled near the fire, looked up at his sons with weary eyes. 'See how we are hunted through our own country – all through your lust, Owain. I am past caring now whether I live or die. Let your cousins come in the night and put out my life.'

The priest looked appealingly at Cadwgan, but seeing the apathy on the old man's face, he turned his gaze anxiously on Owain.

'*Arglwydd*, beseech your father to fly at once. You must be well away by morning. Only Uchtryd's wily tongue has kept them from marching on you this very night.'

The Lion of Powys nodded. 'You are a good fellow, we will heed your advice. I have no desire to be caught by my dear kinsmen like a rat in this trap of Llanbadarn. We will run to fight another day. Let us only get north to Gruffydd and then we shall return to deal with these vermin.'

'They have a great host, *arglwydd*...Llywarch alone has many hundreds of men and he seeks vengeance for your killing of his brothers. I would fear him above the rest.'

Owain nodded, impatient now. 'Come, Lord my father. The rain is now our ally, we can slip across those hills and pass within ten paces of any scouts without them seeing us.'

Cadwgan stirred himself reluctantly. 'We are less than three score Owain...what's the use?'

Owain reddened with annoyance. 'You are the King, this band belongs to you. We are not a few scurvy shoe-kissers of the Bishop of London. Our army may have melted away, but that is the fashion of our people. We are no French or Saxons to fight shoulder to shoulder until we are all slaughtered, like a stampede of stupid cattle! We hit, we run and we return to hit again!' His voice became louder and the men shuffled to their feet, his ringing words already spurring them from their exhaustion. 'We will come back with a host of Danes or Irish…then all our men will appear from the trees like some of Merlin's magic! You, above all, father, should know this, for you have done it yourself often enough.'

The auburn-haired prince shouted his words to the rafters of the little church and every man cried his agreement. Even Cadwgan nodded grudgingly at the reference to his old triumphs. He pulled himself up slowly from his crouch by the fire.

'So be it – though my old limbs are crying out at the thought of journeying in that wet hell out there!' He nodded at the black square of the door, where rain poured down unrelentingly. He straightened up. 'But I am Prince and there is an end to it,' he said in a much firmer voice, pulling his cloak down over his mailed jacket.

Their pursuers caught up with them when they had reached be Dyfi river, some twenty miles to the north of Llanbadarn. As the monk had predicted, the forces of Madog, Ithel and Llywarch made a rendezvous with those of Uchtryd after breaking their camp near the ford of the Corunec* at dawn. The sympathetic Uchtryd, who had already given surreptitious shelter to many hundred fugitives from Cadwgan's lands, had indeed persuaded the renegade allies to postpone their overnight attack on Llanbadarn.

When their whole army of two thousand marched south, they were actually in sight of the fugitives, who had taken the higher inland route up the bleak western slopes of the Plynlimon mountains. On reaching Llanbadarn, Madog and his compatriots were mortified to find the whole countryside emptied of people and animals; only the monks of the *clas* remained, indignantly calling down curses upon the armed men who angrily ransacked the sanctuary, looking for the princes of Powys.

Ithel ranted at Uchtryd, accusing him of collusion and treachery, but the older man shrugged philosophically and advised the hot-blooded Madog and his brother to spend their breath in giving orders to their men. The main force split up into two, one going down into Ceredigion to further violate the *clas* of Llandewibrefi, in case the enemy had doubled back there; the main force retraced their path in the more likely hope of catching Cadwgan and Owain as they tried to slip northwards to Gwynedd.

The fleeing warriors had reached a ford well up-stream from the estuary of the Dyfi before they were aware of their pursuers. The ground was sodden and the river in full spate after the stormy weather of the last few days. The few wretched dwellings known as Machynlleth were well behind them before they could risk plunging their horses into the swirling waters to cross to the northern bank. Their route then lay back along the opposite side of the river, keeping to the narrow belt of flat land along the shore until they reached the Mawddach and safety, another twenty miles further.

A stream north of Aberystwyth.

As they began to plod back along the Dyfi towards the estuary, Morgan sighted the hostile war-band coming up the opposite side.

'Oh, for a host of our own!' he yelled in frustration, wheeling back his horse to the old Prince and Owain, who were travelling behind in the single file that the narrow path demanded.

They all reined up and stared across the river. The enemy had seen them, too, and were yelling threats and urging their own horses and barefoot men-at-arms to greater speed.

'Twenty or thirty of them to each of us,' swore Owain wildly. Cadwgan groaned. 'We are lost now! Either fight to the death or be taken prisoner to be maimed and blinded – or killed, if we are fortunate. Spur on, for God's sake!'

'Useless, sire…they would catch us inside ten miles,' snapped Morgan.

He had his sword out, but it hung uselessly. Though Ithel and his men were less than a quarter of a mile away, they also had to go up to the ford and back, at least half an hour's journey in the mud of the river bank.

The fifty men from Powys clustered together all looking to Owain the Valiant for leadership. Cadwgan had gone to pieces days ago and his eldest son was their only hope of salvation. They were quite willing – and fully expected – to stand there and fight themselves to the death for Owain, but he had the urge to at least salvage something from the catastrophe.

'My father, you must reach Gruffydd and carry on our campaign. No more than a few dozen miles separate you from Gwynedd now. If you strike off with half the men up there, we will draw off these wolves and let you get clear away.'

He pointed with his sword at the steep hills above them which led to the lake of Tal-y-llyn and the huge mass of Cadair Idris towering into the rain clouds.

Cadwgan shook his head. 'Old man and spent king though I be, I'll not leave my two sons to die on my account. It must be the other way. You will fly to Gruffydd and I'll stay to die at these bastards' hands!'

A stubborn gleam came into his eyes, as if the prospect of dying within the hour was the only thing worth living for.

Owain glared back at him, his anger quick even at a time of mortal peril. He started to argue, but the ever-quick brain of Morgan came to divide them.

'While you debate, they will be on us and no one will live to reach Gwynedd,' he said urgently. 'Already those across the river have passed out of sight…but I have a thought, Owain. Let the Prince our father go as you say and the rest of us will take this coast track to draw off Madog and Ithel…for by their banners and shields over there, it must be they and not Uchtryd or Llywarch.'

'That is what I have already said,' snapped Owain.

'And I denied!' yelled Cadwgan. 'You'll not ride to your death on my account.'

Morgan shook his head impatiently. 'When we came up the other side of the river, did you not see a vessel anchored at the mouth of the Dyfi where those few fisher huts stand? It looked a sizeable craft, enough to get to Aberffraw*. We can ride to it ahead of those other swine and board it. With

* *The capital of Gwynedd, in Anglesey.*

either gold or a dagger at his throat, the ship-master can be persuaded to sail at once. And there is no other vessel to pursue us.'

Owain pranced his horse close to Morgan and slapped his brother on the shoulder. 'You should be the *edling*, Morgan, not I! The brains went all into your head!'

'If it's to be done, we have not the space of a heart-beat to lose,' snapped Morgan. 'Father, ride with your Chancellor and Pencerdd this minute – straight up through those trees and lay low until the host has passed by, then make all haste to Gwynedd.'

'And we'll be waiting for you in Aberffraw, having saved our backsides from a long ride!' jested Owain gaily, wheeling his horse around and already starting off on the track towards Aberdyfi, their original route.

Cadwgan looked hesitantly at his sons, then spoke urgently to the several older men who were his ministers. He turned back to Morgan. 'Only if you swear to take ship and not martyr yourselves on my account,' he compromised, and with a raised band of farewell, led his men off the track and up into the woodland leading to the high land.

The others did not stop to watch the Prince vanish through the dripping trees, but hurried on after Owain.

'On to the strand!' he yelled and the fleeing men, now about eighteen in number, slanted off on to the sand that lay immediately below the grass and scrub that lined the lower part of the estuary.

The ship, the only one of any size, was already in sight, anchored near the cluster of mean fishing shacks that was Aberdyfi. The tide was high, though on the ebb. The vessel was moored quite near the shore, which became steeper near the hamlet, due to the approach of the hills to the water's edge.

'How do we get to her?' yelled Owain, over the drum of the now cantering horses.

Morgan swivelled about to shout at the men:

'Do you all swim?'

All but one yelled that they could. When they reached the bank opposite the vessel, their pursuers were but five hundred yards behind. Owain threw himself from his horse, tore off his cloak and sent his sword belt spinning into the deep water. The others followed his example, tearing off their scanty armour and metal-girt helmets, then plunged into the icy waters, keeping only their daggers with them.

The one who could not swim was dragged, half-submerged, by two of his compatriots and slowly the whole band made their way across the hundred yards of bone-chilling sea to the ship.

The first of their pursuers arrived at the bank just as the leading swimmers reached the low side of the vessel. Madog and Ithel themselves were amongst the horsemen, the foot soldiers having been left behind in the chase. Most of the bowmen were on foot and the more aristocratic mounted men, armed only with spears and swords, stood in screaming frustration on the bank. One man had a bow but, thankfully for Owain's band, he was a poor shot. Though immediately pressed into service, he fired a whole quiver of arrows and only managed to inflict a trivial scratch on one of the men who was towing the non-swimmer.

'Throw us a net, you beautiful villain!' yelled Owain to a gaping sailor as he arrived alongside the ship.

The man, reacting automatically to the voice of royal authority, was galvanized into action and slung a strong fishing net over the low bulwarks. Owain and Morgan clambered up and in a few moments all the men were standing shivering in the low waist of the decrepit vessel.

Dripping wet, they stood and gazed gleefully at the shore, where more and more horsemen were arriving, to add to the yells of angry abuse that rang across the noon-tide waters.

'That's Madog – the one with the torc around his neck,' pointed out the keen-sighted Morgan. Owain cupped his hands and roared out a promise...
'I'll be back to kill you, you treacherous kisser of French feet!'

The weak winter sun glinted for a moment on a sword blade waved by Madog. 'Where's that ancient father of yours, that ex-Prince of Powys?' screamed his voice from the distant shore.

Owain swallowed his anger with difficulty and pointed down to the empty deck, hidden by the bulwarks. 'He's here, resting after his swim,' he lied at the top of the lungs. He wished to give his father the best start on his flight to Gwynedd, without setting a blood-hungry pack of frustrated warriors after him.

Ithel's voice came thinly across the sea. 'Tell him he's now a prince without a princedom! And you are the heir to nothing, Owain ap Cadwgan! King Henry is to give Powys and Ceredigion to us in return for our help in ridding the country of you, you crazy ravisher of Norman wives!'

For a moment, it seemed that Owain was going to dive overboard to tear the heart out of Ithel, but Morgan put a restraining hand on his arm. 'We have to get this craft on the move, brother,' he murmured practically. They sought out the petrified ship-master, who was crouching in the mean shelter at the stern which served as the cabin. With an ostentatious display of his dagger and the promise of gold, Morgan got the Irishman to move his wretched crew of two skinny boys into action. One hauled up the large stone that served as an anchor, while the other shook out the single sail.

Owain returned to his slanging match across the water, but the distance lengthened and the voices grew more faint as the ship-master went to the large steering oar in the stern and piloted the ship away from the shore.

The fast-ebbing tide in that most treacherous of estuaries was soon whirling the little craft towards the open sea. Within minutes, the men on the shore were only dots against the grey-green landscape. Before long, the land-bound gentry of Owain's band were starting to feel the first uneasy twinges, as the Irish vessel crossed the bar and lurched into the choppy seas that lay off the river mouth. A stiff north-east wind was blowing and in spite of Morgan's threats and promises, the ship-master was adamant that it was impossible to reach the island of Môn* or any other part of North Wales with the wind in that quarter.

'He says Ceredigion, Dyfed or Ireland are the only places he can make for,' reported Morgan.

Owain gave a short laugh. 'I fear we will get little welcome either in Ceredigion or in de Windsore's domain, Morgan! So let it be Dublin, then. There'll be a welcome of a different sort from Murketagh O'Brien, I'm sure. And I will be seeing Nest ferch Rhys sooner than I had hoped.'

The captain leaned on his great oar and the ungainly hulk slewed around and aimed itself at Ireland, while Owain stood himself in the prow and willed the vessel to move even faster towards Dublin and his new obsession.

* *The modern Anglesey.*

CHAPTER EIGHT

THE TWENTIETH DAY OF JANUARY, 1110
THE flag fluttering from the highest turret of Shrewsbury Castle showed that the King was there.

In the same room that Bishop Richard had commissioned Madog and Ithel's recent campaign, Henry of England and Normandy now held another audience.

He sat at the same table, with the Bishop on his right hand, and faced another two men across its oaken width.

One of these sat and the other stood, though he was by way of being a king himself. It was Cadwgan ap Bleddyn, there under a flag of truce, trying to retrieve something from the wreckage caused by Owain's escapade.

The seated man was Gerald de Windsore, hunched in the chair, staring at his feet as the harsh words of Richard of London cracked across the room at the Welsh Prince.

'But for your precious truce, Welshman, you would now be rotting in our King's dungeon! Considering the treachery of your cursed offspring to our friend de Windsore here, you may consider yourself fortunate that Norman chivalry is so strong as to respect your parley. A lesser bred would have considered his vile acts sufficient warrant to ignore your white-flagged messengers!'

Cadwgan's yellowed face flushed slightly and he shot a glance at the King to see what his reaction was. But Henry sat impassively, his calm features betraying nothing as his Warden of the Marches berated the Welsh ex-ruler. Henry was not a big man, but there was something about him that directed every eye in his direction. He had that undefinable aura of superiority that was vital in a medieval ruler who wished to keep his throne. No one knew just how his brother Rufus had met his death, but many had their suspicions – and were very careful to keep them unspoken in the King's hearing. Henry wasted no words and there was an intensity in his brown eyes that marked him as a man different from the others.

Like Owain, a lock of hair fell on his forehead, though it was dark brown, not auburn.

He sat now immobile, dressed in a rich but sober-coloured costume. His tunic was cream with green embroidery and a dark mantle of green velvet lay around his shoulders. A narrow circle of gold lay on his thick hair, the only badge of kingship he bore.

Waiting until the harsh voice of Richard had finished, he turned to Gerald of Pembroke.

'And what have you to say to all this, de Windsore?' The royal voice was slow and measured, in contrast to the irritable snap of the warrior bishop.

Gerald looked up, slowly, as if waking from sleep. For a moment he seemed not quite aware of his surroundings.

Then he spoke in a dull, lack-lustre voice. 'My only quarrel with this man, sire, is that he begat a son. A son that I shall surely kill, for he has wronged me most deeply.'

With these few monotonous words, de Windsore subsided into his morose silence.

King Henry shifted his keen eyes to the Prince. 'And you, Cadogan of the Welsh....what is it you want from us today? My loyal steward, the bishop here, sent equally loyal countrymen of yours to seek out you and your son and either destroy you or remove you from those lands which we gave into your charge some years ago. What can you say now that might change our minds on this matter?'

Cadwgan held out his hands, palms up in supplication.

'Nothing can I say to excuse the rashness of my eldest son, lord. But this was some madness, inherited from his mother – some affliction of the mind. None of it was any of my doing. It is common knowledge that I forbade his wild escapades many times in the past. Then when this most heinous of his foolish acts took place – this moon madness at Christmas – I entreated him in every possible way to make amends. It was through my intercession that de Windsore's children were so speedily returned to him. I did all I could to make him return the booty from Cenarth Bychan...and most of all, both I and my kinsmen, especially my Norman wife, entreated him to give up the Lady Nest. But all to no avail...and I know nothing of them now, save that they are in Ireland.'

Henry looked from Cadwgan to Gerald, giving the Sheriff of Pembroke a questioning look.

'The Lady Nesta...what say you of her, de Windsore?'

Gerald raised his head, the suggestion of Mongol cheeks being emphasized in the slanting light coming from the slit window opposite.

'I have nothing to say about my wife, sire. She is gone.'

Henry's impassive face hardened slightly. 'Come, man...she is your wife, she has been abducted! You cannot just sit there and say "she is gone!" and leave it at that.'

Gerald rose slowly from his seat and glowered at Cadwgan.

'Her heart may yet beat, sire, but to me, she is dead.'

Two angry spots appeared on Henry's cheeks.

'Listen, sir knight – apart from being your wedded lady, she is also my ward. And you have no small beholdenment to her for her past deeds in your favour. I will say no more, but you are well aware of them. You cannot shrug off a wife like you would throw off an old cloak!'

Though there was sarcasm in the words, Gerald's rare emotion now commanded the scene. He moved a few steps nearer Cadwgan, his hand on the hilt of his great sword. He glared almost crazily into the parchment face of the old Prince, who looked back uneasily at the castellan.

'Sire, I had a castle – a castle of my own. It is now no more – and never will be for many a year. I had a wife...and she will never be wife to me again. If I could benefit my temper by cutting this old man to shreds, I would do it gladly, but he is a poor thing and I store my vengeance for his son.'

Gerald's voice cracked at the end and he stepped back, trembling. Richard had listened impatiently to all this. Now he slammed the table and spoke bluntly to the King, without any veneer of diplomacy or tact.

'The lady went not unwillingly with this Owen, sire – that is the root of the matter. She tricked de Windsore into escaping to summon help – by a most undignified route, I must add. Then off she went into this Owen's arms like some wench being taken to her wedding bed!'

Cadwgan found some strength of voice to shout at this.

'No, my lord, not so! He had not met this lady since childhood. It was some dispute between Sir Gerald here and my son. The ins-and-outs of it are not to be found, but I swear that no plot was made to make off with Nest ferch Rhys.'

The Warden of the Marches sneered. 'A Welsh princess – and a hot-headed Welsh prince to rescue her from the arms of the Norman oppressor? And you try to tell me it was all but chance? Nonsense, sir...there must have been secret messages between them. Her Welsh maid, plenty of Welsh loungers around Pembroke Castle to carry tales. De Windsore suspects it, that's why he is in no hurry to have her back...eh, Gerald?'

De Windsore stood immobile, not answering the forthright bishop. His head sank slowly, and it was answer enough.

Henry's face took on a hint of impatience.

'The day wears on and we have other business besides this...so what is to be done with you, Cadogan of Powys?'

Cadwgan rubbed his hands together nervously. He looked ten years older since last week, when he had failed to persuade Gruffydd ap Cynan of Gwynedd to help him expel Madog, Ithel and their partners. He had been forced to come to Shrewsbury to beg some mercy from his Norman overlords, as he had nowhere else to go.

'Lord King, this is no doing of mine. For the sake of my son's sin, all I have striven for on your behalf these past years has fallen about my ears. I have kept the peace in Powys and Ceredigion and until now, you can have no cause to regret the action that you had in ceding those lands to my care. I beg that you call off these ravaging bandits, Madog and the others, for they have no notion of government and will reduce our lands to wreckage within a few weeks.'

Henry looked up at Richard, but the bishop scowled and shook his head. 'It is too late, even if we wished it,' he snapped. 'Madog, Ithel and Llywarch are in control throughout Powys and Kerdigan. Until at least this mad dog of his son is brought to heel, Cadogan cannot be restored.'

The King sighed lightly. 'So be it…Cadogan, you have a French wife, the daughter of our faithful Picot de Sai in Clun Forest. I know she brought you dowry lands in Knighton, so I banish you from Wales to these estates until our further pleasure be known. From the look of you, you need some months to restore your health – so it may be that we are doing you a kindness by this judgment.' Henry said this easily, but there was a stern undercurrent in his voice that discouraged any argument.

Cadwgan groaned, partly at the thought of being bottled up with Marie in her father's domain, where she could crow over him and endlessly throw his dependence on her family in his face.

'Might I not hope for some leniency in the future, Lord?' he muttered. 'This is a harsh verdict for a man who has ruled his lands well on your behalf for so long.'

Richard snapped an answer for the King. 'Let us first see what befalls your erring son, Cadogan! The scriptures speak of the sins of the fathers being visited on the sons – we shall have to apply the text in reverse for a while!'

Henry rose to indicate that the audience was finished. 'And let us also see if this Madog and Ithel fail to imitate your just rule, Cadogan. My Lord Bishop here will keep me well informed.'

He turned finally to Gerald, who stood all in armour, except for his helmet. 'And you, sir, be not so uncharitable toward your wife. Remember that she is still my ward.'

He walked from the table towards a side door, where two spear-holding guards stood like statues.

Half way there, he turned.

'And remember also, de Windsore, that you suffered my displeasure once before. It was your wife who had you restored, not any valorous act of yours. I am not inclined to go to any great lengths to avenge your loss of a heap of sticks and stones at this Cenarth, but for Nesta I would dare much – and I expect you to do the same!'

He turned and followed his chaplain from the chamber, leaving behind him a white-faced Gerald and a dejected, deposed Welsh Prince.

PART TWO

CHAPTER NINE
OCTOBER, 1110

NEST sat by the open window, rocking the cradle absently. Her mind was far away, thinking of her other four children, whom she had not seen for almost ten months.

Little Llywelyn – Llywelyn ap Owain – had been born early in September, almost a month premature. Now it was mid-October and the dead leaves were blowing over the battlements of Din-geraint, heralding a winter full of war.

Nest could hear Owain's strong voice out in the great hall, arguing with Morgan, as usual. Outside in the bailey, the tumult of men's affairs clashed with her motherly cradle-rocking and with Rhiannon's peaceful sewing on the other side of the bedchamber. For Din-geraint was now a place of war, far different from that seemingly distant Christmas when the *eisteddfod* had been held – that fateful feast when Owain's challenge had changed both their lives.

Now the place echoed with the clash of weapons, the neighing of the war-horses and the excited shouts of young men eager to mingle their blood with that of Norman and Fleming.

Nest sighed and looked down tenderly at the young baby in the crib. It was ironic that both this child and this lust for fighting had come directly from the desire of one man for her. For there was little doubt that all the turmoil in all this western part of Wales could be traced back to that lunatic venture of Owain's against Cenarth Bychan.

His voice came again from the hall and she smiled wanly as she saw his strong chin and forehead in those of the sleeping babe. But for the yearning for her other children, she would have been quite content, though half Wales was up in arms because of it.

Yet the longing for little Angharad and Gwladys and the boys became unbearable at times. Llywelyn's arrival had somehow heightened the *hiraeth** for them, instead of soothing it.

A sudden flurry of wind banged one of the window shutters against the rough frame and Nest shivered. That wind had blown up from Dyfed, passed over Penbroch and brought with it the icy hand of her husband, Gerald. Not a single word had arrived from him since the other children had been returned. Though Owain was now at war with all Normans, there were plenty of ways

---

* *Longing or nostalgia.*

of passing news and messages, but nothing had been heard from the great castle in Dyfed.

She knew that Gerald would never rest until he was avenged for his ruined castle and his smirched reputation – half the Norman nobles in Britain had laughed up their sleeves when they heard how Sir Gerald de Windsore had been forced to flee through a latrine shaft, like some cuckold caught in a lady's bedchamber. Even so, Nest could not understand this complete excommunication of herself. It was weird and perverse and her straightforward mind never for an instant considered that Gerald believed that the whole affair had been planned in advance.

The shutter banged again and Rhiannon, afraid that the baby might be disturbed, sprang up to close it. She stood for a long moment staring out of the other open half, before turning back inside. 'Lord Owain must be planning some other escapade, *arglwyddes*,' she said, her homely face radiating pride. She had enjoyed this past ten months more than all the rest of her life put together – she worshipped Owain and saw him as the saviour who had brought them to live amongst their own kin again, after so many years in the French wilderness.

Nest looked up from the hypnotic rocking of the cradle. 'Why so, Rhiannon...this fortress is always bustling with brave fools itching to go out and get themselves slaughtered.'

The maid jerked her head towards the bailey. 'There are men from Powys and Arwystli there today, lady – men from the north. Maybe they have brought more slaves for Ireland.'

Nest fell silent. This was something she disliked more than battle and bloodshed, though it was well rooted in usage. Selling Welshmen, as well as the stray Norman, Saxon or Fleming, into slavery across the Irish Sea was something she could not take easily...there was something so degrading about being sold like cattle. Since Owain had started his guerilla war against his Welsh and Norman enemies, he had captured and exported hundreds of miserable wretches across to Dublin and Wexford, where they toiled until they dropped, in the fields and peat-bogs of Murketagh and other petty Irish kings.

Owain had only laughed when she had chided him about slavery. 'If the boot was on the other foot, we would all be working ourselves to the death in some Normandy vineyard – those few who escaped gutting and dismembering!'

Men's voices suddenly became louder and the chamber door banged open. Owain strode in, beckoning Morgan after him. 'Let's hear what our beautiful Nest has to say on the matter,' gusted the auburn-haired brother, flinging himself down on the shaggy skins of the bed. Rhiannon rose hastily to leave, but Owain waved her down again. 'Stay, good girl – if all our allies had as much faith and good sense as you, we'd want for little.'

Flushed with pleasure, the servant girl sank down, while her mistress smiled at the two men and raised her smoothly arched brows in question.

'Since when do mere women have a use to men, apart from mothering and sewing, Owain ap Cadwgan?' she mocked affectionately.

Owain grinned from the bed, but the dark Morgan looked even more serious than usual. 'My brother has a scheme even more full of madness than usual, cousin,' he said in his slow, deep voice. 'I have tried to dissuade him, but he's set on it. It will bring down more trouble on us than did his escapade at the Rock of Cilgerran last Christmastide.'

Owain flapped a hand at him, in careless defiance, but Nesta sensed the deep concern in Morgan's words.

'What is it? Anything to do with the Irish ships that came up the Teifi yesterday?' she asked anxiously.

Owain shook his head, a stubborn look on his face. 'It's a matter of revenge, Nest, my love. We have heard from a good Welshman at Abergwaun* that William of Brabant – God rot his black soul! – is creeping across the north of Dyfed tomorrow with a small escort, on his way from St. David's to Shrewsbury. We intend to waylay him and rid Wales of one of its worst tyrants.'

Morgan broke in vehemently. 'I agree that the swine deserves to be cut slowly into a thousand pieces, Owain. But though I have no wish to save his foul skin, I fear the anger that his death would bring down upon us.'

Owain banged the bed angrily with his hands. 'What do you think we are doing at the moment, then...making the French fall in love with us?' he demanded. 'One more carcass will make little difference.'

Morgan wheeled around from the window, where he had been morosely watching the bustling soldiery. 'It *will* make a difference, my brother – a great difference! This Brabant man is leader of the Flemish settlers in Dyfed. On him the French depend for the organization of their flat-footed colonists there. He is rich, he has great power, even amongst the Normans themselves. He is the one who raises Flemish troops for de Windsore and for King Henry. Kill him and the flood-gates of Norman wrath will really be opened up upon us.'

Owain jumped up impetuously and went to put a caressing hand on Nest's shoulder. 'I fear no flood-gates, Morgan. We are strong enough now to hold Ceredigion against anyone.'

Morgan shook his head violently. 'No, Owain, no! Now we fight Welshmen and a few Norman skirmishers. It suits Richard of London to let us squabble with our father Cadwgan and waste our time shedding Welsh blood, even at the price of a few drops of French. But once take any drastic step like slaying this William of Flanders and the full wrath of Henry Beauclerk will fall upon us. He loves these clumsy folk from the Low Countries too much to ignore such a gesture.'

Morgan became more agitated as this long speech broke from him. His black hair swirled about his ears and his eyes flashed below the deep brows as he entreated his stubborn brother to moderation.

---

* *The modern Fishguard.*

Owain shrugged inside his stylish yellow tunic. 'What say you, Nest ferch Rhys? This William of Brabant has urged his men on to many a savage attack on our folk. I have seen homesteads desolated by him and sights that even my hard eyes have wept for. He normally keeps well within the French lands, but rumour has it that he is to escort gold and silver from the taxes in Dyfed up to the King at Shrewsbury. It is a chance too good to miss – we could have him not a dozen miles across the river as he passes through the commote of Emlyn.'

Nest was torn between Morgan's fears and her unswerving loyalty to her lover. She played the middle course.

'I am no soldier, Owain. What Morgan says seems good sense, though I have heard that this William has caused much suffering. I have met him many times at Gerald's table at Penbroch. He is a gross and cruel overlord – even the peasant Flemings fear him. He squeezes the last grunt of work from them and the last groat in taxes. Yet to slay him would set the Normans about our ears in no small fashion.'

Owain looked up at his brother and Morgan raised his hands in despair. He saw from Owain's expression that the matter was already decided. 'So be it, brother! Yet remember that I counselled you against this, when we are skulking in some ditch with the French trampling all over Ceredigion!'

He bowed quickly to Nest and strode out of the room. Owain smiled after him, knowing that Morgan was going straight away to make sure that everything was in readiness to make the attack on the Fleming a success.

'Morgan is the most faithful man in the world,' he said to Nest, 'as you are the most faithful woman.'

This time Rhiannon knew her cue and silently slid out of the room, closing the door softly behind her.

Llywelyn was asleep and the cradle soon stopped rocking.

Morgan went the rounds of the hutments and stables, making sure that all was ready for the morrow and the trouble that must surely follow.

When his inspection was finished, he went to his favourite place on the stockade, the same one that he and Owain had used on the night of Cadwgan's great feast.

Looking down into the swirling waters of the Teifi, he pondered on all the changes that had come about as a result of his half-brother's rashness that Christmas.

Madog, the leader of the men who had hunted them at Bishop Richard's instigation, was now their ally! When their own father had been ignominiously banished to his wife's estate in Clun, Madog and Ithel had taken over Cadwgan's lands. But within weeks they were fighting amongst themselves and governing so badly that King Henry gave orders for their ejection. He reinstated old Cadwgan, who had to pay a ransom of one hundred pounds, as well as promising not to give shelter to Owain nor to assist him in any way whatsoever. The Prince readily agreed and was soon established back in Mathrafal, his main seat in Powys.

Morgan grinned wryly when he remembered the pontifical messages that had come from Mathrafal to Dublin, warning Owain to stay well away from Powys and Ceredigion, on pain of King Henry's displeasure. It was probably these more than anything that had prompted Owain to return to Wales in April, three months after his hasty escape from Aberdyfi.

Together with Nest and the survivors from the attack on Cenarth Bychan, Owain and Morgan landed in Gwynedd and made their way secretly across to Cadwgan's homelands. They took over one of his own hunting lodges, Plas Eliseg, at the foot of some wild crags near Llangollen.

Their father soon discovered that they were there and sent frantic appeals for them to go away, which Owain spurned with contemptuous nonchalance. Cadwgan, afraid though he was of Norman displeasure, hesitated to send armed men against his own sons, and an impasse was reached, until Owain decided to move of his own accord.

In June, Madog fell foul of Bishop Richard again. Already in bad odour because of his mishandling of Cadwgan's domains, he made matters worse by giving sanctuary to some Saxon brigands who were wanted by the Warden of the Marches for crimes committed in England. Richard ordered Madog to hand them over, but the Welshman refused and sought out Owain as an ally. Previous differences were forgotten in the face of the common French adversary and the two cousins swore a great oath never to make peace with the Normans, nor to betray each other.

Morgan, still staring into the fish-laden river, smiled cynically at the memory, knowing that Madog ap Rhiryd was about as trustworthy as one of the slippery eels that lived under the stones beneath the stockade.

Now Madog was in Powys, harrying both the Normans and his uncle Iorwerth, Cadwgan's brother, who had recently been released from prison by the King. Owain and his war band had come south to Ceredigion and in complete defiance of their father had occupied Din-geraint as the most convenient centre for raids into Dyfed and Ystrad Tywi.

Though they had not gone as far as the great fortresses at Penbroch and Carmarthen, they had pillaged deep into the Norman lands and drawn out massive amounts of booty and slaves, leaving desolation among the settlements of Norman, Fleming and vassal Welsh.

Morgan looked thoughtfully across at the dense woods on the opposite bank and his mind travelled to that great castle perched on its rock at Penbroch. Never once had Gerald de Windsore been seen during the sharp fighting that sometimes accompanied these Welsh attacks. Usually, Owain's men appeared from the trees like magic, wrought their havoc and vanished again like will-o'-the-wisps. But now and again an enraged Norman force would smash its way through the woods in a blind search for their tormentors. These columns were always spied upon by Welsh scouts, but never had the red saltire of de Windsore been seen on a shield or surcoat. No massive retaliation had been launched across the Teifi, mainly because the garrison in Dyfed was seriously drained of men for Henry's campaigns in Normandy.

Morgan shook off his reveries and turned back to look at their own fortress. Though the stockade was vintage Montgomery, it had none of the sophisticated Norman defences. No drawbridge, no gatehouse, no keep – just a heavy wooden fence with massive gates, and inside, Cadwgan's new hall with a cluster of outbuildings.

All around were bustling men, a few chickens and pigs, and cooking fires with blue smoke scurrying this way and that in the autumn gusts. Horses, tethered to pegs, churned the wet turf into mud as they kicked out petulantly at a few small boys wearing their father's helmets and carrying sticks as make-believe swords. Morgan smiled in spite of his worries. He loved them all, these children and their fathers, everyone in that place.

Though he was a man of Powys, reared in the north with the loom of mountains all around, he felt equally at home in this sea-girt land of Ceredigion, with its rolling heaths and woodland. Morgan well understood Owain's passion to make their ancient lands free once again, but his brother's rash methods made him fear that one day their luck would run out.

This matter of the Fleming tomorrow, for instance…Morgan sighed and turned towards the hall to rest on his pallet until the evening meal was served.

In the Prince's chamber, where Cadwgan and the fat Marie de Sai had slept last Christmas, Nest was suckling little Llywelyn. Owain lay on the bed, hands clasped behind his head, staring serenely up at the roof beams. His yellow tunic was unpinned to the waist, showing the rippling muscles of his hairy chest.

'Nest, my love – are you happy?' he asked suddenly, in his disconcerting direct fashion.

Nest smiled slowly and shifted the eager babe to the other breast. 'Never more so, Owain…though I sorely miss my other young ones. But for that, I wish these days in Ceredigion would last for ever!'

The auburn-haired prince twisted his neck to look at her, as she sat on a stool alongside the bed.

'You were born into a great house at Dinefwr…you have lived with a King and in another great castle at Penbroch. Surely you miss the company of other gentlewomen and the trappings of a chivalrous court?'

Nest wrinkled her nose at him, her eyes dancing. 'You are casting around for flattery, Owain ap Cadwgan,' she chided him affectionately. 'You wish me to say "Is this not the royal court of Ceredigion and am I not the consort of the princely heir of Powys!"'

Owain grinned back at her. 'Well, are you not, Nest? One day, not far distant, you will be the queen of more than Powys. And our little son there, Llywelyn, will be the heir to far more. One day, all Wales will be under my guidance – even Gwynedd, when old Gruffydd at last leaves this mortal life.'

He grinned suddenly. 'Perhaps we can marry our little lad off to one of his granddaughters and link our lands in that way. It would not be the first time – nor the last, if only we can keep the damned French out for long enough.'

The mention of the Normans brought a cloud over Nest's mind as she thought of the next day's escapade.

'Morgan is worried about this ambush tomorrow, my love…and he is a man of sense and judgment. Must you do it? I care nothing for William of Brabant, but Morgan is right enough about the hornets' nest you must surely stir up.'

Owain's face hardened. 'Enough, Nest – my mind is made up. I saw three homesteads in Dyfed last month, where William's men had been. Even I, used as I am to the ways of men in war, was sick to my heart to see what they had done to women and children alike. For that alone, I will personally cut down this Fleming and be damned to the consequences. These barbarians must learn that they cannot ride rough-shod over a land that was cultured even before the Romans came.'

Nest winced as Llywelyn pulled at her a little too enthusiastically, but her mind remained on war. 'But is this the way to do it, Owain? Richard sits in Shrewsbury waiting his chance to call down the full wrath of Henry on you – only these war in France have delayed it thus long. You have defied the King's edict to your father merely by coming back from Ireland. This six months of harrying the French must have brought the King's patience very near its end.'

'A pox on the King,' muttered Owain, his labile mood taking a violent plunge. He looked at Nest with different eyes an almost haunted expression lurking in them as he studied her lovely face.

'Tell me, Nest ferch Rhys, how was it between you and Henry?'

She dropped her eyes, looking instead at the babe avidly drinking from her body. 'It was a long time ago, Owain,' she murmured pleadingly.

'I want to know, Nest…please.' His voice was supplicating, in an obstinate, almost child-like manner.

Nest sighed. They had skirted around this subject more than once and she again sensed his half-jealous, half-curious need to know what it had been like to be mistress to a King of England.

'Owain, why do you persist? I have told you, it lasted but a brief period and the choice was not mine. I was but a passing fancy of a man whose reputation for using women is as great as his cunning as a monarch.'

'You loved him, Nest?' The words stumbled out bluntly. The raven-haired woman smiled, a madonna of a smile that carried warmth and comfort as well as passion.

'Worry no more, Owain…you have no need of jealousy. No, I did not love Henry. But he was gentle and gallant – we both knew that my graceful submission would smooth a path for both myself and for Gerald.'

She stretched out a hand and touched Owain's knee. He gave a sudden wry smile, then chuckled. 'A scheming harlot, this Nest, subtly twisting the King of England around her finger.' The thought seemed to please him and she sighed with relief that his black moment had passed.

Owain reached out and took her hand. 'And so yonder Gerald was set free to dispossess this churlish Saer. You took your children home from Gloucester and had three more pups by de Windsore?'

The mention of the children saddened her at once.

'I miss them, Owain – especially Angharad and Gwladys, though naturally the boys are dear to me also, little Normans though they be.'

Owain jerked upright on the bed and stroked the soft head of his only child. 'Shall I raid Penbroch and bring them all back to you, my love?' he offered with a gaiety that did not hide the crazy genuineness of his offer.

'No...please, Owain, no! No more rash escapades this week, I beg you,' she said in alarm. 'One day, perhaps Rhiannon and I can travel in disguise to Caer Rhiw or Penbroch and try to glimpse them. Even from a distance, it would be God's gift just to see them once more. But, please, no more talk of raiding Penbroch...that is one fortress that can never be taken.'

'We shall see about that, Nest – we shall see.'

Ignoring his son's squalling protests, Owain bent to kiss the white neck where her robe fell open.

CHAPTER TEN

OCTOBER, 1110

TEN days after the ambush of the Fleming, a weary and mud-spattered rider trotted through the gates of Din-geraint just as dusk was falling. The Doorward of the hall went scurrying off to find Lord Owain and his brother Morgan, as the horseman's manner left no doubt that his mission was of the greatest urgency.

Rhys Ddu, for it was Einion's dark squire who had made the forced ride down from Powys, sat by the great fire and gulped down some hot wine, while the sons of Cadwgan were being found. Around him, servants were setting out the tables for the evening meal and many a curious eye was levelled at the taciturn northerner, whose arrival could herald nothing good.

Owain, as was usual at this time of day, was with Nest and their babe. He hurried out before Morgan could be summoned from his lodging in one of the crowded huts outside. Owain, genuinely pleased to see the hard-faced, but trusty man, went straight to the fire and clasped the newcomer's arm.

'Rhys Ddu. I've not seen you since we returned from Ireland.'

The dark one came straight to the heart of the matter.

'Since Einion persuaded your father to pardon me for the part I played in the Cenarth Bychan affair, I have been riding in Prince Cadwgan's retinue most of the time. Four days ago, the Prince, with his brother Iorwerth ap Bleddyn, went to Shrewsbury to seek the ear of the King, who has again returned from Normandy. I was there also, and for the sake of the bond between us, Lord Owain, I have hurried here to bring you a warning.'

Morgan hurried in just in time to catch the last words.

'Rhys Ddu, welcome! Though I fear to hear what you have to tell us.'

Owain gestured impatiently. 'What is it, then, man?'

Rhys unbuckled the clasp of his riding cloak and let it slip from his shoulders.

'Henry has again dispossessed your royal father of all his lands. He has given them to a Norman, who is already bringing an army into Wales with intent to slaughter you and your kindred and your war-band.'

There was a heavy silence. Then Nest's voice cut in from behind – she had followed Owain from the bed-chamber. 'This Norman – is he from Dyfed?'

Rhys shook his saturnine head, as Owain snapped a command.

'Tell us the whole story, Rhys. You are no alarmist nor would you have ridden alone from Powys to carry some old wife's tale.'

Rhys cupped his cold hands around his goblet and looked steadily at Owain as he told his tale.

'I was attending Prince Cadwgan when he had audience with Henry Beauclerk in Shrewsbury Castle. Iorwerth and he had gone there to ask relief from the ransom they had to pay for Iorwerth's release and the return of their lands. They had to pay three hundred pounds worth of silver, in oxen and horses, as well as giving hostages, including Henry, son of Cadwgan and the fat Frenchwoman…'

'We know all this, Rhys!' snapped Owain, impatient to get at the meat of the story.

'Whilst we were in the tower room with the King and Richard of London and other high-born Normans, discoursing peacefully, there was a sudden commotion and a man burst in, much dishevelled and with wounds on his head. He said he was one Maurice, a Fleming from Brabant.'

Owain and Morgan stared at each other. 'William's brother – the one who escaped us last week!' snarled Owain.

Rhys Ddu went on with his tale of woe. 'He fell down before the King and cursed all Welshmen, saying that Owain ap Cadwgan's host had waylaid them in Dyfed, murdered his brother and taken much gold intended for the King. Henry turned from his usual calmness into a creature of rage. He fell on your father, shaking him and asking him what he knew of the affair.'

Rhys paused to slake his thirst. 'Cadwgan said he knew nothing of it, but Henry said "Since you cannot keep you lands free from your son and his battle-crazed comrades, I shall give them one who can prevent more harm to my men and my lands". Then he forbade your father to ever set his feet in Powys or Ceredigion again. Though he has placed no shackle or fetter upon him, he has commanded him to stay at Shrewsbury until he has decided what to do with him. The King even allotted two shillings a day from his own purse for Cadwgan's sustenance, so that he shall not enter Wales again.'

'And what of this Norman who is coming to destroy us? snapped Owain.

Rhys wearily wiped the grime from his travel-stained face.

'Henry straightway sent a messenger to another part of the castle to fetch the mighty baron Gilbert fitzRichard. When he came, the King said to him "You were always asking me for a portion of Wales for yourself – so now I will give you the lands of Cadwgan ap Bleddyn. Go and take possession of it and cast out every fighting man you meet. Fortify it well against this Owain and any followers who come after him"…and Richard accepted it gladly. He is already in Powys and assembling a great host under his lieutenant Stephen. They are to march south, to ravish and permanently secure the whole country. They intend building strong castles at the mouth of the Ystwyth and here at Din-geraint.'

Owain slammed his hands together in anger, his face livid 'They have it already planned…the only matter they seem to ignore is that we are already here at Din-geraint and Madog is in Powys!'

Rhys shook his dark head. 'Madog ap Rhiryd is at this moment riding down to meet you. He has heard of Cadwgan's possession and has avoided facing fitzRichard's troops until he speaks with you and decides upon a course.'

Morgan anxiously rubbed his bristly chin. 'This Gilbert fitzRichard...he is a man of great power, so I have heard. He has many knights and men-at-arms, recently returned from the wars in France. They will be seasoned and hardy fighters, Owain. We have no happy task in tangling with such as he. I think our friend Murketagh O'Brien had better be approached – and quickly!'

Owain paced up and down before the glowing fire. The Penteulu of Din-geraint and other senior members of the kindred were drifting into a circle around them, worriedly picking up the threads of the fateful news brought by Black Rhys.

'When will Madog arrive?' asked Owain shortly, throwing back his russet lock impatiently.

'Later tonight – or more probably after dawn.'

'And these new French...are they marching already? When can we expect their company?'

'They were assembling in Shrewsbury three days ago. More are to be summoned from fitzRichard's lands in eastern England and will not arrive for at least a week. The main host set off for Powys, then his knight Stephen was to march to Llanbadarn and make a fortification at the mouth of the river there, before pursuing you in this part of Ceredigion. I would say it would be at least two weeks before they are at the gates of Din-geraint.'

Nest, normally silent in front of her men folk when they were discussing war, was again forced to ask the question that preyed on her mind.

'Dyfed...what of Norman forces from Pembroke. Will they also march on us from the south?'

Rhys shrugged and murmured that he had no knowledge of this, but Owain was more emphatic. 'Why should they, after all this time? Apart from skirmishes, we've not seen a whisker of a decent French army within twenty miles of the Teifi. They are too intent on growing corn and vegetables and screwing tithes from the few wretched Welsh folk that are left. We have nothing to fear from Gerald de Windsore, nor his scabby friend de Turribus at Cemais. It is from the north that the danger lies.'

Morgan kept the talk to immediate issues. 'And what of this help we must have from Dublin? Murketagh has already given us ships and their crews – he promised us mercenaries at any time we might need them...and, by David's bones we need them now!'

For once, the Lion of Powys agreed without dispute. 'We have plundered more than enough to pay them handsomely, God knows. As soon as Madog rides in, we'll sail for Dublin and be back within the week with enough Irish and Norsemen to chase this Stephen back to his master at Shrewsbury...and beyond, if needs be!'

Morgan, ever cautious, raised his heavy brows. 'Do we all need to leave this place? With enemies on the threshold, I dislike turning my back, even for a few days.'

Owain, his spirits soaring now that action was in the air, slapped him on the back. 'They should have named you Thomas, my brother – you are ever doubting! Good Rhys here has told us that it will be at least two weeks before the French stumble their way down the coast. With nothing to fear from across the river, what trouble can possibly befall? We may leave the gates of Din-geraint wide open and think nothing of it! Come, servant, bring some mead, we'll drink to a reunion with our old friend Murketagh O'Brien!'

As if fate was tempted beyond endurance by Owain's words, the stronghold of Din-geraint was under siege within three days of his leaving for Dublin.

He had been right in thinking that Gilbert fitzRichard's main force would move slowly down the coast from the Ystwyth, but more rapid danger came from an entirely different quarter. A heavily-armoured force drove eastwards from Brycheiniog and Beullt,* crossing without hindrance the lands of Richard fitzPons at Llanmyddfai** and Rhydderch's tenancy in Ystrad Tywi.

Norman soldiers were in the Vale of the Teifi before scouts from Ceredigion spotted them, and although the warning was raised half a day before they arrived at Din-geraint, little could be done to delay them. It only remained for the depleted garrison to bar the gates and wait for the inevitable onslaught. The fastest ship was sent after Owain, but the defenders knew that it would be at least four days before the Lion of Powys could get back to lead them.

The Penteulu, now in command of the fortress, was almost frantic with worry over Nest.

'*Arglwyddes*, you must flee, you and the child. Only hours remain before the French will be at our gates. Lord Owain would never forgive me, if I were to survive, should I allow you to come to harm in his absence.'

He stood at the entrance to the bed-chamber, wringing his hands in anguish. Nest rose from the chair where she had been cradling little Llywelyn and walked over the rush-strewn floor to reassure him.

'Good man, where shall I go? FitzRichard's men are coming down the coast and now there are Normans between us and the doubtful sanctuary in Cantref Mawr. Would you have me cross the river and return to Penbroch, for that is the only direction remaining?' Her smile and gentle touch on his arm robbed the words of any hint of sarcasm. The Penteulu looked her pleadingly.

'Lady, there is Ireland. You could go up to Caerwedros and they will arrange a passage for you from Llangrannog, as you did once before.'

Nest's great eyes warmed him once again. 'You are a faithful man, Idwal, but have no fear for me. Remember, I am still both the wife of a Norman knight, and even more, the ward of their royal King. No harm will come to me from any invader.'

* *Modern Breconshire and Builth.*
** *The modern Llandovery.*

The Penteulu laid a gentle hand on the swaddled babe in her arms. 'I beg leave to doubt that, *arglwyddes*... but even if it were so, what of your child here?...Lord Owain's child! If the French are baulked of his father's death or capture, they will be all the more eager for revenge on his heir. And Norman men-at-arms are not renowned for their kindness to children of the enemy,' he added bitterly, with memories of pillaged homesteads branded on his mind.

Nest's face clouded at his words. She hugged Llywelyn more tightly and rocked him gently to and fro.

'Think, *arglwyddes*...think,' urged Idwal. He was fully dressed for battle, in which he fully expected to lose his life, but the safety of Owain's lady and their child came before his longing to be with his men at the palisades.

Nest looked into the face of the sleeping babe and sighed. 'You are right about the child, Idwal. I shall stay, as there will be no risk to me and maybe I can do something to aid Lord Owain. But our son must be safe...so send him to Ireland,' she added bitterly. 'Send him to the refuge where most of the royal line of Wales seem to spend their time since William the Bastard came to these islands.'

An hour later, no less a foster-mother than the Penteulu's wife herself – together with an elder daughter who was recently delivered herself and had her milk – set off with a small escort for Caerwedros. Rhiannon stubbornly refused to go, saying that any woman could care for a babe, but only she could attend Nest in such a time of peril.

As the little group slipped through the gates and hurried northwards, Nest followed them with her eyes from the palisade, feeling as if one of her limbs had just been torn off and sent to Ireland. First her children from Caer Rhiw, now little Llywelyn. Her eyes misted over as they strained to catch the last sight of the riders vanishing through the trees. Was she cursed for some unknown sin of hers or her father's? Was she doomed to have every child of her body snatched away from her like this?

She turned from the stockade long after the last sight of them had gone, thinking bitterly that in a few hours she may well be a prisoner again, of whatever Norman knight that fitzRichard sent as a vanguard.

As she entered the chamber again and sat down on the bed, she ran her hand over the furry coverlets and thought of Owain, torn between her love for him and the possibility of being sent back to Penbroch by the new invaders. Would Gerald take her in...would she want him to, anyway? At least, she thought with a desperate surge of hope, she might see Angharad and Gwladys and David and William and Maurice again.

But Owain...her Owain! She had never known such happiness as these last few months. Was this the end of it – she somehow could not believe that. The Celtic sixth sense that was never far below her consciousness told her that the affair could not end as lamely as this, from a mere mistake of military tactics. It would end, there was no doubt of that, but it would be a far more dramatic finale.

Consoled, but still uneasy, she rolled back on to the bed. Her breasts were full and aching and she thought of her new babe, now suckling some other mother's milk. All these troubles, all this bloodshed…poor Idwal was going to die, along with all his men – all to be traced back to that fateful last Christmas. If only Cadwgan had not held a feast…if only Gerald had not brought them to Cenarth…if only…but what was the use, one might as well say if only she had not been born!

Curling up, she quietly cried herself to sleep as armies once again manoeuvred around the fate of the women and the children and the men of Ceredigion.

When Nest awoke, the battle was half over.

She groped her way out of troubled dreams, in which all her children were shouting at her and a rhythmical knocking came on her old bedroom door at Caer Rhiw.

Then she became aware of Rhiannon bending over her, white-faced and shaking. '*Arglwyddes*, the French…they are attacking the stronghold.'

Still heavy with sleep, Nest stumbled from the bed and pulled on a light cloak over her mantle. With Rhiannon trembling behind her, she went to the door and looked out into the castle compound. Men lined the catwalk beneath the palisade, most of them bowmen, who jumped up to loose their shafts before dodging back behind the shelter of the timber battlements. Nest looked for the source of the regular thumping that had forced its way into her dreams. It came from the gates, which were shivering and splintering from the impact of some great onslaught from outside.

So far, there were few casualties amongst the Welsh garrison, as the French were more fond of sword and lance than the long-bow. Until the wall was breached, the defenders were out of their reach. A few bloody bodies lay slumped on the catwalk, where stray missiles and arrows had found their mark, but Nest knew that real carnage would begin once the gate gave way.

Idwal, the Penteulu, saw them emerge from the chamber door and ran across. His face was ashen with the certainty of inevitable death within the next few minutes.

'Lady, I beg you, stay inside. I will surrender myself to the leader of the French as soon as I see that all hope is gone. I must explain who you are before these blood-crazed ravishers burst in.'

Nest seized his hand. 'There is no need, Idwal…I can speak for myself. I am ward of their King…that will protect both me and my handmaiden. You fight as you think fit, good man.' She meant, 'let yourself be skewered swiftly on a Norman lance in the heat of the fight.' Both she and the Penteulu well knew that his fate would be slow and barbaric if he was to allow himself to be taken prisoner in these circumstances, when the Normans found that Owain, Madog and Morgan had not been accounted for.

Idwal pointed to the gate. 'They have fifty men swinging a great tree-trunk against the gate, it cannot last many minutes. We have no means of stopping them, besides our bows.'

The gate began to groan and buckle inwards and Idwal dashed off pathetically ill-equipped with his leather tunic and bare legs. This was no way for Welshmen to fight Normans, cooped up in an out-of-date wooden castle. The warriors of Wales were mobile guerillas, speed and agility being their main weapons. Their way to defend a fortress was in preventing the enemy from getting within miles of it, by harrying them into extinction or retreat before they arrived. Once at the castle walls, the battle was lost.

Nest stood frozen in the doorway, Rhiannon whimpering at her shoulder, as the gate gave way.

With a yell of triumph, a human flood of mailed warriors spewed through the opening, as one great door fell drunkenly off its hinges. Dropping the trimmed bole of a big birch tree, fifty Normans raced inside to cut down the Welshmen who dropped like monkeys from the palisade in a desperate, suicidal bid to stop them. Behind the first wave of the French came more men-at-arms, then horsemen smashed into the compound. Within seconds, the trampled earth and grass was stained with blood – almost all Welsh blood.

In fascinated horror, Nest watched the Penteulu throw away his spear and raise his arms in supplication to the leading horseman, a man in a bright blue surcoat over his mailed hauberk.

Without slackening speed, the plume-helmeted rider raised his sword and gave Idwal a blow that completely severed his right arm at the shoulder, then rode on without a backward glance. Nest saw the Penteulu stagger, look stupidly at his arm lying on the ground, then collapse on top of it with his main artery spurting blood like a fountain.

The blue-coated rider had vanished behind the hall. Nest, with a moaned 'Idwal!' started to move towards the stricken Penteulu, but Rhiannon grabbed her. The maid was a sturdy girl and, with her grasp strengthened by desperation, she dragged Nest back into the chamber and dropped the bar behind the door.

'You can do nothing, lady…we must wait here for whatever fate has in store for us.' Her resolve seemed to have hardened with the actual arrival of mortal danger. Nest, following her example, pulled herself together and nodded as calmly as she was able.

'Come and sit here with me, then, faithful Rhiannon.' She led the way to the bed and they sat side by side, listening aghast to the thunder of hooves in the bailey, the frequent scream of mortal agony and the clash of steel on steel. The sounds did not last long – within ten minutes all the defenders were dead. There were no women, children or old folk there, Idwal having sent them off into the woods earlier in the day…now there were no men either.

A few managed to escape over the palisade when they had loosed all their arrows and seen that the battle was lost. Those who ran on the landward side were almost all hunted down and slaughtered by horsemen, but a few who dived into the Teifi managed to swim downstream and struggle out to safety on the further bank.

Inside the fortress, all was soon quiet, apart from shouting in Norman-French, some ribald laughter and the noise of tables being overturned in the main hall.

For half an hour, Nest and Rhiannon sat clutched together on the bed, almost fearing to breathe. 'Can they know that we are here?' whispered the servant eventually. Nest hardly had time to shrug, when the maid's question was rudely answered.

Without so much as a call or a knock, the door of the chamber was suddenly smashed to firewood with a heavy battle-axe and the remnants kicked aside.

A heavily-moustached man-at-arms peered suspiciously into the room, axe raised expectantly. The nasal on his helmet gave him a diabolical appearance and Rhiannon screamed in fright.

In the dim light from the shuttered window the soldier's eyes searched the room. When he saw the two young women, his lips curled in lecherous anticipation. But his luck was out, as before he could make a move he was roughly pushed aside by another mailed and helmeted figure, one wearing a peacock blue surcoat.

The newcomer strode forward unhesitatingly and grabbed Nest by the chin, his metal-clad fingers jerking her head up. His eyes opened wide in surprised admiration and a whistle of appreciation hissed from his thick lips.

'Well, well – this flea-bitten castle was worth taking after all!'

Nest tried to brush his hand away, but the knight dug his gauntlet painfully into the flesh of her throat and bent to kiss her on the lips with sadistic roughness. The man-at-arms, taking advantage of his master's preoccupation, stole up behind Rhiannon and grabbed her, his hand ripping away her gown and plunging inside to fondle her breasts.

Both the women squirmed and kicked, but they were powerless against the muscular warriors. All they gained were bruises and scratches from the armour-plated leather and steel link-mail.

When the blue-coated knight paused to draw breath, Nest managed to gasp her protests. 'I am Lady Nest, ward of your King, sir. And wife to Gerald de Windsore of Pembroke. Do you dare treat me and my maid…'

That was as far as she got, as the hard-eyed man clamped his lips on hers once again. He lifted her easily on to the bed and was fumbling with her girdle, when a cold, firm voice from the doorway made him pause.

'Sir Roger, the men are already at the Welsh drink…are we to allow them to pillage and destroy this place or are we to preserve it as ordered by our Lord fitzRichard?'

Nest, dazed with the pressure of the knight's body and the ignominy of attempted rape, hardly heard the reply, but her blue-coated ravisher got up and stalked out without a backward glance.

The Norman who had spoken was a young squire, with a cold, prim face that radiated disapproval at the world. Even in her fuddled state, Nest recognized him as the type who often combined religious fanaticism with ruthless secular efficiency, much as Richard of London had achieved. The young man now strode across the room to where the man-at-arms now had the sobbing Rhiannon stripped to the waist and struck him hard on the shoulder with a wicked-looking mace. In spite of his armour, the man yelled and spun round. As he saw the young nobleman he pushed Rhiannon away and jerked to attention.

'Get out, man...there'll be time for that later!' snarled the squire. The soldier stumped away sullenly and the younger man turned to Nest. His face was haughty and unfriendly, but at least he showed no inclination to ravish her, she thought thankfully as she pulled her mantle together again.

'What was that you said to Sir Roger – about yourself?' he asked coldly.

Nest was thankful that someone was willing to listen.

'I am Lady Nesta de Windsore,' she said firmly, using the French version of her name. 'I am ward of King Henry and wife of Sir Gerald de Windsore, castellan and Sheriff of Pembroke. I demand to be treated in a way appropriate to my station and also that my maidservant be likewise respected.'

The squire looked scornfully at her. 'Ward of our King! And lady of a Norman knight? Alone in this Welsh outpost...you expect me to believe that?'

'I do...'

'You are a Welsh woman?'

'Yes...but...'

'Then you must expect to be treated like one. Sir Roger de Hait will no doubt return to complete the treatment before long.'

Nest became very angry. 'Listen, young Norman. How many Welsh women did you ever hear speaking such good Norman-French? Or such Flemish – or Saxon – or Latin?' She rapidly changed into the languages she had picked up either at Pembroke or Shrewsbury or from the tutors at her father's court. 'Does every woman in the castles you pillage have such a command of tongues?'

This rapid demonstration struck home on the fair-haired man. His arrogance remained, but his expression showed that he was impressed.

'You say you are a ward of Henry Beauclerk? How came you to be in this remote place, then?'

'I was captured almost a year ago.' She felt it was unwise to enlarge on the circumstances at the moment, only to say enough to ensure the safety of Rhiannon and herself. These men must have come from either Normandy or eastern England, not to have heard of the kidnapping from Cenarth Bychan.

The squire looked uncertainly at the two women, then over his shoulder at the door.

'I know nothing of this, but I will do what I can to give you the benefit of the doubt until others arrive with more authority.'

Nest frowned as she straightened her hair and tried to smooth her crumpled gown. 'What do you mean by that?' she demanded.

Her air of regality must have got through to the man. He seemed to defer slightly to her by the tone of his voice. 'We are but a flanking party, sent to secure this place for Gilbert fitzRichard. The main host is coming down from the north, under his chief lieutenant, Stephen. When he arrives, all will be well.'

Nest sensed that he was trying to imply more than his actual words.

'What of this coarse master of yours – this Roger de Hait, you said his name was?'

Again the young man looked over his shoulder. 'He is no master of mine…he is a land-owner from Cornwall. I am only assigned to him for this one escapade, thank God.'

He suddenly appeared to think that he had talked too freely and turned abruptly for the door.

'I will attempt to see that you remain unmolested until Stephen arrives, but if these men get at that strong honey drink of your people, I cannot vouch for the consequences.'

Without another word he strode away, but a few moments later a different man-at-arms arrived outside the shattered door and stood with his back to it, obviously to guard against entry rather than to prevent their escape.

Rhiannon was snivelling and trying to repair her woollen gown. Her bosom was bruised from the brutal fingers and although Nest well knew that she was no virgin, the girl was badly upset and outraged by the molestations.

'We can count ourselves lucky for the intervention of that squire,' soothed Nest consolingly. 'Otherwise, we might both have found ourselves carrying French babes in a short while!'

It was now late afternoon and for some hours afterwards the fortress of Din-geraint was relatively quiet. Hammering sounds and axe blows came from the gateway, where the military efficiency of the Normans was busy repairing the defences against any possible counter-attack. From the limited view that the women had from their shuttered window, they could see bodies being dragged away for a hasty burial and French soldiers looting what little remained in the huts of the compound. No one came near them and no food or drink was provided.

'They seem to have forgotten that we exist,' muttered Rhiannon, her stomach rumbling with hunger as dusk fell. The man on the door had been relieved by another, but refused to answer when asked what was going to happen to them.

After several minutes' persuasion he surlily agreed to get them some water. He fetched a pitcher from somewhere, but apart from that, they remained cut off from events.

But with the passing of a few more hours, they wished that their excommunication could have lasted indefinitely. Soon after dark, a growing noise rose from the great hall, together with a smell of cooking that doubled their hunger pangs. Men's voices became louder and more raucous as the time went by, with shouting, singing and the occasional crash of an upturned bench or table. It was obvious that the main store of mead and *cwrw** had been found. The guard at their door became more and more restive as he became aware that he was missing all the fun. Eventually he slipped away in the direction of the food and drink.

Nest and her maid were left alone in the darkness. There was a rush light, but no means of lighting it. They sat hand in hand on the bed, hungry and tired, but too uneasy to try to sleep.

Eventually, the buxom Rhiannon found that her stomach was getting the better of her fears. 'I'm off to the kitchens to get some food for us,' she declared stubbornly, 'and a taper for the light. They can't be going to starve us to death, the drunken swine are just too occupied with their own bellies to give us a thought.'

In spite of Nest's reluctance to let her go, Rhiannon dragged aside the splintered door and stepped out into the gloom of the courtyard. The bed-chamber was connected to the nearby hall by a thatch-roofed passage with only one wall as a protection against wind and rain. At the other end was another door into the upper hall and as she stepped out of the bed-chamber, this further door suddenly burst open. In the smoky light that flickered out, she saw the burly silhouette of a man, swaying in the doorway.

Roger de Hait saw her at the same instant. 'Where d'you think you're going, you Welsh bitch!' he snarled in a slurred, thick voice. Rhiannon ducked back inside as heavy feet came after her.

'*Arglwyddes*...that foul Frenchman!'

De Hait burst into the room, peering around in the dim light that came across from the door he had left open in the hall. Though the women could not see his face, he was obviously drunk.

'Well, my two Welsh virgins...I'd almost forgotten you!' He shuffled to the foot of the bed and reached out for them in the gloom. Rhiannon pushed her mistress behind her, trying to shield Nest with her big body. She was almost as tall as the Norman and stood with her hands up in front of her chest, fingers clawed like some menacing lioness guarding its young.

'Leave us alone...leave us alone!' she repeated over and over, oblivious that she was speaking in Welsh to a Norman from England. De Hait suddenly chuckled and hit Rhiannon a tremendous blow across the forehead with his clenched fist. She fell as if pole-axed, but for good measure he kicked her skull a few times as she lay inert on the floor.

Nest, watching this drama in the semi-darkness, was paralysed with fear and concern for her friend, but suddenly she screamed. As if this was the trigger, the Norman flung himself upon her.

There was no time for protestations about being a king's ward or a Norman's wife...Roger de Hait was too drunk to care. Later, Nest was to suspect that he would have cared little if sober, so crude a fellow was he.

---

* *Welsh beer.*

With a grunt of anticipation he launched himself over Rhiannon's body and tumbled Nest to the bed. Almost suffocating her with a smell of mead, wine and sweat, he clamped his full lips on hers for the second time that day.

She squirmed violently, but his right hand grabbed her by the hair and pulled her head down on the pillow.

Then he began methodically tearing off her clothes, ripping them from neckline to thigh. He had discarded his own armour before starting his carousing and wore only a short, open-necked tunic. As his hands explored her, he muttered drunkenly, but the mead had done nothing to lessen his virility. Nest was raped there in the darkness with the same efficiency as de Hait had ravished Din-geraint earlier that day. Her struggles were as futile as those of a rabbit in the grip of a hound and she soon capitulated, finding that it was better to bow to the inevitable rather than suffer severe pain.

Having lived with three other men and having borne six children, she could not pretend to be terrified and mortified by the experience, but anger and revulsion at being taken by a drunk and fear of immediate physical assault filled her mind, as well as concern for poor Rhiannon, who might well be lying dead at her feet.

But de Hait went on pounding and bruising her…when at last he came to a climax, she had difficulty in suppressing the first awakening of her own animal response. But fury soon drove away this ultimate shame and when he finally climbed off her and stood fumbling with his robe, she sobbed curses at him in a mixture of tongues.

De Hait looked down at the still figure of the maidservant and gave her another vicious kick. 'A pity she's like that – I was looking forward to a double treat,' he mouthed throatily.

Nest flew at him, sobbing and shaking with pain and violent anger. But with a contemptuous snarl, he slapped her face with such violence that she fell back on the bed, blood coursing its salty way from her torn lip.

Crying with mixed pain and impotent rage, she lay on the crumpled coverlets for a while. When she dragged herself up, her ravisher had gone and Rhiannon was mercifully beginning to groan herself back to consciousness.

When the maid had come painfully back to her senses, Nest tenderly bathed her split scalp with water from the pitcher. Much later, when Rhiannon had fallen asleep across her mistress's lap, Nest was left to listen to the wind and the fading noise of the roistering Normans in the hall.

Her infallible sixth sense told her that, once more, she was going to bear a child.

CHAPTER ELEVEN

OCTOBER, 1110

OWAIN AP CADWGAN stood in the prow of the long Norse ship and watched the reddening dawn flood up into the air over the cliffs.

An onshore breeze drove the seven vessels rapidly towards the beach of Llangrannog, where his keen eyes could already see tiny figures waiting to meet them.

Morgan stood behind his brother, as if ready to hold Owain back should his mounting impatience tempt him to jump overboard and swim ahead – though this was unlikely, as they were both wearing mail tunics and full battle array.

All the ships were crammed with men, mostly Irish and Danish mercenaries, apart from the few dozen Welshmen that the brothers had taken with them from Din-geraint. It was only six days since they had left, but to Owain it seemed like six months.

'We chose these long ships because they were supposed be fast,' he fretted. 'But two days and nights it has taken to cross from Dublin.'

'God sends the winds, Owain, they can't blow in the right direction for every traveller at the same time,' answered Morgan soothingly. His brother grunted and turned impatiently to watch the little island of Lochtyn slide level with them a mile to the north. The sandy cove where the Hawen valley sliced through to the sea was right ahead and ten minutes later, the flat bottom of the Viking ship slithered to a halt on the sand.

The other vessels grounded side by side on the narrow beach and all but a few crewmen jumped out into the shallow surf.

With Owain well in the lead, the pebble bank above the sand was soon covered by almost four hundred fighting men, who set about lighting fires and preparing the meagre rations they had brought with them.

Owain had no heart for eating, though he recognized the need for his men to have full stomachs before the inevitable conflict to come.

With Morgan at his side he strode over to the stream, where it babbled down from the wooded valley to spread out across the beach. As he knelt and drank from his cupped hands, the men who had waited for his arrival brought him up to date with events.

'Geraint and I jumped into the river, Lord Owain,' said the leader of the little band, a young fellow who was one of the sons of Idwal, the dead Penteulu of Din-geraint. 'There was nothing more we could do – my father had just been slain before our eyes. Our arrows were all gone and hundreds of Frenchmen were howling below.'

Owain excused him with an impatient gesture. 'I know you are no coward, Ednyfed – but tell me your news.'

The youth fingered the crusted scab where a Norman arrow had removed half his ear. 'The Lady Nest refused to leave, you know. She sent the babe with my mother and sister to Caerwedros and they only just escaped from there, as it was attacked the next day.'

Morgan grunted. 'They arrived safely in Ireland at the same hour that we set off – the other swift ship you sent from Din-geraint came the previous day.'

'But what of *Yr Arglwyddes* Nest?' snapped Owain, cutting across the explanations.

Ednyfed shrugged. 'I heard nothing until this morning, Lord Owain. When we escaped, we took to the woods and in the last five days have been collecting survivors and new men...I have about three hundred up there in the woods at Pont Garreg.'

Owain ground his teeth in frustration. 'Lady Nest, boy...what news?'

'She is still in Din-geraint, Lord, with her maid. We have had men watching the fortress from the woods and no one has left, except messengers.' He shuffled his feet and looked sideways at the boat-strewn beach, as if to avoid Owain's eye 'We captured three such messengers yesterday, who were travelling to Caerwedros.'

His sudden shifty manner made Morgan instantly alert.

'What of it? Out with it, boy.'

'Before we killed them, they gave us news.' No one asked what induced the Normans to speak so freely. 'They said that the first war band to reach Din-geraint was that of Roger de Hait. The next morning, this Stephen arrived from the north having reduced Caerwedros on the way. These scouts said that there had been much discord between the two French leaders.' The late Penteulu's son looked ill at ease.

'What are you trying to say?' grated Owain, already half suspecting the truth.

'This Hait had been in his cups the night of the conquest of Din-geraint...and had...had molested the Lady Nest.' Edynfed gabbled it out, now that the moment had been reached. 'She was taken by force and Stephen had threatened him with dire consequences, because she was the King's ward.'

The two brothers looked at each other, Morgan concerned at the effect it would have on Owain. The elder son Cadwgan was white in the face, his jaw set like a vice. He slid his sword from its scabbard and with a vicious swish slashed an inoffensive briar to sheds, in lieu of de Hait's throat.

Slamming the weapon back into its sheath, he turned to stare grimly up the narrow gorge, where ferns were turning golden brown high on the hillsides.

'We march on Caerwedros as soon as the men have eaten,' he muttered, in a voice like gravel on a wave-swept beach. 'Let the French there send messengers to Din-geraint for help. When part of their garrison there has left to aid Caerwedros, we shall join up with the rest of the Irish who are on their way to the Teifi mouth. Together we will attack Din-geraint...and God grant me that this de Hait has stayed behind, so that I might kill him.'

Two hours before dusk several hundred Normans marched out of Din-geraint and headed north. They went in answer to a frantic appeal for help from the small, ill-fortified palace at Caerwedros, a dozen miles away. The few Welsh who besieged it took care not to press their attack too well and as soon as the reinforcements arrived, they melted away, their decoying task done.

As soon as it was properly dark, Owain's force, who had spent the day moving unobtrusively down the coast to the mouth of the Teifi, lit a great fire on the sea-ward side of the rocky island that lay off the estuary, so that the glare would only be seen across the western horizon and not by the French at Din-geraint, three miles inland.

This pyre was a prearranged signal to guide the main fleet of Irish vessels, slower than the long ships that had sailed from Dublin at the same time.

Three hours later, a horde of wild-looking Irish scrambled ashore from a dozen ships which beached just inside the river mouth at Gwbert. Knowing that the Norman scouts would give the alarm before these new men could reach the fortress, Owain had already set off for Din-geraint with his own five hundred men. There was no moon and the attackers sidled through the woods and reached the stockade before being seen. Then all hell was let loose, as the guards on the ramparts sighted the ghostly attackers flitting from the trees. The watchers sounded the alarm on their horns and men thundered up from their sleeping places to range themselves along the palisade. Though half the garrison had gone to Caerwedros, there was still a formidable force left to face the Welsh, who attacked the fortress wall directly and without preamble. Taking advantage of their surprise appearance and the almost total gloom, Owain's men repeated their tactics of Cenarth Bychan and scaled the wall at a dozen points with the aid of grapnels and ropes.

The defenders brought flaring torches to try to light up the scene, but Morgan had anticipated this and set archers well back from the walls to pick off the flare-holders as soon as they appeared. The Welshmen swarmed up the ropes and started a ferocious hand-to-hand combat along almost the full length of the palisade.

Losses were heavy on both sides and dead and bleeding bodies fell like rain from both the catwalk and back over the outer wall.

The gate had been well repaired and remained invulnerable to Owain's men, who had yet to learn the techniques of military engineering. But by sheer desperation and agility the more lightly-armoured Welshmen soon began turning the battle in their favour.

Owain and Morgan were the first up adjacent ropes and once on top, fought side by side, often back to back. In spite of their efforts to keep a blackout, some of the fallen torches set some thatch alight and an eerie red flicker began to light up the scene. The two brothers fought desperately on the narrow planking that lined the battlements.

Within minutes Owain had a gushing wound in his own arm, saved from being more serious only by the metal-studded sleeves of his thick leather cuirass. As he fought a great ox of a man, another Welshman suddenly materialized from over the rampart and gave Owain's opponent a devastating jab in the back with a spear. The man turned with a cry to face his new tormentor and Owain brought down his sword on to the side of the man's neck. With a despairing scream the Norman fell from the rampart into the bailey and the brothers found they had a moment's respite, as only Welsh stood near them in the confused twilight.

'Time we saw what we were doing,' gasped Morgan, his chest heaving with effort. He stumbled to the palisade and shouted some prearranged orders to the archers standing below.

A moment later, a fusillade of fiery streaks arched up into the sky and curved down into the castle bailey. Many of these fire arrows found a mark in the thatch of the buildings, both hall and smaller hutments. As the straw and turf was damp, no great blaze began, but a series of fitful fires and smouldering patches appeared, enough to give sufficient light for them to see that the palisade was all but won. A few struggles and duels were still going on along the catwalk, but men were still swarming up the ropes and clambering over the wall. Owain looked around at the bloody scene, lit by a ruddy, demoniacal glow from the fires.

'If Nest ferch Rhys is in one of those huts, or the hall chamber, we had best get to her before a real blaze begins,' yelled Morgan above the clash of steel and the shouting.

Owain looked over his shoulder and saw that the latest wave of invaders were all Irish, presumably from the second force who had just arrived. He yelled to his own men nearby and pointed down into the compound, where the Normans who had escaped from the palisade were collecting themselves and preparing to counter-attack. There was no ladder at this point, but the impetuous Owain jumped straight down on to the muddy ground, a dozen feet below. With wild, banshee cries, a score of his followers launched themselves after him, Morgan amongst them. A party of Normans saw them and came running, maces and swords flashing, but a solid mass of Irishmen flung themselves down right behind the French and began savagely attacking their rear.

Owain left them to struggle and waved his own men towards the hall, screaming encouragement at the top of his voice. He had lost his helmet in the fall and his left arm was hanging almost useless at his side, but his enthusiasm was undimmed. His red hair flared out as he ran ahead of his bodyguard through the churned mud of the compound. Most of the fighting was now along the inside of the wall, but the bailey was almost as noisy, with moans and screams of wounded men and the neighing and rearing of maddened horses dragging at their tethering pegs.

Owain streaked across to the hall chamber, which seemed to be free from fire, though a hut nearby had its roof in flames.

'The bed-chamber...both sides,' bellowed Owain hoarsely, pointing with his blade. Morgan raced round the other side of the small building, some of his men following him. There was a guard on the door, but as soon as he saw the flying shapes coming, he bolted in the opposite direction, right into the path of Owain, who cut him down with a single vicious blow. As the man fell, two other Welshmen leapt on him to vent their fury for all the harm done to their own families.

Owain charged the repaired door with his good shoulder and smashed through without slackening speed. It was pitch black inside.

'Nest...my Nest, are you here?'

There was a movement of white in one corner and in a second she was in his arms. 'We were afraid that the guard would have had orders to kill us rather than let us be recaptured,' she sobbed into his chest. Rhiannon stumbled out behind her, sobbing with relief.

'Take the maid out, Morgan, keep her safe for the moment,' commanded Owain, after pressing his lips fervently against Nest's cheek. 'Then take the hall and see that the French are not able to rally from their remnants near the wall.'

Alone with Nest, he held her tight with his sound arm, the pain from the other at last making itself felt.

'Nest, this French swine, this de Hait...he ravished you?' His voice was like a steel blade being ground on a millstone.

She quivered in his grip. 'I would have kept it from you – how can you know?'

'I know,' he rasped, 'and I intend to kill that man, if he is still living.'

Nest shook her head in the darkness. 'He took out a war-band some hours ago...there is only a squire left in command here. Stephen left yesterday, to go back to the Ystwyth where they are already building a castle.'

Owain was not interested in castles at the moment. 'You are not injured, Nest? I want that man...was he mad, that he ill-used a ward of the king and wife of a fellow knight?'

'He was drunk,' said Nest simply. Her fingers caressed his shoulder and suddenly felt sticky blood. 'Owain, you are hurt!'

He pulled away abruptly. 'Only a scratch – I must go to the fight. We shall kill every man and then fire the fortress. It cannot be held against them, now that they are in Ceredigion in such numbers, but at least we can deprive them of the use of it until we have found strength enough to drive them out for ever.'

He turned and strode into the mêlée that still raged outside.

Nest sank on to the bed in the gloom, her intuition wriggling like a serpent in her mind. She knew that the thought of her having been taken by another man had stabbed deeply into Owain's heart. The joy of being rescued and re-united with him was submerged by a flood of misery as she knew that, for him, her body would never be the same again. Though she had had children by another Norman before she came to Owain, this new defilement, unwilling though she was, had cast a deep shadow on their love. She sat forlornly in the gloom and her head sank lower as she wondered how she could eventually tell him that there was going to be a child from the ravishing of Roger de Hait.

CHAPTER TWELVE

NOVEMBER, 1111

THE King turned from the window embrasure and stepped down into the tower room that had been the scene of so many of his decisions about the turbulent Welsh situation.

It was now late eleven-hundred-and-eleven and the cares of almost a dozen years of ruling England and Normandy were beginning to show in Henry's face.

He strode to the high-backed chair behind the table and threw himself into it. 'What in the Holy Mother's name are we to do with these bickering tribesmen,' he sighed. 'You can never tell from one day to the next who is on whose side or who is your enemy, they change allegiances so quickly.'

Richard, Bishop of London, smiled cynically. 'That is our strength and their weakness, my Lord. If the Welsh were to combine for but a few short months, they could drive us back to London. Only their eternal family feuds save us from constant war with them.'

Henry nodded. He well realized Richard's worth in his crafty tactics these past few years. Without the military force of the Montgomery brood, he had achieved far more by clever manipulation of the Welsh tribal vendettas.

The bishop, in a plain red robe with no ecclesiastical trimmings, sat on the opposite side of the table and poured some wine for himself and his monarch. 'The present matter needs some careful thought, your majesty. This man Madog, son of Rhiryd, is a wild dog and no one knows who he will bite next. I think that we can play him off against Owen ap Cadogan.'

'The *late* Cadogan, Richard,' added Henry, with a wry smile. 'I think that your masterly inactivity helped towards that end and to the demise of his brother, our unlamented Prince Iorwerth.'

Richard allowed himself an icy smile of self-congratulation. 'That was well done...without getting blood on our own hands, we have rid the Welsh lands of two of their major princes.'

'This is mainly why I have progressed to Shrewsbury, my bishop. Tell me the ins and outs of the matter,' commanded Henry, settling back in his chair with his glass of wine. His big, calm face gazed steadily at the Warden of the Marches, as the craggy churchman told of the latest bloody intrigues.

'You will remember, Lord, that when you were last at this castle, you had Cadogan before you when the news of William of Brabant's assassination came to us. You straightway deposed Cadogan and sent him to exile in

England on twenty pence a day.'

Henry nodded and drained his goblet. 'He was an old fool – yet when this damned Madog slew Iorwerth there was no one with Cadogan's experience to look after Powis and not challenge our overlordship.'

Richard grunted. His King was well up on local affairs, in spite of having all England and part of France to rule. Cadwgan had indeed been recalled to fill the gap left by the barbaric killing of Iorwerth by his psychopathic nephew, Madog ap Rhiryd. Madog coveted his uncle's lands in Powys, which Henry had restored to Iorwerth after letting him out of prison the previous year. The nephew lay in wait for him at Caereinion, surrounded the house where Iorwerth was sleeping and set fire to it. When the uncle appeared in the doorway of the flaming building, Madog himself forced him back screaming at the point of a spear, and a blazing roof beam soon made a horrible end of the older man.

When Henry had heard of the affair he was so incensed with Madog for deliberately upsetting the *status quo*, that he gave Iorwerth's lands into the keeping of Cadwgan, rather than let Madog have them.

'I offered a pardon to this Owen at the same time,' he mused. 'Young devil though he is, he seems to have the seeds of government in him. But no one could – or would – tell me where he was at that time.'

'He was in Dublin, from where Madog returned before him, saying he could not stomach the crude ways of the Irish,' supplied the bishop sarcastically. 'A fine sentiment, coming from that savage. Within a month of murdering Iorwerth he had done the same to his other uncle, Cadogan ap Blethin... probably in jealousy for your giving Cadogan the lands he coveted.'

Madog, baulked of reaping any benefit from his first uncle's death, had lain in wait for Cadwgan when he was visiting Trallwng* to survey it for a new palace. In another ambush where, as with Iorwerth, the prince's companions had fled to safety, the old man had been left alone to be cut to pieces on Madog's sword.

'He then had the temerity to come straight to Shrewsbury to seek audience of me,' grated Richard. 'He asked for the lands that he had twice killed for!'

Henry gave a slow smile. 'And you gave them to him, you fox in prelate's robes!'

The bishop smirked. He was proud of his underhand subtleties in his dealings with these Celtic aborigines. 'Better for them to slay each other than to spill good Norman blood in achieving the same end. I told Madog that he could hold those lands that had once belonged to him and Ithel his brother.'

Henry rose and went restlessly back to the window, as if seeking some rider along the road that led to the castle.

'And then yet another of this brood of Blethin's came and asked for the land...this Meredith.'** Richard poured more wine. 'He came to you, I under-

---

* *Modern Welshpool.*
** *Cadwgan's brother.*

stand, thinking perhaps that I had some private pact with Madog…and you told him wisely, sire, that he should hold it in preference to Madog, but only till Owen ap Cadogan should come and claim it, having been offered your pardon.' He guffawed. 'That should set every one of them at each other's throats.'

Henry continued to stare through the window…'And now they are all gathering here, to fight for the crumbs we throw, like a pack of mangy dogs under a table.'

'They are all here except Owen, sire. After his many misdemeanours, small wonder that he is cautious about approaching the King's castle. But I have sent emissaries into Powis to assure him that you grant him safe passage here. My spies tell me that he arrived from Ireland a week ago, together with the Lady Nesta…and her latest bastard, begotten by that drunken ravisher, Roger de Hait.'

Henry's brow clouded. 'I should have had Hait hung…instead, I made Gilbert fltzRichard send him off to the thickest part of the Normandy war, where he should speedily have perished. But he still lives, damn him.'

'The devil looks after his own, sire,' said Richard piously. 'But speaking of the Lady Nesta, there is another matter to finish before we see these Welshmen. Gerald de Windsore is here again at your command, though unwillingly. And also Stephen, who is holding the new stone castle at Kerdigan, which the Welsh used to call Din-geraint. You asked for them both, I know not why.'

Henry wandered back to the table and slumped down, swinging the full skirt of his dark velvet mantle over the arm of the chair with a grand gesture.

'I fail to understand this Gerald. He was fully forgiven for the Montgomery treachery and has been a most faithful and able sheriff in Pembroke, but he has acted most strangely over this affair of his wife. It is what…two years almost, since she was abducted? Yet de Windsore makes no move to get her back, either by ransom or force of arms. You and others – especially Walter, Justiciar of Gloucester – informed me that he wants nothing more to do with her…and she a woman as fair as any other in my kingdom.'

'You know her well, sire?' Richard made the words a statement more than a question, but the result was the same. Henry spoke in a monotone, almost oblivious of the Warden's presence.

'I have had many mistresses, but to me, she was the most memorable. Both for her beauty and her character. She was a true princess and was fitted better for a queen than the brood mate of a Florentine castellan.'

Richard rose from his chair and straightened his robe.

'Perhaps if you wish it, we should see these various parties, sire. De Windsore, fitzRichard and his man Stephen are in the outer chamber.'

Henry nodded curtly and Richard beckoned his clerk, an elderly cleric who stood dutifully next to the immobile guards at the door. After whispered commands, the clerk went out, but returned almost immediately and bowed to the King and the Bishop. 'Your Grace, there is word that Owen the Welshman and a retinue have just arrived at the castle gate.'

Richard looked at the King, who shrugged. 'Let us get on with the others. We have some business with them that does not concern this Lion of Powis.'

A moment later there entered the hall the lean figure of Gilbert fitzRichard, son of Richard Bienfaite who had been at Hastings with the Conqueror. He was a regal, austere man, chronically ill with some wasting disease, but still painfully erect. Behind him came his lieutenant, Stephen, a dark, handsome man in his fortieth year. His origins were something of a mystery, being the bastard of a lesser Norman baron.

The third figure was Gerald de Windsore, as tight-lipped and even more inscrutable than the King himself. He was in full armour, unlike the others who wore more decorative court robes. His right hand kept straying to his sword hilt and Henry's astute eye noticed that he had developed a nervous twitch in the corner of his mouth since they had last met in this same chamber.

The three men dipped their knees to the King and then grouped themselves in front of the table, de Windsore well in the background. But it was to him that Henry first addressed himself.

'De Windsore, I understand that when the Lady Nesta was taken at Kerdigan last year, Stephen immediately sent word to you, asking that you straightway came to deliver her...and you refused?'

Gerald's narrow eyes looked steadily at a point behind the royal chair. He spoke in a low monotone, as if to himself. 'My King, I have no wife. Children of a woman who was once my wife, yes...but I became without a spouse on the night that Cenarth was destroyed.'

Henry slapped the table impatiently. 'You reject the Lady Nest because she was ravished? Or because a handful of rude Welshmen razed both your castle and your pride?'

'And sent him sliding through a privy!' murmured Bishop Richard with malicious frankness.

Gerald's mouth twitched spasmodically. His waxen complexion seemed stretched tightly across his Tartar features, but he held his tongue.

The King played with the stem of his empty goblet. 'The matter resolved itself, as we know...our Welsh hero once more showed his prowess at reducing Norman strongholds and gained the lady back. But now the problem of Nesta may arise again and I want to know your intentions, de Windsore.'

Gerald's eyes slid into focus and a troubled, enquiring look crept into them. 'What do you intend, my Lord?' he muttered.

'I am going to pardon Owen ap Cadogan and return his father's lands to him. Better the devil one knows than a succession of snarling brigands. I think I can gain his allegiance – and your wife might be one of the tools I need to employ. Now, will you take her back to Pembroke?'

Gerald's mouth twitched again as all eyes turned on him in the silent room. Then he stood motionless, except for his fingers, which opened and closed upon the hilt of his great sword.

'Lord, I owe you much,' he croaked at last, in a strangled voice. 'If you command me, then I must. But I pray you, sire…do not ask me to take her into my house as a wife. Wife she is no more and I have sworn to revenge myself on her paramour.'

Henry frowned in irritation. 'You do indeed owe me much, de Windsore. Nine years ago, I was all for sticking your head on a pike above the gate of Pembroke. You owe Nesta even more than your life, as she later interceded for your return to favour…and, I might remind you, this fly-blown castle of Cenarth that you doted on, that was also granted to you at her behest. Without your wife, you would have nothing, Gerald…no honour, no castle, no life!' His voice had not been raised, but had developed an edge of steel that convinced the others that his kingship was well earned.

De Windsore trembled slightly, from his own emotions, not regal fear. To hear all the facts that he submerged in his own mind snapped across a roomful of nobles, was castigation far worse than flogging. 'Lord, you are my liege master, you may do what you will. But I would rather lose my life than spend the rest of it in the company of the emblem of my disgrace,' he muttered in half-defiant stubbornness.

Henry turned to his bishop and lifted his hands in exasperation. 'So be it…I will not force any man into domestic strife against his will. Force him into bloody battle and certain death, yes! But God knows that the whisper in the bedchamber can be more destructive of a man's soul than any lance can be to his body. Stay celibate then, de Windsore, and be damned to you!'

Several of those in the chamber listened to this bitter royal outburst and wondered how Henry fared with his queen, Matilda.

Their musings were interrupted by a stirring at the door, where the clerk was whispering to some messenger.

He came forward and stooped before the king. 'My Lord, Owen the Welshman is in the antechamber.'

Richard of London quickly broke in, 'Lord King, this other native, Madog, is waiting in another room. I suggest we have them here together; nothing but our own advantage can come of their inevitable disputes.'

Henry looked hard at his Warden of the Marches, thinking what a flinty and scheming mind the bishop possessed. But he saw the wisdom of Richard's words and nodded his assent to the clerk.

As the messenger left, Gerald de Windsore stumbled forward, his eyes wild and his emotions driving him to ignore the strict protocols of the court. 'Sire…Lord King, let me leave this place…I beg you, make me not stay where this Welshman will come, if I cannot smite him to cleave his hellish flesh from his bones.'

Henry looked at him coldly. 'You are a Norman, sir…your private feuds have no meaning in our presence. You will stay and you will conduct yourself chivalrously.'

There was no questioning the King's words and Gerald shuffled back, his twitch worsening. A moment later, the door swung open to admit Owain ap

Cadwgan; at the same time, a smaller entrance in the opposite corner allowed a young page to usher in Madog ap Rhiryd.

Owain's wary eyes lighted almost simultaneously upon Gerald de Windsore and on his treacherous cousin and one-time ally, Madog. He stopped dead and his hand moved uselessly towards his empty scabbard, his sword having been taken from him at the gate.

De Windsore spun around to stare through the window, with his back to Owain, unwilling to even look upon the man he had sworn to kill. As for Madog, he looked sheepish, but nothing more. Even with the blood of Owain's father fresh upon his hands, he was here to squeeze the best bargain he could for his old lands.

With Gerald ignoring him and Madog trying to appear nonchalant, Owain's blood pressure dropped slightly and he looked elsewhere. For the first time, his eyes fell upon the King – and they stayed there. With his reverence for kingship in any form, he was fascinated by the first sight of this monarch of all England and much of France. He hardly knew what had expected…he half imagined some ethereal being with a halo hovering over the crown but instead saw a solid, calm face with a direct gaze and a bearing that set him apart from any other person in the chamber.

'So you are the notorious Owain,' breathed Henry softly. 'Come near and let me survey you. You have done me much harm, but there is that about you which helps explain your exploits.'

It seemed that some mutual bond of respect had joined these two ruthless, courageous and efficient men, though they had been but a few seconds together.

Owain walked quickly forward and bent his knee. He straightened up and looked Henry full in the eyes. 'We have much in common, sire. You are sovereign of England and I intend to remain premier prince of my country…when I have dealt with certain vermin that at present infest it!'

He shot a venomous look sideways at Madog, who pretended not to hear. The cousin was a burly, thick-necked man, far from looking the typical Celt. He had a rough appearance, and a badly broken nose did nothing to improve his looks. In spite of his boorish appearance, he had a quick and cunning mind, but was utterly devoid of scruples, even in an age where political or personal tolerance was almost unknown.

Henry Beauclerk looked from one to the other. 'You have not met for some time, cousins,' he said with sarcastic sweetness. 'Are there any matters that you wish to discuss, Madog?'

The son of Rhiryd rolled his big shoulders uneasily. 'I last saw Owain a year past, when I left Dublin. I could stand the rude manners of the Irish no longer,' he added irrelevantly.

Owain's face was scarlet with rage in an instant. 'Their ways are like the children of angels compared to yours, swine of swine!' he snarled. 'You had better hide in the deepest pit you can find when we quit the King's peace of

Shrewsbury, for I shall start seeking you out to avenge my father's death the minute our feet cross this drawbridge.'

Bishop Richard's eyelid flickered at the King and Henry took the hint. 'You should temper revenge with mercy, Owen. I have brought you here to consider what is to be done with these lands now that Iorwerth and Cadogan, your father, are no more. Meredith ap Blethin, come forward.'

Maredudd had entered with Owain – yet another son of Bleddyn and brother to Cadwgan, Iorwerth and Rhiryd. He was a small grizzled man in his fifties, who had previously been to Henry to ask for these disputed lands of Iorwerth's. The King had given him only a stewardship of them until Owain appeared from hiding and now the time seemed ripe for yet another change of ownership.

Maredudd nodded surlily to the King. He was not one for bowing and scraping to these French pigs, but he knew when to avoid open hostility.

'Meredith, what did I give you, three months past, when you came to me?' asked Henry.

'All Powys, except for Caereinion and a third of Deuddwr and Aberriw,' growled Maredudd.

'And you, Madog, did you not receive those latter lands from me, the same ones that belonged to you and your brother Ithel?'

Owain boiled over at this, not even the awe of a major king keeping his tongue in its place. 'Those lands were stolen from my father and his brother Iorwerth in the first place…what right has this bloody assassin to be given land he took by treachery from a man he was soon to murder?'

Henry held up a hand as the heated Owain leaned on the table and breathed fire into the royal face. Several of the guards, having good reason to distrust Welshmen, moved a step nearer.

'This is the fortune of war, Owen,' said the King gravely. 'Now, to business. You have been a costly and aggravating enemy, Owen. I would far rather have you for an ally – and it would be cheaper in my soldiers' pay and blood! On due consideration, I am willing to grant you pardon for the many wrongs you have done to us and to restore Powis to you – apart from those lands of Madog. The ones that Meredith ap Blethin now keeps in care for you shall be yours in return for five hundred pounds in silver and the giving of certain hostages.'

Owain cooled down rapidly. He made lightning calculations of the loot he had won during two years of campaigning and the profits on the slaves he had sold to Ireland. Five hundred pounds was a stiff penalty, but it still left a handsome profit for him. The return of most of Powys and an amnesty was a generous offer after the havoc he had wreaked on the French.

'What of hostages…you mentioned them as well as silver?'

Henry's eyes stared evenly at the mercurial Welshman. 'I want every Norman prisoner returned.'

Owain snorted, 'Then about ten you shall have…there are no more. My men, who have seen their families ravaged before their faces, have not been in the habit of taking French prisoners!'

The royal eyes stared unblinking. 'I think you have one such with you today, Owen,' he said softly. 'Is not the Lady Nest with you?'

There was a silence in the chamber as tense as a harp string.

Owain's jaw muscles clenched until the muscles bulged in his cheeks. Slowly, his head turned to look at the back of Gerald de Windsore.

'She is not here, sire…she is in Powys, where no treachery can befall her.'

Like a taut bow suddenly released, Gerald de Windsore swung around and almost ran to the table to stand before the King. 'Lord, release me, I beg. I wish to hear none of what passes. I plead with you, let me go.'

He was like a man demented. The impassioned, wild words were all the more dramatic coming from a man normally even more inscrutable than Henry himself. The King looked at his castellan for a moment, then nodded.

As Gerald swung round and began loping towards the door, Henry called after him. 'Wait, de Windsore…one last time. Will you take back the mother of your children to Pembroke?'

'Lord…NO!' The half-crazed anguish in the voice was unmistakable.

Henry waved his hand in final dismissal and watched with a frown as de Windsore almost ran from the room.

When he had gone, the King turned again to Owain. 'Well, my Lion of Powis, as I have heard you called?'

Owain ap Cadwgan waved his head slowly from side to side, almost uncomprehendingly, looking as if he had just recovered from a blow on the head. 'You want Nest?…the Princess Nest? As a hostage?' He sounded incredulous.

Henry nodded impatiently. 'I want the return of my ward…the wife of that Norman knight. She was taken from him by force…by you. It is more the *return* of a subject I require, than the taking of a hostage.'

Owain stood chewing his lip. 'This cannot be!' he said brusquely, rapidly recovering his poise. 'She is no prisoner, she is not with me by force. Nest is the mother of my child, she has been my true wife for two years. She will be my queen when my lands are rightfully regained.'

Henry shrugged. 'I also hear that she is the mother of another bastard…a Norman this time, one de Hait.'

Owain flushed lividly. 'Another instance of your rapacious followers, Lord King.' His awe of the royal presence seemed to be rapidly fading. 'They ravish Wales and respect not even she who is your ward, as you are fond of reminding me.'

Henry calmly returned the flashing glares of the Welsh prince. 'Take all or nothing, Owen ap Cadogan. I must have the return of those prisoners, twenty hostages that I shall describe – and the recovery of the Lady Nesta – in return, you shall have peace and the return of Powis from Meredith here.'

Owain pounded his hand on the table, careless of majesty.

'Impossible! To hell with your so-called generosity. What true man can trade his wife for land, as if she were a horse? Nest ferch Rhys would herself have no part of it.'

'Have you asked her?' rapped out Henry.

Owain was pulled up short. He desperately wanted the lands of his ancestors, upon which to start building his dream of a united Wales with himself as its leader. Yet his pride, if not his love, prevented him from even countenancing the pact.

'Well, have you asked her, Owen?' barked Richard, knowing instinctively that this was the right moment to sow doubts in Owain's mind.

Henry, a king himself, knew that Owain needed a respite, a pause for face-saving.

'Go back and think…go back and speak with the Lady Nesta. Let us know within three days what you intend to do. There will be no second chance. The alternative is annihilation.'

'You can have my answer now…it is "No",' snapped Owain in a surly growl. He shot a filthy look at Madog, his boorish cousin. 'This is partly your doing, you scurvy fool! Apart from being my father's assassin, I could kill you for this alone.' He looked back at the King. 'Perhaps you wish to reclaim your mistress, sire,' he said spitefully…'the young princess that came to your bed after you had locked up her husband.'

Richard took a threatening step forward. 'Remember you speak to your King, Welshman!' he thundered.

Owain glared back at him. 'He is not my King, priest. He is King of England and Normandy. I acknowledge him no more ruler over my land than this worm-ridden knave here.' He jerked a thumb at the glowering Madog.

Henry held up a hand, regally. 'Let us not descend to bickering like wives at the wash-stones…we are kings and princes. Go home to Nesta, Owen, and talk with her. She shall be received into the care of Stephen of Kerdigan, as that husband of hers seems to have had his senses desert him. I shall be gone by tomorrow, I have other things to do than wait to ogle old lovers.'

Richard of London smiled to himself, as he knew that Matilda had been raising the dust over Henry's incessant affairs with half the pretty gentlewomen of the realm – Henry was going out of his way to declare his virtuous intentions.

The King rose to indicate that the audience was at an end. As he left the chamber, Owain turned to throw a last virulent dart at Madog.

'Look on me well this day, Madog ap Rhiryd…the next time it shall be but a short glance before I tear those lamps of your rotten soul from their sockets!'

With a final vicious look, he turned and marched from the turret room, with old uncle Maredudd close on his heels.

That same night, Owain, Morgan and their uncle reached the hunting lodge near Llangollen where Nest was staying. Under the grim, rocky skyline of Cefn y Fedw, the small house stood in isolation, part wooden, the rest rough stone. It was named Plas Eliseg, after the ancient stone pillar of King Eliseg which stood in mysterious loneliness further down the valley. There was none of the formality of the courts here. All ate together around a crackling fire in the centre of the single large room. Afterwards, Owain and Nest retired to their cubicle in the corner, divided from the rest only by a partition and a thick woollen curtain.

Rhiannon had the two babes with her in another cell at the other end of the room – Owain could hardly bear to look at the de Hait baby, though he was a finely built child.

The Prince of Powys slouched on the edge of the bed, the only one in the building, while Nest sat quietly alongside him. Her hands were folded in her lap and she did not touch him, only waited passively for what was to come. Though no word had yet been spoken, she could sense the gap that was already opening between them.

Then Owain began to talk, tonelessly outlining the ultimatum that Henry had put forward.

'He says he has no interest in you himself, Nest. He will be gone from Shrewsbury tomorrow and in any event, wishes to send you back to Dingeraint. The corrupt tongues of the French now call that 'Kerdigan' and he wishes that this Stephen should be your guardian there.'

Nest nodded dutifully. 'He was the one who saved me from further molestation by de Hait. He is the only gentle Norman I have ever met.'

Owain was silent but his hands tore at the fur on the bedcover until bald patches appeared.

She felt him receding from her.

What was she to do, oh God? She loved him, but since the affair of de Hait and the birth of his bastard...a French bastard...she had seen Owain daily getting more remote from her. The bonds were slackening and snapping, thread by thread. Nest sighed, a sigh that came from the depths of her soul. She knew at that moment that she was going to lose Owain, lose the torch of her life. But if it was to be so, it might as well be now, as lovers still, rather than strangers later.

'You must make this pact with Henry, my love,' she said softly, 'and I will go to Ceredigion.'

'Never – I will not allow it,' he muttered gruffly, not looking at her.

She laid a hand softly on the back of his, the first contact they had had that day. 'Owain, you are the hope of Wales. Gruffydd of Gwynedd is old and now you are the new light. To get a foothold, you must regain all of Powys. I will not be the barrier that stops you, not for your sake nor for that of our people. It is my right and duty as much as it is yours,' she ended firmly.

He shook his big head stubbornly. 'Never! You are mine. We will stay together for ever,' he muttered, but they both knew that his voice carried false conviction.

Nest tried to intertwine her fingers in his, but his hand lay unresponsive on the bed.

'It must end sometime, Owain. I have many children – I have not seen five of them in almost two years. At Din-geraint I shall be able to arrange a meeting through this Stephen, who is a good man. And little Llywelyn, he must stay with you. I shall leave Rhiannon with him, but there will be plenty of opportunity for me to visit him, if I am under Stephen's care.'

Owain stared stolidly at the floor between his feet. 'And what of the de Hait child?'

She sighed again. 'We have already had many demands from his father for his return. Even a bastard child, if a son, is dear to the parents – we should know that,' she added with a tinge of bitterness. 'I can even see this babe when I am with Stephen.'

'You seem to have it all worked out,' snapped Owain, suddenly turning his sullen face towards her. 'Where do I fit into these schemes of yours?'

She recoiled inwardly at the lash in his voice, but outwardly stayed calm. 'You are and always will be my only love, Owain. But I am married, a mother to other children – and you are to be the premier Prince of Wales. There is far more in these matters than my own wishes and desires. I am not flying to someone else's arms, Owain ap Cadwgan…my husband will not have me, the King rushes in another direction…and as for de Hait, I would rather throw myself from the walls of Din-geraint into the Teifi, than set eyes on him again.'

Owain rose to his feet and paced the tiny cell. 'I will go to Henry again and prevail on him to accept a different ransom. Another twenty hostages, instead of you!'

She flushed with real anger at this. 'Twenty good Welshmen? You think I am worth that, Owain? I would not see a single one taken into bondage for my own sake. I may not be able to wield a bow or a sword for my country, but I have valour enough to use myself in the cause of my own people.' She was on her feet now, her eyes flashing into his. 'I will go to Ceredigion and you will triumph and prosper as a Prince. That is the reward I want and if you love me, you will accept our destiny without argument.'

But argument there was, which lasted another hour. Owain became more and more angry, not because he really resisted her arguments, but because he was fighting his own desire to agree with her and let her go to Stephen.

Nest knew this well enough and would not yield an inch. She knew him well enough to realize that anger might succeed where logic would fail.

Eventually, he broke.

He stopped his pacing and stood in front of her, quivering with a rage that was all the more acute because he recognized his own guilt in wishing her to have her way.

'Then go, Nest ferch Rhys, and be damned, to your Norman friends!' he hissed. 'If you desire so much to flee to your precious Stephen, this paragon amongst French swine, I shall not stop you.'

Nest smiled gently, though the bottom had just dropped from her soul. She had kept a little corner of her heart to hope for some miracle that would make her sacrifice unnecessary – but the age of miracles seemed over.

'It is the right thing, Owain,' she said in a soft voice. 'It is right, though God knows I love you and leaving you is only a step from death itself…but the alternative is worse.'

'What do you mean now?' he glowered suspiciously, still rough with her because he was hating himself.

'Our affection would wither away if I stayed. You would begin to hate me for keeping you from your kingdom. You would hate me for making you remain an outlaw. And you would begin to hate me for being the wife of de Windsore, the mistress of King Henry and the victim of de Hait. All these things were not of my doing and you know it – but it would not stop them from coming between us, once the seed of discontent was sown.'

Owain did the only cowardly thing in his whole life. He snatched up his cloak and prepared to run away from a situation he could not handle.

'I'm going to the court at Mathrafal. If you are here when I return in two days, then all will be well. If you are not – then I know that you have defied my wishes, Nest.' Illogically, as he reached the curtain he turned and spoke. 'My uncle Maredudd ap Bleddyn is here, should you wish escort to Ceredigion or Shrewsbury.' Without another word, he turned and went through the curtain.

'Owain!'

She heard her own voice scream as if it belonged to some other person. Suddenly she knew he was going and that she would never again see him in this life.

He hesitated and turned back into the cubicle. Nest threw herself at him, her usual restraint abandoned. She kissed him as she had never kissed a man before, then through her sobs she pushed and pummelled him away. Bewildered, he stumbled through the woollen drapes and disappeared, whilst Nest fell on to their bed and cried softly until sheer exhaustion sent her into a merciful sleep in the small hours of next morning.

PART THREE

CHAPTER THIRTEEN
JUNE, 1114

A ROYAL procession was winding its way down the coast from Aberystwyth to Kerdigan. Several thousand foot-soldiers, hundreds of mounted men and many score of armoured knights were strung out along the beaten track that led from the new Norman castle at Caerwedros towards the south.

In the centre of the cavalcade, the silk banners of King Henry fluttered in the late spring breeze and dozens of red and yellow pennants streamed out from the tips of upraised lances. There was no fighting to be done and the King of England wore only a light cuirass of armour, his helmet resting on the pommel of his squire's saddle.

This was Norman dominated country, but in any case peace – albeit an uneasy one – had settled on the whole of Wales these two weeks past.

The regal company had stopped at Caerwedros for refreshment, having left Razo's new castle at the mouth of the Ystwyth early that morning. Though it was now late afternoon, Henry wished to push on to Kerdigan by nightfall, anxious to complete his tour of the new Norman fortresses that had been erected in the three years since he had given Cadwgan's lands in Ceredigion to Gilbert fitzRichard.

It was now the middle of eleven hundred and fourteen and Henry felt that at last he had settled the 'Welsh problem' – a problem mainly created and maintained by the indomitable Owain, for whom Henry had developed a grudging admiration.

As he jogged along on his great black horse, Henry Beauclerk thought of this Owain and all that had passed since he had bargained with him three years ago in Shrewsbury castle.

The Lady Nesta had been restored to Norman guardianship and was actually in residence at Kerdigan, their next stopping place, where she had been in the care of Stephen ever since she had forsaken Owain ap Cadwgan.

The Prince of Powys had been as good as his word and had ruled his father's possessions in the north with a ruthless efficiency that Henry admired. He had reigned there with the staunch help of his brother Morgan and his uncle Maredudd ap Bleddyn, who acted as captain of the household guard.

There had been internal feuds in plenty, but until lately none had split the Welsh enough to suit the wily Bishop, Richard of London. There had been a vendetta between Owain and Madog, as Owain pursued his promise of vengeance against his cousin for causing the murder of Iorwerth and Cadwgan. Madog had been betrayed into Owain's hands in the previous year and the usual punishment of burning out both his eyes had been carried out to even up the score.

From that time on, Owain seemed to have slipped back into his unruly ways, though even the King suspected that Bishop Richard had engineered various provocative situations to discredit Owain's reputation.

The venerable and doughty old Prince of North Wales, Gruffydd ap Cynan, had once more rallied the men of Snowdonia to come out against the English, his excuse being the accusations of the Norman Lord of Chester that Gruffydd had been filching his land. With the Warden of the Marches aiding and abetting, the sick and ailing Gilbert fitzRichard joined in with further allegations that Owain ap Cadwgan had been conducting raids into his lands of Ceredigion. The whole squabble rapidly escalated until the fiery Owain, forced to leave the indefensible lands of Powys, fled to Snowdonia to range his men alongside those of old Gruffydd.

Henry sighed as he recalled all the commotion that he had had to face at Westminster and Woodstock, when he returned from his Normandy campaigns earlier that year. Richard of London had deliberately let matters proceed to such a point where there was no option but to mount a full campaign against the Welsh of the north. This was just what the Bishop, fitzRichard and Hugh of Chester wanted, as a final crushing blow against the leaders whose remaining lands they so much coveted.

Reluctantly, Henry diverted effort and money from his wars on the continent to make his first military excursion into Wales.

Yet in the event, hardly a blow was struck nor an arrow shot in battle.

Sensible discretion overcame suicidal valour as Henry's great army – drawn from as far afield as Cornwall and Scotland – marched into Wales. This host had vowed to exterminate the Welsh from the face of the earth or cast them into the western sea and the wily Gruffydd decided that it was better to come to terms and live to fight another day.

Even before this, Henry had tried to split the Welsh by sending Owain's uncle, Maredudd – who had seen the wisdom of surrender earlier than anyone – to seduce him from the cause of Gruffydd. The whole affair was soon settled bloodlessly and when tribute and hostages had been handed over, the great army broke up and went its various ways.

The King, who had never before set foot in Wales, took the opportunity to make a circuitous return through Kerdigan, Pembroke and Glamorgan to see the results of the work of the new defences of his western realm.

As the quarter-mile long cavalcade plodded down the last long slope to the Teifi river, Henry beckoned to a young squire, one who had led a party out from Kerdigan to meet them.

The youngster peeled off from the host of outriders and drew his horse alongside the King's, his face flushed at the honour of being so singled out for the royal notice.

'Sire?' he enquired respectfully.

'You are a lieutenant to Stephen, the castellan of this Kerdigan?'

The young man nodded energetically. 'Indeed I am, sire. I went there when it was captured and sacked by the Welshmen over three years ago. I have seen it rise up in stone from the ruins of the old fortress.'

Henry's square, calm face was thoughtful for a moment.

'You were there, then, when the Lady Nesta returned?'

'Yes, sire...she was sent into the charge of my benefactor and patron, Stephen. And there she has remained ever since.'

'She is well?' asked Henry curtly.

'In good health, my Lord, though I think not so well in spirit.'

Henry turned his head to look at the eager youth.

'And why not?'

'The lady has had many troubles over the past few years, sire. She has lost her children no fewer than three times. Her elder sons and daughters are with de Windsore in Pembroke.'

The squire broke off momentarily to look cautiously back along the cavalcade to where Gerald's red cross on its silver banner fluttered at the head of his Flemish troop.

'Then she had her first bastard by the Welshman and that babe was left with foster folk in Powis when the lady returned to Kerdigan.'

Henry finished the sad catalogue for him. 'And the bastard by de Hait's ravishment has gone, too, I suppose?'

The young man nodded. 'The father demanded it when it was eighteen months old. Stephen was loth to let it go, as the Lady Nest was so much in need of a babe to mother, but although she had the natural affection for her own flesh and blood, the circumstances of its birth were so well known that eventually he let de Hait take it to his own wife at St. Clears.'

Henry pushed out his full lower lip. 'So now the ever fertile Nesta is without any of her seven children. It must indeed go hard with her, she was a woman born to be a mother.'

Later, he repeated the same sentiments to Stephen, the custodian of Kerdigan castle, when they were settled down and dined in the new hall. Though the Lord Gilbert fitzRichard owned the territory, he had been taken back to his English domains a week ago, suffering from yet another stroke which had left him almost without speech and with a palsied right arm. It was left to Stephen to entertain the King and to show him the new fortress that had been built to keep the Welsh of southern Ceredigion and northern Dyfed in subjection.

They sat now at the high table, with Bishop Richard, Ranulf the

Chancellor, Walter the Justiciar of Gloucester and several of the premier barons of the land. The lower tables were packed with knights and squires, and outside, the bailey was crowded with soldiers sitting around camp-fires, singing and drinking after their meat.

The triangular promontory was now surrounded by a battlemented stone wall and the centre third of the compound was occupied by the keep. Outside, a cluster of huts and stables was already growing up and Normans and Flemings were already settling to business, no Welsh folk being allowed to trade in the shadow of the castle walls.

A bridge across the Teifi was half completed, to replace the old ford. In the three and a half years since Owain's desperate attack to rescue Nest from de Hait, the place had changed beyond all recognition. It was ironic that she was back in the very same spot, this time of her own free will, but almost as much a prisoner in that she had nowhere else to go.

Some of these thoughts came into the King's mind as he listened absently to the earnest gossip of those around him. Eventually, as some of the noblemen became sleepy or raucous with drink, he beckoned to Stephen, who was hovering in the background to make sure that the servants were doing their work with alacrity.

The castellan came across to the King and bowed. Henry had never met him before today, but was impressed by his calm and masterful bearing. He was a tall man with tawny hair, having much of the looks of the Northmen who gave the Normans their name.

Henry crooked a finger at him and Stephen bent over the royal chair.

'The Lady Nesta – she made no appearance at the feast tonight?'

The castellan shook his head. 'Apart from a few lower women and serving wenches, there are no other ladies in Kerdigan, sire. Lady Nesta did not wish to place her solitary presence into such a masculine gathering as this.' He motioned briefly at the somewhat disorderly throng that shouted and guffawed across the tables.

Henry nodded his understanding. 'You have no wife, then?'

Stephen shook his tawny head again. 'None, sire. I think these frontier castles are no place for a tender family. With the fortunes of war, they can become bloody battlefields overnight. I have never been quite happy to see Lady Nesta here, especially with no female company of her own standing. But there seems to be little choice for her.'

Henry frowned. 'In what way, Stephen?'

Like the eyes of the young squire that afternoon, the castellan's face turned towards the hall and sought Gerald de Windsore, sitting alone and aloof at a centre table in the main body of the hall.

'My brother castellan from Pembroke, sire…I have made many efforts to secure a reconciliation between them, so that the lady might return to her rightful place among her family. But de Windsore will not even discuss the matter and has never even deigned to visit her or this castle. He is only here tonight because he cannot avoid it by leaving your majesty's retinue. But half an eye can tell how ill at ease he is.'

Henry looked down from the dais at the sallow-faced knight who stared so grimly at the opposite wall, obviously calculating how soon he dared rise and leave for his pallet in the crowded gatehouse.

'And the lady,' asked Henry slowly, 'how did she view any reconciliation?'

Stephen pulled at his rather prominent chin. 'Without enthusiasm, as far as her husband was concerned, I feel. But she aches for her children and would go back for them alone. De Windsore has grudgingly allowed them to visit her on two occasions and her joy was pitiful to see. Though when they had gone, her black depression seemed to make the exercise less than worthwhile. I have been trying for some time to negotiate for the elder daughter to come and live with her mother; it might have come to pass if this campaign had not thrown affairs to the winds again.'

Henry looked up over his shoulder at the castellan.

'You seem to have a great compassion for the lady – and have worked hard for her happiness. I shall not forget, for she has a deep place in my affections, too. I would like to see her again – we leave for Pembroke in the morning as soon as I have inspected the new fortifications. Only tonight remains, if she has not already retired.'

Stephen inclined his head. 'The Lady Nesta has told me that it would give her great pleasure if she could once more meet you, sire. I am sure that she waits in her chamber in the hope that you might honour her with your presence.'

Henry rose and immediately those on the top table who were still able to either stand or see, began staggering to their feet.

Henry stopped them with an upraised hand. 'I shall be back – let us have no ceremony here, this is still a campaign of war.'

Those who bothered to think of it imagined that the King was going to the nearest latrine shaft – all except de Windsore, whose mind, fermenting with jealousies, correctly divined the purpose of Henry's departure.

Stephen led the way through a small door at the back of the dais and began climbing a narrow spiral staircase cut in the thickness of the wall. In spite of the lax circumstances, one of the King's personal esquires and two men-at-arms tramped up the stone steps behind him.

The castellan tapped on a stout wooden door at the end of short, arched passage and then opened it for the King.

'I will wait here, my Lord,' said Stephen tactfully, and pulled the door shut after Henry had passed through.

The small tower room seemed empty, lit only by two wavering candles, but there was a rustling at the further end and from an adjacent robing room, Nest stepped into the candlelight.

Henry stood stock-still, gazing with sudden fascination at this figure from his past. He had come up to visit her merely from courtesy mingled with curiosity to see how his casual mistress of twelve years ago had survived seven childbirths.

But one glance at the more mature Nesta brought admiration and sudden desire flooding back, stronger than it had ever been in the old days.

She knelt gracefully before him, the light gleaming on the black sheen of her hair where it escaped from the white silk of her head-dress.

'It is good to see you once more, sire,' she murmured.

Henry strode across the room and held his hand for her to touch briefly with her lips before he helped her to her feet. As he tore his eyes for an instant from her lovely face and figure, he was aware of a well-built maid-servant lurking in the background, but she bobbed out of sight as he glared at her.

'Will you sit, my Lord?' Nest waved towards a cross-legged chair near the empty fireplace, but Henry led her to it and saw her seated before drawing out another for himself. He sat right in front of her, and leaned forward, hands clasped in his lap. His eyes studied her face intently.

'I see countless people every day, Nesta. I hate some and like others, but have to be civil to all except my open enemies. Words of pleasure and welcome roll easily from my lips as a kingly duty, but I swear that I never meant them more than when I say now how much pleasure it gives me to see you again.'

From anyone else, these words might have sounded laborious and pedantic, but the slightly husky tone and the drilling force of his eyes caused a tingling to flutter along Nest's spine. Though she had never loved this man, he was the King of England – and the first man to show her what love-making could really be like.

If twelve years had ripened her own beauty, it had given this man a ten-fold increase in character. Always direct and commanding, his personality was now almost overpowering.

'Nesta, is all well with you here? I learn that you grieve for your children.'

Henry reached forward and took her hands into his. 'Life has not been too kind to you, Nesta. Even before we met the turmoil had begun. Since then, ill fortune has dogged your steps. It seems that the people most deserving of happiness receive the least.'

Her chin came up almost defiantly. Her dark eyes returned, without flinching, the stare of the most powerful man in Europe.

'Please do not pity me, sire. In that very unhappiness, I found my ultimate happiness, the only real love I shall ever know. Though even that is now lost,' she added in a low voice.

Henry had no need to ask who she meant. 'I too have a great regard for that man, though he has sorely tried my patience and that of my ministers. Yet he has a certain wild charm.'

Nest smiled, not wanly, but with a warmth that rose from the deep places of her soul. For a few minutes they spoke of Owain ap Cadwgan, though Nest did most of the talking.

But no man likes to spend his time with a beautiful woman in listening to her raptures about another lover and Henry soon changed the subject.

'And you Nesta – you cannot stay cooped up in this frontier fortress like a dove in a cote!'

She smiled, more thinly this time. 'A dove is free to fly – but where could I fly? I am still part of Owain's ransom for Powys – I am still your ward. Where could I go?'

Henry frowned. 'I can command this idiot of a husband to take you back, if you so wished it.'

Nest shook her head emphatically. 'I am still a princess with a princess's pride. I will not be forced on a man who has refused to acknowledge my very existence for over four years.'

Henry looked faintly troubled for the first time since he entered. 'I cannot reverse the pact with Owain, not even for you, dear Nesta. Only a few days ago, I was forced to extract even greater penance from him for his revolt against us with old Griffith. I have lost count of the times that he has thrown over treaties and ridden against my barons. We cannot afford any gesture which other Welsh princes might interpret as weakness.'

Nest shook her head slowly. 'That is understood, sire. And is of no consequence, in any event.'

'Why not? Would you not wish to return to your kinsmen, your lover and your son?'

'My son – yes. I would go for him. I would do almost anything for any of my children. But I can never return to Owain, not even for Llewelyn. Like Gerald, he has been unable to face the thought of another man possessing me, even though it was by force.'

Henry's face tightened. 'That damned ruffian, de Hait. I should have had him hanged. If only I had been here – I spend so much of my time in France. It is the price of trying to be king in two countries at once.' He sighed deeply and took her hands again in his. 'But Nesta, surely your Owain cannot hold a rape against your honour to him. And you lived with him for long after this ravishing took place.'

Nest nodded. 'He has fought his feelings for a long time, but I have felt him slipping away from me. It was only his honour that held him so long. He did his best, but the arrival of little William, de Hait's bastard, was too much for him.'

Henry's intense gaze held her eyes. 'He sounded very loth to let you go when I presented him with the ultimatum at Shrewsbury.'

'He protested his love, sire – and I think he loves me still. But not in a way that will let us be as we were before, like one mind and one flesh. And without that whole, I want nothing, painful though it be.'

Henry got up and moved restlessly about in front of the gaping, empty fireplace.

'I cannot have you rotting your fair life away in this outlandish place, Nesta. We must do something – and quickly. Tell me, how has this Stephen been? Have you anything to complain of in his actions or manners?'

Nest jumped up, almost in alarm. 'No, nothing...the reverse in every way. Stephen has been the one support in a barren life. Please, Henry, think nothing but good of him.'

The royal eyebrows raised a little. 'You sound fond of your jailer.'

Nest used her prerogative as a princess to look impatiently at a king. 'Surely you cannot be jealous,' she asked with unconscious archness mixed with a little impatience. 'He was the one who saved me from further insult by de Hait. Had it not been for the return of Owain and the battle, Stephen would have sent de Hait to you in fetters. He almost slew him on the spot – only drunkenness formed some excuse. Since then, that knight has been kindness itself. He has tried to intercede with Gerald and has managed to let me see my children.' Nest paused, hesitating about how venturesome she could be with her tongue. 'Though you are a Norman, sire, I have to say that my blood rebels at many of the deeds wrought on my people by your kind – but of all Normans, Stephen is the first I have met who is good in all he does.'

Henry looked blank for a moment, as if deciding whether or not to be annoyed. Then he gave a rare grin and slipped an arm about her shoulders. 'That relegates me to the ranks of the French monsters – perhaps I should make this paragon Stephen my heir!'

He swung her around to face him and his eyes travelled lowly down her slim figure dressed in its robe of pale green linen.

'We must be serious, Nesta. I will not have you lingering here, with no prospect of salvation. I shall send you to Cairdyf in the care of Mabel fitzHamon for the time being, until I make up my mind what to do with you. You will still be in your precious Wales, but within easy reach of Gloucester, where I sometimes hold court.'

His meaning was quite clear and Nest again felt the ghostly tinglings caressing her neck.

'Will you go, Nesta?' His eyes shone into hers like torches. She dropped her own gaze. 'You are the King – and I am your ward, sire.'

He gave a short laugh. 'Come now, my Nesta. You and your kindred spend half your lives proclaiming to the world that you owe fealty to none but the Welsh princes. I'll not command you – I am *asking*. Will you come to Cairdyf?'

She raised her head and nodded. 'For how long, sire?'

He shrugged impatiently. 'God knows...until my dear wife Matilda discovers, perhaps,' he added with jovial sarcasm. 'She and Archbishop Anselm have been laying down the law about my necessary amours these past five years, but I usually manage to dodge them for a time.'

Something hardened deep in Nest as she realized just how deeply this affair went into Henry's soul. She would be just another furtive toy for as long as propriety allowed. A haughty rejection was half-way to her lips, when she checked it. A princess by birth she may be, but where was she now? Without her royal father, without her lands, without her husband and even without her Welsh lover...what grounds had she for haughtiness before the King of England?

'Will you come to Cairdyf, Nesta?' Henry asked again and by his tone she knew that he was not going to ask again.

She paused, then nodded once, her lowered eyes staring down at the hem of his dark red robe.

Henry put out a hand and lifted her chin. 'You are beautiful, Nesta – if I realized how beautiful you had become, I would have campaigned in Wales long before this.'

Nest had no love for him, but the nearness of such a man thrilled her. She had come close to loving him once and the hot feeling of anticipation of being taken by him again crept through her. One last faint reservation came softly to her lips.

'My husband…what of Gerald?'

Henry looked down at her with those unfathomable eyes and said: 'I am the King.'

Stephen of Kerdigan himself escorted Nest to Cairdyf. Before Henry left for Pembroke, he charged the castellan to spare no effort in making her journey as safe and comfortable as possible.

Two weeks after Henry departed they left the castle on the Teifi and travelled by a route which included as many Norman settlements as possible. On the insistence of Stephen, Nest travelled in a litter rather than rode and their progress was slow, but eventually they reached the end of Welsh-held territory. Once beyond the River Afan they were in Morgannwg, amongst the numerous estates of the knights who came with Robert fitzHamon to displace the natives from the lush Vale of Glamorgan. FitzHamon, one of the Conqueror's right-hand men, had died of an old wound some seven years earlier, leaving no male heir. Until his daughter Mabel married, the castle and great lands at Cairdyf were under the direct guardianship of the King, who had no intention of ever letting it leave his own family.

The small cavalcade continued along the track of the old Roman road, the Via Julia Maritima, until they reached the wide horseshoe of hills that encircled the landward approaches to Cairdyf.

Riding at the head of the party, Stephen raised his gauntlet to halt the riders, then turned his horse back to come alongside the litter. Nest was already peering with interest through the curtains at the panorama spread below in the summer sunshine.

'Within sight of our goal, my lady,' said Stephen gravely, his usual dry humour absent. He kept his feelings well under control, but he was sad to see this lovely woman tumbled into yet another man's arms even if that man be his own liege majesty.

He pointed down into the green bowl below them, where marshland lay around the tidal course of the central river. 'There lies the stream called the Taf which gives the place its name…on its further bank, the castle and the new borough. Another hour and we shall be at its gates.'

At the end of that hour, they were crossing the rickety wooden bridge and approaching the great castle. It was great mainly through the efforts of the Romans, but Robert fitzHamon had made use of the fortifications built by the ancient empire, though they had been abandoned for almost seven centuries. Nest, being used to the massive pile at Pembroke, was not overawed by the Cairdyf fortress, but appreciated that it was still a formidable structure. The great Roman square had been too large for Norman needs, but they had deepened the old ditch and thrown the soil inside the ancient walls to form a twenty-foot ramp, on top of which was a stout wooden stockade. The huge arena inside, where legionaries once paraded, had been cut in half by a palisade. In the western half, fitzHamon had thrown up the usual moated mound, forty feet high and topped by a massive timber keep. The outer stockade and the foot of the mound had drawbridges and gates, making it appear impregnable, though in a few years the Welsh were to repeatedly prove this faith unfounded.

But for Stephen and his train, the defences were thrown wide open by the time they reached the cluster of houses and shops that marked the beginning of the settlement outside the castle gates. A troop of men-at-arms under a very deferential squire had ridden out to welcome them, as they had been expected since Stephen's advance messenger had arrived the previous day.

Their escort was led off to quarters in the numerous outbuildings in the inner ward, whilst Nest, Rhiannon and Stephen were conveyed straight up to the towering keep.

At the top of the steep flight of steps that led up from the inner drawbridge, a woman waited for them in finery that made Nest feel a country bumpkin, rather than a princess and a favourite of the King. This was Mabel fitzHamon, the true owner of the great fitzHamon lands. Since her father's death, she had lived alone either in Cairdyf or in one of her many estates in England and Normandy. She was almost thirty and still unmarried. Nest, though the most charitable of souls, could quite understand why, when she got far enough up the steps to see her hostess's face. There was no avoiding it – Mabel fitzHamon was not just plain, she was ugly. A round pug face with a flat button of a nose, stared out from under mousey hair that no maidservant's art could prevent being thin and lack-lustre.

Mabel watched Nest climb the last few stairs, then moved forward to take her hand. 'Welcome, Lady Nesta…I am glad to have some suitable company in this dull place.'

In spite of the words, Nest felt that Mabel's tone held more of duty than genuine warmth, but both then and later she had no cause to complain about her hostess's hospitality and kindness. The Norman lady had spared no trouble to make her as comfortable as the spartan fortress allowed. She conducted her up to a fair-sized chamber facing the main gate, with a view southwards to the sea. Ironically, it was the same view that poor Robert of Normandy was to gaze at for eight long years until his death there – Henry, wary of further efforts of his brother to seize the throne, incarcerated him there for safe keeping. But this was a decade in the future and Nest found herself in a pleasant enough chamber with the summer sun streaming through the window slit on to a bowl of wild flowers that Mabel had placed there.

While Rhiannon busied herself putting Nest's clothes in a curtained alcove, Mabel fitzHamon was running an appraising eye over her guest as they exchanged small talk about the rigours of the journey.

She saw a strikingly beautiful woman, a few years older than herself. Her clothes had been of the first quality, but were now worn and dull with use. Nest had been out of touch with other ladies and the changes in fashion since she left Pembroke, now almost four years ago.

'We must call in the silk traders and the peddlers to deck you out properly,' fussed Mabel, becoming almost effusive on the subject of finery. Nest secretly realized that fitzHamon's daughter tried to make up for her sad lack of good looks by an almost pathetic devotion to gowns and fine fabrics. She did not know that Henry, in his personal letter to Mabel informing her of the coming of her new guest, had told her to spare no pains nor expense in giving Nest whatever she might require. Though Mabel was not jealous on account of Henry – he was already securely married and also forty-six years old – she slightly resented having to play landlady and procuress to his latest mistress, a mere Welshwoman.

There was also the business of young Robert of Gloucester, Henry's eldest bastard, whom some wagging tongues alleged to be the son of this Nest, though that was patently impossible unless she had conceived at the age of ten.

Mabel pushed aside these thoughts, especially of Robert, and allowed herself to enjoy the welcome company of another educated, civilized gentlewoman. Mabel had never met Gerald de Windsore and had hardly heard of Owain ap Cadwgan or the Welsh princelings of the west, so there was little fear of treading on delicate ground. Mabel soon forgot her minor piques and the fact that Nest was only a Welsh lady, as conversation came around to mutual Norman acquaintances, of Pembroke, Shrewsbury, of Stephen of Kerdigan and of course the King himself, of whom Mabel had an obvious and unselfish admiration.

Stephen managed to divert the conversation away from Nest's relationship with Henry. 'You had two brothers, I think, Lady. What of them?'

Nest smiled sadly. 'I have seen neither since the black day when our father died. Gruffydd was the heir, though two years younger than I. My kindred smuggled him straightway to Ireland but I fear he will never now return to claim his kingdom.'

For once, Nest spoke only a half-truth, but the others were unaware of it.

'What of the other brother, Nesta?' asked the indefatigably curious Mabel.

'Hywel was but a baby of two years when the blow fell. He was captured at our house of Caer Rhiw in Dyfed. I have never seen him since – I think he is now in exile in Amorica*, after being sorely treated by his captors when he tried to escape some years ago. He is maimed and has his manhood taken from him.'

Stephen was silent. Though a Norman knight himself, brought up to regard torture and maiming as a natural part of life, he revolted against it deep within his soul. For the hundredth time, he wished that he had been allowed to follow his early inclinations and take holy orders – then he looked across at Nest and somehow felt glad that he had stayed free of celibacy.

Pleading fatigue after this last day of a long journey, Nest escaped further questioning by retiring to her lofty room in the tower on the mound. There was no ante-chamber attached to it and Rhiannon slept in a niche in the corridor, curled up contentedly on a blanket like a dog on the threshold.

Nest sat for a long time at the window, staring out above the palisade to where a distant headland stood black against the moonlit sea.

She felt more lonely than she had for years. This land of Morgannwg seemed as remote from Ceredigion as had Shrewsbury or Ireland, though she knew that a few miles to the north, the land was as Welsh as it had ever been, untrodden by a Norman foot.

But down here on the lowlands the atmosphere was different. A few yards away beyond the castle wall were prospering French, Fleming and even a few Saxon traders, busy building up the new town of Cairdyf where nothing but a few fishing huts had existed since the Romans left. She closed her eyes and tried to send her thoughts winging westwards. There were so many people there for them to seek. Owain, her Owain, was always the first. Though, against her will, she could feel his image growing dimmer as the months passed, he was something that only death itself could completely erase. She had heard nothing at all from him since that day in Powys when he had ridden off and left her to make the inevitable decision.

Tears filled Nest's eyes as she watched the yellow moon slide through the same sky that hung over Owain and her children. Would he take a wife, she wondered? He had been settling down well, until this recent trouble that had brought King to Wales. Powys had never had such a strong prince. Owain had learned from his father's mistakes and she drew some comfort from the thought that her decision to leave him to govern his princedom had been amply justified. That was about the only thing that had gone right, she thought, in a sudden welter of self-pity. Apart from that, her presence had plunged West Wales into repeated blood-baths, ever since Owain had carried her off from Cenarth Bychan. The ravages of Madog and Ithel had led to hundreds of deaths in Ceredigion and Dyfed; she thought bitterly of the fighting at Din-geraint and the guerilla wars of Owain that must have pushed the death roll well into the thousands, to say nothing of the misery from pillage, rape and destitution that had overtaken women and children as well

* The modern Brittany.

as the fighting men. Perhaps she could find obscurity and some peace as the latest clandestine diversion of her old master, the King. She raised her face to the night sky and prayed to the vague God that she had been brought up to worship. She prayed for deliverance from her unwilling rôle as the focus of men's restless cruelties.

As if in answer to her prayer, a sudden commotion down at the main gate gradually penetrated her abstraction. Torches were flickering and men were running about. Beyond the wall there were more moving lights, and horses' hooves sounded on the rough road that came from the east and England.

A horn blew several times and the great gates were slowly creaked open, a most unusual happening after sundown.

There were more trumpet blasts and a double line of flambeaux jogged into the outer ward, revealing an advance guard of a dozen armoured horsemen, their spears erect. Though there were no banners or gonfalons in a night-time procession, there could be no doubt that this was a royal cavalcade.

A moment later, a solitary rider on a great grey horse entered the castle, followed by another half-score rearguard.

It was the King, eager to be re-united with his old flame, at the end of a forced ride from Gloucester to claim his new plaything.

In spite of herself, she felt a flicker of anticipation and even fear running through her body: fear that Henry would find that twelve years had dulled her attractions for him more than he expected. She moved back into the chamber and quietly called Rhiannon from the corridor. There was time enough for the girl to help her into one of the dresses that Mabel had laid out for her – the poor light would disguise the doubtful fit for this first evening. As she let Rhiannon comb out her long, black hair, she knew that they need not hurry, as the impatience of the King would have to wait on the courtesies of Mabel fitzHamon's rank. Henry would have to suffer the conventions of some conversation and have refreshments pressed upon him before he could decently escape to his new mistress.

It was almost an hour before the expected knock came upon her chamber door. When Nest opened it, she found Henry standing there alone. He came in without a word, still in his riding clothes, though without arms or hauberk.

With no preamble, he put his arms about her shoulders and kissed her passionately upon the mouth.

Then he pushed her to arm's length and looked down upon her with those deep, unnerving eyes.

'Nesta, we are both too old and too knowing in the ways of love to waste time in coy dalliance,' he murmured. 'I get no younger and the time gets shorter. I almost killed my horse to be with you before you slept this night. I want you and I wish to make up quickly for those years when I foolishly forgot how beautiful you really were.'

He pulled her close again and one hand slid down to her breast. She shuddered as the familiar old feeling crept through her veins. Let a man – any bold, handsome man – hold her like this and she would acknowledge that she was lost, though he be the devil himself.

And this was no devil – this was England's King.

During the following months Henry came frequently to his mistress. His visits to the high keep of the castle at Cairdyf were usually furtive – nights stolen from official business at Gloucester, where the King's presence was seen more frequently than ever before.

Walter, the Justiciar of Gloucester, was well aware of the sudden attraction of the place over Shrewsbury, but otherwise the secret was tolerably well kept. The Queen spent much of her time at Woodstock or Windsor, but as far as anyone knew, no word of her husband's latest interest reached her. His amorous wanderings were well known – at least twenty bastards could call him father by the end of his reign – and Matilda did all she could to keep her royal consort on the narrow path of husbandly duty. But his eternal rovings up and down his kingdom as well as his even more frequent visits to France, left him ample opportunity for illicit love affairs.

But for the first time for years, he remained faithful to Nest, in that his interest in other paramours ceased while she was in the ascendancy in Cairdyf. He would arrive in the twilight of an autumn night, with only a squire and a few armed soldiers, departing for Gloucester as unobtrusively in the pale light of the next dawn. Mabel had left for Normandy soon after Nest had arrived and the morose castellan took little interest in anything but the running of the castle business.

Twice Stephen arrived from Kerdigan, the first time on some faint pretext and the second with no excuse at all. He was the only contact she had with her homelands in the west, though there was little news that he could bring her.

'My only knowledge comes from Pembroke,' he told her gravely on the second visit. 'Your children there are well and I also hear from St. Clears that the child fitzHait is growing into a sturdy infant. Though there is no gossip of your sudden disappearance from Kerdigan, I know from squires who have visited the great castle on the Haven that de Windsore knows of your present situation.' As delicate as ever, in contrast to the usual bluntness of the Norman, Stephen avoided any more exact description of Nest's status at Cairdyf.

She looked at him with a frank smile. 'You need not tread delicately on my account, sir. I am Henry's mistress, as I was when I was twenty years old. I was also Gerald's wife then, as I am now. It was a bitter draught for him to swallow then and I am sorry that such humiliation must come to him a second time – apart from other matters.'

Stephen nodded understandingly. 'The Hait episode casts no shame upon you, lady. De Windsore is not to be admired if he adds that to his list of reasons for spurning you. Better that he had sought out this Hait and challenged him.' His voice suddenly wavered with emotion. 'If it had been I, I would have gladly lost every drop of my life's blood on the tourney field for the sake of your honour.'

As if embarrassed by this outburst, Stephen dropped his eyes. 'As for your kinsman, this Owen, I am not blind. That was the love of your life and though I can have no regard for him save as a royal prince and a brave warrior, I am sorry that the grief you felt at parting was a grief that can never be healed by any other man.'

Nest stepped nearer and took Stephen's hand affectionately. 'As you have little cause to love my Owain, neither can I be enraptured about the French who have ravished my homeland. But you, Stephen, are a true friend and my only anchor in these shifting sands that are called life.'

The castellan of Kerdigan rode out of Cairdyf feeling as if he had two hearts in his breast, leaving Nest to sew in her window until the next time her royal lover should canter into the outer bailey.

Nest had been at Cairdyf for some seven months when Henry braved the winter mud and slush to visit her in the New Year of 1115. His coming had been announced this time a sealed letter to her, borne the previous day by a troop of soldiers on their way from Gloucester to Carmarthen.

Nest was expecting him when he arrived late on a filthy night. She had dressed with particular care in the finest gown that she possessed. Her wardrobe had increased in number and quality, thanks to Mabel's gifts of fine silks and linens, which she had brought on a brief visit from her French states.

Rhiannon had spent long hours with comb and tongs, dressing Nest's raven tresses and crowning them with a thin gold headband to keep her veil in place. This extra care was for a special and saddening purpose. Though Nest was not in love with her royal master, she respected and admired him, both for his magnificent virility and his unmatched regality. Though Owain, still her only love, could equal the first attribute – and with his youth, even surpass it – that same youth robbed him of the august magnetism that Henry Beauclerk possessed.

This affection and respect, containing everything but the mysterious magic of love itself, was precious to Nest and tonight she knew it must come to an end.

After the late evening meal, they went as usual to Nest's chamber. Unsuspecting of the approaching finality, Henry kissed his mistress with his usual expertise and between kisses removed Mabel's finery and destroyed Rhiannon's patient work with her hair.

Eventually they lay naked between the heavy blankets and rugs of the bed, sheltering from the January winds that sought the cracks in the shutters. When all passion was spent and they lay trembling but quiet, Henry pushed his lips against her ear and kissed it.

'Tonight you surpassed yourself, my love. Perhaps you have been visiting some old dame for some invigorating potion?' he teased idly.

Nest smiled wanly into the darkness. 'I have been visiting some old dame, sir, but she was skilled in things other than love potions.' He gave a sleepy, questioning grunt. 'It was a midwife, Henry. I am with child again. Your child

– a royal one.'

She felt his arms stiffen, then relax again. He sat up straight in the cold air of the chamber and spoke to the gloom.

'It had to happen, Nest, it was but a matter of time. You were built to be the mother of many and neither am I any laggard in fertility.'

They were silent for a moment. There was no constraint between them, only a calm acceptance of the inevitable.

'What is to be done, sir?' Nest slipped back into a formal address now that they were speaking of practical matters.

'How far are you gone, dear one?' Henry slid back under the clothes and put a strong arm about her shoulders.

'Well into the third month. I suspected it some time ago, but waited until it was beyond doubt.'

Henry laid his head against her soft hair. 'This will be my fifteenth child and I know that it will be a son,' he mused. 'It must have a good home and no better upbringing could be found than the one you could give, Nest.'

'But I have no home, only that which you have provided these past few years.'

The King kissed her neck below the black tresses. 'Then you shall have your old home back again. My son will be a fitzHenry and half a Norman. I shall acknowledge him fully and be damned to my Queen and old Anselm. He shall live in your Wales, but have a Norman upbringing.'

Nest failed to see what was meant at first.

'Back to Din-geraint…Kerdigan?'

Henry shook his head on the pillow.

'No, Nesta – Pembroke.'

It was Nest's turn to sit bolt upright, heedless of the icy draughts on her naked body. 'Pembroke! You know that is impossible!'

'Impossible?…nothing is impossible. I am the King,' he retorted with a trace of irritation.

'But Gerald…he has rejected me, disowned me these four years.'

Henry turned over with a bounce and thumped the pillow under his head. 'Then he had better learn to accept you again…and that quickly, if he knows what is good for his neck.'

Nest subsided slowly on to the linen alongside the King and stared up at the night-shrouded rafters.

'You would command him?'

'I do command him…as soon as a messenger can reach Pembroke,' snapped Henry. 'You know well enough that your dear husband owes his position, his wealth, his very life, to me. I usually have little patience with underlings who array themselves alongside traitors…only your intercession, years ago, saved de Windsore.'

Nest's mind was whirling. She had expected nothing like us. Discreet banishment to some obscure outpost was the usual reward of a pregnant royal mistress. Pembroke, though remote, was certainly not obscure, being one of the most important royal castles and a place incessantly visited by ships from the western coasts of both Britain and France. She suspected that Henry wished to rub Gerald's nose in the dirt a little, to remind him once again of his proper place in the Norman hierarchy.

But it meant home...the nearest to a permanent home that she could ever hope for now, with Owain unattainable and her Welsh contacts shattered by time and events. But Pembroke – which almost certainly meant Caer Rhiw as far as she was concerned – would have her first children within sight and sound and Henry's child to nurture for some years at least. Even little William, the innocent result of rape, would be in the locality...only Llywelyn, the sole love-child, would be absent.

She was almost afraid to believe that this could actually happen. 'Will Gerald agree, sire?' she whispered again.

Henry snorted. 'You are going home to Pembroke, Nest, to have my son. De Windsore can stay on there either as castellan or rot in one of his dungeons. I am not particularly concerned which he chooses.' He slid a hand on to her bare stomach and held it there. 'I thought that familiarity would breed indifference,' he murmured, 'but once again I find it thrilling to know that a new part of my body and soul is growing within you.' He turned and kissed her again. 'I am very glad, Nesta. Our affair had a short time to go, as Matilda is growing suspicious again. It is good that I have left you something for you to remember me by. And on my part, I am proud to have a son from you. He will be one of the best and shall have preferment while I live...would that he was not to be another bastard!'

He spoke the last words with a deep bitterness and Nest sensed his frustration that he had borne only one legitimate son. In days when hold on life was so uncertain, both from war, accident and disease, it was a near disaster for a King to have only one male heir.*

'You are certain it will be a son, sire?' she whispered.

'Of course! I may not have your Celtic foresight, Nest...but I know this child will be a boy. We shall call him Henry for you to know the special regard I hold for his mother.'

Nest's mind worked quickly. Henry was in a magnanimous mood and this might well be the last time she would ever see him alone.

'Henry, my master, I promise to do all in my power to raise your child as you would wish. Will you grant me a favour in return, as we both know that we shall never again lie together?'

Cautious as ever, the King gave a qualified answer. 'If it be reasonable, Nesta. What do you wish?'

'Owain, my kinsman. He has been unjustly accused by Lord Richard of London and has fallen foul of your wrath.'

Henry groaned. 'My God, girl...you are in my bed, with my child inside you and yet your mind still swings like a lodestone to that wild and unruly prince.'

* *William, his heir, was in fact drowned in the 'White Ship' disaster five years later.*

He pinched her thigh, hard enough to hurt, but she sensed that he was still in an amiable mood.

'Sire, you have said yourself that he has a certain charm even in your eyes, though he has so often been your adversary. All I ask is for you to nurture that charm and take him into some position of trust, so that this unending bloodshed that ruins our land may cease.'

Henry gave a loud sigh of mock exasperation. 'She asks me to forgive my enemies, Oh, God! You should have been a nun and a saint into the bargain, Nesta. You ask me to take your last lover and make him my squire! Or would you prefer to have him Chancellor or Justiciar of England, this bold and arrogant Welshman?'

She smiled secretly, for she knew she had succeeded. 'Owain would be no pretty court ornament for Windsor or Westminster, Henry. I mean that you should ask him to lead a troop of Welsh soldiers to your wars in Normandy. You know better than I that none in Europe can match Welsh archers and nowhere will you get a more dare-devil captain for them than Owain ap Cadwgan. I would but weld his loyalty to you, for I know that he admires you, Norman though you are. And with him at your side, your French wars would be won in half the time.'

Henry, now a soldier again and already forgetful of his new prospective fatherhood, mulled over her suggestion.

'Please, Henry...my last and only favour,' she said in a low voice.

There was a moment's silence, then he smacked her hip under the coverlets. 'So be it, Nesta! The Lord Christ said that one must turn the cheek and forgive thine enemies. This man of yours, who has sorely tried me over the years – I will take him, if he will come. Sleep now, Nesta, before you persuade me to knight him!'

In the morning, the King galloped off for the east and a messenger left for Pembroke, in the far west.

CHAPTER FOURTEEN

JUNE, 1115

NEST was near the time for her confinement when her brother first came to Caer Rhiw.

She had heard rumours, even when isolated at Stephen's castle at Dingeraint, that Gruffydd ap Rhys had returned to his native land. Out of fear for his safety she had made no attempt to communicate with him, though Rhiannon, her ears and eyes ever to the Welsh ground, assured her that Gruffydd was in hiding in the depths of Cantref Mawr.

He had slipped ashore some time in the thirteenth year of the century but for eighteen months had been reluctant to come out into the open. There was good reason for his caution, Nest had thought, as he had been deprived of his inheritance by the Normans and was fortunate to have escaped the fate of poor little Hywel, who was crippled for life.

As the months went by, a year, then almost two without signs of his being hunted down, the heir of Prince Rhys ap Tewdwr became bolder and began to travel about in both Deheubarth, his father's old kingdom, and in Gwynedd, where he was said to be seeking after a wife.

Until Nest returned to the unwilling bosom of her husband, she had heard nothing of her brother, but in the hot, early summer of 1115 a messenger arrived from the court of her uncle Rhydderch at Dinefwr. He carried a letter from Gruffydd asking if he might enjoy the hospitality of Caer Rhiw.

Nest had last seen him at her wedding and yearned for another sight of him, the brother who was so close to her in childhood. She was hungry for a taste of family companionship that was so much a part of the Welsh way of life.

She bid the messenger from Cantref Mawr wait until the next day, then hurriedly wrote another message, politely requesting her husband to attend on her to discuss a matter of some importance. This note was sent from Caer Rhiw within the hour, going the few miles to where Gerald de Windsore insisted on living separately in his beloved castle on the great rock of Pembroke.

This peculiar domestic arrangement had been adopted by the castellan when he received the royal command to take back his pregnant wife. In a single stony interview, the white-faced, tight-lipped husband made it clear that he was going to do the absolute minimum to fall in with the King's instructions.

Nest was to live at Caer Rhiw and never to darken the doors of Pembroke except when some unavoidable public function demanded that he made some show of appearing alongside his spouse.

Gerald never visited Nest unless there was pressing business connected either with the fabric of Caer Rhiw or the children. The daughters and little David lived with Nest, the elder boys with their father at Pembroke or at Maenor Pyr. Once, Angharad had a severe fever and a bloody flux. Fearing for the girl's life, Nest sent for the father, who sat immobile at the bedside for some hours, hardly uttering a word, until signs of recovery allowed him to escape. Matters concerning the actual buildings of the house at Caer Rhiw forced him to appear on two other occasions, but he had disposed of even that slight aggravation by installing an efficient Flemish steward.

This time, she felt that Gruffydd's request could only be met after Gerald's approval. Though she felt nothing for her husband, neither hatred nor contempt, she stubbornly clung to the convention that whilst she was under his protection and in his house – though it had been her own dowry gift – she was beholden to ask his leave to invite guests to stay within its walls.

Late that evening Gerald rode up to the court on the peaceful river bank and sullenly greeted her in her bower, which faced the grassy courtyard.

He tried not to look either at her face or at the great swelling beneath her gown, which concealed the royal child.

Gruffly, he muttered words which asked the reason for her message. Nest looked up calmly, almost pityingly, at his tortured profile.

'My brother Gruffydd asks us to give him shelter for a while. He has been with my uncle Rhydderch ap Rhys at Dinefwr and desires to visit me. I wondered if you have reasons why this might be objectionable?' She spoke gently, unable to return hatred towards this strange man who had treated her with such unremitting humiliation and contempt for so long.

The Sheriff of Pembroke stared over her head at the blank wall above them.

'I have no quarrel with your brother, madam. He has stayed with me before – he can come again if he so desires.'

Nest's eyes opened wide with genuine astonishment.

'He has stayed with you, Gerald? When was that?' she asked incredulously, her surprise driving away her awareness of the strain between them.

'He was in Pembroke when…when you were…were away.' Gerald's voice faltered, the impediment in his speech, which had come with the twitch of his mouth, disturbing his words 'He has been back from Ireland these…these last two years, almost. He came to me at the first, seeking you. I gave him a bed and some meat for…for some weeks.'

'You never mentioned this before, sir…and he is my brother!' Her voice shook now with mixed indignation and surprise.

Gerald made no reply for a moment and jerked his riding mantle across his chest as if to leave. Then he suddenly addressed the rose bush a yard to the left of his wife. 'I was beholden to him for help when I visited Ireland at the turn of the century. Though he was but a youth then, he was reasonable when I sought his sister as a wife.' The wooden face suddenly distorted and he shook with angered self-pity. 'Though why in God's name I should now be grateful to him for that act, I cannot tell!' He shouted the words, looking at his wife for the first time. 'Have you any other business with me, lady?'

Nest shook her head, her eyes filling with tears in spite of herself. 'None, sir. Your daughters are well, though you did not ask. I know that William and Maurice are in good health, for they called yesterday, to take David riding.'

She gave this family report with a bitterness that matched Gerald's usual contemptuous disdain, but it was lost on him.

He turned sharply on his heel, so that his dark cloak flung out like a great wing, and strode away to the gate without so much as a backward glance.

As Nest heard the hooves thudding across the soft turf towards the road, she signalled Rhiannon, who was waiting in a doorway opposite, her paling face creased with dislike for the man who so mistreated her mistress.

'Rhiannon, fetch the messenger from Dinefwr.' It was good to slip back into Welsh after crossing French words with Gerald. 'He can ride at dawn with an invitation to my brother Gruffydd…It will be good, Rhiannon…so good to see him again, this time in Wales.'

Nest and her brother had a feast of talk, which lasted a whole week after his arrival at Caer Rhiw.

She cried at the joy of seeing him – partly because now, at twenty-nine, he so strongly resembled her father, the great Rhys.

Tall and slim with rather pointed chin and the same black hair that so many of the family possessed, Gruffydd was the reincarnation of the man who had died so gallantly at Brecon Gaer twenty-two years before. Rhydderch, their uncle, also had the same look, but there was a strength in Gruffydd's face that the Lord of Cantref Mawr just missed possessing.

Though Nest had been in Ireland with Owain for many months, she had not met Gruffydd there, as he had been staying in Wexford, whilst they were guests of Murketagh O'Brien in Dublin.

There was so much family talk, saddened by that about Hywel, their younger brother, whom Nest had not seen since infancy.

'I have sent to him these five months,' said Gruffydd as they sat talking in their favourite spot, the sunlit bower. 'I have told him that it is safe to return, but I have had no word yet. He was in a priory in Amorica when I last had news of him.'

'Has he taken Holy Orders?' asked Nest sadly.

'I think not. It was just a place where such as he might have sanctuary, as he is unable to work or even look after himself properly.'

Their brother, born two years before the death of their father, had been maimed and castrated at the age of seventeen when attempting to escape from Baldwin's castle, where he had been imprisoned since the time of Brecon Gaer.

'Is he much deformed, our poor Hywel?' asked Nest.

'I hear that apart from losing his members, the French hamstrung his legs so that he can barely walk. They also performed their favourite trick of striking off the thumbs and first fingers of each hand, so that he could neither hold a sword nor draw a bow to fight his tormentors.' His handsome face hardened at the thought. 'No wonder the generous French let him go the following year…he is hardly a danger to their armies now.'

Gruffydd's voice held a tone which surprised Nest. It contained more than anger for a brother's agony. There was a steely bitterness and resolution in it, that reminded her of her own loved one, Owain. Here was a man who was going to do something about the state of affairs, not merely sit and mope about the past glories of Deheubarth. She felt excited and afraid at the same time.

The impression that Gruffydd was back in Wales for a real purpose was strengthened during the following weeks, as he stayed on at Caer Rhiw. At night, furtive figures slipped into the courtyard and talked behind his chamber door until the small hours of the morning. Then her brother took to melting away for days on end, offering no explanation or telling of where he had been.

On one occasion he was gone for two weeks, this time admitting that he was off to Gwynedd to see Gruffydd ap Cynan, the veritable warrior of the North. When he returned, full of high spirits, he announced that he had successfully negotiated for the hand of Gwenllian, the old prince's daughter.

Immediately after his return Nest was brought to child-bed. Though it was her eighth birth, she found that the process did not get any easier with repetition. For a week she was weak from loss of blood, but the fateful fever did not strike and within a month she was back to normal.

As the King had confidently forecast, it was a boy – a strong little babe with nothing about him to mark either her features or those of his illustrious father.

Gerald stayed utterly aloof, neither sending a messenger nor attending himself to ask if she was in need of anything. Though in practical terms this was unnecessary – as every event in Caer Rhiw was reported to Pembroke within hours – it was the patent disdain that angered Nest so much. Henry had commanded Gerald to take her back, yet apart from the proximity of the two castles, she might as well be in Rome or Babylon as far as her husband was concerned.

She knew that this was not what Henry had intended. He wished for a home for his child, not just a roof over his head. He would want little Henry, when older, to have the company of other Norman lads, like William and Maurice and David.

Nest knew that if she sent a message to the King on this score, his retribution would descend on Gerald within a week, but her own pride and nature forbade her from returning evil with evil.

Nest sent news of the birth to the King via Gloucester, as well as to Mabel fitzHamon. Within the month, messengers returned from both with birth presents. From Henry there was a warm letter, confirming his wish that the babe should be named Henry fitzHenry. He further commanded that as soon as the child was six months of age, he should be brought by his mother to

Gloucester, where his royal father would come to see him for the first time.

The letter had come from Normandy, where the King was waging his endless war. A mischievous footnote read – 'Your plea and advice concerning our mutual friend Owain has proved fruitful. When he fights, it is as if the rampant lion on his shield comes to furious life! For my part, Nesta, I shall keep my promise and send your lion home as an English knight.'

Her heart beat faster just to see Owain's name written on a piece of parchment. She had heard nothing direct from him since they had parted. It was now almost a year since she had heard any news of little Llywelyn, now almost five years old.

Gruffydd was with her when she read the royal letter.

'Why do you tremble, sister?' he asked gently. 'Does the King of England, chief of our oppressors, mean that much to you?'

She smiled at him through misted eyes. 'It is Owain…Owain ap Cadwgan, our cousin. He went with Henry to France and the King has promised to make a knight of him.'

Gruffydd snorted, 'A fine reward for the Prince of Powys! Why does he go crawling after the leader of the Normans? He spent years fighting them more ably than any man since our own royal father, then he turns around like a dog and licks the spear that wounded him.'

Nest bridled at his words. 'That spear has been brandished for too long in our lands, Gruffydd ap Rhys. Ever since we were children, we have been hounded and harried, living with the stench of war in our nostrils. If you go to Ceredigion, you will see nothing but the ashes of homesteads, devastated fields, widows and orphans!' She rose from the chair in her room and went to the open window. 'Look out there, Gruffydd…look at our poor Wales. The land is like a desert north of here. We may be a great sport for a few armoured hot-heads, but is it so funny for the farmer and the herdsman who sees his crops ruined, his flocks destroyed, his women ravished and his children slaughtered or sold into slavery?'

Gruffydd glowered at her back. 'You, too, are going soft, are you, my sister? The easy Norman life has seduced your spirit and dried up the blood of Rhodri Mawr that runs in our veins. Don't tell me about war, Nest, I've spent a lifetime hiding from this race that maimed my brother! Our father kept them back, it was fools like your Owain's father and idiots like our uncle Rhydderch who opened the floodgates. But the time is coming when the tide will begin to run the other way!' he added darkly.

Nest swung around and looked at him keenly. 'What are you plotting, Gruffydd? Are all these comings and goings at night and your liaison with Gruffydd ap Cynan part of this scheming?'

The brother looked at her as if appraising her discretion. 'You are still the Princess Nest ferch Rhys, my sister – not Lady Nesta de Windsore! If the need arose, I am sure you would be like my wife-to-be, Gwenllian. She declares that if someone would only give her a sword, she would ride to battle alone against the French!'

Nest stared at him. 'And what battle do you think of attending, then?'

He gestured impatiently. 'The time is not yet ripe. When I came from Ireland two years ago, I had not thought of revolt. I was weary and wanted to see this kingdom of heaven that is Wales…the kingdom that should have been mine. But since I have been in Dyfed and Cantref Mawr, scores of young men have come to me secretly, then openly, imploring me to take up my patrimony and restore the Kingdom of Deheubarth.'

Nest sniffed, but in spite of herself, something stirred deep in her breast at the mention of her ancient kingdom. Aloud, she said, 'Silly hot-heads! They will end up without their thumbs and members, too.'

Gruffydd ignored her, pressing on with a gleam of fervour now in his eyes. 'Even Rhydderch has the glimmering of ambition in this direction, though he is so cautious, like an old man in his dotage. But we can do without him. Preparations are being made. Men and arms are being gathered in the deep woods and the wilds of Cantref Mawr, Emlyn and even Cantref Bychan…throughout Ystrad Twyi, the old fire is being re-kindled. I had hoped that this Owain of yours would have added his fire, but it seems that he has been seduced by this smooth-tongued King of yours.'

'He's not *my* King!' retorted Nest sharply. 'I am his ward – and as is well known, was his mistress, though from circumstance and necessity, not choice.' She doubted that herself, but pressed on with her defence of Owain. 'What chance has a band of barefoot boys, fighting the armed might of the barons? Owain tried for years, as you say, but at length maturity made him see that he was only prolonging the agony of his people. What can you hope to gain, when he failed?'

Gruffydd leaned forward eagerly. 'We have what Owain had five years ago, Nest,' he said fervently. 'We have the will to win back our homeland – no price is too high for that.'

Though Gerald did all he could to convince the world – and himself – that he had no wife, there were certain occasions when no amount of pretence could prevent him acknowledging Nest's existence.

Towards the end of that year of 1115, when Nest had regained her figure after the birth of little Henry, there was a great feast at Pembroke, attended by the most illustrious in the land – only the King's absence in France prevented it from being a most royal occasion.

Whether he liked it or not, Gerald had to produce his wife for the feast and swallow his pride and humiliation.

The reason for the celebration was the installation of the first Norman Bishop to the See of Menevia. The last incumbent, Galfridus*, had recently died, much mourned by the Welsh. To their bitter disgust, King Henry – in effect, the Queen and Anselm – had contemptuously brushed aside their choice

* *or Wilfred.*

of a native successor and appointed Bernard of Normandy, the Queen's chaplain, in his place.

Though Henry's grant was made on September 19th, it was mid-November before Bernard arrived by sea at Pembroke, en route for his ceremonial induction at the ancient cathedral of St. David's, on its rocky peninsula twenty miles to the north.

The King had sent detailed orders for a great feast to be held two nights before the induction. Barons and nobles from all over England and the Marches congregated at Pembroke and the royal castle was ready to throw its greatest party since the days when the Montgomerys held the fortress. Gerald, as castellan and sheriff, was the reluctant major-domo of the whole affair. Three days beforehand, he made one of his rare appearances at Caer Rhiw.

A thick mist was swirling over the tidal marshes outside and Nest was confined to her chamber next to the bedroom where Angharad was contentedly rocking the cradle of the slumbering fitzHenry.

The house of Caer Rhiw, in its first stone version as built by Gerald, was a simple square enclosing a courtyard.

It was into this yard that Gerald de Windsore rode on that November afternoon, to set in train the fateful chain of happenings that were to close the most tragic part of Nest's eventful life.

The steward rushed from his dwelling to seize the castellan's bridle as de Windsore dismounted, his escort remaining under the arch of the gateway.

Gerald, with only a light chain corselet over his tunic, strode off through the wreathing mist towards the main living quarters. He marched through the deserted hall and up the spiral staircase at the back, his spurs clinking and the tip of his scabbard banging on the unyielding treads.

Nest heard him coming through the oaken door and hurried to open it for him. Though she was by no means thrilled to have his company, she was still his wife – also, a feminine curiosity made her hasten to discover the reason for this surprise visit.

Gerald stooped to enter the doorway. He wore no helmet, only the hood of his light armour covered his head, but the small passage-like entrance made him bend as if bowing to her. She dropped briefly to one knee, then rose quickly.

'You are welcome, Gerald,' she said steadily. 'Will you sit at the window?'

He shook his head curtly. 'I come only to ask you to attend at Pembroke the day after tomorrow, madam. There is a feast in honour of Bernard, the new bishop, and it is fitting that you should be at my side.'

Her eyes opened wide. She had heard of the celebration, but had not expected to be drawn from her exile because of it. Social events were a thing of the past for her, so she had thought.

'Do you wish this, Gerald?' she asked, wondering if this was some awkward first gesture at a reconciliation.

'The King will expect it,' he grated, his taut face flickering with a fleeting trace of emotion. 'There will be many Marcher Lords and other nobility, all with their ladies. It is necessary that you appear at my elbow – just for that evening,' he added with cruel and unnecessary candour.

Nest felt as if her face had been slapped, but she gripped her lip between her teeth and tried to dam back the tears of angry shame that welled up.

'You make yourself very plain, Gerald,' she said bitterly.

He looked at her with his pale, cold eyes, his mouth twitching grotesquely. 'As plain as you were to me, more than once, lady – though you did it with actions, not words.'

This was the nearest that he had ever come to actual recrimination. As if flayed by his approach to emotion, he swung around and started for the door again.

'Our daughter is well, Gerald,' she said with defiant sarcasm, determined that he should not leave without being reminded of his lack of fatherly interest.

He stopped, turned slowly and looked back at her. 'And so is your new son, no doubt,' he sneered.

She flushed scarlet, unable to help herself. Once more he turned for the door and if she had had a knife, she would have plunged it into his back, heedless of the steel links that lay under the dull green surcoat. Seething with shame and anger, she watched him stoop again to leave.

Then for the second time, he turned around and straightened up. 'Another matter comes to my mind, lady. Is this brother of yours still in this place?'

She stared at him, taken off balance by this sudden shift of topic.

'I have had many disturbing reports of this Gruffydd,' went on de Windsore, harshly. 'He has been causing unrest and discontent among the Welsh in Ystrad Twyi and elsewhere…he is no longer welcome in my house.'

Nest thought of the furtive nocturnal messengers that came when Gruffydd arrived and the many mysterious trips that he made himself.

'Why should it disturb you, sir…your compatriots long ago made sure that he had no lands, no armies to be a threat to your conquest.'

Gerald looked at her with scathing dislike. 'I am the castellan and sheriff of Pembroke, madam – anything that may break the King's peace here is my business. I ask you, have you seen your brother lately–do you know where he is?'

She returned his stare with equally haughty contempt. 'I have not seen him these past three weeks. I have no notion of where he might be, and if I had, I doubt that I would tell you. You were willing enough to offer him hospitality in the past – are you turning against him now, as you have turned against others even nearer to you?'

Gerald refused to answer directly, but threw a last warning shot. 'Your foolish kinsman seems to be attracting too much attention to himself. If he thinks that he is going to raise a rebellion against your King, he had better tread softly.'

Gerald deliberately accentuated the 'your' when he mentioned Henry, but before she could think of a suitable retort, he had turned swiftly and clattered down the stairs with no further hesitation. As the sound of horses' hooves thudding on wet turf faded into the distance, Rhiannon came out of the bed-chamber, where she had been keeping Angharad company.

'*Arglwyddes*, I could not help hearing what he said about the Lord Gruffydd. I have a great fear in me for your royal brother.'

Since de Windsore had rejected Nest, her maidservant had refused to refer to him by name – he was always either 'him' or 'the castellan'. When Gerald appeared, Rhiannon refused to stay within sight of him. After so many years with Nest, the usual relationship of mistress and maidservant had become blurred and Nest would have felt as if she had lost an arm if the faithful woman ever went away. She listened to her as the girl went on.

'In the kitchens and market place I have heard much of the Lord Gruffydd these past few months – especially so when I went to visit my kindred in Cantref Mawr. Many young men look to him as your father's spirit, come back to restore the House of Deheubarth and drive out the French, whom surely the devil himself must have sent upon us.'

Nest heard this confirmation of her suspicions with concern. 'Is this notion of rebellion a real thing, Rhiannon, or but the yearnings of dreamers who sit whittling at twigs?' She walked to the window and stared out at the drifting fog coming up the haven. 'Gruffydd has never said anything to me about raising a rebellion, only vague longings about our old kingdom. Is he really collecting an army, Rhiannon?'

The servant nodded vigorously. 'There are many who hide in the forests, outlawed both by the French and by the Welsh tenants who fear the invaders, *arglwyddes*. They are scattered and ill-armed, but many in number. But even our own princes would join them and rise, if they thought that the others would help, especially old Gruffydd ap Cynan from Gwynedd. I hear that your lord brother is trying to persuade him, even to the point of taking his daughter to wife.'

Nest paced up and down before the mullions of her window. The further up the social scale, the less one knew of events, she thought bitterly. Her own maid was more abreast of local politics than she was herself. Gruffydd had made many threats and promises, but had never disclosed any concrete plans. A germ of excitement at the prospect of a new Deheubarth arising from twenty-two-year-old ashes fluttered in her breast, but fear for Gruffydd soon overpowered it.

'And this is now well known to the French?' she asked Rhiannon.

The servant-woman shrugged philosophically. 'All has been done in secrecy, at night and in distant glades. But traitors are as plentiful as heroes. The castellan seems to sense how the wind blows.'

'And is any date planned for a rising, I wonder?' mused Nest.

'I would not know, but the nods and secret smiles in the homesteads, and even on market days in Penbroch, tell me that something will happen soon.'

Nest was silent for some time, staring out into the mist. She turned at last and found Rhiannon moving awkwardly from foot to foot, as if she wanted to say something, but feared to broach it.

'*Arglwyddes*, I wondered, in this matter…what would the Lion of Powys do?'

Nest frowned. It was the very reason that she had been staring out into the blankness of the mist for so long – Rhiannon seemed to have penetrated her innermost thoughts.

'You mean, would he join with my brother against the French?' she asked bluntly.

Rhiannon nodded, looking both eager and uncertain as she tried to size up her mistress's reaction.

Nest sighed and toyed abstractedly with the gold pendant that hung around her neck. 'I do not know, girl. Owain fought for so long and was beaten in the end. Now he is Prince of Powys and rules with little interference as long as he acknowledges the King. How many times, Rhiannon, were Ceredigion and Powys ravaged by Norman and rival Welsh alike, because he persisted in fighting back? It is less than two years since he was last hounded from Powys into Eryri* at the point of ten thousand French and Scottish spears.'

Rhiannon scowled and muttered to hide her angry embarrassment. 'Some in the market place say that the Lion of Powys has been bought off with a Norman knighthood and no longer has the stomach to fight for Wales.'

Nest flared up at this, her face glowing with righteous indignation. 'If you think that with them, girl, you are a stupid fool! Has anyone, since my father Rhys, ever fought harder or longer for his people? God knows I have enough blood laid at my feet through love of Owain ap Cadwgan…but he is older and wiser now. He sees that it is better to lead Powys to peace, rather than have every man, woman and child put to the sword by continuing to fight against impossible odds.'

Rhiannon stared sullenly at the floor. 'Gruffydd ap Rhys does not think so,' she muttered in a surly voice.

Nest's anger evaporated as quickly as it had risen. She sighed and laid a reassuring hand on the maidservant's arm.

'Gruffydd has spent almost all his life in Ireland and has never lifted a sword in anger. He sees things as they should be, not as they really are.'

She had a sudden pang of fear and her previous daydreaming at the abstract thought of a new Welsh uprising turned to sheer horror at a mental picture of more burning homesteads, more slain men and mutilated women and children.

'God grant that my brother fails to even begin this venture,' she whispered.

But God granted not that the rebellion be prevented, but only that it be delayed.

Two nights later, at the great banquet in the hall of Pembroke Castle, rumours of a fresh uprising of the Welsh were being bandied about at the high table amongst some of the most exalted Normans in the land.

* *Snowdonia.*

Walter, the Chief Justiciar of Gloucester, Ranulf of Durham, who was the King's Chancellor and Bishop Richard of London had their heads together before too much wine had flowed.

They called Gerald de Windsore to them, from his place on a side table of the upper dais, where he sat stony faced alongside his incredibly beautiful, but utterly silent, wife.

He came to them and stood respectfully attentive behind their chairs, while they questioned him to add further local knowledge to what they already knew of Gruffydd ap Rhys' activities.

'This man is highly dangerous,' mumbled Gilbert fitzRichard, who slumped in a nearby seat. His illness had worsened and now he spoke and dribbled through a corner of his paralysed lips. He spoke of the son of the King whose territory in Ceredigion he had usurped, but his arrogant manner made it sound as if he was now being threatened by some new invader.

Walter of Gloucester, a full-bellied man with a deceptively mild face, added his news gleaned from the royal castle at Carmarthen, over which he kept a watching brief for the absent King Henry.

'It is not now a matter of secret words behind the trees in Ystrad Twyi,' he proclaimed in his rolling bass voice. 'There have been bold outcries, even in the town, and many more are reported in the surrounding countryside. They are already proclaiming this Griffith the new saviour. I have already caused word to be sent to Rhydderch ap Tewdwr, the fellow's uncle, advising him that if he wishes to keep his tenancy in Cantref Mawr – as well as his eyes and his members – he had better act with discretion and stop giving his nephew the shelter of his court.'

Richard, the vulturine Warden of the Marches, looked around the glittering company, now warming up under the influence of unlimited food and wine. The ecclesiastical throng, further down the high table, were laughing and joking with Henry's two sons, William, the legitimate heir and Robert of Gloucester, the bastard of whom ridiculous rumour had alleged to have been mothered by Nest.

The honoured guest and new incumbent of St. David's, Bernard of Normandy, sat in their centre, with Urban of Llandaf and William of Winchester on either side. Richard, though a bishop himself, sniffed scornfully. He was a soldier, who found it advantageous to wear holy robes in the exercise of his political power. But he despised these soft professional priests. There could be no help from them when the fighting started again – this Bernard was a boudoir creature of Queen Matilda's and Richard wagered that Henry had had little real say in his appointment. He turned to Ranulf, the man with even more power than himself under Henry the King.

'This Welsh brigand is in theory a ward of our Lord Henry, or should have been, if he had not slipped from Rufus' clutches when Neufmarche felled the father.' He shot a cold eye across at Nest, sitting isolated and withdrawn in her finery at the other table. 'There is the other ward of that campaign…a pity that our Lord Henry showed more interest in the daughter than in the son.'

Ranulf, a heavy-jowled, dark man, followed Richard's glance, then shrugged. He had little interest in local Welsh feuds. This was the first time that he had been dragged into Wales and he hoped that it would be the last.

'Have this Griffith slain, then, if he distresses you all so much,' he muttered disinterestedly.

Gilbert fitzRichard nodded, his palsied left side flapping as he struggled to turn in his chair. 'Yes...slay him!' he slobbered thickly. 'I want no upstart princeling aspiring to my lands!'

Richard of London beckoned the respectful Gerald to come near again from where he stood against the shields and tapestries that decorated the wall behind the dais.

'De Windsore, is this Griffith at present in Dyfed?'

'No one knows, my Lord Bishop. He vanished three weeks past – no one knows where he has gone to earth.'

Richard scowled. 'Then tell all your knights and garrisons in your shire to have their eyes sharpened for a sight of him. He had better be seized, not killed at sight, until the King's wishes be known.'

FitzRichard gave another nasty, lop-sided smile. 'No...keep him alive for the moment, de Windsore. After all, he is the brother of your good wife, to say nothing of being the uncle of the King's latest son!'

The evil shaft struck home and the two familiar spots of colour glowed again on Gerald's sallow cheeks. Yet his features remained expressionless. 'It shall be done at once, Lord Bishop,' he murmured, swinging away so that he need not look at the sneering face of Earl Gilbert.

'You try a man too hard,' murmured Ranulf, who, for all his lack of interest in Pembroke, knew well enough how matters stood between the King and the de Windsore family.

Gilbert fitzRichard spat clumsily on to the floor. 'A castellan without a Lord gets ideas above his station. It was different when Arnulf was here. I am not sure how far I trust this Gerald – I have heard that he received this Griffith as much as two years ago and gave him shelter until very recently. De Windsore was one of the Montgomery traitors...and with his wife the sister of this new rebel...' He turned again and looked across at where Nest sat, dressed in white silk with a gold girdle and a gold-trimmed cloth over her jet-black hair, this time braided up in true Norman fashion.

'It was her brother who aided these Montgomerys from Ireland, and helped Arnulf get the daughter of the Irish king for wife,' he muttered thickly. 'I distrust the whole affair.'

Richard drank his wine down and banged on the table for more. 'I have given a direct order for this Welshman's arrest. You must do the same when you return through Carmarthen tomorrow, Walter, as he is just as likely to be in those parts as here.'

Gilbert fitzRichard laughed moistly, wine running from the corner of his mouth. 'Excellent…excellent,' he slurred. 'The next time he bobs up to goad these natives to treason, we'll have him like a fox in a trap. With luck, he'll accidentally fall on a spear, trying to escape us!'

Two nights after the banquet, the misty weather gave way to a tearing storm that exploded from the Western Ocean and hurled itself upon the tip of Wales in a fury of wind and rain.

Nest had gone to bed, though it was only early evening. In the pitch darkness, with the wind making draughts that blew out the candle, there was no comfort in staying up longer. Rhiannon had settled little Henry for the night in the ante-room where she herself now slept, then secured all the shutters and jammed cloths into the cracks to keep out most of the rain. Her jobs done, she left Nest dozing in bed. The noise of the storm and the creaking and banging of doors and shutters through the building made it impossible to sleep properly, though she dozed off fitfully from time to time.

Nest had gone back to her old habit of sleeping naked between the warm coverlets of soft fur. With her head buried beneath these heavy wraps, she failed to hear the sound of hooves on the wet ground, as they competed with the scream of the gale.

But a few moments later, she had no chance to miss the crash of her door opening and heavy feet marching across the floor of her chamber. Half-awake, she raised her head above the coverlets in time to see a menacing figure appear in the arch of her doorway. The only light was from a dim, wildly flickering horn lantern above her bed, but the remaining slumber fell from her in an instant when she saw that the figure was Gerald, soaking with rain, his mantle clinging to him like a wet sack.

'Gerald, what brings you here? Is there anything wrong with the boys?' She sat up, clutching the bedclothes around her bare breasts.

Her husband advanced to the bedside, and though the light was so poor, she could see the pure hate in his eyes as he glared down at her.

'My sons are well, lady.' His voice quivered above the whistle and howl of the tempest outside. She suddenly knew what was wrong.

'You have come about Gruffydd,' she said steadily.

He threw off the soaking cloak on to the floor and wrenched the sodden leather hood from his head. 'Yes, I come about Gruffydd,' he snarled with cruel mimicry. 'And I come about a wretched wife who, not being content with being a whore and an adulteress, now has to try her hand as a traitor! You sent a warning to that damned brother…admit it or not, I know the truth!'

He was in a rage, showing more emotion than she had ever seen before. All the pent-up jealousy, shame and hate of the past five years was at last breaking through the dam that he had so laboriously built in his mind. She faced him with defiance, tossing back her disordered hair with a proud tilt of her head.

'Oh, I'll admit it, Gerald…I'll admit it with pride! He is my brother and he has been your guest. He has broken bread and drunk wine with you in your house…he did you good service in Ireland, and whether you like it or not now, he gave you a wife.' She sat bolt upright in bed now, quivering with excited anger. 'You are a slave to your masters, sir, but my loyalty lies with my kindred! Yes, I sent word to him after the feast. I was the one who told him to flee from you and Walter's men at Carmarthen. He has gone north, Gerald, to Gruffydd ap Cynan – well beyond your reach.'

De Windsore leaned over her, now in a healthy towering rage, such as he had not enjoyed for years. His hands opened and closed as if seeking her throat. Oblivious of the water which still trickled down from his drenched hair, he hissed meaningless oaths at her, the flood-gates of his hate now wide open. 'You are a bitch, woman…a thing from hell itself. Since we married, you have been a millstone about my neck. You whore!…with the King when I was in prison, then with that Welshman who so humiliated me…and Hait! Were you so ravished then, by Hait, or did you open yourself to him willingly, like all the others.' His gaunt face looked skull-like as he leant nearer to spit the words into her face. 'Then back to your royal lover, to make me a laughing stock in every Norman court, as you did in every Welsh one with that Owen! And now this final treachery…worse than any you committed with your foul body! Treachery against me and those I serve. Even your beloved Henry will not take kindly to this act of wantonness!'

Nest became equally as angry as her husband. She raised a quivering hand to point at him, the heavy furs falling away to reveal half her bosom.

'You French have had the best of one of my brothers…my Hywel, mutilated, castrated, ruined for the one life that God gave him on this earth. You shall not have the other son of Rhys my father! I heard two of your squires talking at Pembroke the other night, about the orders you had just given to seize Gruffydd. What would you expect me to do…turn my ear away, you fool! Husband, I am a princess of Wales first and a French concubine a long way second. Yes, I sent a message that night – it matters not how. And I would do the same again tomorrow – and every day of my miserable life, if it were necessary.'

Her eyes flashed and her voice rose, but suddenly she realized that she might as well have been talking to herself. Gerald was still there, but he was not listening. He was staring it her with a blank, yet almost crazed expression. His mouth vas open and his eyes were moving slowly from her face to her hair and then down to her exposed breast.

With sudden awareness she jerked the bedclothes up to her neck, but it was too late.

With a vicious jerk, Gerald whipped the covers right back to her knees, revealing her white body etched against the dark furs in the fluttering lantern light.

She squealed, and with a mixture of anger and fear fought to cover herself again. But with a moan that seemed to burst up from the bottom of his soul,

Gerald de Windsore threw himself on her, his cold, soaking clothes crashing down on her bare skin. His mouth clamped on hers and as she wriggled under him, he tore at his own garments in a frenzy.

When she managed to move her head aside, he began a sobbing monologue of curses and foul language, hardly intellgible, but obviously directed at her.

As she fought and squirmed, his hands made painful excursions at her body and once more she knew the bitter experience of a revulsion of the mind, but a yielding of the body.

Husband though he was, he raped her as harshly and thoroughly as had the drunken de Hait at Din-geraint. His heavy body bruised and ravished hers and though he was silent at the end, as soon as he lifted himself from her, his curses and blasphemies came back in redoubled viciousness.

As he pushed himself up from the bed, he began slapping her face with a hand made horny from the sword-hilt. Rhythmically he hit her and swore between each blow.

'You whore, you have done me harm so often,' he gasped, 'but this is the worst thing of all! I had sworn never to touch you, never to speak to you unless I must, never to kiss you, never to caress you for all time. Now you have made me do this…you have the body of a witch, you are the evil itself that divides a man's body from his soul!'

He struggled into his lower garments, scrabbled on the floor for his mantle, muttering and sobbing oaths all the time.

Nest lay battered and almost paralysed with fear. She knew that he was on the very edge of madness, if not already gone over the edge. Gerald angry, or aloof or contemptuous she could understand, but this sudden collapse of a man's mind was something that terrified her beyond measure.

Still muttering, he threw his cloak clumsily around his shoulders and with some return of coherence, stood for an instant with his eyes wild and haunted as he stared at her.

'I will do you harm, somehow, lady…to even this score,' he snarled, and stumbled away to the door.

Almost afraid to move in case he should return, Nest lay shaking on the bed until she heard a distant door slam in the howling wind. By the time a sleepy and bewildered Rhiannon put her head into the room, the sound of hooves again echoed faintly through the storm.

CHAPTER FIFTEEN

MARCH 19th, 1116

'HE is a fine child, Nesta...with you as his mother and I the sire, how could he be otherwise!'

Henry, King of England and Normandy, rested a strong arm across her shoulders and looked down at Henry fitzHenry, who drooled and gurgled contentedly in his wicker crib. The casual embrace of his parents was almost platonic. Two squires, Rhiannon and another lady of Gloucester Castle were in the room and Henry was treating his late mistress like a sister.

They walked slowly to the window embrasure, leaving a beaming Rhiannon to fuss over the swaddling clothes with pride almost as great as if she had borne the babe herself – her hatred of Normans stopped abruptly where any child was concerned, especially if that child belonged to her mistress.

Looking down into the bustling inner ward of the castle, Henry spoke in a pensive mood. 'I seem to have a surfeit of bastard sons, Nesta, all of them more sturdy than William, my only true heir. Yet he is all I have to entrust with the care of England.'

Nesta looked up at the side view she had of his strong face: her inexhaustible compassion flooded up for him. 'Why have you called this congregation today, sire? Surely you have no premonition of death in France?'

So used was she to her own sixth sense that she easily accepted that others might be equally fey, but Henry shook is head. 'I have none of your Celtic foresight, lady! But these are troubled times. My brother Robert of Normandy still yearns after the throne and I must make this public declaration today to put the seal on my William's right to this kingdom, if any stray arrow or lance comes my way in France.'

Nest was silent. She knew that he had already made his barons in Normandy swear fealty to young William and acknowledge him as the heir. But Henry was still not satisfied and had called the nobles in his English lands here to Gloucester, to make them bow to the same command. It was the eve of his return to France, from where he was not to return for over four years.

Nest secretly wondered whether he had summoned her to take little fitzHenry to the place where the barons were congregating or whether the reverse was true...whether he had made the great ones travel so far west instead of going to Woodstock, Winchester or London, as this was so much nearer for the infant son to travel.

At all events, he was using the occasion to clear up much business of state before leaving for the continent. The full extent of the business was yet to be made known to Nest.

Henry looked down again at Nest's supple figure and smiled wryly. 'I had reports after Bishop Bernard's consecration feast that you and de Windsore were married in name only…the man is a greater fool than I took him for!'

Nest flushed furiously and for a moment almost hated him, before reason told her that he could not have known what had happened on the night of the great storm. How could he know and so how could he avoid trampling so harshly on the tender raw edges of her sensibility.

'Speak nothing more of that man, sire,' she snapped. 'It is only the fear of you that stops him from doing me some great harm.'

Henry's face darkened suddenly. 'I heard tales from Pembroke, Nesta. It was you, then, that confounded de Windsore and Walter of Gloucester. I heard that that damned rebellion-maker had escaped us. I hope you are not proud to see what desolation he is making throughout your land?'

Nest was defiant, though her anger subsided with the King's sudden change of mood.

'He is my brother, Henry. Would you have me stand by and see him chained and blinded and hurt like your barons did to my other brother? You are the leader of those who took my father's lands…would you not have tried to regain them if you were he?'

Henry turned and walked abruptly across the room, unwilling to cross words with her. He looked down for the last time at his most recent bastard, then across the room at Nest.

'Lady, our lives are inextricably entwined. I have not forgotten that this latest rebel is your brother, but such feelings can have no place in affairs of kingdoms. If you have any communication with him, tell him to flee away to Ireland or Amorica as fast as his legs and ship will carry him, for today I have resolved to set an enemy against him who will most surely stop his marauding.'

Nest's chin jerked up defiantly. 'Gruffydd is the son of Rhys, my lord. He has the same greatness as that old warrior who was our father. What man can you send against him who is so surely bound to triumph?'

Henry moved towards the door, his squires scurrying before him. As he reached it, he turned and with an almost sad smile looked upon Nest for what they both knew was to be the very last time.

'What man, Nesta?' he repeated her words. 'A man who waits in the hall below, a man who has proved himself to both you and me that he is almost invincible…a man I took to France and knighted for his valour.'

Nest stared at him, her eyes wide. Her hand slowly stole up to her throat.

Henry nodded. 'Yes, my princess…yet another link in the chain which binds us. That man is the Lion of Powis…Owen ap Cadogan.'

* * *

In the great hall of Gloucester Castle, a large throng waited for the King. Groups of nobles, with satellite knights and squires, stood about, heatedly discussing the forthcoming campaign in Normandy or the current unrest in Wales.

Other smaller knots of men were weary litigants, hopefully following the King's court about the countryside, trying to get some civil dispute settled before Henry vanished overseas again for some unknown period.

The hubbub of talk was in four or five languages, from Flemish to Latin, from Welsh to Saxon and French. The babble was increased by the yapping of dogs chasing each other over the rush-strewn floor and the clank of armoured men moving up and down the steps to the great doors at the end of the hall.

The two elder sons of the King stood with their young bloods in the most splendidly arrayed group. William of Normandy, a tall pale youth, was to be the leading figure in today's proceedings, as he was to be accorded the fealty of all the barons present there. His illegitimate brother Robert, who lived much of the time at this very castle, was more sturdy and had the dark hair and skin of his mother, an un-named concubine of Henry's, who had died in childbirth.

In a corner of the hall a group of equally dark Welshmen stood uneasily, most of them a full head shorter than the surrounding Normans and Flemings. One of them stood out from the rest with his russet waves, and it was he who was nudged by his nearest companion.

'Brother Owain, is that Henry's elder bastard? They say he is the offspring of our cousin Nest.'

Morgan was unused to being in the company of Normans without a sword swinging in his hand and the novelty of standing unmolested in a royal castle made him acutely uncomfortable.

Owain, looking harder and older than the reckless brigand who had terrorized West Wales five years earlier, looked across the hall and snorted with derision.

'Morgan, you act like a swineherd on his first visit to a fair! How could a lad that size have come from our cousin's womb?'

Morgan's pride was pricked by his brother's patronizing manner, but he held his tongue. Owain had been moving in higher social circles these past few months, with almost a year in Henry's camp in Normandy, which ended with the touch of the royal sword on his shoulders. Morgan and his other brothers were none too pleased by this change of heart and would rather have seen the knighting sword being parried with an angry counterthrust.

Yet Owain had brought peace to Powys and already the homesteads were being built and the land giving out its bounty again. Derelict fields were tilled and new flocks had appeared on the uplands this spring. Compared to the smoking desolation and bloodshed of the last half decade, peace was a welcome novelty to the old kingdoms of central Wales, though the price of this subjection was lying uneasily on many of the princely line.

Morgan looked around at the swelling throng. 'Why have you been called all the way from Mathrafal for this purely French celebration, brother?' he muttered. 'Knight of England though you be, I feel that Henry could have had his brat acknowledged as our next oppressor without your presence being so vital.'

His sarcasm was lost on Owain, who was searching among the throng with his eyes. A few Norman ladies were scattered here and there, well chaperoned by their maids and companions, but the raven hair he sought was not to be seen.

Morgan had to repeat his words in less cynical tones before he could get a response from Owain.

'I am not here for William's sake, Morgan,' murmured his brother. 'The King wishes to give me some task concerned with Wales…that is all I know.' He turned to scan the crowd again. 'Have you seen any sign of Nest ferch Rhys, or that lumpy maid of hers?' He tossed his red hair, now grown longer in the recent fashion, as the Normans had long since given up shaving the backs of their heads as they did in the Conqueror's time.

Morgan picked his teeth morosely with a fingernail. He was bored with it all and felt a constant nag of resentment at loping around under a Norman roof.

The mention of Nest gave him something more pleasant to set his mind upon. 'You know that she is here, then?'

Owain nodded curtly. 'She has brought Henry's bastard for him to see,' he snapped.

Morgan whistled pensively through his teeth. 'Our cousin is a prodigious mother, Owain. That will be five children by de Windsore, one by Roger de Hait, your little Llywelyn and now this sprig from King Henry.'

His brother's face darkened in a hint of the old temper that he had learned to cool in France. But the listing of Nest's maternal achievements was no pleasure to him. 'None of those but my Llywelyn was born of her free choice, Morgan,' he rasped. 'She had only one love match, for all her fecundity.'

As they stood together uneasily on the rushes, a young Flemish squire pushed his way through the throng, picking the Welshmen out easily by their different physique and the plain, unadorned clothes of Morgan, who spurned his brother's adoption of Norman fashions.

'Sir Owen of Powis?' queried the messenger, looking at Morgan.

The dark brother jerked a thumb at Owain. 'There's your man – though I'd call him Prince Owain, if I were you… "sirs" are ten a penny here.' He jerked his head at the throng around them, but the Fleming only smiled blandly.

'The King wishes to see you in the antechamber, before the main audience and affirmation, sir. Will you follow me?'

Morgan strode behind Owain as they went to a small door at the side of the empty dais of the hall.

Inside, the King stood in greater finery than usual, drinking from a silver-banded horn, talking with Ranulf the Chancellor and Richard of London. Gilbert fitzRichard slumped on a chair, having just been assisted from a litter which stood in a corner. His paralysis was rapidly worsening and did he but know it, this was to be the last year of his quarrelsome life.

As the two Welshmen entered, Henry broke off his conversation and strode across the chamber towards Owain, his hand outstretched.

'Owen…Sir Owen, you are welcome.' His voice held genuine warmth.

To Morgan's annoyance, Owain dropped to his knee, though very briefly. When he rose, he gestured towards his brother.

'Sire, this is Morgan, of whom you have heard me speak in praise.'

Morgan made a surly and jerky bow, refusing to drop to any floor for a Norman. He sensed the antagonism in the chamber towards them both, only Henry seeming to have lost the enduring suspicion and hate that the two races felt for each other.

FitzRichard especially was glowering across the room with arrogant contempt written plainly on his twisted face.

The King took Owain by the arm and led him to the table, where a servant stood ready with wine. 'Come, drink and wash away the dust of England from your throats…it must be choking you, brother Morgan, by the surly look on your face.'

Henry grinned at Morgan and in spite of himself, the dark brother began to feel a grudging liking for this scheming Norman.

But Henry's next words were to strangle at birth any seeds of affection for the royal person.

'Owain, you have served me well in Normandy – will you serve me equally well in your own Wales?'

Owain wiped the wine from his lips and looked steadily at the man who had once been his enemy and was now almost his idol.

'When you laid the sword on me, sire, I swore fealty to you for life,' he answered simply.

Henry paused, as if searching for the right words.

'You know better than I, that Wales is on the edge of war once more. The son of old Rhys is rampaging through the south and west, stirring up quietened passions and opening old wounds.'

Morgan looked sharply at Owain, but the elder brother's eyes were on Henry, who continued to speak his mind.

'I had thought him no danger and allowed him to roam alone in Dyfed, in spite of his past dealings with the Montgomerys. But he became too restless and outspoken, Owain…but for yet another folly by that damned knight de Windsore, my orders to seize Griffith would have stopped all this trouble.' Henry's face darkened. 'Though I have heard that he was warned in time to escape to Griffith of Gwynedd…and we both know well the one who advised his flight!'

Morgan looked uncomprehendingly from one man to the other, as secret thoughts passed wordlessly between them. Two men, one king and one prince – bound by the ties of battle and one beautiful woman.

Owain stayed silent – he had nothing he wanted to say.

The King pulled himself together briskly. 'Thanks to the lesson I taught old Griffith of North Wales, two years ago, he was circumspect in receiving Rhys' son – even though his wayward daughter had promised to marry him. On my orders, Griffith was going to deliver the young fool to me, to keep him out of further trouble, but once more some treachery warned him off.'

Owain spoke at last. 'I heard of this, sire. He escaped to the church at Aberdaron and found sanctuary there until he slipped on board a vessel that took him back to Deheubarth.'

Henry shrugged impatiently. 'I care not how it was done. But since then this petty prince has been mauling my lieutenants all over the south-west. Castles at Narbeth, Llandovery, Swanzey, the Ystwyth, Blaenporth...all attacked and some razed to the ground. I even fear for my own fortress of Carmarthen and there I would like to have you in the company of my son Robert and his men, to drive this Griffith away. I will make Llywarch ap Trahearne a comrade for you there, too – another stern fighting man, as you only too well know! It is in you two that my hope lies in this matter – when you return, I will worthily repay you for it.'

Morgan, his temper rising rapidly, waited for his brother to repudiate angrily this outrageous suggestion of treachery. Then his own anger was suddenly switched as he listened incredulously to Owain's reply, as his brother straightened up and looked steadily at the King.

'It is hard for me to agree to stand against another of royal Welsh blood – and a kinsman into the bargain, sire. But partly for my debt to your own person, and mainly because I wish to see peace maintained in Wales, I will do as you request.'

Morgan, normally the least quick to anger, exploded in wrath. He grabbed his brother's arm and shook it violently. 'Are you losing your wits, man' he hissed. 'This is Gruffydd we are talking about – the brother of our Nest, the uncle of your own son! A man who has the steel in him to carry on the fight we began that night at Cenarth Bychan. Think, Owain...for God's sake, think!'

There were growls of anger from the Norman lords grouped around, who had followed every word that passed between Owain and the King. The guards at the door shifted uneasily and through his anger Morgan felt the hairs on his neck begin to prickle.

Owain shook his hand off impatiently. 'Morgan, let it lie...I know what I am about.'

Morgan, hopeful for the moment that Owain had some devious trickery up his sleeve, subsided into silence, but followed the rest of the treacherous talk with heightening mistrust as Henry continued.

'I have already appointed other Welsh chieftains to guard Carmarthen. Three of them are taking turns of two weeks a-piece at the castle. One is your kinsman by marriage, Rhydderch ap Tudor. He is uncle to this damned Griffith, but has no scruple as to where his first duty lies.' Henry glared pointedly at Morgan.

'How would you have me act in this affair, sire?' asked Owain woodenly. He had decided what he thought best for himself and his countrymen and was determined to carry it out to the letter, however unpopular he might become amongst his kinsmen and followers.

Henry tossed down the last of his wine and threw the empty horn to a hovering servant. 'Seek Griffith out and bring him captive to me – or rather, to Bishop Richard or Walter the Justiciar, as I will soon be over the sea again. If he runs far enough, let him run – to Ireland, preferably. But see that any support he now has is completely crushed. He is hiding in the forests of the Vale of Towy and is being supported by the folk that live there. You will send your hosts in bands into those woods and spare no person, neither man nor woman, boy nor girl. If his sustenance is deprived him, Griffith will be flushed out like a hare from a thicket.'

Owain flushed slightly. The hard, cruel details of such a campaign against his own folk were not to be swallowed without an effort.

'This is a painful instruction, sire. It was to avoid more despair among my people that I fell in with your commands.'

Henry gestured impatiently. 'If you fail to frustrate this rebellion, have you thought of the consequence? There will be another army in Wales, one from England, Scotland and Cornwall as before. Then more than a few forest folk will perish, Owain. The whole country will be in flames again – and as you can see, my barons are in a mood to extirpate the Welsh from the land and settle their own there completely. One has to trim the proud-flesh to avoid losing the festering limb, my friend.'

Owain capitulated with a sigh. 'I shall have Llywarch with me, you say – and your son Robert?'

Henry, knowing that he had won him over, smiled grimly. 'Yes – and a large force of Flemings under de Windsore. I shall send him to hunt for his erstwhile guest as a penance for all his past mishandlings.'

Owain's face set like a rock. 'De Windsore! I have no wish to consort with that man. We have a point of contention, as I am sure you know, sire!'

Henry's good humour returned in full flood, a wide smile creasing his face. 'You need not ride with him, as long as you ride not *against* him! Now go with that esquire there, who will guide you upstairs. There is a face there that you would rather gaze upon than mine.'

He dismissed them with another grin and turned to his barons. The two Welshmen left the chamber and outside the door a thunder-browed Morgan snapped at his brother, 'Yes, go tell your kinswoman that you have accepted a Norman commission to hunt down her brother and butcher a few score Welsh children...I'll see you back with the horses.'

With a final contemptuous glare at his brother, he turned abruptly and stalked angrily away.

* * *

In an upper room, Owain stood before Nest for the first time in four years and knew afresh that he loved her.

They looked at each other across the width of the chamber, each too full of emotion and whirling thoughts of things past, to break the moment with mere words.

To Owain, the woman looked lovelier than ever, her braided black hair framing the sweet oval of her face. He saw a woman more mature than he had last known, but more than ever before he saw the lover that had made almost two years of his life worth all the rest put together.

Nest, on her part, felt the old familiar trembling in her legs as her one and only man faced her. He, too, looked older and there was a tiredness and a hardness in him that she had never seen before. Yet this ageing only enhanced his attraction. His hair was longer and the russet shades showed even more strongly. He wore fine clothes in the Norman fashion, but in his confident, proud bearing, he was exactly as she had remembered him.

They were alone in the room, as Rhiannon had taken fitzHenry away and the ladies of the castle had retired. When their long appraising looks were satisfied, the two lovers started forward at the same instant and grasped each other's hands.

'Nest ferch Rhys, you are more lovely than ever,' said Owain, hoarse with emotion.

She smiled gently. 'Our lives touch again, Owain, my only love. But much has happened since we last saw each other.' She sighed and dropped her eyes. 'Things that must drive us apart again, I fear.'

Owain shook his impetuous head angrily. 'I have never married, Nest, because of you. All other women have lost their appeal these days. There is no call to talk of being driven apart. Come back with me to Powys, you have no need to return to Penbroch, if I hear the situation correctly.'

She shook her head sadly. 'That can never be, Owain. You are as bound by Henry's wishes today as much as you ever were at Shrewsbury, four years ago. And the wedge has been driven even deeper by the advent of little fitzHenry. It was because of him that the King sent me back to Gerald...the royal child must have a Norman home. I could not leave all my children again...not another time, Owain.'

Owain's eyes dropped and there was a stubborn sadness in his voice. 'Neither has little Llywelyn a mother, Nest. Why must the only child born of love be himself deprived of it?'

Tears welled up in her eyes in an instant. 'There are seven of my children living in Dyfed, Owain – for I even see little fitzHait now and then. Much as I love Llywelyn, how can I give up seven for one? He never knew me, he was too small when he went to your kindred.' She sniffed back the tears and ran a knuckle across her eyes. 'Do not ask the impossible, my love. And were I willing, you are too beholden to Henry to cross him again – you have some honour to think of, too.'

The mention of Henry and honour in the same breath suddenly brought back the recent memory of Morgan departing in furious anger. Owain abruptly dropped Nest's hands and stepped back a pace.

'Nest, I was never one to mince matters, nor to seek an escape for things I have done. I was called by the King today to perform a duty which is painful to me and may cause you not to wish to see my face before you ever again.' He took a deep breath. 'But if you will leave all and come to Powys with me, I will cut myself off from Henry and throw his knighthood back on the ground at his feet, whatever the cost.'

He spoke with deliberate harshness, implying that there would be only this one offer and one chance to accept or refuse.

Nest paled, suspecting what was coming, but she held his gaze steadily. 'I feel that I know what your task is, Owain – but tell me. I have to hear you telling me.'

He hesitated, then plunged.

'I am to seek out your brother Gruffydd and seize him or slay him.'

Suddenly, he lunged forward and pulled her almost violently into his arms, covering her with fierce kisses, on her face, her eyes, her neck, her lips. They were almost the actions of a man in a frenzy. When he paused to draw breath, he pulled her head against his shoulder and muttered desperately into her ear.

'Nest, until I saw you just now, my path seemed so clear. Gruffydd must be stopped or all Wales will be plunged into fire and bloodshed once again. I gave you up before so that there might be peace, but now your brother jeopardizes the balance that has been so painfully struck between Welsh and French. Yet, Nest, one look at the pain on your face and I am lost again.'

She twisted in his arms and returned his embrace and kisses with the desperation of one who knows that this is to be the last time. Twice this day she had known what it was to look finally on a man who had been both lover and a father to her child, but this time it was anguish such as she had never known before.

She pushed him to arm's length and with tears running like brooklets down her face, spoke through her sobs.

'Why must it be you, Owain. Henry is not a cruel man, not unnecessarily cruel. There are plenty who could be sent to frustrate Gruffydd – so why you?'

Owain smiled grimly. 'Plenty have been sent – and more will go besides me, Nest. That is the measure of the danger that your brother poses. I have brought this on myself by being too efficient in Normandy.' He laughed bitterly. 'I am the Lion of Powys, Owain the Valiant – knighted for foolhardy courage across the seas. Would that I were Owain the Craven, the Lamb of Powys…it would have saved me this, at least!'

She clung to him again and laid her head on his chest. 'You cannot hunt down Gruffydd…he is my brother, your kinsman, a Welshman as good as any alive. He is doing now what you were doing when I first met you. Do you think that he would have raised arms and sought you out to kill, if the rôles were reversed?'

He grasped her head gently and raised her face to his.

'Then come to Powys with me...now! I will defy Henry, raise a war-band and march to join Gruffydd. Nest, it must be done clearly, one way or the other. Wales cannot afford to bleed slowly yet again.'

He felt her shudder in his arms. 'No...no!' she sobbed into his chest. 'I have been the cause too often of waves of bloodshed and misery in my own land. There must be a curse on me, Owain,' she wailed, lifting her face again. 'Ever since Brecon Gaer, when my father died, the sword has followed me wherever I went. And how often since you came under the gate at Cenarth Bychan has fire and pillage swept Deheubarth! The peace which our father Rhys sought has been wrecked over and over again by his daughter – now his son is taking up the torch of violence!'

Owain shook her gently. 'What would you have me do, Nest?' he murmured in anguish.

'I do not know...I do not know, Owain. Let someone else be the instrument of my Gruffydd's downfall. Or let him have the chance to abandon his scheme. He could still obtain the King's pardon, as you have, more than once. He could slip away to Ireland, his second home.'

Owain released her with a sigh and they stood apart, suddenly strangers once again. 'It must be me, Nest. You say, once and for all, that you will not return with me to Powys to be my wife?'

She smiled wanly. 'I have been wife to so many, Owain – and still am wife in church and law to Gerald de Windsore, though there is hate between us. I cannot come,' she ended firmly.

Owain straightened himself and hitched his mantle over his shoulder in a gesture of finality. 'Then I will do all in my power to allow Gruffydd the chance of an honourable settlement – or to vanish to some sanctuary. That much I promise you, Nest. But I must carry out this commission for Henry, to scour Ystrad Tywi for those who succour Gruffydd. Perhaps if I flush out those sufficiently well, he will abandon his rebellion. I can do no more than that, Nest, not even for you, for whom I would venture more than anyone on this earth.'

She held out a hand impulsively and he grasped it tightly.

'This is farewell, Owain. Would to God that I were a purer woman – then I might look forward to a chance in the next life of being with you always.'

There suddenly seemed nothing further to say. Owain kissed her hand and swung out of the room without risking a backward glance.

Nest, her heart almost choking her throat, watched him from the window as he crossed the courtyard to go out of her life for ever.

CHAPTER SIXTEEN

APRIL, 1116

'WHAT do we do with these beasts, Lord Owain?' shouted Alun, his young squire, 'we are warriors, not cow-herds.'

Owain dropped his reins on to the saddle and pulled off his helmet to wipe his brow. A score of cattle milled around, lowing and stumbling at the edge of the river, where his ninety soldiers took the opportunity to drop their arms and paddle around in the clear waters of the Tywi, under the pretext of rounding up the calves and young cattle.

It was a month after the visit to Gloucester and the spring had suddenly decided to turn warm. For two weeks Owain, Morgan and Llywarch ap Trahearne had been dodging in and out of the dense woods of Ystrad Tywi, rounding up the peasants who were suspected of giving shelter and assistance to the forces of Gruffydd ap Rhys. So well had they harassed them, that a stream of refugees was filtering down the wide valley of the Tywi to Carmarthen, six miles away, preferring to camp under the inhospitable walls of their Norman adversaries than to risk the hanging or mutilation that Henry's Welsh agents had promised to any folk even remotely suspected of giving succour to the rebel son of Rhys ap Tewdwr.

Owain, knowing well the uselessness of large forces in the surrounding forests, had split his host into small groups of not more than a hundred men apiece. Morgan had one force and was reluctantly chasing down the broad vale towards this place where Owain was now waiting to rendezvous with him. Here, the main Tywi stream was joined by the little Cothi, the river that came down from the old Roman gold mines. The cattle had been seized from a group of fleeing peasants – as they had run away in a guilty fashion, Owain had taken the beasts as a salutary warning. Now he was hard put to know what to do with them.

'Let them stand in the water, Alun,' he commanded. 'The men may as well eat their mid-day bread, while we wait for the war-bands of my brother Morgan and Llywarch to join us. They said that they would be here at Ystrad Rwnws just after noon.'

Alun, the only other man with a horse, slid from his saddle and lay gratefully on the river bank, dipping water with his hands to quench his thirst. Downstream, the cattle had stirred up great clouds of mud, but above them the river was crystal-clear. Some of the men were merrily trying to dip trout from the shadowed pools against the banks.

Owain slid from his own horse and lay on the mossy turf, feeling in his pouch for bread, meat and cheese. He lay on his back and stared up at the white clouds scudding across the blue Welsh sky, seeing the face of Nest etched on every one.

He thought of his little Llywelyn back in Mathrafal. He was not a robust child, but his foster parents did all they could to build him up as befitted the only son of the Prince of Powys. The boy knew little of his mother, whom he never remembered – Owain felt a knot tighten in his breast as frustration overtook him. The eternal questions of what life was all about flooded over him...Why did he labour as he did, when all that happened was that he lost his love, had a child who knew no mother? He moved remorselessly towards the grave so that another generation could take over the endless task of playing out another series of fruitless lives.

The thought of Nest and little Llywelyn came back again to torture him. The twisted web of politics kept even a mother from her babe. If he were to take Nest back to Powys – and he thought that if he really forced the issue, she would have come – he would undo all the patient and often distasteful work with the Norman leaders that had achieved this balance of power – a balance which Gruffydd was within an ace of upsetting. It was all or nothing – either they rose as one man against the French and cast them out – or came to terms with them and ruled by proxy in Wales.

Morgan and Gruffydd were all for the former path, thought Owain moodily as he stared at the sky. And deep down, in his heart though not in his mind, he would like to have agreed with them. But it was impossible – until the Welsh were willing to forget their family feuds and unite, any rebellion was doomed to failure – a failure that would again ravish a countryside already weak from innumerable previous scourges. Better that a few should be put to the sword or chased to Carmarthen town with their mangy cows taken from them, than have unleashed upon them the madness that Gruffydd proposed.

Owain rolled over and sighed as he munched at his hard bread and tainted meat. Owain, though he would not admit it to Morgan, felt the urge to abandon this respectable rôle and throw in his lot with the rebels, however hopeless their mission. Indeed, he ought to lead the rebels, for he knew that he was a far better warrior than Gruffydd ap Rhys, who had hardly lifted a sword or a spear during all those exiled years in Ireland.

If he were to do this, the prize would not only be Wales, but Nest herself, the only woman he had ever wanted for more than a night's frolic.

But the risks were too great. He had felt himself grow older and wiser lately – that year in Normandy with Henry had aged him quickly and formed a vague yet compulsive bond with the King that stifled feelings of revolt.

His troubled mind was suddenly interrupted by a cry from young Alun.

'Lord Owain, there are men approaching in the distance.' Owain grunted, not bothering to take his eyes from his gloomy study of the clouds. It would be the band of either his brother or of Llywarch, his old enemy, coming down the valley to their rendezvous at the ford of Rwnws. He had arranged for all of them to join up here and march together to Carmarthen to meet Robert le fitzRoy – as Henry had recently taken to calling his eldest bastard.

The young man, though quiet and retiring, was an excellent soldier, especially in strategy, though he lacked nothing in courage. Henry had sent him down to the royal castle on the Tywi to gain experience under the watchful eye of Owain, who had a genuine fondness for the young man. He liked Robert and a grin lifted his depression as he recalled the young man's reluctance to pay court to Mabel fitzHamon of Cairdyf, a match which his father was determined to arrange.

Alun called again, more urgently this time.

Owain jerked himself up on to one elbow. 'Now what is it, boy?'

'There are many men, *arglwydd* – they are not ours, they look more like French or even Flemings.'

Owain squinted up at the sun, then dropped back on to the grass. 'As long as they are not Gruffydd's men, Alun, it makes no matter. Though if they are Flemings, they can take these damned cattle from us.'

The beasts were an embarrassment to Owain, as he had no particular wish to march into Carmarthen to meet the King's son looking like the leader of a band of drovers, rather than warriors.

But Alun was not to be so easily reassured. 'They come after us from the direction of the town, lord – not down from the valley. There are a great many of them, almost upon us now.'

The boy sounded so worried that Owain hauled himself reluctantly to his feet, to look for himself. At first he saw nothing, for they were camped in a slight hollow at the water's edge. Alun had climbed to the rim and was pointing across at the farther side.

Suddenly, as Owain's eyes were upon him, the squire crumpled like a broken doll and fell slowly off the grassy bank, rolling faster and faster almost to the spot where Owain stood.

Still no one was in sight and incredulously Owain stared at the broken arrow shaft sticking out of the chest of the jerking body at his feet.

With a great roar of alarm, which brought his men splashing desperately out of the river, Owain lunged for his discarded hood of mail and his sword, which lay on the grass.

As he struggled frantically to put them on, he glanced up apprehensively at the bank above, just in time to see a solid rank of armoured Flemings appear in a semicircle, raising bows to take careful aim at the Welshmen trapped in the hollow.

In anguish, Owain yelled at the top of his voice.

'Stop...stop, will you! We are King's men, not the rebels of Gruffydd.' He shouted instinctively in Welsh then, realizing that they were Flemish, he repeated it stridently in Norman-French.

Dimly he noticed a mounted figure riding behind the foot archers, his shield carrying a diagonal red cross on the silver of the polished metal.

His own men were also yelling at the tops of their voices as they scrambled up the gravel from the water. Like Owain, they feared that the Flemings had mistaken them for a party of the rebel Welsh. Separated from their arms and at a great disadvantage down in the hollow, there was little else they could do except wave their arms and shout to avert a terrible misunderstanding.

Yet the silent bowmen did not waver and a split second later, a devastating hall of arrows hissed down into that fatal ford of Ystrad Rwnws. Shouts turned into screams of mortal agony as throats, chests and limbs were pierced by the steel-tipped shafts.

Owain's men wore only leather jackets, their arms and legs being bare. The slaughter was immediate and terrible at that point-blank range, with all the Welsh crowded together in the little dell.

Two arrows hit the steel links of Owain's Norman hauberk with force enough to make him stagger, but they did not penetrate.

He had his hood almost on and was yelling in a frenzy, still convinced that some awful error had been made. Then, as the Flemings re-strung their bows and let fly again, an arrow hit him in the side of the neck, at the very spot where he had failed to pull down the armoured hood to meet the hauberk.

In that instant, he knew that his life was at an end.

There was no pain, only a noisy pumping, as his life's blood spurted out on to the soil of the Wales he loved so much.

Slowly, he sank to his knees, both hands clutching the shaft of the missile that was so unexpectedly ending his twenty-nine years of life. Rapidly, his vision darkened as the blood left his brain, but somehow in his final fleeting seconds the figure of the man on the horse glowed almost brilliantly against the blurring background.

With weird clarity, Owain ap Cadwgan recognized Gerald de Windsore as the man who sat watching behind the archers. Almost the last thing his mind was able to do before eternal darkness closed in, was to know that this was no tragic mistake, but a cold-blooded assassination, a long nurtured revenge.

The very last thing to fill his dying brain was the vision of a lovely face.

'Nest...my Nest,' he bubbled through the blood in his mouth, then he sank dead on to the banks of the Tywi river, which was to run tinged with pink for the rest of that tragic day.

It was growing dusk that evening when the messengers rode up to Caer Rhiw, their horses flecked with foaming sweat.

Five men-at-arms from the garrison at Carmarthen escorted a young esquire, his shoulder swathed in fresh bandages.

He first sought out the steward and made sure that Lady Nesta's maidservant was with her, before asking to be admitted to the lady's presence.

Nest, conscious from his manner that something was amiss, sat herself in the window of her room, bathed in the last red light of evening. The young man, whom she had never seen before, was obviously ill at ease and his pallor was more marked than was merited by his slight wound.

'You have news for me, sir?' she said quietly, her dark eyes scanning his face and already reading the news in them – some of the news.

He gulped and nodded – he could not have been more than seventeen. 'Bad news, my lady – the worst.'

He was right, though he did not know in what manner.

'My husband?' she asked quietly.

He nodded and his eyes looked moist. The day had been filled with too much death for his years to bear. 'He…Sir Gerald…he is slain, my lady.'

Though expecting the news from his manner, Nest sat very still, her fingers ceasing to flick the needle back and forth through her tapestry. Though she had no affection for Gerald and came as near to hating him as it was possible for her to hate any human king, she suddenly found that sixteen years of marriage could not be shrugged off like an old cloak and be forgotten where it lay.

Sir Gerald de Windsore was dead – and now she was a widow with five fatherless children.

'Tell me how it happened,' she said at last.

The squire, sighing with relief that he had no wailing or woman's tears to suffer, stumbled on hurriedly with his story.

'Sir Gerald left Pembroke some days ago, as you know, lady. He had two hundred Flemings to join Lord Robert le fitzRoy at Carmarthen, to assist in hunting the rebels.' The young man hesitated in some embarrassment, as it was well known that the leader of the rebels was no less than the brother of this lady. 'When we had almost reached the castle this morning, we met with some Welsh who were fleeing to the town to avoid some other loyal men of the King. Sir Gerald questioned them, but I know nothing of what was said. Then for some reason, we turned and headed quickly up the broad valley that lies in those parts. Our knight urged us on and we soon surprised a band of Welsh, who were encamped with cattle at a ford. Our archers slew almost all within sight, but a few must have escaped and brought others upon us, for no sooner had we turned back towards Carmarthen, than we were attacked on two sides by an equal force of Welsh.'

Nest frowned at this. She was worried that Gruffydd himself might have been involved in a conflict on such a scale as this.

'Do you know who these Welsh were?'

The youth shook his head and winced as the movement hurt his shoulder. 'No, my lady…I have only lately come to these parts, but I can say that the form of attack upon us was odd…the main body of the Welsh seemed content with holding back our men-at-arms, whilst three or four of their leaders made straight for your lord and dragged him from his horse, he still fighting valiantly.' He hesitated, then gulped. 'They held him on the ground lady –

then one, a shorter, very dark fellow...he...' His voice faltered as the image still burned a nightmare in his mind.

'Then what, boy? Come, tell me it all.' Nest's voice was distant.

'Some held him, my lady, while this other raised his sword and struck off our lord's head, taking many savage blows at it, like a man possessed of a demon!' His voice began to shake. 'As he did so, he was shouting something in Welsh – all I could understand was a name...Owen.'

An icy hand reached into Nest's body and grasped her heart.

'Owain? What else did he say, lad? Come, tell me for God's sake!'

The squire shook his head miserably. 'I have no Welsh, madam. All I remember is that name.'

All her fears for Gruffydd were suddenly turned upside down. The appalling death of her husband already forgotten, she moved towards the messenger and gripped his sound arm. 'Then tell me this – the attack you made at the ford. Was any Welsh leader struck down there?'

The youth nodded vigorously. He felt on surer ground here. 'Yes – the best archers were commanded by Sir Gerald to strike down the leader before any other. The foe were resting and had little armour – they were surprised completely, having cattle still in the river.'

Nest shook him with gentle urgency. 'This leader – what was he like?'

The squire shook his head again. 'I have been but a month in Wales, lady – and this Welshman had a hood of mail half on his head, hiding his face. But he wore a fine yellow surcoat, unlike most Welsh, who dress like peasants.'

The icy hand squeezed her harder with a grip of ultimate doom. 'Did this surcoat carry any device?'

The young man nodded. 'A red lion, madam, a lion rampant.'

Nest turned and walked slowly back to the window.

'Go to my steward, sir, and see that he feeds you well and attends to your wound...and thank you for your speedy message.'

The boy stammered some thanks and feeble expressions of sorrow, then thankfully vanished from the bower.

Nest stood at the window for a time, then went slowly to the small door in the corner which led up on to the flat roof above the chamber.

Outside, she leant on the low parapet and looked westwards into the crimson orb of the setting sun, as it fell into the Western Ocean.

With it, she saw Owain's life and soul vanishing.

That same sun had seen him rise early that morning, full of life and plans for the future. That same sun that had seen him born, now must set on a world devoid of Owain ap Cadwgan, the only man who had made her life worth living.

As she watched, the fiery rim finally disappeared. As the great pink rays shot up from the horizon, a part of her own life went with it. Turning, she looked north across the flat lands of south Dyfed, her eyes and soul drawn instinctively towards the distant Teifi and the lands beyond. Ceredigion and Powys, the lands of Owain...where they had met, made love – and finally parted. Where little Llywelyn stayed, now the only living reminder of his father.

She was filled with sadness, rather than pain, for the pain of final parting had already been suffered.

Her eyes sought the north again and saw Cenarth Bychan, where it had all begun. From that place had started the madness of hate that had consumed Gerald all these years – a madness that had today exploded into his treachery and horrible death at the hands of Morgan and his brothers.

Northwards, too, lay Llangrannog and Din-geraint, full of memories of her Owain. As she thought of Din-geraint, that place now called Kerdigan, a vision came to her of Owain cutting his way into a castle for the second time, to carry her off with him...then the vision changed to the face of Stephen, the castellan of that same Kerdigan, the only man since her father to treat her with courtesy and consideration that was not tinged with open desire.

Stephen...a name to cling to, when life seemed to have lost all meaning.

She glanced northwards for the last time, then turned to go down. She would grieve a while for Owain, finish the grieving that began four years ago...then perhaps she would go north again, to Kerdigan.

HISTORICAL POSTSCRIPT

THE Lady Nest herself is not heard of again in history after the events recounted in this book, but one of her many famous children was Robert fitzStephen. We do not know if she married Stephen of Cardigan or if their Robert was illegitimate, but Stephen was Constable of Cardigan in the year 1136, and Hait was Constable of Pembroke – Gerald's old position – in 1130.

Robert fitzStephen had lands in Cemais and succeeded his father as Constable of Cardigan. He went to the assistance of Henry II when the latter invaded North Wales in 1157 and was badly wounded in the same battle in which his half-brother, Henry fitzHenry, lost his life. In 1165, Cardigan was taken by the Welsh under the 'Lord Rhys' (son of Gruffydd, Nest's brother) and Robert was taken prisoner by his cousin, remaining so for three years, until another half-brother, David fitzGerald from our story, successfully pleaded for his release. Robert then crossed to Ireland as a prominent member of the Norman invasion of that country and played a significant rôle in its conquest. He was granted lands in Wexford and a joint grant of the Kingdom of Cork, where he died in 1183.

Henry I, Nest's royal lover, lived until 1135, when he died on December 1st of 'a surfeit of lampreys'. His first wife, Matilda (mother of his only legitimate son, William, who was drowned in 1120 in the White Ship disaster in the English Channel) died and Henry married the daughter of a German prince in 1121, in the interval being 'wont to use concubines'!

Henry fitzHenry, Nest's royal bastard, had lands in Narbeth and Pebidiog, in Dyfed. He was killed fighting alongside his half-brother Robert in 1157, when 'he fell beneath a shower of lances' whilst plundering churches near Moelfre, Anglesey.

The children of Gerald de Windsore and Nest were also to find a firm place in history.

William fitzGerald became the Lord of Emlyn, the estate in which Cilgerran (our Cenarth Bychan) lay. Together with his brother Maurice fitzGerald, he came into prominence as a leader of the Norman settlers against the great revolt of the Welsh in 1136, which was led by Gruffydd ap Rhys, their uncle, on the death of Henry I. As mentioned below, they unsuccessfully led their French and Fleming troops against Llanstephan Castle in 1146.

Maurice is best known, however, for his prominent part in the Norman invasion of Ireland, together with his half-brother, Robert fitzStephen. It was Maurice who founded the Geraldine dynasty, from whom sprung a line of famous men right down to our own day. A recent President of the United States – John Fitzgerald Kennedy – could trace his ancestry back to Princess Nest. It was Maurice who took his father's emblem to Ireland and which was adopted as 'St. Patrick's' Cross – today, the diagonal red cross forms part of the Union Jack.

In 1169, Maurice landed in Ireland and led the Norman contingent against Dublin. He settled in Kildare, which 'Strongbow' – Richard fitzGilbert, great-grandson of the Gilbert fitzRichard in the story – granted to him. His wife was Alice, granddaughter of Roger Montgomery, one of the traitors against Henry I. Maurice, said to be a brave and modest man of few words, died in Ireland in 1176 and William died two years earlier.

David fitzGerald, the youngest of the three sons, unlike his military brothers, became a cleric of some renown. He was first an archdeacon of Cardigan – again suggesting a close bond with his half-brother Robert fitzStephen – and a Canon of St. David's. After the death of Bishop Bernard, a conflict arose between the Welsh canons on the one hand and the English and French canons on the other, concerning the succession. A compromise was reached by the election of David, for he was both Norman and Welsh by birth. He was consecrated Bishop of St. David's in 1148 at Canterbury. In 1162, he assisted Nicholas, Bishop of Llandaff, in the consecration of Thomas à Becket, the Archbishop of Canterbury of famous memory.

In the last years before his death in 1176, he was in frequent conflict with the Welsh canons of St. David's, apparently acting contrary to Welsh interests in matters of property and the status of the bishopric.

Angharad, one of the daughters of Nest, made a good Norman marriage with William de Barri, who took his name from Barri Island in Glamorgan. They lived at Maenor Pyr (Manorbier) in Pembrokeshire and are mainly notable for giving birth to the very famous Gerald de Barri. This grandson of Nest (with her husband's Christian name) is of course, 'Giraldus Cambrensis' or Gerald the Welshman, cleric, historian, commentator and chronicler, to whom we owe much of our knowledge of life in twelfth-century Wales and Ireland.

William fitzHait, another bastard of Nest's, became Lord of St. Clears in present-day Carmarthenshire; he was noted as 'leading a multitude of French and Flemings at the siege of Llanstephan Castle in 1146, fighting alongside the sons of Gerald' – his half-brothers, Maurice and William.

Robert of Gloucester, the bastard of King Henry (who has wrongly been called another son of Nest) was married to Mabel fitzHamon about 1121. He was favoured by Henry after the death of the legitimate heir, William, and created Earl of Gloucester in about 1122, the name le fitzRoy being dropped. He was often called 'Robert the Consul'. He was largely instrumental in rebuilding Cardiff Castle in stone and was a patron of literature: the famous writer Geoffrey of Monmouth dedicated his 'History of the Kings of Britain' to him in 1139. Robert of Normandy, Henry's brother, was imprisoned in Cardiff Castle under Robert of Gloucester's care for eight years until his death in 1134.

Llywelyn ap Owain, the love child of our story, is difficult to trace because of confusion over names, but it seems very likely that he was the one who was seized in 1128 by his great-uncle, Maredudd ap Bleddyn (Cadwgan's brother and Owain's uncle), who delivered him over to the Norman Payne fitzJohn who interned him in the castle of Bridgnorth. He must have been returned to Maredudd, for we know that in 1130 poor Llywelyn was castrated and had his eyes gouged out by his great-uncle.

Morgan ap Cadwgan, after the death of Owain, ruled Powys in conjunction with his uncle Mareddud ap Bleddyn (the one who so misused Owain's son Llywelyn) and his brothers Einion and Madog. Henry I invaded Wales again in 1121 and Morgan was in the forefront of resistance – one of their men managed to hit Henry with an arrow. It recoiled from his armour, but gave him 'a great fright'!

We next hear of Morgan in trouble; in 1125, there was some treachery between him and his brother Maredudd (not the uncle). Morgan killed his brother with his own hand, though the reason is not known. As penance for this deed, Morgan went on a pilgrimage to Jerusalem, but died in Cyprus on the return journey in 1128.

It is of interest to know that Oliver Cromwell is a descendant of our Morgan ap Cadwgan – it is somewhat ironic that the arch anti-royalist, who helped behead Charles I, was himself descended from royalty with a far better claim to the throne of Britain than the Stuarts!

Gruffydd ap Rhys, the brother of Nest, rampaged through Wales in the fateful year of 1116 in which our story ended, but late in that year he came to a truce with the King and retired to a quiet retreat at Caeo, in what is now northern Carmarthenshire. But the restless patriot was waiting his chance. As soon as Henry died in 1135, he was prominent in the great revolt which exploded in Wales. He had married Gwenllian, a daughter of the doughty old Prince of Gwynedd, Gruffydd ap Cynan.

When the revolt started, Gruffydd hurried off to his father-in-law in North Wales, to enlist his support. While he was away, his wife Gwenllian led an attack on Cydweli (Kidwelly) Castle, but was killed there along with her young son Morgan; the spot is still known as Maes Gwenllian.

Gruffydd re-lit the torch of revolt that had been smouldering since 1116, the year of our Owain's death – he stormed castle after castle and routed the Normans at Crug Mawr, just outside Cardigan, though failed to take Cardigan itself at that time.

It was left to his sons, especially the very famous 'Lord Rhys', to consolidate these victories. The Lord Rhys, a nephew of Nest, rebuilt Cardigan Castle and lived there, holding the first organized National Eistedfodd there in 1176.

The ramifications and influence of the kindred of Nest are unique in Welsh history and play no little part in the history of Ireland after the Norman Conquest – many facets are also of importance even in English History. The present owner of Nest's dower house, Caer Rhiw (Carew), is a direct descendant and her Christian name is Nesta!

KINGDOM OF
POWYS

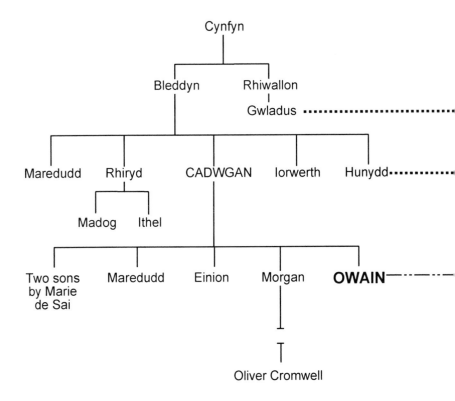

Marriage lines ················
Illicit liaison —·—·—·—

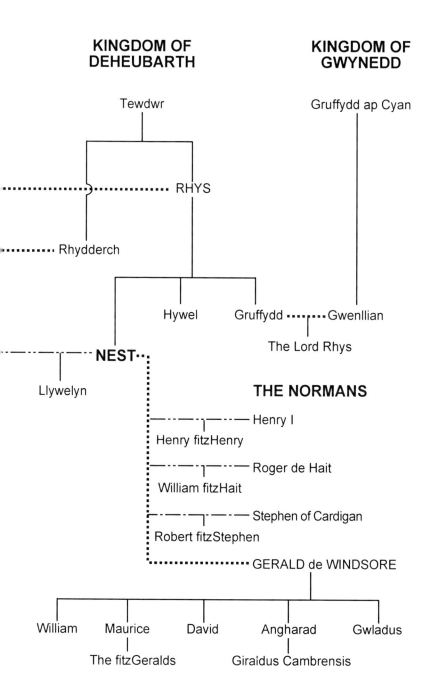

KINGDOM OF DEHEUBARTH

KINGDOM OF GWYNEDD

Tewdwr

Gruffydd ap Cyan

RHYS

Rhydderch

Hywel   Gruffydd ·······Gwenllian

The Lord Rhys

NEST

Llywelyn

THE NORMANS

Henry I

Henry fitzHenry

Roger de Hait

William fitzHait

Stephen of Cardigan

Robert fitzStephen

GERALD de WINDSORE

William   Maurice   David   Angharad   Gwladus

The fitzGeralds   Giraidus Cambrensis

Printed in the United States
212311BV00001B/59/A

9 781903 552476